THE VALLEY, THE CITY, THE VILLAGE

The author loves words – but more than words he loves Wales...

Trystan Morgan comes of peasant-farming stock, though some of his kin have moved from the hillside to the valley to work in the mines. He is brought up by a loving, hardworking, deeply religious grandmother whose early widowhood has made her life one of endless toil, willingly accepted. Trystan can just remember his early days in the hill cottage and remains in touch with the countryside by going to stay with kindly aunts and uncles there.

We journey with Trystan from childhood, to a Welsh university, to the threshold of a career as a painter...

THE VALLEY
THE CITY
THE VILLAGE

by

Glyn Jones

Magna Large Print Books
Long Preston, North Yorkshire,
BD23 4ND, England.

British Library Cataloguing in Publication Data.

Jones, Glyn
    The valley, the city, the village.

    A catalogue record of this book is
    available from the British Library

    ISBN   0-7505-1665-8

First published in Great Britain by
J. M. Dent & Sons Ltd., 1956

Published in Large Print 2001 by arrangement with
The estate of Glyn Jones, care of Laurence Pollinger Ltd.

Magna Large Print is an imprint of Library Magna Books Ltd.

Printed and bound in Great Britain by
T.J. (International) Ltd., Cornwall, PL28 8RW

INTRODUCTION by DAVID SMITH

From the moment we read the title we know we are embarked on a Welsh Odyssey. That trinity – *The Valley, The City, The Village* – evokes a journey in time amongst thickets of conflicting values. This movement has been the central experience of the Welsh people since the swarming, internal migration off the land and into industry began in the nineteenth century. The cultural dislocation for Wales, both social and linguistic, has proved bewilderingly complex. Glyn Jones's three locales promise, and deliver, an investigation of the different modes of living and understanding manufactured by the Welsh in the first half of the twentieth century. And yet this book is not a 1956 throwback to the melodrama of naturalism of those urgent 1930s narratives.

What gives his novel its startling freshness is the pattern he uses. No other Welsh novel selects, from the impressionistic shoals of images that flood the mind, by darting, like a gimlet-eyed kingfisher, to spear the exact metaphor or simile that will convey the visual and tactile *sense* of Wales. Glyn Jones understands the surrealism of the actual history of Wales. He finds a language to match its fantasy and a cast of characters who express the fishes-out-of-water cultural limbo of their lives. Occasionally the farrago of words he has assembled leads him into a stylistic fandango that recalls the whirling intoxication of Dylan Thomas, high on epithets. Always, though, the glittering style calls attention to more than itself, for his first-person narrator, Trystan Morgan, moves from place to place, from childhood to maturity and his consciousness is shown, rather than analysed, in a succession of incandescent episodes; often a momentary flashing cameo, lit up by Trystan's painterly eye.

It is Glyn Jones's greatest achievement to present South and West Wales as a landscape of the mind in which literal, palpable reality is transformed, never beatified, to convey impalpable, but no less real, meaning. No matter how harsh the conditions of life in the Valley (the account of a blackleg miner hauled by rope through a river is stunning in itself and for its execution), Trystan's perceptions are constantly sharpened there. Only the social posturing and deadened intellectuality of the university-town threatens what he knows to be 'the visionary and necromantic power of art.' Removal to the countryside in the final section is, then, no retreat but merely a

6

stage in that self-discovery which has been, obliquely, the re-possession of a culture.

At the end, Glyn Jones confronts the accusation that Trystan's obsession with himself and his art are evasions of the wider duty owed to others, perhaps to Wales itself. The painter discusses a 'Wales free and Catholic,' and admires the courage of those intent on this 'fruitless' course; he reiterates his youthful views that the enemy is 'capitalism, not England,' but he also remains defiantly true to the tangible presence of Auntie Tilda who sits silent while others talk of 'the state of our country, its language, its history, its future.' Trystan's art will be dedicated 'to the prisoner with whom I am captured, to the exile with whom I am banished ... to the incurable ... to dwarfs and monsters, and to their parents; ... to the repressed, to the un-regarded, to the cheaply held.' He cannot tell this directly to either his idealistic or his cynical friends, but he can represent his humane vision in his art. Equally, in a closing dream sequence that is at once richly comic and studded with the glint of irony, the necessity of holding together both concrete matter and those abstract concepts that, alone, give 'impressions' shape is ham-mered home by the dead Grandmother who ends her catalogued chronicle of Welsh generations with the instruction, 'You shall learn and remember.'

Glyn Jones, in this bravura novel, has taught the lesson that a literature, or any other art, alive to its own impulses is a latimer to life.

The Valley

1

Rosser's Row, to which my grandmother and my Uncle Hughie had brought me to live, was a colliers' terrace, standing on the bank of the black river oiling down the *cwm*. The houses, very tall, four-storeyed in the backs which overlooked the river, were built of bare grey shale with an occasional slab showing up brightly ochreous; they were, to the rear at least, irregularly, squarely, and minutely windowed, and here and there the whole barrack-like structure was protected against the dangers of subsidence by large iron disks and rusty embossments bolted like cyclopean coinage into the external walls.

Trefor and I came out of the Row and crossed the iron bridge over the river, but we were not going to school because we did not like Knitty Evans. Knitty was our teacher, a bellower and a bull-roarer, always very masterful and intolerant towards us, threatening to report our malpractices to our families. At the end of every lesson he rose up and came skirmishing amongst the class with his dirty cane, bellowing and bringing bad feelings and oppression, his

11

long black hair displaced and dangling down over his ears like a pair of wings.

We hid in the Greyhound passage until all the village children had gone to school. Trefor, a passionate micher, was a boy with an impenetrable mop of dusty fur on his head, a decaying seat to his corduroys, and a choirboy's cassock cut off at the waist for a jacket. He had the best shooting *cymal* in school for playing marbles, but his mother was a widow and he had to gather nettles for making small beer or collect horse-dung in an old pram. He had picked up a broken umbrella-stick on the ash-tip as we came by, and now, placing his forehead on the crooked handle, he walked round and round it to make himself giddy. Then, spreading his legs, he made water behind him like a mare.

When the school bell stopped ringing we found some soft tar on the road and we walked about on that for a bit. Then we sat down at the roadside where the kerb was high and watched the people and the traffic. Trefor pulled half a plate of rhubarb tart out from inside his shirt and we ate it between us. Sam the baker's bread-cart passed very slowly and the front wheel went over a big shining gob that we had seen Harri Barachaws, the rag-and-bone man, spitting on the ground.

('Get your hair cut, Harri,' Trefor had

shouted after him.)

As the rim turned, a long thread of silver stretched up from the road in a bright elastic line, until the wheel moved too far and the shining wire of sputum snapped back on to the dust. By this time the rear wheel was passing over it and it did the same thing again, the glittering string stretched up from the road, fastened to the wheel, dithered with the increasing tension, snapped silently, and sprang back to its original position.

'Whip behind the cart, Sambo,' Trefor called out, although there was nobody there.

When we got home at dinner time my granny knew I had not been to school because Knitty Evans had sent a boy to ask why I was absent. All she said to me was, 'God sees everything. It is possible to *act* a lie without telling one.'

When she had gone into the middle room my Uncle Hughie, who was always compassionate towards me, took me on his soft knees. 'Don't you cry now, boy *bach*,' he said. 'Every time *I* miched she beat the soul out of me.'

Before the deaths of my parents my granny and my Uncle Hughie, who was a bachelor, had lived in a cottage high up on the mountainside, a place where all the people spoke

Welsh and all went to chapel. Every Saturday I left Pencwm, the town at the head of the valley where my father was a schoolmaster, and visited them. I got out of the train at Ystrad Halt and climbed the steep path to my granny's cottage. On both sides the grass shone with the lustre of brushed silk. Ahead of me I saw her dwelling with a row of martins sitting on the warm roof. In the boughs of her gate-side rowan a blackbird was heard with metallic chink-chink, in the morning silence he made a stithy of his tree. The long green flank of the hill, brilliant rows of white-washed cottages and lonely steadings scattered upon its slope, curved smoothly down into the broad mining valley, where the small engine, still immobile at the Ystrad Halt, erected a gigantic white elm of steam into the clear sunshine. At an immense height a smooth blue roof had slid over the warm view and a few chalky clouds also, small and fragile as the air-bones of a bird.

When I knocked, my granny opened the door, her brown face wet, one eye shut and a bar of red soap in her hand.

She gave me a wet kiss, and welcomed me into her kitchen, dim even in sunshine because a bush of window geraniums always shut out the light. The aromatic air was strong with the scent of resinous firewood baking in the oven, and I could recognize too the acrid smell of drying pit-clothes. On the glowing fire a large iron kettle boiled and a finished meal lay upon the table oilcloth. The dim cosy room had all the furniture common to the cottages of the miners – the floor sacks, the corner 'bosh,' the wire drying-lines, the china dogs, the stand and fender, the row of brass candlesticks, the window-sized friendly-society calendar.

My granny was a big heavy woman dressed in black, and as soon as she had returned to the kitchen sink she began talking to me about Uncle Hughie. He had only just gone out to work on the middle shift. It was easier, she said, to get a Jew to drop his bag than to get Hughie out of bed in the morning. He was hanging the alarm-clock on the peg behind the bedroom door now to hear it better; and every morning after calling him she had to saucer his tea to cool it, and even blow on it for him, or he would never get to work at all. Then she laughed and began to use the towel from behind the door on her wrinkled oak-bark face.

Often in her dim sweet-smelling kitchen we sat as now by the fire together, while she held her mangled hands heavily upon her aproned knees. They were red and rugged, the hands of a labourer, their knotted erubescence evidenced familiarity with the

15

roughest work, they seemed as though the coarse substances at which they had laboured had become an element of their conformation. Often, when I was older, and knew the meaning of those bony and inflexible knuckles, the large inflammatory fingers, I turned my gaze from them with shame and pity and watched my own painter's hand, culpable, indulged, and epicene, as it moved adroitly in the perfect glove of its skin. Often I stared at those hands and remembered the way they sought, in her bitter childhood, the warmth and comfort of her pig's wash burden. Potato peelings, loaf-ends, plate-scrapings, all pulped together in a wooden pail with an admixture of hot skimmed milk, she carried every morning from Ystrad up to the pigsties isolated on the colliery refuse tips, earning a few pence weekly from a neighbour for doing so. Often, in winter, when the wind was rough and cold on the bare mountain slopes, she rested with her burden beside the steep path, and held for a moment her frozen hands deep in the warm slop of pig's food.

But it was always with reluctance, seated with me beside her kitchen fire, that she spoke of her childhood's sufferings, her stern, untutored upbringing, the humiliations of her life of youthful poverty; she preferred to divert me then with humorous recitals of her rare girlish pleasures and of her silliness and vanity. She did not wish to recall her childhood's struggles, the grim grammar of the school she had learnt in, instructing herself in loneliness, and in secret even, to read and write; she did not wish me to know how she had sat on her bed night after night, a simple Welsh book on the seat of her chair before her, and the shadows of the bars falling in candlelight across it as she tried to read. She did not wish me to know of the monotonous food, the cast-off clothing, the drudgery of that time, and then the encaustic history of her widowhood, her laundering, her chapel-cleaning, the endless sharing of her home with strangers.

And she hid from me also how she had sensed, with the brooding divination of motherhood, an unusual acuity and pro-mises of intellectual pre-eminence in her younger son, my father, and how she had determined that under God's will nothing in the mastery of her endurance should be left undone on his behalf. She did not describe to me the morning my father entered college, when, at last, she bore his roped-up trunk from this hillside cottage in a manner ennobled by the porterage of balanced basket, water-stane, or clothes-bundle, *upon her head*. She walked the path to the railway halt that morning under her heavy burden with the erect bearing of some at last triumphant wet-eyed queen, wearing her jet, her white collar, and her chapel black. She did not tell me how bitter to her was my father's early death, and my mother's within the year. When I came to live with her down in Rosser's Row she would say rather: 'When I could read Welsh quickly I began to learn English, and there was one thing in that language I could *not* understand then. M-o-u-n-t-e-d is *mount-ed,* isn't it? And w-a-n-t-e-d is *want-ed*. What I could never find out was why l-o-o-k-e-d wasn't *look-ed* and p-o-k-e-d wasn't *pok-ed*. There's a stupid little girl I must have been, mustn't I?'

To me my granny was always a warm and visionary being. Sometimes, the whole sky ablaze, and the crimson sunball dissolving hot as rosin upon the hill-top, a tall black figure seemed to float out of that bonfire as though riding a raft of illumination. Her heavy progress was laborious, her shoulders rose and fell against the dazzling hump of hillcrest radiance with the rock of a scale-beam. She shepherded her rolling shadow down the slope; returning from the prayer-meeting she wore over her vast flesh her long black boat-cloak, with the brass buttons like a dramatic row of drawer-knobs down the front of her. Her feet were in clogs, her head in a black cloth hat with hanging tie-tapes and a cart-wheel brim sweeping the broad spreads of her balancing shoulders.

She would reach the rowan at her garden gate and pause there, eyeing with mildness and benediction the wide sweep of the mining valley below in the moments of sunset. Then, as she turned to the cut sun and the afterglow, her lined face became lit up, illuminated as though from within like a rock of clear crystal; her opaque body glowed, momentary starlight inhabited her glistening form. And I, shouting at the sight of her, reached her side with singing limbs, she was my radiant granny, my glossy one, whose harsh fingers lay gently and sweet as a harp-hand upon my curls.

As we stood together, watching the valley, the sun sank, and from behind the hill the invisible ball cast up the powerful glow of its illumination like a huge footlight into the flawless blue sky above us.

2

The valley was full of excitement.

Trefor lived in the first house in Rosser's Row, and one day during the Easter holidays he came up along the front pavement to call for me. He wanted me to go over into Ystrad again to see if there were any fights on, or if the shop windows were being broken.

We had long since left Knitty Evans's class behind and we never miched now, we were under a nice teacher called Deller Daniels. Soon we would be trying the examination for the grammar-school for which Deller was coaching us. If I passed I would have to travel up to Pencwm every day by train from Ystrad; but Trefor, I knew, even if he got a free place, would not be able to take it because his mother was a widow and she could not afford any longer to be without the money he could earn working underground. Trefor's father had been killed in Ystrad Pit and his mother had to make a living selling at their side door bottles of small beer which she made out of the herbs and nettles collected by Trefor and his sisters. She also took in washing. Their house was always full of steam from the iron boiler of clothes on the kitchen fire, and often great clouds of it blew out through the front door and across the pavement.

A few weeks before we broke up the miners in the coalfield had come out on strike for extra pay and Trefor wanted to go over again to see if there was anything exciting happening in the main street of Ystrad. Although my granny repeatedly told me I was not to, we had already been over several times and had stood near the crowds listening to the speakers. We had heard Rutter Shadman speaking on the ash-tip, urging the colliers not to give in or return to work. Shadman was a miners' leader from Pencwm and whenever there was trouble in the valley he was to be seen standing on a kitchen chair on some open patch waving his banana hands and bawling to the crowd around him about 'We members of the working classes of these islands.' He was a big, red-faced man with bushy eyebrows like blacking brushes and a voice people said you could hear in the next valley. My Uncle Hughie had a story about Shadman's famous voice. Once, according to him, Shadman was up in London negotiating in a wage dispute. He asked at one point if he could use the phone in the next room to consult the valley lodges before coming to a decision. While he was phoning, one of the coal-owners who had been out of the room returned and asked what on earth the shouting was going on next door.

'It's Shadman,' said one of his friends, 'speaking to the South Wales miners.'

'Heavens,' said the coal-owner. 'Why the devil doesn't he use the telephone?'

But Shadman never made you laugh like some of the speakers we had been listening to. Harry Hughes the barber, for example, who always began with a joke: 'Comrades, now let us analyse the position in which we now find ourselves,' he would say; 'we can see its origins as far back as 1649, that cold morning, you remember, and Charles the first in two pieces.' Or Sioni Lewis who we heard ending his speech the other day with: 'And don't forget the match to-morrow boys. On the river field this time. Married versus Singles. Ha'penny a man.'

'How much must we pay to come in, Sioni?' one of the strikers shouted.

'Let's see now,' said Sioni. 'Grand *stand* – a penny. Grand *sit* – tuppence. Starving coal-owners admitted free!'

You could even get some fun out of old Dai-go-to-Work, because although Dai was supposed to be one of the leaders of the men he was against striking and his speech was as monotonous as cuckoo-song. 'Men,' he would shout at the crowd before him, 'Men, go to wurrk!' And all the young miners would jeer at him and drive him into a frenzy.

But Shadman was serious and ferocious, he never made any jokes, and the only thing we liked about his speeches was that he used a lot of bad language. It was exciting to hear him shouting out words at the top of his big voice that our teachers punished us for using at all. 'Shut your bloody mouth,' he bawled at someone in the crowd who had been heckling him. 'Shut your bloody mouth, or I'll come down and shut it for you.'

'Good old Shaddy,' the young miners shouted.

It was Rutter Shadman, so people said, who had painted the banner carried at the head of the procession marching down the valley a few days before the strike started. On a sheet of tent canvas, twelve feet by three, we had seen in red paint the words: 'The wages of sin is DEATH, but the wages of the worker is HELLISH.'

I went out with Trefor as before but I did not tell my granny where I was going. She was consistently reluctant to approve of a strike, she condemned the bitterness and the violence that always arose during the stoppages, and she grieved at the idleness of the men and the sufferings of the women and children, and the debts which mounted up even for good families. She told me at the beginning that if I saw an open-air meeting, or a crowd of men talking together, or the police marching, I was to keep away because I might get into trouble or be injured.

My Uncle Hughie was unlikely to become involved in the strike. Although he worked at the Ystrad Pit he was not now engaged in cutting coal. He was called a winder. I had been down to see him at work more than once. His engine-room was a huge place, very high and empty, and the noise in it was deafening so that the iron sheets with which it was floored vibrated under your boots.

My uncle smiled in the middle of it all; seated up there plump and shining in his shirt-sleeves, he saw everything from his elevated wooden chair. On either side of him were large polished levers, in appearance resembling those I had seen in the signal-boxes; squares of leather were tied to his hands and by moving the levers to and fro he controlled the vast metal drums and the great shining cables that raised and lowered the iron cages in the shaft, with their loads of coal, or debris, or men. The job of winder was always given to someone reliable, to a man connected with a chapel often, to someone who was known not to drink; it was responsible and well paid. In my uncle's hands daily were the lives of hundreds of men.

This walk along the river bank which Trefor and I now meant to take was a favourite one with my Uncle Hughie, and sometimes he went along the whole six miles of it up to Pencwm. After the present strike was over two of my aunties from Llansant, my Auntie Rosa and my Auntie Tilda, my mother's sisters, came to stay with us for a little at Ystrad. On the Saturday night my Uncle Hughie went for a stroll along the river bank with my big-nosed Auntie Tilda, while Auntie Rosa, whose legs even then were not good, stayed in with my granny and me. About a mile up the river

24

my uncle spotted Anna Ninety-houses coming along the bank towards him. Anna was an eccentric friend of my granny, living alone in a little canal-side cottage, a great talker, toothy, always dressed in queer clothes. Leaving Auntie Tilda's side Uncle Hughie went hesitatingly across to her.

'Anna,' he whispered, 'don't tell my mother, will you?'

'Tell her what?' asked Anna in a puzzle.

'That you've seen me with *her*,' jerking his head at my Auntie Tilda.

'Who is she then?' asked Anna.

'A little widow,' he answered. 'I'm courting her. Don't tell, will you?'

Anna agreed with a nod, frowning darkly.

'You know what my mother is, Anna.'

Anna nodded again.

'All right, Hughie,' she said. 'There's lovely. I won't say a word. And I wish you joy. I hope you'll be very happy.'

The next night Anna saw my Auntie Tilda sitting next to my granny and me in chapel and she heard the announcer in the big seat welcoming to the service and to Ystrad the relatives of 'our respected precentor and his mother, with whom they are spending a few days in our valley.'

Anna realized my uncle had taken her in again and for the rest of the service she could hardly contain herself for laughing. When Uncle Hughie came down into the crowded chapel after the Second Meeting she laughed so much and pummelled him on the chest that people began to wonder what was the matter. 'You old fool,' she said to him. 'You old fool, you've diddled me again. Oh, you do jade me, Hughie. "Courting," indeed. "Don't tell my mother," indeed. I'll give you "don't tell my mother."' And then she tried to explain to my granny what had happened.

Trefor and I crossed the iron bridge and walked along the river bank towards the village. Opposite us, on the other side of the river, we could see the tall, bolted backs of the Rosser's Row houses from which we had just come, and as we passed along we tried to say who the occupants of each house in the terrace were. In the first, the one nearest the bridge, lived Trefor's mother, and next door, in the house with the ten-foot hollyhocks, were the Prydderchs, a big family with a mad father. Mr Prydderch used to wander about Ystrad muttering and I knew he had done something terrible to his wife before she died. It was to do with having a baby but I didn't know what. My granny was called in to see Mrs Prydderch the night of her death and I overheard her tell my uncle that the stairs were blood from top to bottom.

Next door to them were, first, Mrs Preece

and then, Mrs Watkins, whose house was white-limed. You could see these two, when they were friends, gossiping for hours over the back-garden wall, even standing out there with umbrellas over their heads when it was raining. But frequently they would quarrel about the children and then, while the neighbours enjoyed themselves listening in the pantries, they stood on their garden paths and called each other names like 'dirty cow' and 'sow-face' and 'black belly,' using very high voices and beating meat-tins and frying-pans in each other's faces. 'You can go to hell,' Trefor and I once heard Mrs Preece shouting over the wall, 'and in case it's not hot enough, here's some coal to take with you.' With that she flung a shovelful of small coal over Mrs Watkins.

The garden of the house next door up was completely covered in with a twelve-foot-high cage of wire netting. ('I don't know where that poor woman dries her washing,' my granny used to say.) Here lived Emlyn Preston, a collier, whose hobby was keeping a lot of small birds in this enormous aviary. Sometimes Mr Preston invited the children from the Row in to look at his birds, and it was a pretty sight to see the canaries and the budgerigars and the lovely little Indian finches flashing about from perch to perch inside the wire cage. He bred curly Bedlingtons too, and although our houses stood on the bank of the Ystrad River we never had any trouble from rats because of Mr Preston's terriers.

The Lewises lived next door. Mr Lewis, a fireman in the Ystrad Pit, used to get a bit drunk on Saturdays and in this state he loved to play his melodeon. From across the river we used to watch him sitting on a kitchen chair in the middle of the back yard and playing on calmly while his wife, a large, fat, red-faced woman, shouted around him and threatened him with her fists. 'Shut up, you fool,' she screamed at him in Welsh. 'You tin ape, haven't you got any sense? You're dull as a broom-leg. Do you want everybody to know you're drunk?' We could hear her right across the river and we enjoyed it until she saw us listening and drove us away with her shouts, shaking her fists at us. But Mr Lewis took no notice at all, with a lovely smile on his face he went on calmly playing sad hymns on his melodeon.

Next door again were Mrs Price and her husband, a family the people were calling the 'Evan annwyls' now, since the strike, which means 'dear Evan.' Evan Price was a blackleg and had to have police protection for the mile and a half walk between Ystrad level and Rosser's Row. One day at the beginning of the strike when I was coming home from school I had seen him approaching the bridge surrounded by a red-faced sergeant and three constables, and followed by a jeering crowd of strikers, mostly boys and young men. Evan Price walked in the middle, his face black with coal-dust, wearing his pit-clothes. He walked hurriedly and in silence, clutching his tin box and jack to his breast, his head bowed, not looking to right or left. I had felt very excited to see him like this, a man I knew surrounded by policemen, but the shouting and jeering of the crowd made something happen in my stomach, it was like the weakness of hunger. At the entrance to the bridge the police drew up to prevent the crowd going any further so that Mr Price was able to pass over alone to Rosser's Row. Just then Mrs Price ran round the corner of Trefor's house and on to the bridge. 'O Evan annwyl,' she shouted, throwing herself upon her husband. 'Evan annwyl, are you safe, are you safe? O Evan annwyl.' I could hear her clearly from where I was standing and so could the crowd of miners. They began laughing and jeering. 'Evan annwyl, Evan annwyl,' they chanted. 'How are you, Evan annwyl? O Evan annwyl, Evan annwyl.' They were no longer angry, everyone seemed to be laughing, enjoying the fun. The big sergeant began to clear them away.

'Go on now, boys *bach*,' he shouted, crimson in the face and grinning. 'Go on, get off home. And don't forget the match to-morrow. By God, I'm looking forward to that.'

The crowd of men laughed and jeered for a little as they drifted away, and then one of them said: 'Come on, boys, let's go up the Pandy for a kick about. Coming Charley? Coming Rhysie?'

Slowly they left the bridge, shouting: 'So long, Sarge,' and, 'See you to-morrow, Sarge'; and someone from time to time made the others laugh by mimicking Mrs Price crying: 'Evan annwyl, O Evan annwyl, are you safe?'

When everyone had gone I crossed the bridge and went home. I described what I had seen to my granny, who heard me out solemn-faced and shaking her head; but my uncle's nose began to twitch and he went into the front room.

But that had been a month ago, before we had started our school holidays. Evan Price now stayed on the pit company's premises, and did not come home at all, since the police could no longer guarantee to protect him. In the meantime things became more serious; almost every day now we heard of stone-throwing and window-breaking and fights and chases and baton-charges by the police. But most of this violence was reported from Pencwm, the town at the top of the valley, and in our village of Ystrad very

30

little that was exciting had happened. But every day my granny reminded me to keep away from strikers and police alike.

Trefor and I continued our way up the river opposite Rosser's Row. In that house without curtains, where the bottom garden wall had fallen into the water, lived the O'Learys, a lovely family of seven or eight children all wild as bears and with no parents. One of the children, Mikey, had a withered arm and the smallest had an iron on his leg. It was the best house in Rosser's Row to go into to play because there was hardly any furniture in it and you could dig holes anywhere in the garden and knock nails into the walls even in the parlour and no one would say anything to you. And every now and then all the O'Learys would go on the stage for a few months and travel round the country acting in a comic play called *Casey's Court* which had a lot of children in it.

Past Mrs Bowen Black-hair's we went; past the Brass-Knocker's; past Ben the Barley's; past Mam Evans's, the last house. Mam Evans, an aged widow, lived there with her mother who was supposed to be nearly a hundred. They were very respectable, members at our chapel, Caersalem, but they liked a drink every night, quietly, in the secrecy of number twenty-four. Past the two dozen houses of Rosser's Row and past the ivy-grown and derelict engine-house at the end of it.

Past our own house too, our garden bereft now, almost, of its wonderful show of tall sunflowers. In the morning a dozen young strikers had wandered in the sunshine along the bank of the Ystrad, and admiring the great golden dishes of our blooms had shouted across to us, to my Uncle Hughie and me, mending the clothes-line in the garden, telling us how fine the flowers were and how was it looking? Presently they came across the bridge and up the back of the row and after a lot of laughing and joking my uncle gave them one each, and a bunch to take away. They pinned the enormous medallion-like blooms with difficulty on to their shabby jackets and went away happily.

'Take care of yourselves to-day, boys *bach*,' said my uncle to them. 'Use your heads, now. Don't do anything foolish.'

'Foolish!' they said. 'Too true we won't, Mr Morgans. We been foolish long enough, slogging our guts out down under, and for what? Getting wise we are now, Mr Morgans. So long, and thank you. Come on, boys, up Pont-y-ffyn for a swim.'

They went happily towards the mountain.

Trefor was telling me a rhyme he had learnt about the strike. He could sing it. It went:

In the upper Ystrad Valley
Sticks and stones are very handy;
If you run about or shout
You're sure to have a heavy clout
Off the Bobby.

As I was learning it we saw a man coming towards us along the river bank. He had no hat on, but although the day was warm he wore a thick white scarf and a long black overcoat too big for him. It was Mr Prydderch. He came on, muttering, his eyes on the ground. His crinkled hair stood up in disorder on his head and the cuffs of his overcoat came down over his hands. I was always afraid of him but Trefor spoke to him as he went by.

'Hallo, Mr Prydderch,' he said.

Mr Prydderch didn't look at him. I had once passed him with Jimmy Prydderch, his own son, and he had not even noticed us.

When he was a long way behind I said to Trefor: 'Why is he like that? What's he muttering all the time for?'

'Don't you know?' said Trefor. 'He's off his head. He pulled a baby out of his wife with a iron hook and she bled to death. That's what he wears a scarf for. He tried to cut his throat because of it. My mother told me, but I'm not supposed to tell. Say, "Red Hatchet."'

'Red Hatchet,' I said. 'What's "Red Hatchet"?'

'Well, if you tell what I told you now, you know that little trap-door in the ceiling of your bedroom? In the night it will open and the Red Hatchet will come out and kill you. What are those men doing up there?'

The men Trefor was pointing to were clustered in two groups, one on each side of the river. They were shouting in excitement. As we got nearer we could see that a man was standing between them up to his waist in the middle of the coal-black water. It was at this man that the group on each bank appeared to be shouting. I recognized the men, they were strikers; several of them still wore the huge sunflowers that my uncle had given them that morning. I remembered what my granny had told me but I could not tear myself away until I understood what was happening. The men on the banks were moving towards us and presently I saw the ropes. The man in the river was tied round and round with ropes, his arms were bound to his sides, and a length of rope stretched out from each side of his body to the nearest bank. By means of these the strikers were forcing him to walk along in the middle of the river. As we watched he stumbled forward, fell, and disappeared under the black water, but the ropes were pulled taut and he rose again quickly, soaking wet, and continued on his lurching way towards us. At last, in spite of the drenching he had had, I was able to recognize him – he was our neighbour, Evan annwyl, Evan Price the blackleg. Slowly he came along and the men on each side shouted and swore at him and shook their fists. And then there was a loud cry, the ropes dropped into the river and the men fled, some up into the tips on the far side and some jumping the hedges and scattering across the fields. We knew the police must be coming around the bend in the river so we ran back along the bank in the direction of Rosser's Row. We were breathless by the time we reached the bridge and each of us went hurriedly into his own house without saying good-bye.

'What's the matter?' my granny said to me. 'Why have you come back?'

I sat down on a chair by the fire-place and put my face into my hands.

'What's the matter?' she said again. 'Has someone frightened you? Trystan, what is it?'

I began to sob. My granny tried to comfort me.

'You're like ice,' she said. 'What is it, *bach?*'

I went into the bath-room behind the kitchen and vomited.

3

Beside me on the sunny mountain top lay Evan Williams, the shy and freckled darling; and Benja Bowen, called Rosie Bowen, with rounded, glazed-fruit cheekskin; or Cochyn, which is Ginger, Bowen, with dense kinked hair the orange of new coconut-matting; or Benja Brag; or Bowen Bighead; or Bowen the Bootmaker's boy: beside me lay Bouncy Bowen, Esquire, the celebrated donkey-buyer, the big fool – and bigger liar.

We three, Benja, Evan and I, had passed into the Pencwm grammar-school, to which we travelled up every day by train from our village halt at Ystrad. This grammar-school was the one at which my father had once been the Welsh master.

Benja was at the moment singing rude quatrains to the tune of 'Mochyn Du' before our summer-holiday cookery.

Somewhere, far below us in the valley, Ystrad, our village, lay amongst its few and vulnerable fields. It was entirely hidden from us now by the eclipsing swell of the hills, but as we had climbed up we had seen the sunny pewter of its roofs shrink beneath us, and watched the drifting smokes and the silver-backed streams of the coal-field covering them. For the strike had been over a long time and all the miners were back at work again. And now as the three of us strove together among the huge volumes of moving air, as we reclined upon the great muscular back of the sun-swilled mountain, Ystrad itself was remote and unreal in our memories.

I had left Rosser's Row early to meet Evan and Benja, bearing food, billy-can, and sketching-block in my schoolbag. The sun was lowish but already bright. A few white clouds, clotted and bumpy, trekked down the *cwm* through the dewy brilliance of the unsoiled morning. Each small stone or dislodged pebble, isolated on my sunny path, had a tapering, elongated comet's tail of shadow clearly marked behind it. I passed a stepped-on slug with his bowels on his shoulder. Long grasses leaned out of the breeze-brushed banks like slim fishing rods fishing in the road. As I walked my face felt the floating webberies of the nightshift spiders; the sequined poplars clattered softly above my head; the hedge beside me tossed out its vibrant blackbird.

'Don't you *hear* me, don't you *hear* me, don't you *hear* me?' asked the cream-breasted thrush. '*Here* I am, *here* I am, *here* I am. It's *me*, it's *me*, it's *me*.'

A group of bed-bound colliers, beautiful blackened men, their scarlet mouths and liquid lustrous eyeballs glistening in the sunshine, ground out a cud-chewed sound as their hobnailed boots grunted past me on the road. One of them carried a bunch of large lemon dahlias in his hand. They were neighbours, Ivor Preece and Phil Watkins and Emlyn Preston, so I greeted them and they readily replied, leaving me a sweet and thrilling whiff of pit-clothes in their wake.

In the distance were the clustered slag-heaps like a township of smooth grey roofs in the sun, high-pitched and apsidal, some of them overgrown with the green velvet of moss-like grass. And behind the tips, barren under their vaporous shadows, were the mountains for which we were bound, monstrous, treeless, cliff-cut, under a shabby fur of turf and ling.

At the level crossing I met elate Evan and buoyant Benja carrying their food in their leather satchels.

'Hail,' said Evan.

'How be?' said Benja.

Together we went forward towards the busy coal-mine which we would have to cross to get to the mountains. This was not a pit, the place where my Uncle Hughie worked, but a 'drift,' a sloping tunnel driven into the side of the hill.

We went through the steam-swept colliery ground, avoiding wire ropes, and running trams, and coal-trucks. From the house-high stacks of carrot-red pit-props came a woody pine-smell. Here, when I was small, I often sat down in seclusion with Trefor, within hearing of the mine's metallic dissonance, and with pocket-knives we carved rough boats from the rugged lumps of red log-bark that everywhere littered the ground. We smoothed the little hulls, sometimes as much as three inches in length, by rubbing them on the shale-like walls of Rosser's Row. The masts of our little ships were matchsticks, their shrouds and rigging cottons, their seas the edge of Ystrad River or the grey waters of the daily wash-tub.

Passing a derelict tram, with a splintered sprag still in its wheel, we went among the blinkered ponies and the grimy surface men, we walked the coal-glittering ground of the colliery, while the confluent and dissolving streams blew about us. No one shouted at us. Presently we stood in the fine drizzle of coal-dust right on the archway above the mouth of the mine itself, the dark tunnel driven into the hillside. There we saw the down-tilted rail-track disappearing under the earth. One glittering wire rope ran swiftly down the slant over its rollers out of sight into the tunnel beneath us, and its fellow, of equal glitter and rigidity, passed up in a counter direction. As we watched we saw the noisy journey come clanking up the slope out of the mine, six trams loaded with lump coal were tugged up the declivity into the sunshine at the end of the taut rope. A young collier, wearing a naked light flaming in his cap, rode hunched on the last tram.

At that Benja began to boast that his Uncle Benny was a rider with an oil-flare burning on his head, and what *he* used to do was to take up his stance where we were posted now and make a flying leap down into the last tram as the journey pelted down empty into the darkness of the drift.

Whenever Benja told us a thing like that he watched our faces cunningly, out of the narrow of his eye, to see if his statement had provoked that grinning scepticism, that confederacy of disbelief, to which he always responded with a spell of punching or arm-twisting, accompanied by abuse and per-verted laughter. But Evan and I were acquiescent; frowning, we directed our gaze steadily at the felt-like mountains.

We had a crabby walk to climb over one of the tips that put a squalid paw down into our village, and when we had scaled it we went up through the green-hearted grove of airy birches and tall bracken. At last we were at the mountain top where shoals of cloud-shadows were skidding over the grass and the old rocks pushed their glittering bones out into the sunlight. Here, once, the eagles nested in the broken-brinked cliffs: here the legion-vanquished hillmen had encircled with rock their puny encampments: here the conventicle's pious vedette had sentinelled the pathways leading up from the valley. No one lived here now and nothing grew except an occasional crippled thorn-tree, fidgeting in the wind, and casting a deformed and tatty shadow on the sheep-shaved turf.

We had sweated as we had climbed, hungry and burdened, and with hammering pulses, the steep and windy gradients near the mountain's summit; we were petulant and blown. But once on the long crest we dropped our burdens and performed in the high wind a shouting and boisterous tripudiation in honour of our achievement: we crowed like dawn-cocks: we wallowed like tingling dolphins in the showers of wind: we bit like exultant pit-ponies put out to grass: we covered the mountain's sunlit back with the patterns of our exultation and delirium, with the bedlam choreography of our dizzy eleutheromania. And then, when at last we sat down, we were silent and a little awed. There was no living soul within miles of us. There was no dwelling to be seen anywhere in the glass-like clarity of the air, not Ystrad our village nor Pencwm the town at the valley's end. Once, so Benja said, a lost boy had starved to death on these mountains. When they found his body he had eaten his hands to the bone. We all laughed again and having lit a grass cooking-fire the three of us sat laughing beside it.

To me the mountain was painter's

country. Over our heads, as we cooked, large masses of lathery clouds were blown through the blue like frondent soap, silvered and convolved, sloshing vast bucketfuls of brilliant light over our whole mountain. The majestic swimming ridge on the far side of the wide valley rose convulsively into the sunshine; as I watched I saw it constantly sloughing the teeming cloud-shadows off its head and shoulders. And there, between the driven foliage of swift shade, was the stone-quarry's amphitheatre, taken out of the hill as it were at one bite.

Benja, singing his quatrains, leaned back against the ruined dry-built wall. He was wearing his shrunken white-boiled holiday suit, a pair of button boots, and a motor-bike helmet. As he waited for our food to boil in the billy-can he sang of the strange behaviour and misfortunes of eccentric local females. He sang of his sister Mary who was working in the dairy: and his sister Elin who was courting in Llwyncelyn: and his sister Liza and his mother couldn't rise her...

'For I had a sister Anna
She could play the grand pi-anner;
She could also play the fiddle
Up the side and down the middle,
    Wass you effer see,
    Wass you effer see,

42

Wass you effer see,
Such a funny thing before?'

'On a fine day,' he said, when our counter-songs had brought to an end his interminable stanzaic cycle, 'on a fine day you can see all the county of Glamorgan from by here, aye.'

'And all Monmouthshire,' I said. 'You can see the fairies dancing on Twyn Barlwm.'

'And all Carmarthenshire,' said Evan. 'You can smell the laver-bread in Carmarthen market.'

Benja looked with dislike from one of us to the other, uncertain whom to start horsing first. But we went on and baffled him by our fluent collaboration; we named in progressive inconsequence Cardiganshire, where all the girls have big noses; and Pembrokeshire, where the bugs ate the sailor; and Breconshire where King Brychan Brycheiniog put the shovel down. To secure the postponement of our penal thumps and fierce retroflexions of the arm we then bestowed nonsensical attributes upon all the other Welsh counties we could remember and the English boroughs and the transatlantic colonies where our countrymen still utter the tricky mutation of our native speech – London, Liverpool, Vermont, Scranton, Pa., and the Chubut Valley of Argentinian Patagonia.

Benja waited and our stratagem was successful. 'Don't talk so damn daft, will you?' was all he said. 'Don't talk so damn daft.'

Then he dropped his eyes, which had flickered with uncertain hostility between Evan and me, and became silent and absorbed. For the moment he appeared to be confronted with the futility of all his aspirations and enterprises. He watched in silence our dinner bubbling above the grass-and-twig fire, staring at the flames which stamped upon it or blared sideways in the breeze.

We had forgotten to bring water and we were boiling our potatoes in lemonade. Far down there under the calm curtains of the birches we had come across a limpid little stream, but Benja forbade us to take water from it. He interrupted his narrative to stop us, a tale of what he did with a live bullet he had found.

'Gudge, don't drink that,' he said, as we stood beside the stream. 'An old hag spits and bathes her bad leg in it every morning. She's got green teeth and' – here he bent down and struck the mid point of his shinbone – 'her foot is purple up till here. Come on,' he urged us, spitting into the current himself. 'There's clinking water further up.'

'What happened to the bullet after?' asked Evan.

'When my old man was out in chapel,' Benja went on, 'I fastened it in a hole in the stitching-machine and then I gave the what-you-call at the back a whang with the rasp and hammer. You ought to have heard the bang, aye, it sounded like a frigging thunderbolt, aye.'

'Did it do any harm?' asked Evan.

'No, no harm,' said Benja. 'Only it went through two doors and out through the parlour window. But my old man hasn't noticed the holes yet.'

I always wondered about Benja, he was so wayward, so boastful, rebellious, untruthful. I remembered his flow of obscenities after a calamitous examination, when he cursed the entire Welsh begetters of the infixed or post-vocalic pronouns. I remembered his zeal in collecting synonyms for the word 'brothel'. I remembered him, at a hint of salaciousness, hounding smut through the collected works of Chaucer. I remembered his endless lies to me, to Evan, to the masters, to his parents. And yet I always wanted his company. Evan and I never enjoyed ourselves so much as when Benja was with us.

Now, after eating his share of stale cakes and potatoes, he lay back and closed his eyes. The sunlight was clear as a beam directed down upon his face, revealing every flaw and blemish, and my eye, like a high-powered microscope, travelled carefully over the absorbing territory of his shining and unshaved cuticle. In the intense illumination I noticed every dry scale of skin upon it; every blackhead, ink-blue or coal-black with age; every pustule in whatever development between incipience and maturity; every pole-like hair planted in its little hole. I laughed at the endearing comicality of his brassy lashes, his hat-fruit cheek-glaze, his protuberant Adam's apple, and his hulking head surmounted by the leather helmet. I bent over him, feeling helpless in a flood of affection and delight.

We spent some time after dinner clouting one another with our school-bags and talking about our form and our masters. I made one or two drawings, but in the end Evan and I found ourselves as usual listening to accounts of Benja's experiences and to his opinions and reflections. Principally that afternoon he related a long and digressive tale which Evan and I punctuated with disingenuous questions and open jeers. And our barracking resulted as usual in assaults, scufflings, suppressions of free speech, and the triumph of preponderant muscularity.

Benja was brave; Benja was clever; something exciting was always happening to Benja, especially when he was unaccompanied by sceptical and derisive witnesses. Benja one dinner hour got drunk on invalid port and had to be locked in the Head's room until a taxi could come to take him home; Benja swanked he always used the masters' lavatory; out with the form surveying, Benja 'accidentally' upset Geoger James's tripod into the lake; Benja filled the pockets of the new games-master's overcoat with sheep's droppings and helped him to wipe the mess off his hands. Benja shouted 'Sit' in morning assembly a split second before the Head, and half the school sat. Benja did things so that he could describe them to you afterwards. He had the faculty of describing many things which he had not done also.

After the upheaval of his narrative he lit a cigarette-end in the fire and fell back again silent and pensive. His cherry-cheeks glowed, his toothy hake-like underjaw hung unlocked, and a thin thread of spittle began to creep out over his plump protruding bottom lip. His pendulous septum nasi glowed rosy in the sun and as the smoke poured out of his nose the gusty wind blew it sideways. I knew by his rapt expression he was thinking about girls, and presently he said that in France they had bro-thels, did Evan and I know that? He would bet we didn't even know what a bro-thel was, but if we had heard of a red lamp, or a leaping-house in the play of Shakespeare, it was all right because it meant the same. If we were in France would we go to a bro-thel? Did we think Froggy had been to a bro-thel? It was funny they had bro-thels in France and not in any other country. Did we think we ought to have bro-thels in this country as well?

Benja's questioning disturbed me, my heart resisted and yet welcomed his words and the passages to which they were prelusive. I felt at such times in my mutable and bewildered blood both repulsion and the awakening of some new authoritative power which impelled me to listen. The desired hold of innocency was still then powerful upon me. The generations of my grandmother and my uncle, faithful to the reticent and fastidious puritanism in which they were nurtured, saw childhood as symbolic of some Edenish innocence and so cherished it, accepting regretfully the signs of its departure. So in the serene and mellow atmosphere of their home I awaited, with instinctive misgivings, manhood and initiation. I dreaded lest these should mean my exit from the angel-encircled garden of which I felt myself to be an occupant. And yet I could, at the same time, never be merely the reluctant mystes. Puzzled, I yearned for knowledge, for more complete emotional understanding, for initiation. There was brightness to an eye, hair flowed, hands touched, a wet lip could be an enchantment. 'Trystan,' Bolo Jones had said to me in school one day, 'a girl was asking me who you were. Dilys Phillips. Do you know her? "The dark-haired boy on the Ystrad train," she said.' These words were sweet, a revelation, and yet disturbing. There was the presence of Mair-Ann also when I spent my holidays with my uncle and aunts at Llansant. In the window of a Pencwm art shop stood a large reproduction of Rossetti's 'Beloved'. This I gazed at daily in enchantment and complete absorption until on my seventh or eighth visit the pretty girl who worked in the shop smiled out through the shop window at me. That smile disenchanted and yet pleased me. And what was it I had felt in the Caerdaf theatre once, seeing the pink uplifted hands of the beautiful dancers, delicate, fragile, of unearthly loveliness? As they swayed in unison to the stringed music, with the rose-warm illumination upon them, I felt new sweetness flooding my heart, the drinking of unaccustomed draughts of miraculous milk was an ecstasy I was conscious of experiencing.

I got up and put some more dry grass on the fire although it was almost time to go home. Benja's talk had set my mind in a turmoil. When we were collecting kindling we had laughed about Caersalem our Ystrad chapel, and our Pencwm school and about the manikins Evan had invented for his latest play. The dwarfism of these little

49

creatures was so complete that their chained bandogs were brass-collared bacilli. When they found the bones of a dead gnat or midge, they crept in between the lipless teeth of it and lit their tiny floor-fires in the hollow cave of the skull, letting their frail smoke fume out through the portals of the empty eyesockets. Also, with great hardihood, they resisted the mammoth stampede of their implacable enemies, the massacring money-spiders, whose hairy bellies went over them as they trampled them to death.

Why couldn't we go on talking about these as we had been doing and making up more nonsense about our other creations; for instance the gigantic figures of the *Ardderchocaf Ach Anac*, the *Bechgyn Beilchion Bendigeidfran*, the *Cewri Cedyrn Cymru* which we had invented, whose false teeth were set in horseshoes, who had telegraph poles for peg-legs, and organ-pipes for drinking straws. Why couldn't we go on laughing about Benja's essays, especially the one on 'The Seasons' which he sent in to Thomas English. 'Spring,' wrote Benja, trying, as Tossy said, to be original or poetic, 'Spring is on the hills! Hooray! The daffodils, the emblems of Wales are a-bloom! The golden gorse-bushes are a-bloom, the hills now wear those golden bloomers!' Why couldn't we go on rolling and wrestling, why couldn't we be eternally warm and breathless, our pulsing ears burning with our exertions, our chests tight where we had been kneeled upon, our wrists hot and raw where we had gripped one another in hysterical horse-play?

Taking out my sketching-block again I went to the cliff edge. The wind was sharper and I was entering a mood of growing dejection. I wanted to go home but Benja and Evan held it was too early. As I sat looking down the smooth side of the mountain I remembered again a bitterness of a week ago. Benja, Evan, and I were in our classroom with our form waiting for our French master's entry. Evan tossed Benja's ruler neatly on to the top of a high cupboard as a reprisal. Benja threatened him.

'Look here, Evan,' he said. 'Nark it. Are you going to get that ruler down or not?'

'What do you think I am?' asked Evan. 'A steeplejack?' He was safe from assault because the master's step was expected every moment in the corridor outside.

Benja laughed.

'Well, I suppose I'll have to get it myself,' he said.

He placed the master's stool against the cupboard and then inverted the waste-paper basket on top of it, shedding chalk, chewing gum, and refuse over the floor. Standing on top he was able to swing himself up on to the cupboard, where he sat like a red-headed ape with his short legs dangling over the edge. Titty Taylor slipped to the door to watch for Morley and the whole form were Benja's audience. He began to enjoy himself, clowning among the white and wooden solid geometry. He lifted up from the depression in the top of the cupboard a plaster cast of some naked goddess. The boys were enchanted. Benja wiped its nose and leathered its behind. Grinning and his eyes like stars he tried to draw suck from its plaster breasts and the form rolled in their desks with uncontrollable laughter. Titty Taylor ran to his place, giving a warning. Benja grinned and climbed down without his ruler.

Morley, the French master, entered, young, immaculate, sardonic. After spending some time on the verbs he called me to translate the passage set for preparation. I never liked doing this and I was poor at it. When I came to the word 'niais' I stopped.

'Come on,' Morley said, 'what did you get for "niais"?'

I was silent. I could not remember.

'Have you prepared this?' he asked me, and when I said I had he asked again:

'Well, what did you get, my boy?'

The mental effort to recall the meaning of the word was nullified by the distress and disappointment I felt at failing in the estimation of a master I liked. I could sense the other boys looking at me and I coloured. Then, taking hold of my book to show me the word in the glossary, Mr Morley turned to the end. It was a new book and the pages containing the words 'miel' to 'plupart' were uncut. Morley looked steadily at me for a moment and then said: 'Did you prepare this?'

'Yes, sir,' I answered.

'I'm afraid, my boy, you don't keep strictly to the truth,' he said. 'Go on, Edmunds.'

At first I could scarcely see. I sat down in misery and confusion. From time to time I could hear Edmunds's steady voice translating and then fading again. Benja turned round and grinned.

I heard little of the rest of the lesson. At intervals I made an effort to clear the torturing thoughts from my mind, and for a short time I would succeed and follow the translation with intensity. But the strain was too exhausting and presently they had completely occupied my mind again. As the afternoon wore on my resistance to these thoughts became less effective, and by the end of the lesson I was incapable of dismissing them: I remained conscious of their existence in a mind dazed and numbed, but able to perform its ordinary functions without betraying their presence. The question constantly arising in my mind was: 'Am I a liar?'

On the way home to Ystrad in the train I tried to speak to Evan and Benja as usual, but I paid little heed to what they were saying. I saw dimly the shops and people in Pencwm High Street and the fields and houses from the compartment window, but I was only half aware of their presence. When I left Benja and Evan and made for Rosser's Row I felt relief at being able to call before me the agony of the whole scene without interruption. But I could not do this for long because the question of whether I was a liar kept breaking in, and I found it impossible to think of anything which did not quickly lead back to this agonizing consideration. Instead of going home I walked along the lane that led up the mountain where I had lived for a short time with my granny. A good distance up the hill I came to a little hollow I knew about and lying on the grass there I tried to settle this question.

'Was I right,' I said to myself, 'in telling Morley I had prepared my French? But then I had. When Benja called for me I told him I had to finish my French homework before I could go out with him. Benja could tell him that. I wish Morley knew. But he thinks I'm a liar. What exactly did he say? I sometimes don't tell the truth? It was worse than that. His exact words were: "I'm afraid, my boy, you don't keep strictly to the truth."'

This was followed in my mind by a momentary blankness as though my reason had been completely wiped out. And then in turn an overwhelming sense of anguish and despair swept over me, and my mind was in confusion. Presently dry sobs began to shake me and my throat burned and tightened. I buried my face in the grass and struck the ground with my fists in an agony of shame and remorse, I cried in silence, without attempting to restrain myself. Then, relieved, I was weak and helpless. When I got home my granny had gone to chapel and my uncle not yet returned from work. I ate my tea and went to bed.

I had remembered these bitter things lying upon the mountain turf, the ground wind hissing along my body and the intermittent sun at my throat, fastened soft and warm upon me. I rose. Down the slope, beside the outcropping crag of granite glittering in the sun, a sheep was giving belly to her lamb. Everywhere around me, smooth in the sun, were the unshawled shoulders of the hills. The clinging, flexible cloud-shadows, surging in dark random areas of tattered transparency, continued to dip and swell at every earth-fold, curve, or smooth protuberance. I walked slowly back to our fire, feeling the chill. Over our heads some bird was winching his sweet and wheezy song. A little engine very far below us puffed into sight, following his leading-string of steam blown ahead of him down the valley.

'Come on, Benja,' I said. 'Come on Ev. Let's go home.'

Benja got up and put the fire out, giving the performance a mock benediction in a nasal and liturgical sing-song.

'Yn enw'r Tan,' he said, dropping a big charred stone upon it.

'A'r Mwg,' dropping another.

'A'r Yspryd Drwg. Amen,' finally extinguishing it.

4

In the gaslight of my granny's kitchen I sat on the couch, decorating, with a flight of swans, the margins of my Caesar and waiting for my Uncle Hughie to come from the parlour so that he could test me in my lesson. My granny was there too, ailing by the fire, watching Joe the jeweller cleaning the workings of our grandfather clock.

A soft green chenille cloth, folded for the time being across the back of one of the redwood chairs because Joe was there, always covered our kitchen table now; and here, in Rosser's Row, the floor newspapers and the sugar-sacks of my granny's mountain cottage had been replaced by rugs and vivid strips of coloured coconut matting.

My Uncle Hughie had worked hard to make our house bright and comfortable. He had grained all the wooden doors and cupboards with an amber paint and varnished them over. The sink or 'bosh' and the roller towel had been removed to a bath-room which he had built with his own hands out over the back yard. We had a brand new cooking-range with green tiles instead of the old blackleaded bar-and-brick grate with the fire roaring half-way up the chimney. And the brown beams above our heads had been boarded over flat and covered with thick white ceiling paper.

There were pictures on the walls too. One was of my grandfather whom I never saw, and one of my father and mother on the day of their wedding. In a thin gold frame appeared a picture in black and white which I had wondered at a good deal. It was large and at the bottom of it an open Bible was pictured firmly gripped by the claw-like roots of an enormous oak. The trunk of this oak, although of great girth, was squat, and the greater part of the picture was taken up by the gnarled and heavily foliaged branches which grew out of it. Among the branches were inset the photographs and pictures of perhaps a dozen men, most of them bearded and venerable; they were the ministers of Caersalem, our chapel, from the time it was founded at the end of the seventeenth century to the present day.

The room had become very bright and cosy now, especially when, as at this moment, the dark-red baize curtains were drawn over the little back window; and the frost was hot in the fire; and the bright greenish gaslight shone silky on the sleek yellow woodwork. I always liked the gaslight, I liked to watch it strike a glittering reflex from the brass about the fire-place, the drying rod, and the row of candlesticks, and glint on the glasswork and the flowered crockery of the kitchen dresser.

My granny and I sat there keeping our eyes on Joe, who had all the workings of the grandfather clock laid out on newspapers on the table before him. She, my granny, large and brooding in her thick black bodice, her red-plum paisley shawl, and her hair-net, sat in distasteful and unaccustomed idleness upon her arm-chair with her feet on the steel fender. She felt too indifferent, she had been telling Joe, even to make a few spills for Hughie's pipe.

I watched her, she was old and stately, despite her face-rag she seemed to me a princess, an ageing empress, she looked as though a kingdom were under her governance, as though she should receive the devotion of many, the homage of embassages tributary to her. Her large thighs beneath her black skirt and darned apron were spread out, and I thought how lovely it used to be when I was smaller, to feel, in chapel say, her warm haunch, firm and yielding against me; how sweet to drowse then in the fulfilling contiguity of her flank and bosom, her soft-as-sponge-or-wadding side and shoulder.

Now she had a wide piece of scarlet petticoat flannel tied round her swarthy face, and her ribbed workman's hands, reposed upon her lap, held a red neckerchief drenched with eucalyptus. Whenever she was ill I fell into despair, my bowels yearned to hear her say her pain was remitted; always, so long as her sickness continued, my anguished bed was made in hell beside her. But now, apart from her irking idleness, she was mutely reposeful, she laughed at herself in the kitchen mirror with her grooved face swollen and encircled in its loop of scarlet flannel. And her interested eyes, although overflowing behind her gold-rimmed glasses, were bright and watchful over the movements of the little jeweller.

Joe appeared small and shrivelled behind the table, he was so short compared with my granny that he looked as though he was sitting in a hole. He had the reputation of being a clever workman, but he was a spree-drinker and he always had to clean our great clock in my granny's presence; she distrusted him, she felt sure he would be tempted to steal the big brass bell out of the workings of it to sell for drink.

Now Joe had all the parts with his oil-bottles and his shirt-cuffs on the table before him, the clock-face painted with some summer scene, the iron chains, the huge black weights, the shining pendulum, and the big noisy bell like a brass basin that could be heard striking the hours in every house from one end of Rosser's Row to the other.

Joe the jeweller was rather a querulous chap: sour, touchy, a bit of a know-all; he had a bloodless body, a blanched albino face, a small bleached moustache, and little colourless eyes whose achromatism suggested slimy orbs cut from the back-flesh of a jelly-fish. The only dab of colour upon his features showed in the winy saddle of inflamed veins across the hump of his nose. He always wore a black suit, a wing collar too big for the calibre of his chicken's neck, and a black knitted tie with a glass pin on it. Although his starched cuffs stood upright on the table, no one could persuade Joe to take his bowler-hat off indoors, and he was wearing it now, just as he did working in his shop window, pushed on the back of his head as he sat with his oily rags before him by the table.

Joe had been all over the world repairing clocks and watches, so he bragged, and while he scraped the cogs and toothed wheels he began telling my granny about the clocks he had seen in China.

'Now you know,' he said in his heavy brass voice, 'we have a type of a clock in our country and the hands are always going round as we say from left to right. You have noticed that now, haven't you? Well, China is a funny country, and do you know what the hands of the clocks are doing in that part of the world?'

'What?' I said, although he had not been addressing me. 'I suppose they are going round from right to left?'

He laid down his rag and looked at me in astonishment.

'From right to left?' he said, puzzled. 'How do you make that out? No, of course they are not. From right to left, did you say? No indeed. They are not going round at all. The hands are standing still and the *faces* are going round. How do you make out they are going from right to left?' he complained. 'I never heard of that in my life before.'

'Go on with your cleaning now, Joe *bach*,' said my granny in a husky voice, 'so that I can have the table and get you a bite of something to eat.'

Every now and then as he used his rags and his jeweller's screwdrivers, the little man would look up at me frowning and cogitating, his white shrunken face puzzled

61

under the bowler-brim, perplexed at the perversity of my remark.

Presently my Uncle Hughie came out into the kitchen. He acted as the pitcher and leader of the singing in our chapel and he had been in the parlour preparing the hymns for Sunday. He had a curved red mark half-way down his nose because that was where his glasses always ended up when he was reading music. He came over the coconut matting with a slow rolling tread, bulky-bodied, stooping, slant-shouldered, slapping in his leather house-slippers. He placed his worn hymn-books and a sheaf of choral manuscript on the book-case he had built in the recess where the tap and the sink used to be.

'Did you turn the parlour light out, and the gas-fire, Thomas-Hugh?' asked my granny, as he handed her a slip of paper with the numbers of the hymns on.

'Tut, tut, clean forgot to, *tawn i marw,*' he teased, pretending to be genuine and winking at me.

He sat in the other arm-chair on the opposite side of the fire to my granny and reached his pipe down from the brass-fringed mantelpiece above him.

'How are things by now, Joseph?' he asked, taking his brass tobacco-box out of his trousers pocket.

Joe only grunted.

Uncle Hughie was a soft-fleshed, round-shouldered plumpish-trunked man, one who was always about the house, after bathing, in a khaki cardigan worn *under* his braces, through which a green silk muffler was tied. Always there was a broad strip of flannel underpants showing across his belly. I knew that belly of my Uncle Hughie well, my hands and the cheeks of my face remembered it from my childhood. Often then, in the kitchen of the mountain cottage, when he was eating his dinner before going out on the night-shift, I would stand small and sleepy between his whip-cord knees and, as though I were a nestling, he would feed me with juicy titbits off his steaming plate, a piece of bread dipped in the thick gravy perhaps, or small pieces of meat soaking out of his steak and kidney pie. As I stood there, hardly awake, my ear against his soft body, I heard the sounds that went on inside him, the hinge-whine, the gravel-trickle, the rock-roll, the bowler-plap, and sometimes a strange grinding noise as of someone chewing gristle.

'Hughie *bach*,' my granny would say to him, 'eat your dinner yourself. You'll give that child the moon.'

Earlier in the evening, because my granny was sick, my uncle and I had been out in the back yard to fetch a lineful of big washing in. It was cold and dark out there, moonless, the sky black and the brilliant stars active. I looked up and saw the glittering constellations pulsing like buoy-lights around us, and the row of equidistant dots of illumination, dim and motionless, which showed where the long mountain road crossed from Ystrad into the next valley.

From the other side of our back-yard wall came the washing sound of the river. The air was bitterly cold and I felt the chill of the flagstones seeping up through the soles of my slippers.

'*Tad*,' said my uncle, 'even the stars are shivering.'

The galvanized wire line, the clothes-prop, the inverted washing-tubs, were all furred with a deep nap of hoar-frost. When we caught hold of the clothes to unpeg them we found them stuck to the line and starched out by the frost into shapes of comical rigidity; the frozen canvas aprons and the flannel drawers, held aloft by the hems or the ankles, stood flat and upright in our hands like velvety garments supported by whalebone or buckram. And, as we handled them, a cold, blue, frosty glitter, as from minute sequins, sparkled faintly over their chilly surfaces. We had fun cracking this hard and cardboard-like clothing to fold it into the clothes basket, the starlight was upon us and the clean cold of the river-washed night.

Suddenly, as we hurried at our chilly task, a light tenor voice somewhere in the darkness began to sing an aria from *The Messiah*. My uncle straightened himself and listened, I sensed that, as he stood silent and motionless beside me, the singing, above the soft undertone of the river, was a delight to him. I could see the whites of his eyes gleaming like fish-scales in the starlight. The young voice came warm and full through the darkness. My spine, with cold and glory, seemed to thrill, my flesh received the compounded melody and the flashings of the night. And then after a few bars, the song broke off as suddenly as it had begun, and in the water-washed silence a distant engine clinked.

Without a word we carried our creaking basket up the steps into the warm kitchen. There our frozen clothes, our rough men's drawers and flannel nightshirts, were transformed into vestures spangled with minute, electric-flashing brilliants, to our joy they glittered in the bright gaslight like the tinselled garments of stage fairies.

The skin of my uncle's pinkish face always shone like polish in the gaslight after his bath and shave; it seemed soft, supple, and moistened, and his washed hair above it rose up thick and grey off the top of his brow like a fortification. He had a plump oval face with two hairy arrow-heads prominent upon it. His grey moustache hung over his lips and sloped up from the extremities of his mouth as though acting as an indicator directed upwards towards his nostrils. Then his heavy grey eyebrows were, in shape, colour, and almost in bulk, a duplication of them; they too rose upwards at a steep pitch from the outer corners of his eyes to a point directly above the bridge of his nose.

But these two down-turned embellishments were not indications of unhappiness or hypochondria on my uncle's part; they gave his fattish, twinkling face, rather than any appearance of discontent or melancholy or querulousness, an amused and quizzical expression. He liked telling minute jokes; he would tease people, playing innocent affectionate tricks upon them, and gently mimic their behaviour. When I was smaller he would stand before me, smelling richly of shag, or carbolic soap, or violin resin, and make me laugh by imitating the Englishmen with oiled hair and bell-bottomed trousers who had crossed the border to work in the Welsh pits.

'Dost thou knaw John Divis?' he would say, acting both parts in a suitable dialect. 'Dost thou knaw John Divis?'

'Knaw him? Aye! Where beest he working now?'

'Why him's dead, ten-eleven year ago.'

He knew a large number of such little dialogues, about the coal-men, and the scavengers, and the bug and the flea, but my granny would lose patience with him for repeating them. And I remember when I awkwardly dropped a pound of candles into his bath-water, he pulled them out and solemnly handed them back to me; I asked him what I should do with them now, and he was so grave telling me to put them into the oven to dry that I obeyed him.

He sometimes used his whimsy to effect. A newly married couple came to live in Rosser's Row. The husband was a clerk up in Pencwm, and the wife for that reason imagined herself superior to her working-class neighbours in Ystrad. To emphasize her salaried position she would sometimes go into a house or two in our Row just before pay day and ask the colliers' wives if they could change a pound note for her.

My uncle heard of this from my granny.

'She will have to come from b'there,' he said.

One Thursday morning, after the night-shift, he was cutting sticks on the pavement in front of our house. Presently he saw the young woman coming along with the pound note in her hand. While she was in another house further along the Row he laid down his axe and slipped into our kitchen. We were at that time collecting for a new pipe organ in Caersalem and my uncle, the chapel precentor, was the treasurer of our

67

fund. Until the collections could be banked they were kept in the lustre jugs on our kitchen dresser. My uncle stuffed as much of this money as he could into his trousers pockets and then returned to his stick-chopping at the front door. Presently the young woman came up to him and asked if he could change her a pound note because she was expecting the butcher.

'Change?' says my Uncle Hughie. 'Of course I can change it. Any time you like, young woman,' and he pulled out three or four handfuls of organ money from his trousers pockets and piled them on the doorstep.

That was the last time the young wife tried to establish her social supremacy in the Row. Presently she and her husband left for a suburb in Pencwm where salaries and clerkism were duly respected and were not subject to the insensitive derision of wage-earning manual workers like my Uncle Hughie.

Joe clinked away at his clock, his long nails full of dirt, and my granny, recognizing the hymns by their numbers, began to hum quietly to herself. My uncle leaned back and puffed his pipe in silence by the blabbing fire, one of his fat thighs thrown over the arm of his chair.

'How are things by now, Joe?' he asked again.

'Everything is all right,' Joe said at last.

Little Joe had a very heavy voice, his narrow weasand never seemed to me capacious enough to contain all the organs necessary to produce so resonant an articulation.

'Uncle Hughie,' I said, 'test me in my Caesar, will you, please, if you are not going to do anything?'

I pitched the book across to him. He failed to catch it squarely so that it splashed the lighted tobacco from his pipe over his cardigan and struck him a blow in the chest.

'Oh, sorry I was clumsy, Uncle Hughie,' I said. 'Did I hurt you?'

'I enjoyed it,' he answered gravely. 'What page is it, *bach?*'

He put on his spectacles from his snap case. The lenses were flat against his eyes and his shaggy brows grew down behind them like a heavy crop raised up under glass. He gave me a long test in vocabulary, doing his best to read out the words in English and Latin, and as he read his glasses crept further and further down his polished nose.

'You read Latin and make it sound like Welsh, Uncle Hughie,' I said.

'I have heard,' replied my uncle, 'that Sion Gymro always read Latin as though it was Welsh, and he was the best scholar in this country.'

'The Latin people,' said know-all Joe, '*are*
a sort of Welsh.'

'I don't see,' I said, 'why I must learn
Latin, Uncle, when I am going to be a
painter. And everybody knows all Romans
died a long time ago.'

'Williams Pantycelyn knew Latin,' he
replied in his soothing way. 'Howell Harris
knew Latin – I read it somewhere. All great
Welshmen have to know Latin, Trystan
bach.'

'And Mabon the miner's leader,' said
pithy, bull-brass Joe, 'he was a great one for
the Latin.'

My uncle winked at me. 'Does it tell you
in this book,' he asked, 'about how Julius
Caesar and his army came to these parts,
Trystan?'

I knew my uncle was only beginning to
talk nonsense, I could tell by the sparkle of
his plump, pork-pinkish face and by the
pitch of his upsloping eyebrows. I said no, it
did not, as far as I knew.

'Well,' he said, 'there is a story in one of
those old Latin books about Julius Caesar
coming up this very valley and capturing
two Ancient Britons called Dai and Shoni.
He took them back to Rome with him and
at last they were thrown into the arena.
You've heard about that arena, now, haven't
you? Well, as they gazed around Dai said to
Shoni, "There's a place is here, Shoni!"

70

"Aye," said Shoni, "the crowd is like an International in the Arms Park." "Indeed you are right," said Dai. "I wonder who that chap up there is, Shoni? With the leaves round his head." "Don't be so ignorant, mun," said Shoni. "Don't you know who that is? That's Nero!" "Nero, is it," said Dai. "Well, who is that red-headed piece sitting next to him?" "Don't you know her, mun?" said Shoni. "That's Cleopatra." "Cleopatra," said Dai. "Who's Cleopatra then?" "Hush now," said Shoni, "the lions are coming. I'll tell you after."'

I laughed, Joe scowled, and there was the first reluctant layer of a succumbing smile on my granny's face. But the smile did not come.

'Did you ever hear such rubbish?' she said in disgust, tossing her head at my uncle. 'Can't you ever talk to the boy with sense for five minutes? Will a lot of nonsense like that help him to keep his feet on the Rock? If we can't say anything to benefit people we ought to keep silent. A grown man talking such frivolity. But there, the same you've been from the beginning.'

My uncle continued to puff at his pipe in silence and imperturbable good humour. At my granny's words I remembered her telling me, in a reluctant mood once of amused affection for him, that the first time he saw me, a few hours after I was born, he carried

71

me to the window in the shawl and, pointing with his pipe through the glass panes, had said to me: 'Look, little one, there's *out.*'

'Ah, well,' said my uncle at last, as he stood up with a droll expression on his face and his hand scratching deep in his hard hair. 'I think I will get my things ready for the morning.'

He put his pipe back on the rack, but before he had time to leave there was a knock at the front door and in a few minutes Anna Ninety-houses brought her big teeth into the kitchen.

And at her entry the heavens were opened and the great deeps were broken up; passively, in a boiling deluge of English and Welsh, we were overwhelmed and mutely engulfed. Undaunted Anna, without precursory interchange, disembogued her spectacular floods and thaw-waters upon us, she deluged the whole room, the whole valley, the drowning universe, she rode the lawless torrents of reminiscence, intention, and parenthetic exposition, she gambolled and wallowed in the explosive and hurly-burly oceans of her own eloquence, she riotous Leviathan, unrestrained by mandibular cord or iron hook. In the presence of this lovable monologist, the ear of the stunned soul became at last horny, the spirit in stupor withdrew its antennae as the molested garden-snail retracts its sensitive

72

feelers. But Anna talked on, a long row of white biters hanging out of her mouth like a lineful of infant washing.

Yet, where is your boasted street of ninety houses, affable Anna Protheroe, you the occupant of a canal-bank cottage cracked in half by subsidence, you, spied upon by Evan and me as you lie in bed wearing white cotton gloves and with your umbrella open above you?

Your face is thin, you have a minute brow under the black straws of your dusty hat. Out of the red-veined wings of your nostrils, now, pure water issues upon your upper lip, a lip drawn up as ever from white teeth spotted whiter with starchy fleckings. From your chinpoint to the base of your neck there is a soft slope of flesh, like the under half of a chute or gutter, down which bread might slide from your mouth into your food-pipe and your belly.

You wear a green double-breasted over-coat, belted and buckled, with puff sleeves, flap pockets, and large bone buttons; it is trimmed with bunches of broken braid and cut from green tweed patterned with gigantic herring-bone. On your peeping apron there is hen's-mash; on your elbows, dub-lime; on your welts, cow dung. You wear boots with the thick soles of an insurance agent and, unlike my granny who is always zealous for the custody of her shining clogs, you arrive at your destination with cow-fouled footwear.

'But,' says my granny in charity, 'the one without fault has not yet been born. Anna's father had the sow through their grocer shop more than once because of strong drink. He died penniless. Much has happened to Anna which might have embittered her and did not. I remember,' she went on, 'that we once discussed in Sunday-school lending our boiler to Carmel for their tea-party. Many were against it because the dishes we lent them previously they returned to us broken. But Anna stood up and said we should lend to another cause whatever we had, and if the boiler came back to us with a hole in the bottom, well, the great Providence would supply us with a new one. She is a humorous creature with much faith. Judge not.'

Anna hadn't seen my granny in chapel last Sunday. 'And that service sacrament too,' she said, 'nor in prayer meeting the night before last and there's feel the want of you we did, girl, don't rise from b'there now indeed, Mary Lydia, don't rise, I tell you.'

(I remembered Anna hurrying into chapel late, as was her custom, singing the first hymn at the top of her voice as she stamped big-booted up the oilclothed aisle.)

'Here's a cold night,' she went on, 'it's giving me the earick and the frost is like a knife in my right knee again, I wonder if it is the old condition and I would have come yesterday to see you only I had to go up to Pencwm to Davies the druggister, a tonic I wanted for the winter.'

(I imagined her harrying dyed-haired Davies, whose fingers were spatulate, so my uncle maintained, through an excessive counting of his plentiful money.)

'But I met Maria Penrheol by the Greyhound and she said it was only a chill you had and there's bad that poor dab is looking, like a rush, and I didn't know her without her wens, I passed her, girl, not saying a word. "There's proud you are," Maria said to me, "there's proud you are getting Anna Protheroe."'

(Maria, de-goitred and no longer goggle-eyed, nearly nods the hat off her head with affability.)

'Hallo, how is Joe, and Trystan with his lockses, when are you coming down to see my new cockerel, Trystan, a black Minorca, haven't you got any delight now, there's an old frit, you are looking well, Thomas-Hugh.'

'Why not?' slipped in my uncle.

'Red flannel is sure to be wise and soaking the feet in mustard to make water come through the pores, with a boiled onion, I have brought a bit of batch and a few sweetbreads, try them indeed, Mary Lydia,

75

put them on the stone now, will you, Trystan, for your Mamgu, it's nothing, girl, what was I telling you about?'

'Sit down by there now, Anna *fach*,' said my uncle, getting her into a chair, 'and take a bit of wind.'

'Oh yes, I had to go to Pencwm, and I was not a-willing to go up there by train without washing my hair and my feet first for fear and I always cut my toe-nails the night before, if I have to go to the doctor's-shop or the solicitor about my houses, I must settle with the milkman first and with that old Sam the baker, and I make sure my insurance is paid up for the fortnight.'

(I remembered watching through the keyhole taciturn and weary-handed Watkins the milk, receiving and returning milk-jug after milk-jug, accepting all with invariable, 'Pleasethankyou's'; I saw Sam the baker with the wheatsheaf emblems of co-operation painted on his bread-cart, his raw-boned and eccentric cart-horse at a clatter over the level crossing; and on our hearth-rug I remembered cadaverous Ted the Celtic, standing in his leggings and johnny-fortnight mackintosh, his umbrella on his arm, and his cash-book open in his hand; Ted the insurance, who never displayed before you a handful of change but sifted the coins in his breeches pocket and dredged out unerringly the due amount of cash.)

'Because you never know what will happen, I will never forget that smash by the crossing with the coal all over the road and the engine lying on its side making a crinkling noise like a hobbed kettle, and there's a day I had of it, don't talk, girl, I started out wrong, I had to gallop up the breast to the Ystrad Halt like the company horses to catch the train, and a click of collier boys just off the *cwbs* were shouting on me, making fun: "Come up, Anna, your mother won a duck," and cetra, I was tamping mad but I had to laugh, and then Dai the Fan was driving, he's enough to give anybody the worms, that Dai the Fan, I don't think he's quite plumb, hooting his whistle and waving to all the young women doing the washing in the back, and him with a houseful of children and a gammy leg.

(Dai the Fan, wearing a ten-gallon hat and hearth-rug trousers, puts his swarthy film-face out of the engine cabin, his teeth in a grin like a parson's collar.)

'Something is sure to happen with him showing off up and down the line – Poo – hoohoo-hoo, tie-tiddly-om-pom.'

(Out of the halt rattles Anna's little train, ducking under the salmon-pink footbridge and clucking over the points. I get up and put my head out of the carriage window. This is a trip I do every day to reach the grammar-school at Pencwm. The grey day lowers, the wind aims a powerful blow at our coach, we are on the sloping side of the barren valley scuffling round the curves to Pencwm. The decaying wool of the engine's smoke bumps over the bare hillside. Long sagging cables of chewing-gum stretch from pole to pole. Anna squints out uneasily at the roly-poly slope and the river below us, apprehensive of Dai the Fan, the fool, for whose dereliction we might pay with our lives, landing in the water with our wheels in the air.

Now we are diving down into the dimming valley. No lights appear. The labouring coaches crowd after one another with long rhythmic tugs, crashing into the gloom, and the dim shine on the telegraph wires sweeps by like impetuous flocks of spectral swallows. In the deepest part of the valley we cleave the bricks and mortar and the bridges bark at us as they clang over our heads. We dive in the darkness on dithyrambic wheels through a gathering crescendo of jangling gongs, bells, and deafening siren-shrieks, we clamour two hours for Pencwm and hear the calliope slinging out its pent-up bedlam like the skirl of a gigantic bagpipe.)

When I wake up Anna is still talking but has not yet reached Pencwm. Joe stands up, ready to go into the passage to put the workings back into the grandfather clock.

My granny smiles across the fireside at my Uncle Hughie. He also has fallen asleep; his pipe is on the hob and his chin deep in the cross-over of his green muffler.

5

My mother's three sisters, my Auntie Rosa, my Auntie Tilda, and my Auntie Cutty, lived with their brother, my Uncle Gomer, in a house called Môr Awelon in Llansant, a village on the coast of southern Dyfed.

During my holidays from the grammar-school it was usual for me to stay with them for a few weeks every summer, and these visits, because of the kindness and endearing oddity of my relations, and the beauty of their village, I always looked forward to and much enjoyed.

My Auntie Rosa, the eldest of the three sisters, was a dark, hawk-headed invalid, very handsome and shining in her wheeled chair, beautifully enshrouded on special occasions in the endless whisperings of her black silks; her duty was to reply to letters and deal with the money matters of their home, and although she was bossy and dignified and did not laugh much, I knew to the thickness of a hair how far I could go with her and I could usually wheedle her to do what I wanted.

Auntie Tilda was the one who did all the hard work, digging the garden, mending the roof, cooking, cobbling, white-liming, she was very strong, with long arms and dyed hair, and she was my favourite of the three. In spite of the way she slaved she always had time to talk to me and have a laugh, and sometimes when I happened to be in the garden at the back of the house, munching an apple or drawing, perhaps, I would hear the coloured glass landing window tapped and see a hand behind it beckoning to me. I always knew that could only be my Auntie Tilda, and if I went inside the house I would see her on top of the stairs with the blue-and-red window behind her, the great bony forefinger of her right hand to her lips and her left hand, holding a paper, waving me up to the landing. Then, secretly, in her bedroom, when she had found her glasses, we would sit together while I helped her with a picture competition, set in her woman's weekly magazine. We whispered to each other and wrote with a blunt inch of indelible pencil which she wetted with her spittle, leaving blue stains on her lips. When our attempt was completed I took it out and posted it in the Llansant post office after I had put six penny stamps, the entrance fee, inside the envelope. These six stamps were the reason for our secrecy. My Auntie Rosa, the Môr Awelon treasurer, objected very strongly to this sixpence being spent un-profitably week after week; and it was of no use my Auntie Tilda pleading that one day she was sure to win a hundred-pound prize or more. 'Now, Trystan,' she would say as I tiptoed out of her bedroom, 'be sure the road is clear. Don't show that letter to anybody, will you? Do you know, my sister Rosa is the devil on me. Take care now.'

She had a strong face under the dye of her many-coloured hair, with a great nose on it, but if I kissed her or hugged her or thanked her for something she had done, she would look around quickly in all directions and then tell me very sharply to buzz off. The first time she did this I was started, but always after I couldn't help laughing at the top of my voice and she laughed in the same way too.

There was only one thing I disliked about her. Every morning, usually when I was doing a bit in the garden or helping Auntie Cutty with the vegetables, she would appear and shout out: 'Trystan, have you had your bowels down yet?' At first I used to blush to the roots of my hair because she would ask this question even in the presence of visitors. I decided to bring my embarrassment to an end by making up a sort of duet with her and asking her exactly the same question at the same moment. The first time this happened she looked astonished, scowled, and then went off in a huff; but the next day she tried again, grinning, and she laughed at the top of her voice when I joined in with her. After that she gave up asking me.

My Auntie Cutty spent most of her time in the basement. She was narrow and pale and angular, with thick spectacles and a red nose. She talked to herself and was a great plum eater. It was many years before I realized that she was quite dotty and could not do much more than peel potatoes and wash up the dishes. I first began to think there was something queer about her one Sunday night when she was walking down Water Street with me to chapel in her little cape. 'Oh!' she said suddenly, 'I have forgotten my glasses. Never mind,' she continued, 'I've got my apron on!'

Môr Awelon was one of ten or twelve villas that formed the south side of the village square of Llansant. The house was large, rambling, and blue, the outside walls coloured an eggshell blue and the woodwork of the doors and windows painted royal blue. These windows, seven in number at the front, being pointed like those of a church, caused me much wonder when I was small. The ivy-covered wall of the churchyard ran along the eastern boundary of the square and I suspected some connection between Môr Awelon windows and the gravestones I saw in it. Were the lights of my uncle and aunts' house so shaped, I wondered, because they had once been shuttered with those pointed headstones? Thick shutters of white marble, I felt, hinged and with iron catches, would be entirely appropriate for so remarkable a dwelling. Because Môr Awelon was not like any other house I had ever been in. For one thing no object in any room seemed to have been bought at first hand and there were no complete suites of furniture or sets of crockery. Everything had a history which my Uncle Gomer could recite, all the tables, chairs, carpets, and curtains – one set of curtains was made of leather – all the clocks, mirrors, ornaments, curtain-poles, spittoons, and picture-frames had come in incomplete and defective lots, through the saleroom, from decayed mansions, taken-over hotels, and steamship companies in liquidation. What my uncle brought he repaired, painted up, and varnished for the use of visitors. Some objects, like the handless but still working eight-day ormolu, had proved beyond his skill, and some he had tackled in ways which showed more his determined frugality and inventiveness than his sense of style; for instance, the round face of the hanging wall-clock looked out through an oblong picture-frame.

I enjoyed staying in Llansant also because of the great freedom I had there and because I saw how wonderful a place it was for painting. My aunts, all of them without husbands, earned a living by taking in visitors who wished to spend their summer holidays in the village. Every year before I visited them my granny in Ystrad impressed upon me that I was to assist as much as I could with the work of the house. I used to help short-sighted Auntie Cutty to scrape the vegetables in the basement, or do a bit of white-liming in the back for Auntie Tilda, or carry in a load of coal or dig the potatoes before dinner; and once I scrubbed out the big soft-water barrel when a lodger, who felt my Auntie Rosa had overcharged him, leaned out of his bedroom window and emptied his chamber-pot into it.

It was lovely there, and after I had helped my aunts a little they would drive me out and then I would go down to the beach to idle or swim, or up to Trenewydd or Pentywyn, farms on the hills where there were always food, enjoyment and welcome. I was allowed to do exactly as I liked, to come in and go out just as I pleased. And however late I returned at night I was sure to see my three aunts and my Uncle Gomer still at supper, seated around the kitchen table steadily eating with the oil-lamp shining in the middle of them.

They always went to bed very late, governed, as they were by the times of their visitors. It was lovely, at the end of a day up at the Pentywyn fields, to sit by the table in the big Môr Awelon kitchen and listen to my uncle talking. My big-nosed Auntie Tilda would be there, frying kidneys with her hat on, or standing before the fire with her hands holding her skirts up at the back to warm her behind before going to bed. She worked all day like an engine but she was never too tired to listen and laugh aloud her high bell-like laugh. Cutty sat near, her red nose deep in a schoolgirls' paper which she read through her thick glasses while she ate up the stewed plums the visitors had left over from tea. During my schooldays my Auntie Rosa had not gone permanently into her wheeled chair, and she used to sit on the couch after supper with her hands resting on the crooks of her two walking-sticks. In the soft light of the oil-lamp, hawk-beaked and leather-lidded, she looked like a sleek and severe eagle, listening, with impatience or disapproval, to the inexhaustible talking of my uncle.

What *he* liked was to take out the family album from under an ornate but unusable oil-lamp on top of the cupboard and talk volubly about the people whose photographs appeared in it, gesticulating, acting, dropping into guttural tones, and waving his pipe about – Auntie Rosa allowed him to smoke in the kitchen. His narratives proliferated. He was incapable of recounting a simple, uncomplicated story which proceeded step by step from beginning, through climax, to conclusion. Every person he mentioned in any particular narrative became himself the subject of a story, and before he returned to his central theme the people referred to in the digression were also in turn described and explained and what was of interest in them was recounted. His talk rose like some magical and glittering tree expanding into the dimensions of a grove before one's eyes and heaving itself visibly bough by bough towards the heavens. But he never lost his way in the bewildering webwork of his narratives. If he began with Dafi Ty Isa, to Dafi Ty Isa he returned after each digression, and, given sufficient time, with Dafi Ty Isa he finished.

'Here now,' he would say, indicating with his fractured pipe the photograph of a grey and rigid individual with long oiled hair like wet feathers, clad in a suit of tailored iron – 'Here now is Wiliam y Foelas, your great uncle, Trystan *bach*, your grandfather Thomas's brother. Very fond of the drink he was, poor fellow, always after something to wet the root of his tongue. And the ladies. And there is no doubt that they brought him and his box together sooner than there was need. They are telling about him that the only time he went past the Ship Aground without making a call was when he fell in the river and got carried past the back door swearing. The vicar, God bless him, tried his blue best to reason with him but it was no good. I ought to tell you about this Vicar Jones for you to understand. When Twmi Nantfach was having trouble with some old knocking in the bedroom night after night, a ghost they were saying it was, it was the vicar who got rid of it, indeed to God he went up to Nantfach and a big struggle he had, but he brought the ghost away in his tobacco box. And Twmi was so delighted – he had a peg-leg – and to show how pleased he was he painted it green. If I was to drop down dead by here. Only one fault the old vicar had. They are telling about Harri the Lan when he went to the vicar for advice about who he ought to marry because he had been courting two young women and now the time had come for him to choose. One of the young woman, Harri told the vicar, was well-off, with a house and everything, he was only wanting to put his hat on the nail, but the other was the one he was really sweet on. What should he do? "Well, my boy," says Vicar Jones, a widower himself twice. "Well, my boy, there is no doubt at all about what you must do. You must marry the one you love. To marry for money would be a great sin. Remember that now. Good-bye, my boy, and God bless you." They shook hands, and as Harri was going out of the vicarage, Jones says to him: "What did you say the name and address of the other young woman was now, Harri?" Before I tell you what happened at Harri's wedding I must go on about Wiliam y Foelas. One night, they are telling, he was coming home in the trap in his usual state from Tremyrddin. On the top of the ridge up there near Pentywyn he began to hear the clock of Llansant church striking – twelve, it struck – and as soon as it finished the big clock in Tremyrddin began. "Get up, Fancy," says Wiliam to the old mare, "I've never been out so late as this before." A good kind man Wiliam was, the kindest man in Dyfed they used to say. Look at all the brats he brought up that nobody wanted – Dafi Wernddu is one of them. Of course, many people were saying that they were his own and indeed I would have to know he was dead three days before I would believe he couldn't–'

'Gomer,' my Auntie Rosa shouted, dark as a gipsy. 'What are you talking? Have you taken leave of your senses? You have got no more manners than a ram. Put that book away and get ready for bed. The idea!'

My uncle's narrative had been accompanied by large actions, grimaces, pauses, spittings, and pipe-wavings. With his hand he had stirred the air. Now crestfallen, he put the album back under the ornate lamp with the frilled glass and the fluted leg and went limping clumsily outside the kitchen.

My uncle was tall, handsome, and lame. With his curled hair and his long, lined face I felt I had never seen a man anything like as handsome and majestic as he was. He had had a smithy about a mile outside Llansant to which he limped every day, but it seemed to me that even there he talked a lot more than he blacksmithed. At one time I often went out to his smithy so that I could walk back to Llansant with him, and it was a joy to sit down waiting for him and listening to the wonderful stories he told the farmers who wanted a couple of horses shod, or a boot-scraper made or a reaper-and-binder knife repaired. Although he kept them waiting with his talking they did not seem to mind because his stories entertained them, sometimes made them laugh, sometimes disturbed or frightened them. He was a great clown and actor. One of the stories I heard more than once was about Wili Pontlliw, a trooper buried in Llansant churchyard, who had a horse shot under him in the charge of the Light Brigade. Wili, according to my Uncle Gomer, got up and continued the fight against the Russians by swinging his horse round his head at the end of his tail. And he would have won that

89

battle only the creature's tail came out. As my uncle was telling this story he went limping round the forge stabbing and cutting and mastering his steed so that it was only when he sat down on his stool again that you remembered you were not in the battle of Balaclava. War stories suited his dramatic method of narration. One which always filled the forge with complete silence concerned an action in South Africa during which our boys, deprived for many days of water, were reduced to drinking their own. I saw the listeners to this sit there awed or astounded but never incredulous.

I knew many of the village children of Llansant, I saw them summer after summer and I played with them regularly on the beach or at the farms. They seemed different from Trefor and Evan and the Ystrad boys and there was no one in Llansant, certainly, like Benja Bowen. The village children were quieter, they played different games, and they smelt differently. They never breathed on a glass taw before shooting. They had not heard of a large number of things that all the boys in Ystrad knew, and when I spoke to them about a 'sprag' or a 'cheeky,' or said 'oppo' or 'fen mennance' they became silent and looked in front of them. They could not understand. But they laughed together at jokes concerning bulls and stallions and having babies before you were married which, because of the unfamiliar words they used, I could not understand either.

One of the first places I went to each summer was Mr Anthony's farm, Pentywyn, a place high up on the hill overlooking both Llansant and the bay beyond it. There was a son of my own age living there, called Densil, a powerful boy with a coarse, handsome face and slashed-back hair; he was swarthy and vital and as hairy as a rope. His teeth, dirty and with irregular edges, were like small sheets of corrugated zinc. Densil was dirty-minded but I liked him very much because he could tell me a lot about foxes, badgers, otters, and the buzzards that mewed like flying cats behind the hill – creatures common in the Llansant countryside but seldom seen or heard of in Ystrad. Also, his dirty conversation sounded so natural that it fell innocent and ordinary, rather attractive than shocking upon the ears. The first time I ever saw him he was crying. His father had given him a beating because he had boiled five mice in a tin of tar.

Every holiday Densil and I spent a lot of time on the sands, or working in his father's hayfields, and this I liked very much. I loved to see, with the scent of warm hay filling my nostrils, perhaps two dozen men and women at work together in a high sunlit field of Pentywyn. In the distance was the blue sea or the sea silver in a new skin, and the smooth hills crowded around like a plump wallow of green-backed whales. The gathered grass lay emerald under the long wet paint of sunlight. The men working at the hay harvest were often naked to the half, but the women wore hats and long black skirts and sometimes even a cloth about their faces to keep off the sun. They advanced, men and women, in a sloping row across the vivid field, turning the hay-swaths with their wooden rakes or gathering them into heaps which the men lifted into the *gambos* on their flashing pitchforks. The job I always fancied was standing on top of the mounting load of hay in the *gambo* and receiving the loads which the men tossed up on their forks, and arranging and distributing them trimly; but if Mr Anthony was present I was not allowed to do this. He was afraid, not being used to the job, I might fall off the top of a high load or take a pitchfork into my stomach. So instead I used to lead Flower, the skewbald shire, about the field, pulling the *gambo* from one mound of hay to the next.

Densil had a twin sister, now called Mair-Ann. Densil had been to the grammar-school a few years and then had left to help his father because Pentywyn was a big farm milking thirty cows. But although Mrs

Anthony had been dead many years Mair-Ann, because she was supposed to be clever, had been kept at a boarding-school for girls. During her holidays she did not come with us to work in the fields and I never saw her doing anything in the house beyond laying the table, or arranging the flowers or cooking a few fancy cakes for tea.

When she was small and called Mary or Mary-Annie I used to play with her and Densil, both at Pentywyn and down at Môr Awelon. My Uncle Gomer and my Auntie Tilda were always glad when she brought her blue eyes down the hill, because she was comical and made them laugh. She used to recite several pieces of nonsense very rapidly and try to get them to do the same. 'I met a man on the road, he asked me where I was going, to the shop said I, for what said he, for snuff said I, for whom said he, for Mari Twm Tatws said I,' she would say at a great rate. Uncle Gomer made many mistakes in repeating the lines and that delighted both Mary and my uncle. 'My birthday is to-morrow, I've come to you to borrow, bread without butter, no knife for the cutter, no sugar in the tea, no napkin for your knee, a-hum, pig's bum, you shall not come.' Uncle Gomer and Auntie Tilda would laugh and Densil and I try to learn it from her. 'When are you going to die now, Auntie Rosa,' she said, 'for me to have a go in your wheeled chair?'

When she became a little older she always wanted to play with boys. She was strong and could hold you down on the ground. Once when she was wrestling with me in one of the Pentywyn fields she stopped struggling suddenly and when I looked up from the grass at her she was staring down, scowling angrily. 'What's the matter?' I said, puzzled by her frown. She got up and walked away. 'Nothing,' she said. 'Have you got your best clothes on?'

As she got older I liked her less. She had become very pretty, tall and slim and with thick golden hair, and although she was often lovely to talk to you never knew when you might offend her by something you said or did. Sometimes she would walk out of the room slamming the door behind her and not show herself again for the rest of the day. Sometimes she sat and stared at you for a long time, you felt as though she was having a good meal off your face. But it was always enchanting to watch her take a tail of hair that had fallen over her eyes and tuck it back into her thick golden mop.

At the end of my first year in form six I went as usual to Llansant for my summer holidays, and on my visit to Pentywyn I found Densil on a ladder in the orchard. He was among the apples, each hanging a burning cheek to the sun, gathering the fruit into large baskets. Although the end of the holidays was near, the day was bright, very calm and hot even in Pentywyn, which was high and exposed.

'Hallo, Densil,' I said to him. 'Busy at it.'

He had false teeth now and his skin was brown as a cut apple. 'Hallo, Trystan,' he said. 'That's right. Where've you been till now? I thought you weren't coming this year.'

'My granny hasn't been well. I had to stay in Ystrad. I called up because I thought perhaps you'd come for a swim. Feel like it?'

'Yes, I do. It's hot enough. And I haven't been in for a few days. But I've got to fill these two baskets first. Old man's orders. You can help me if you like. We'll finish quicker.'

I began to pick.

'How's Mair-Ann?' I said.

He laughed.

'She's all right.'

I could see that one of the full baskets stood on her special blue stool, under which her ginger cat lay fast asleep.

'I see she's about,' I said, nodding to the basket.

'Yes. But I upset her. As usual.'

'What happened?'

'She's been out with that Stephen Thomas. You know him.'

'Stevie Ty Croes? What's *he* doing now?'

'He's doing engineering in London. Last night he walked Mair-Ann for two hours in the dark without a stop, right up over the Ciliau and down the Roman road. And he talked hard at her all the time.'

'What about?'

'Gas engines. She tried to get a bit of a rest by developing a bad ankle. But it was no good. But she wouldn't let him come on here from Ty Croes. She stopped by the gate. "Good night," she said to him, "you bloody fool."'

'How do you know?'

'She told me. But when I teased her about it just now she didn't like it. I think she fancies him really. Plenty of money there too.'

Presently I saw Mair-Ann coming back into the orchard wearing a vivid blue cotton dress. I had never seen her with earrings before but now she had small red ones in her ears. She was hatless and on her feet were new scarlet sandals. She was the prettiest girl I knew then, her bluebell-blue eyes had a clear look, she had pale, unsunburnt skin, and long, dense hair swinging to her shoulders golden as Bible edges, and she strode over the grass towards us on long beautiful legs, her stride was like the soft resilient pacing of a beautiful animal. But although she did not seem in a bad temper any more I remembered what Densil had said and I was not at ease with her. She was gay now, laughing and tossing back her bright hair; she had waded to her waist in sunlight, standing beside the tree. She had lovely white teeth, but one of them, near the corner, was a little out of line so that after her laugh her upper lip caught upon it and did not immediately meet the lower. That was a delightful thing which I always liked to see happening. When she knew we were going swimming she asked if she might come too.

'That would be lovely,' I said. 'It's terribly hot, isn't it?'

'It is. Dreadful. I've had to go back to the house to dress more suitably. I couldn't bear to have more than two garments on.'

'We can see what one of those is,' said Densil from the ladder, 'and we can guess what the other one is.'

Mair-Ann turned and walked away at once. As she passed the basket of apples on the stool it turned completely upside down. How she did it I was unable to see, but the apples were well spread out over the grass and Densil and I took some time to collect them up again. We went swimming gladly without her.

Because of the illness of my granny that year my visit to Llansant was short, and only four more days remained to me before my return to Ystrad. On each of these days I was up at Pentywyn and saw Mair-Ann. She appeared to have forgotten completely what had happened in the orchard and was always gay and happy. As far as I knew she saw no more of Stephen and seemed to want now to be with Densil and me all the time, in the front room at night, on the roads, down on the Llansant beach, wherever we went Mair-Ann was with us. She was beautiful in the lamp-light of the Pentywyn parlour with her large lustrous eyeballs and a vein prominent in her neck. When Densil jeered at her she no longer pouted, she only laughed or answered him back in a witty way she had. And she was a wonderful describer of what she had witnessed, she made things vivid by the details she told you. She had been watching two tall hunters fighting in the Trenewydd fields, a white horse and a black horse, and after a lot of biting and pawing the black horse had turned round and kicked out viciously with his rear hoofs. The blow landed loudly on the white horse's face and with a horrible scream he fell to the grass dead. She described things like that seriously, as a boy would describe them, but if she had something funny to tell us, she mimicked and acted and made us laugh, seeing and hearing what she was telling us – about Harri Groeswen the shaker, or Thomas the minister who visited the sick and ate their bananas. She was so clever and gay and open I liked her again, I felt a sort of exhilaration in being with her, and every day as I came up the hill from Llansant to Pentywyn I hoped that she would be able to come with us wherever we decided to go.

The last day of my holiday I was up at Pentywyn working in the cornfield. It was still very hot and my trunk and my arms were sunburnt pink. When the two young women were seen with their large baskets crossing the stile into the field, everyone working there welcomed them because their arrival meant a rest for a meal in the shade of the trees growing in the hedges, and plenty of food and great drinks of hot tea, something for the tired, the hungry, and the thirsty. The two women were young maids at Pentywyn, and for the last hour I knew they must have been busy in the farm kitchen preparing this meal for the twenty people working at the harvest, and carrying it out to them in their large, square, flat baskets, normally used for taking butter to market. They laid out the food on white tablecloths spread over the grass in the shade of the elms. I came across the field stripped to the waist and sat down with the other men and women, looking forward to the mounds of home-made bread and buttered slices I could see on the cloths, and the cheese and jam and treacle and tins of fish. I was ready for great drinks of tea out of one of the crocus-decorated mugs set in rows on the grass. But when Anna Price, one of the young women, came to pour me my tea out of the large tin jack, she said: 'Oh, Trystan, I nearly forgot. I've got a message for you.'

'For me?' I said. 'From whom?'

'From one of your aunties. She wants you to go down to Môr Awelon as soon as you've had your tea.'

'As soon as I've had my tea?' I said, puzzled. 'Why, what's the matter?'

'I don't know. It was Mair-Ann received the message. She was coming across Parc-isa when she met someone coming up. Charlo Pil Glas, I think it was.'

'Thank you, Anna,' I said. 'Perhaps I'd better go now.'

I got up and told Densil what had happened. I fetched my shirt and jacket from the hedge and then went over the stile eating a piece of bread and butter. I was puzzled. I could not think what my aunts could want me for. Was one of them ill? They had been quite well when I left them at midday. Had they heard that my granny was worse. That thought pierced me like an edge of ice and I hurried. But they said I was to come after tea. Did not that suggest the matter was not urgent? What could it all mean? As I crossed the Pentywyn fields I tried to solve the unexpected mystery.

To reach the main road to Llansant I had to go through the farmyard of Pentywyn in which the farmhouse stood. Mr Anthony and the four servants were in the field from which I had just come and the whole place lay silent and deserted in the warm sunlight. The two black-and-white sheepdogs, mother and son, lay dozing against the pigsty and did not move. I went across the stackyard, through the flower-garden, and up to the farmhouse, a large building with a semicircular porch supported on two wooden columns, all painted white. I very much hoped that Mair-Ann was still there and could tell me more of the message. The white front door stood wide open. The house seemed fragrant as a rick of honey-suckle. I knocked on the heavy brass knocker and shouted into the hall.

'Yes,' came a voice from inside the house. 'Who is it?'

It was the voice of Mair-Ann.

'It's me,' I called, 'Trystan. I'm going down to Môr Awelon. Thanks for the message.'

'That's all right,' she shouted. 'Can't you come in for a minute? I'm in the parlour.'

I went over the brass, across the hall, and into the big room on the left, still carrying my shirt and jacket. The room was full of sunlight. The goldfish went round and round in its bowl with the newspaper over it. I was dazzled. Mair-Ann lay outstretched on a sort of wicker couch with her ginger cat sleeping on a cushion beside her. The sunlight fell smoothly over her face with the glow and softness of a beautiful red-lipped mask, radiant and faultless. She was wearing a yellow silk dressing-gown with wide sleeves. Because her hands were behind her head her arms were bare.

When I saw her a torrid current shot through me, it was as though a great hot lightning had dropped upon my flesh and in an instant burned its way through me, from head to foot, leaving me numb and uncomprehending.

'Hallo, Trystan,' she said.

'Hallo, Mair-Ann,' I answered. I felt shocked and confused. I wanted to put my jacket on, but I seemed unable to move. I stood before her, my pink-burnt body bare to the waist, staring down. She looked beautiful lying there in her thin yellow silk and her yellow hair melting in the sunglow, but there was something I could not understand.

She was telling me to wait.

'I had the message,' I said. 'I'm sorry I can't stop. My aunts may be ill. Or my granny in Ystrad.'

'Perhaps they're not ill,' she said. 'Charlo Pil Glas gave me the message. You know what Charlo is.'

'But I must go. It wouldn't be right for me not to go.'

I began to put my jacket on. She lifted down the cat, got up off the couch, and came and stood close to me. Around her neck, on a silver chain, was a little silver heart, very plump-looking, with a stone of blue glass set in its plumpness, and there were blue stones in her ears. We were the same height. 'If there's nothing wrong then,' she said, 'will you come back up this evening?'

'Yes,' I said. 'Yes. But I must go now.'

She took hold of my hand. I turned to go. She held my bare arm against her silk gown along the front of her body.

'When are you going back to Ystrad, Trystan?' she asked.

'To-morrow,' I answered. 'This is my last day.'

She took hold of my arms and turned me towards her. She placed her brow against mine. Her hands were white and cool on my breast.

'Trystan,' she said. 'Come up to-night, will you? There will be nobody here. You can do anything you like to me to-night. You will come up, won't you?'

Gently I moved away.

'All right,' I said. 'I'll come.' I felt confused and without understanding. 'I must go now.

103

My aunts have something to say to me. Good-bye, Mair-Ann. I'll come back and see you later on.'

'Don't go,' she said again, but I hurried out of the house and into the sunlight. I saw the hard sea and the soft hills. My heart pounded. What did it mean? Why had Mair-Ann taken my hand? Densil had told me a few days ago that she liked Stevie Thomas. If she was in love with Stephen why had she held my arm against her body? My thoughts and my feelings were in confusion. I thought of her dressing-gown and my naked arm lying against it; I felt the softness still upon my flesh. I felt again the sense of her presence; as I hurried down the road I felt her face close to mine and her brow resting a moment against mine and her hair falling close to my cheeks. Often when we came up in the darkness from Llansant under the dry harvest moons we linked arms together, the three of us, Densil, Mair-Ann, and me, but that contact was only sweet and cool, like the touch of another boy. Why had she called Stephen a bloody fool? Why had her ankle failed? 'You can do what you like to me to-night.' No explanation I could think of revealed the meaning of these words to me. They had a meaning but some resistance in my own heart withheld it from me. Before going into Llansant I put on my shirt and jacket.

I reached Môr Awelon at the visitors' tea-time.

'Hallo,' said my Auntie Tilda, surprised. 'Why have you come back?'

'You sent for me, didn't you?'

'Sent for you? What for? Who said so?'

'Anna Pentywyn. She said Charlo had brought a message up. You sent him.'

'No, I never sent him. Or anybody else. Have you had tea?'

I waited until the visitors had gone out again and then I had tea with my aunts in the kitchen of Môr Awelon.

I did not return to Pentywyn that night. The next morning I left for Ystrad.

6

The building in which the Pencwm grammar-school was now housed had once been the dwelling of a family which, without much effort on their part, had made a fortune out of the coal-pits in the valley. Before the discovery of coal in Ystrad, these people had been small landowners with a barren mountainside on their hands, living in what was only a large farmhouse. But presently both royalties and dividends began to pour into their pockets, they built an enormous castellated mansion in a park overlooking Pencwm, and then, when the

105

fourth generation heir was raised to the peerage, they left our valley for a more feudal area in southern England. It was their mansion that the people of Pencwm had acquired and converted into a grammar-school for their sons.

Before I had reached the sixth form Benja Bowen, feeling that his great gifts would never receive due recognition in a place of learning, had left school and become some sort of clerk on the railway. On my way to and from the station I often met him in the Pencwm high street with a shiny-peaked cap covering his ginger head and a company pencil behind his ear.

'How be?' he would say to me distantly, passing in a cloud of cigarette-smoke. A wage earner now, he had no time to waste talking to those who were still only school-boys.

Evan was in my form, freckled as he had always been, and continuing to write his plays and poems. His parents were unable to send him to the university and he was to work in a solicitor's office. But that did not dishearten Evan. He knew I enjoyed reading the nonsense he wrote, and he used to show me his pieces in the prefects' room before school, an expectant smile on his face; as, '"The Merry Whores of Windsor"; a Tragedy of Terrors; Scene One. A room in Whitechapel. Chublock the Jew paces the boards as one weary of daughters, ducats, and second Daniels. He opens the window (L) and throws out his chest. Fleance, his accomplice, enters.

'Flea: Master, there is a young damsel without.

'Chubb: Without what?

'Flea: Without food and clothing, my master.

'Chubb: Give the damsel food, and bring her in.'

As I read this stuff aloud fresh idiocies suggested themselves to Evan and these he scribbled in between the lines. We were together a great deal, and since his family too were members at Caersalem we saw each other on Sundays also.

Several of the masters at the grammar-school had been my father's colleagues and were kind to me. Only one matter disturbed my happiness and that was a difference beginning to arise between my grandmother and me.

'Trystan, darling boy,' she said to me one night during my last year at school, 'have you thought any more about what we were discussing?' She spoke in Welsh, which was always the language of our Rosser's Row home as it had been of the mountain cottage.

I looked at her and was in misery. She sat facing me across the kitchen table, her lids lowered behind her gold-rimmed spectacles and her gnarled hands clasped before her on the green cloth. Her face was heavily guttered, all the lines and wrinkles of her swarthy features ran down vertically from hair to chin like graining in wood; a few faint horizontal lines were drawn lightly across her brow, but they were hardly perceptible, all the folds, lines, and flesh-grooves of her dusky skin seemed to run in rough parallels from top to bottom of her alien features. I yearned towards her; the thought of behaving in a way of which she did not approve was agonizing to me.

And I *had* thought, I was tormented by the matter she referred to. But I still wished to be a painter and not a minister. This variance was a torment, this conflict between my own artistic aspirations and the disturbed questioning of my grandmother concerning them. In the austere theology of her faith, music and poetry, traditionally employed by hymnist and sacred composer, had received, as surely as Magi gift or pascal offering, the divine approbation. But painting, an idolatrous art, appeared by its nature to fall under the Mosaic ban. Furthermore, how was the dedication of an entire life to the vain pursuit of worldly fame, through the application of colours to paper or canvas, to be justified? Was so dubious an activity anywhere, in parable, or epistle, in mountain, plain, or seashore sermon, was this anywhere held to be a furtherance of the divine plan, the Eternal's *arfaeth fawr* for humankind?

To me she said little at first, but I sensed the dilemma of her doubt and her tender solicitude at my growing absorption and increasing mastery.

For in my later adolescence I seemed to suffer from a phrenetic urge to sketch and decorate; an unremitting itch to draw, copy, shade, design, colour, and represent possessed me. In my despised science text-books, for instance, in one illustrated experiment after another, my pencil wove lacily together the diagrammatical burners, bell-jars, and retorts depicted there; it connected them with dewy threads and delicate nets of cobwebs like the inter-weavings of a Celtic spider. The extensive margins of my geometry book were also of ineluctable attraction and these I en-garlanded with promiscuous decorations of wall-cats, turret clusters, volant swans, and Texan stars. I surrounded the prim logics of congruency and parallelism with borders of starry blossomed bushes or pinioned helmets, or amputated limbs; I threw about them bunches of poppies, lilies, and balloons and hung them with sagging festoons of Chinese lanterns. Elsewhere an archipelago of blots and ink smudges became a bee-swarm disappearing into a pair of working-boots and where logical concision produced the greatest liberality of blankness I had row upon row of patch-eyed pirates, or files of bowler-hatted Jews, who rose out of the shrinking perspectives with an increasing kidnification of their noses.

This unending decoration did not go by without official reproof. The cover of my physics exercise book I embellished with a central motif of branching vines, supplemented with twisted liana-ropes, python-cables, plentiful coils of giant tendrils, and so on.

(In the centre I left a blank space, bevelled like an ornate lapidary tablet. On this Benja, having borrowed my book for cribbing, inscribed: 'Sir Lord Trystan Morgan, Esq., Rosser's Row, Ystrad, Nr Pencwm, Wales.')

When our physics master, a sort of dyspeptic Philistine, was confronted with this disfiguring and sinuous wilderness he coloured and was affronted. Threatening me with a heavy imposition he ordered the removal of the 'disgusting tangle' before the next period.

Since I had inked in my design this was not easy, but before I handed the book in I pasted a sheet of brown paper over the cover. A few weeks later, however, still in the grip of my decorative mania, I forgot offended looks and minatory words and decorated even this over-cover with a still more repellent mass of snake-like forms which secured for me in double measure the threatened dosage of penal verse.

But not all, or even most, of my art was decorative, it was not all fantasy, or absurdity. I drew also from life, and my studio, although I was careful my grandmother remained ignorant of the ironic circumstances, was the gallery of our Ystrad chapel, Caersalem.

Here, in a corner pew, I had complete peace to observe and to copy the bored, reverent, or indifferent heads around and below me. In the borders of my hymn-book where 'Joanna,' or 'Constance,' or 'Arweiniad' left wide margins, I sketched our minister, venerable Mr Prys Huws, and the visiting preachers, and the deacons and the members of the congregation; Williams the tailor, just beneath me, with his parrot beak, polished ivory bald-spot, and black-dyed moustache; Anna Protheroe, or Ninety-houses, in her puff-sleeved overcoat; Richards the overman, sad-faced and leaden-eyed, a raw hairy lump like a meat-loaf glaring across the back of his neck; Watkins the milk, chewing; Doli Vaughan, Caersalem's Nest and Sheba's Queen; dignified Treharne Tai Mawr wearing a tall collar and braided eyeglasses; Ten the Celtic; Dai Edwards, or Half-past Four; the

Montishes; Mrs Rees the Bank, chains, gold rings, and corpulence under a cherry-loaded hat; saintly Robert Harris, a blue-marked collar who taught me in Sunday-school; Niclas y Glo; Dai Badger, shooting pellets; my Uncle Hughie in the precentor's seat, a quizzical twist to his brows as he confronted the congregation.

These faces which I saw Sunday after Sunday, the handsome, the grotesque, the suffering, the pitiful, the serene, these were the faces of the valley, the mothers and fathers, the lovers, the children; and through them, what was odd in them, or sorrowful, or noble, or comic, or beautiful, I learnt the love to which the sermon of Mr Prys Huws, which I was ignoring, exhorted me.

But in time I understood better than my grandmother could have explained to me, that what she desired on my behalf was a life of dedication and service, service to God in our own country if that were possible, or perhaps in Africa, or India, but service to God, and not the exalting of self. When, with gentle words, she hinted that she considered my drawing had become too absorbing an activity, I felt hurt and bewildered. And it was an induction service at Caersalem that revealed finally to me the poverty of my spiritual, or rather my religious life, and convinced me that I had no vocation of the sort my grandmother desired so passionately for me.

Mr Prys Huws our minister, grown old, his powers in decline, wished to retire from the care of our church. He was a handsome old man, his face, with its white beard and silvery hair, beautiful in its perpetual expression of purity and innocence and serenity; but many members of Caersalem were relieved when he first intimated his intention to leave us, because for one thing, although his sermons were lengthier than ever, they were now little more than prolonged and inaudible mumbles issuing from a head which for forty minutes never ceased to shake as though in incessant denial of his message. His garrulity had become well known throughout the valley and he was less and less frequently asked to preside at meetings, or even to propose a vote of thanks. He had never spoken very much English but, with great aptness, the lines he most frequently quoted were those from Lord Tennyson's famous poem in which the brook, despite the comings and goings of men, claims to go on for ever.

When his retirement finally came about a testimonial was arranged for him. So great was the veneration in which he was held in the valley that our chapel on the night of the presentation was crowded as though for a *cymanfa ganu*. He was much moved by the speeches made by the Ystrad people in his praise, and early in his reply he broke down and wept so that we had not to endure another of the poor old gentlemen's interminable mumbles. But the meeting lasted several hours all the same. Mr Prys Huws's ne'er-do-well son had arrived home from his wanderings in South America that very week, and he described to us at great length, and with spirit and colourful eloquence, his adventures among the Indians, cougars, and anacondas of the upper reaches of the Amazon.

We were five or six months without a minister and at the end of that time it was decided at a meeting of chapel members to give a call or invitation to a young man then in his last year at the theological college of our denomination; and whose preachings in our chapel while we had no pastor had greatly impressed us. His name was Dafydd Hanmer, and before entering college, it was said, he had been a shepherd on one of the enormous moorland farms beyond the edge of the coal-field.

He was a dark-haired, rosy-faced young man with meeting eyebrows and blue eyes. It was hearing the answers he gave to the questions put to him by my uncle the day of his induction as our minister that showed me the meaning of true vocation and dedication.

The thirty or forty boys who came up to the Pencwm grammar-school by train from the Ystrad valley were always getting into trouble, the masters complained, and giving the school a bad name. They were impudent to the guards and porters, threw the electric-light bulbs out of the windows, tried to implant a perfect set of muddy footprints across the white ceiling of a compartment, left one compartment while the train was in motion and, clawing their way along the running-board, entered the one next door. Faloon, then only in form four but six foot tall, once even made an attack upon the station-master for shutting the platform gates in his face.

One day when I was in the lower school I said to Evan in our form room before lessons: 'I've broken the strap of my bag, Evan.'

'Sammy,' Evan said to one of the train boys, 'Trystan's broken his strap.'

'Yes?' said Sammy.

'Give him yours,' said Evan.

Sammy grinned and went on unpacking his books into his desk.

'Have you got a spare strap, Sammy?' I asked.

He grinned again and continued to put his books away, not uttering a word.

'Show it,' Evan said.

Sammy pulled out of his pocket a thick

wide strap used, until that morning, for raising and lowering a carriage window. The end that had been hacked from the brass attachment was still white and clean.

It was of no use to me. 'Where did you get it?' I asked.

'Titty bit it off,' he said.

'You damned Ananias,' said Titty. 'You know you said your old man couldn't afford a razor strop.'

The bell rang and we hurried into the hall for morning service.

Now, since I had become a sixth former and a prefect, I was supposed to help to keep order on the train between Ystrad Halt and Pencwm. It was an impossible task. There were no corridors and none of the bad boys would ever enter the same compartment as a prefect.

The morning of Dafydd Hanmer's induction as our minister, I went into the prefects' room as usual before school and found Roger Lewis lying there on the couch with his red hair in the sunlight. He had been absent, marooned by floods and landslides in his isolated mountain village. I pretended to pitch into him the week-end case in which I carried my books and that brought him upright. Roger was the slowest and solidest boy in the school, he looked and moved as though his skin was loaded with flesh of supernatural weight and density. He lived in a hamlet so remote in the hills above Pencwm that it was without light, water, or drainage, and Evan used to tease him that the babies were now born up there with bucket rings already imprinted on their bums.

Roger always came to school on a horse.

'Who's reading to-day, Trystan,' he asked.

I had looked it up on the way in.

'You are,' I said.

His expression changed again. He was very slow at everything, particularly at the reading aloud of scriptural English. His own Bible was a Welsh one. Reading the lesson in the school hall during morning service was a nightmare to him. The last time he did it he practised assiduously beforehand; on the morning he paused half-way through the chapter and looked indolently around the hall to show how much at home he was in this job. But when he returned his glance to the Bible the expression of airy indifference vanished from his features. He had lost the place and there was a long agonizing pause while his finger searched in panic up and down the verses.

He went heavy and worried out of the room to look up what portion he was to read, and as he did so several other prefects came in: Islwyn Viner, the school swot and horseface, who for a birthday present had had his text-books bound in leather; Carlos

117

San Martin, our little Basque; Sammy Evans, cutter-off of window-straps, now regenerate; Evan Williams; Dicky Adler; fat, spectacled Aby Bernstein, who claimed his father's business had only two branches, one in Pencwm and the other in Jerusalem; and three or four other prefects. They sat down getting their books in order for the day.

'Hell of a fuss on the station,' I heard Sammy saying.

'What happened?'

'I don't know the details. It seems Rawlings is mixed up in it.'

'He's a proper marvel, he is,' said Dicky.

Rawlings was a sixth-form boy who hadn't been made a prefect. He smelt of hair-oil and stale tobacco. He was cool with the staff, especially Crumpy, our dwarfish classics master. A day or two before, when they were sitting round Crumpy's desk listening to their lesson, Rawlings took his penknife out and began sharpening his pencil very loudly. Crumpy stopped talking and waited. After a time Rawlings looked up. Crumpy had coloured.

'Have you finished now?' he asked.

'Not quite,' Rawlings answered. 'You go on.'

Roger Lewis came back unhappy under his ginger hair into the prefects' room.

'You're right,' Sammy said. 'I can't stand him. Never could.'

118

'What was he doing?' I asked.

'I don't know it all. Messing about with Agnes, they say. Somebody said he got some kids to hold her down on the seat while he put his hand down her blouse.'

We all laughed.

'She hasn't got anything there,' Carlos said. 'Berny's got more than her, haven't you, Berny?'

Bernstein grinned and felt inside his jacket with both hands at his hanging dugs.

'Surprised it was necessary to hold Agnes down to do that,' said Evan.

Sammy glanced round in silence through his gold-rimmed glasses.

'Agnes is daft, I know,' he said. 'But what the devil did Rawlings want to mess her about on the train for? And get those kids to help him. She was crying in the station, I saw her. She went to the station-master. There'll be a hell of a row, I'll bet there will.'

'The flamer deserves it anyway,' Dicky began; but the bell went for morning assembly.

Just after break that afternoon as I was sitting reading my Tennyson in the prefects' room a little boy came in and said the headmaster wanted to see me.

I never liked visiting him in his room. I went uneasily along his private corridor where the floor was hollow and gave out an ominous echo under my tread. I knocked at the door.

'Come in,' he shouted, and I entered.

He was sitting, not behind his desk, but in his arm-chair by the fire. He motioned me into another arm-chair opposite him.

Our headmaster was an Englishman with some sort of grand accent, but in his twenty years in our valley he had learnt to speak more Welsh than many a native. Everything I knew, everything I was allowed to hear about him, made me respect and admire him, but I was never at ease in his presence. I felt shy and tongue-tied every time I entered his room, very much overawed and unable to behave or express myself naturally and easily. He was a very tall and upright man, bearded and bald, but with a thick layer of long greying hair brushed over his scalp. He always rang the first hand-bell himself in the mornings, and on a rough day it was rather comic to see him stalking about the school yard with his gown blowing about, vigorously ringing the hand-bell with one hand, and with the flat of the other preventing this lid of hair from lifting off his scalp in the wind. His beard, clipped severely back, was greying, and brilliant blue eyes glittered incessantly in what I thought was mockery, or disapproval, behind the round panes of his glasses. To me he was only dignified, austere, and awesome, hardly a human being at all, cold and distant. Carefully he hid from us, his pupils, until the end, the grotesque elements in his character and his sense of mischief.

'Sit down, Trystan,' the headmaster said.

His elbows were on the arms on his chair, his legs crossed and his finger-tips together.

He began questioning me closely, in very great detail, about the Agnes affair, but he soon saw that although I had been on the train I knew nothing of it. He puzzled me by seeming not to care and when I rose to go he said:

'Have you a lesson now?'

'No, sir,' I answered him.

'Sit down a little, will you?'

'Thank you, sir.'

'You haven't much longer in school now, Trystan.'

'Less than a year, sir.'

'And what's going to happen then? What would you like to do?'

Satisfying him about Rawlings and Agnes had been hard, but this was an agony. I was silent. Then I said: 'I would like to be an artist, sir.'

'A painter? You are very good at it, I know. Exceptionally. I remember the Valleys' schools exhibition. Your work was outstanding. Quite outstanding.'

'Thank you, sir.'

'I take it you'll enter one of the art schools

and train as a teacher of art first.'

Again I said nothing.

'What do they think at home about your becoming a painter?'

'My grandmother is very much against it, sir.'

He nodded. 'And your uncle?'

'He doesn't mind, sir.'

'Your grandmother's a very remarkable woman, Trystan. You know that.'

Blast it. I could feel my eyes filling with tears.

'Why doesn't she approve?'

How could I tell him, an Englishman with a class accent, a foreigner, and a member of an alien Church. But somehow I tried to explain that my grandmother felt painting to be almost a frivolous occupation in a world where so much required urgently to be done. Although what my grandmother believed made me unhappy I explained her objection as fully and as earnestly as I was able, because I found it unendurable that he should think her wrong or her principles contemptible.

'I see,' he said. 'And what does she want you to be?'

'I should think a missionary, sir. Or a minister. Something like that. We don't talk much about it, sir.'

'And what do you feel about that?'

'I feel attracted to it, sir. I mean being a

122

missionary. Especially when I hear my grandmother talking. When she describes the conditions in which millions live, especially coloured people, sir, I want to go out to help them. But I'm afraid I soon forget. And I'm afraid if I were ever in some of those beautiful sunny countries I might be more interested in painting what I saw than in helping, sir. I know I should, sir.'

'You like your school work, Trystan?'

'I do, sir. But the thing I enjoy most in the world is looking at things and light and handling paints and paper and trying to put down what I can see, sir: I hope that's not wrong, sir.'

He was silent for a moment.

'This is a very difficult matter for me to discuss, Trystan. I am very loath, for one thing, to give you advice contrary to your grandmother's wishes. And, in any case, the final decision must be your own. Could your decision be postponed? Could you go to the university in the ordinary way and decide at the end of your period there what you wish to do?'

I said nothing.

'You know, people change a good deal, and perhaps this love of drawing and painting is something that will pass.'

'I don't think so, sir. But I don't want to hurt or disappoint my grandmother if I can avoid it, sir.'

'No, I understand that. Will you let me know what you have decided when you *do* make up your mind? I am most interested in this question, Trystan. Tell your grandmother about our talk, will you?'

'Yes, sir,' I said, getting up.

'You have something important on down there at Caersalem to-night, haven't you?' he said, smiling up.

'Yes, sir. Our new minister is being inducted, sir.'

'Are you going to the meeting?'

'Yes, sir. All Ystrad will be there to-night, sir.'

'Well, I hope everything goes satisfactorily. Ring the bell as you go through the hall, will you? Thank you. Good afternoon, Trystan.'

I went back along the corridor, disturbed and yet exhilarated. I had spoken to the headmaster almost forgetting my shyness and my awe of him, and he on his part had acknowledged my dilemma and treated it gravely. The conflict in my own heart seemed less. That my consuming desire to paint might be impermanent I had not until then considered. Was my sympathy with the downtrodden, the neglected, the oppressed, the exploited, really deep and abiding and my love of this external world ephemeral? I thought more kindly of my grandmother's words than I had ever hitherto done.

That same night Evan and I hurried over

our homework and then went to Caersalem. The building was already packed with people, many of them strangers from Pencwm or from down the valley; and since this was the second crowded meeting to be held in the chapel in one day, the atmosphere was hot and oppressive and a good deal of moisture ran down the green walls. We found a place to squeeze into on the gallery in a sort of square pen above the upstairs doorway. From there we had a good view of the packed congregation, row after row of men and women in their best clothes in the body of the chapel and in the curving gallery. Our new electric lights were on, and the seats full of people, without a gap anywhere, and the long, narrow windows and the great brown tie-beams, and the vast, grass-green chapel walls was all round were things I could remember for my sketch-book. We sang hymns with gusto, and prayers were offered by ministers of neighbouring churches in the valley who had come to Caersalem to welcome a new colleague; and then my Uncle Hughie, as the senior deacon of Caersalem, came down from his precentor's seat on the front of the gallery and stood in the pulpit where everyone could see him. This pulpit was an offence to me, a shiny wooden structure, almost black, very ornate and ugly, with carvings and hideous handrails. He invited

Mr Hanmer up from the big seat to stand beside him and there they were beneath a hanging electric globe, my uncle with his hard hair, his arrow-head moustache and eyebrows, and his plump body; and Dafydd Hanmer beside him, fresh-skinned, dark-haired, handsome, lovable, wearing a new minister's suit of black.

It was my uncle's duty to tell the great congregation the reasons for our having given Mr Hanmer an invitation to become our minister, and this he did carefully and soberly, having spent many evenings in the parlour preparing his speech, but he could not help, all the same, making people laugh from time to time. Then he had to question Mr Hanmer publicly, asking him to describe the course of his spiritual life and his career until this moment; asking him why he had entered the Christian ministry; why he had adopted the credo of our denomination; why he had decided to accept the call we had given him, and other matters. I had never before heard any man speak with such simplicity, certainty, and sincerity as Mr Hanmer in his answers, and it was clear that this frankness, and integrity, conveyed by both his words and his bearing, greatly impressed the intent congregation listening to him. After each exposition and reply the people, being unable to applaud, broke out into mutterings of satisfaction, praise, and approval. Men and women turned to those sitting beside them and nodded their heads in sober pleasure at his acceptable words. When the questioning and the answering were over my uncle shook hands with the young man and descended from the pulpit, leaving him there alone, our minister now, to ask a blessing on the congregation.

My grandmother had not been well enough to come to the meetings and when I went into the kitchen at Rosser's Row after the service I found her sitting waiting for me there expectantly.

'Well,' she said, 'what was it like?'

'It was wonderful, Mamgu.'

'Were there many there?'

'The chapel was packed. They had to bring chairs into the aisles. The Roberts boys were sitting on the windowsills. And Evan and I got a seat in the *cwtsh y geifr*.'

'How was your Uncle Hughie?'

'Wonderful, Mamgu. He explained everything from the first proposal in the deacons' meeting until Mr Hammer accepted the call. Of course, he had to make them laugh once or twice.'

My grandmother frowned. 'And Mr Hanmer, how did he speak?'

'He's absolutely sincere, Mamgu. He told us about the way he had always wanted to be a minister, ever since he was a little boy, and how he worked at his Greek after finishing every night on the farm. His parents couldn't afford to let him stay in school and college and he had to go out to work early. But he never gave up and now he's what he's always wanted to be. I hope he'll like it here, Mamgu.'

'What did he say about his call? Didn't he say anything about a call from God to do this work? I mean, Trystan, apart from his own desire to do it.'

'Oh yes, Mamgu. That was one of his best answers to a question of Uncle Hughie's. He said he knew quite well that only fancying the job of minister was not enough. He said that he was as certain he had been called to it as he was of anything. But he refused to talk about it. Not in public. But he said that as we listened to his sermons and to his talks in the week-night meetings that we would learn something about it.'

'He is right. You liked the meeting, Trystan, and you liked Mr Hanmer. Will you think about what he said, darling boy? I would like you to think about these things. Ah, here's your uncle. Go and open the door for him, *cariad*.'

My grandmother did not refer again to Mr Hanmer in this way, but her words were like a blow to me. During the whole service I had not once thought of it as anything concerned with my own problem. I had enjoyed the singing and the sight of the crowded chapel before me, and the faces and the strange ministers, but I had seen in Mr Hanmer's replies only a reflection of his own honesty and not an illumination of the problem which so often tortured me. But after my grandmother's words I began to see the meaning of dedication, and the more clearly I understood it the greater was my own uncertainty, dissatisfaction, and alarm. There was nothing in my own experience to match the single-mindedness and conviction of Mr Hanmer. My life seemed to be lived minute by minute, I enjoyed or endured things as they happened to me, but I had experienced no burning sense of vocation such as Mr Hanmer had described. Although I could not define the distinction to myself, I felt profoundly that a difference did exist between Mr Hanmer's call to a life of service and my own self-indulgent desire to be a painter, intense as that was to me.

But still, in my confusion and my uneasiness and my flashes of resentment, I had at all times the whimsical encouragement of my Uncle Hughie. He, I knew, quoting to my grandmother such verses as those of St Paul commending things of good report to the Philippians, used on my behalf always his droll and tolerant advocacy. And it was he who finally brought about the compromise by which the next three years of my life were governed. I was to go, not, as I had wished, to the art school, but to the university at Dinas to qualify as a teacher; but if, by the time I had taken a degree, I still had no clear vocation for the ministry or the mission field, I was to be permitted to follow my own inclinations with regard to a career.

My grandmother told me her prayers would be that nothing in my life during the next three years, no hardness of heart, no pride or carnal-mindedness or worldly desires, would make an impossibility a vocation to serve among the called and the chosen. I acquiesced in, rather than welcomed the compromise, and prepared myself for a further three years of academic study.

The City

1

When I had been in that place, Dinas, a fortnight, I still wondered what there was to like in it.

My lodgings were in 87 Boundary Villas, a long hillside terrace looking down over the roofs of the university city and its trees and smoke-pall, and the distant sea – a hundred and more houses dressed into a strict rank of military alignment and uniformity. Every morning, as I looked out of my bedroom window, I saw the risen sun run a guard-inspecting eye along them, swinging unimpeded his glance across the playing park. For Boundary Villas, these tall, narrow, three-storeyed structures, overlooked one of the city's recreation grounds.

The houses had doorways in pairs and small tessellated areas before them. Together they formed an uninterrupted façade of pale grey and steak red; that is to say, the walls were of local brick while the mullions and transoms of the bay windows were of some rough pumice-like rock. Each door-porch also was framed with the same pallid and unsmoothed material.

I ate and studied in the dim bay-windowed front parlour downstairs, and slept in its first-floor duplicate. The depressing shadows of this sombre parlour, and the heavy monochromes of its grim furnishings, sobered me abruptly when I first looked into it over Miss Machen's arm. I was chilled. My heart sank. When I introduced the pachydermatous Alcwyn to it, right in the mid kiss of a sexy story of his, he halted suddenly, called twice upon his Maker in alarm, and then fell silent, even he, dismayed by its chilly influence.

For the muddy wall-paper of the room displayed the boring arabesques of some drab and heavily foliaged creeper, and the highly polished oilcloth repeated underfoot in monotonous khakis the tortuous and melancholy branchings. Over the bay window hung dreary chenille curtains of severe purple, approaching black, dividing a heavy penumbral gloom amongst its many corners. All the chairs and the window sofa were stained a tarry black and upholstered in unyielding and funereal mohair. The nigrescent tablecloth seemed cut from the same dismal material as the window curtains but from a remnant of a dowdier and swarthier purpuration. The iron grate, the hob, and the mantelpiece, together with the fire-irons, had been indiscriminately stove-enamelled by Miss Machen to a gloss of even and inhospitable black; and the whole repellent structure froze the new entrant to the room with its bleak angularity and its cold, clean, and anthracitic glitter.

One other feature fascinated and repelled me. Behind the sofa, in the bay window, stood a tall wooden pedestal, painted, I would say, with a thick coating of Welsh gravy; and upon it rested a kind of cauldron with cracked earth in it like a block of indestructible concrete. No fern or flowers.

But there, in spite of this atmosphere of perpetual dolour and half mourning, I found at least cleanliness, quiet, and a sufficiency of food.

But I hated the university from the beginning.

I arrived there on a Wednesday. On the Thursday I paid a visit to the college to see the dean. What a building! What architecture, as Alcwyn had taught me to say.

To a front view the college appeared as a large, grey Tudor manor-house, genuine, dripstoned, and ogee-arched. But this was only a façade. Behind it was concealed a huddle of low modern structures built of steel and glass; these were the lecture rooms and laboratories. As I came up from Ystrad to Dinas by train I saw in my compartment a picture of the university I was about to attend. The old residence was there, dignified and attractive, and some of the park which surrounded it, but I did not guess that what I looked at was to play very little part in the lives of students and was occupied almost entirely by the rooms of professors and the offices of the college administrators.

I went up the steep drive from the city and found myself on the terrace before the college. Above the main porch was a heavy metal shield bearing the university arms, complete with motto. This was in Greek and I could not read it, but Alcwyn told me it meant 'Avaunt, obscurity!' I turned back and looked at the view. Before me was the huge park, and then the university city, and then the sea. I regarded them in deepening unhappiness. The sun was shining, and students, passing and repassing behind me on the terrace, were laughing and talking and greeting one another boisterously after their long vacation; but I was seized with this powerful emotion that I remembered many of my countrymen to have experienced in sadder circumstances than mine and to have movingly described.

I was not alone, I saw, in feeling this sadness and yearning. The dean's room was in the old manor house, the shabby, badly lighted, and depressing part of the college. I took up my place at the rear of the queue of students in the corridor outside the professor's door and nodded to the man before me. He turned away, rude and unresponsive. All the students in the queue, men and women, were silent and subdued; they appeared in that gloomy corridor as depressed, anxious and unhappy as I was myself. As I stood there waiting I thought of my drab rooms and of Miss Machen, my vulture-like landlady, whose appearance had at first staggered and then enthralled me. I thought of my bewilderment trying to find this college, passing in our suburb through street after street, all, to my Ystrad eye, identical in every detail with Boundary Villas, all beef-red and bay-windowed and baileyed with tile-work. I thought of my own entry into this shabby building, where the air seemed warm and used, and of my loneliness and homesickness.

And then Alcwyn came to stand by me. He was slim and spectacled, with wavy albino hair and a cast in his eye. His invisible eyebrows worked and the corners of his mouth were unsteady, he seemed to have difficulty in keeping a straight face.

'Is this the dean's, brother?' he said to me.

I nodded. I had to smile at him and he grinned back.

'Been here long?' he continued. 'I've tramped all over this damn building looking for it. What are you doing? In college, I mean.'

'History. History of art. English. Welsh.'

'Welsh, ay. I'm Welsh but I can't speak Welsh. I'm from Trenewydd. Radnorshire. Ever heard of it?'

'Yes,' I said.

'Where do you live? Near here?'

'No. Outside Pencwm. In the Ystrad Valley. Coal mining.'

'Why the devil did you come all the way up here then?'

'I wanted to do the history of art and it's only here I can do it. There's no department nearer than this.'

'Are there many people from your school here?'

'No one. All the boys from Pencwm go to Caerdaf. I'm the only one.'

'I expect I shall see you then. I'm doing English too. You did tell me your name, didn't you?' he said, grinning. 'But I didn't quite catch it.'

'Morgan,' I said. 'Trystan Morgan. What's yours?'

'Mine's Meredith,' he said, 'but I keep that dark, a complete cryptonym. Everyone says, "Oh, are you related to the great George Meredith?" And then I have to reply: "I *am* the great George Meredith!" And I'm sick of that joke now. I've got myself called Alcwyn. Wonder where my old man got it from? Where are you in digs?'

When I told him he said: 'You're lucky. I'm told a brisk student can quit his bed there at eight-thirty and still arrive in college washed and shaved for a niner. Not that I've got to shave much yet.' He rubbed his chin wryly.

More students were arriving and taking their places in the queue behind us. Even when my eyes were not on him I could feel Alcwyn searching my face and smiling to himself, and every time I glanced at him and caught his eye his grin broadened and became rectangular. He was untidy, and some sweet foreign smell came off his person.

'Where are *you* digging?' I asked him.

He laughed. 'I haven't got any digs yet,' he said.

'Where did you sleep last night then?'

He laughed again. 'I'll tell you. This is what happened. To get here I had to change in Bodrhys and there's always a couple of hours to wait there so I went into the refreshment place. It's a hell of a station, Bodrhys. Do you know it? But there's a lovely waitress there, pretty, ginger hair, lovely figure, you know, so I started talking to her, the usual rot. I told her I loved her and all that, and that I couldn't live without her. I thought perhaps I could see her in the holidays but she kept blushing – she's a lovely blusher – and telling me no, she was courting a Bodrhys bus conductor steady. Anyway, I was so busy loving her that the train came in and went out again without me. So I had another two hours to wait. I left the station and went to the pictures. It was awful. *And* stuffy. *And* I'd seen the films before. *And* I had to stand for an hour. When I got a seat I fell asleep. I woke up and found I had about five minutes to get back to the station. I ran like hell through the town and saw the train just steaming out. I galloped and fell into the last compartment. Phew!'

The surly man who had been standing in front of me came out of the dean's room. But I wanted to hear the rest of Alcwyn's story so I nodded to the girl behind us to take my turn.

'What about your luggage?' I asked.

'Didn't have any, except a week-end case. That's all I've brought so far. Anyway, when I got here it was dark, gone eleven o'clock, so I began looking for a police station. I saw a woman leaning over the gate of a big house, middle-aged, you know, and as I passed her she said: "Excuse me, are you looking for someone? I've noticed you passing up and down." Well, I told her I'd just come up to the university and had nowhere to sleep and I asked her if she knew anyone who would put me up until the morning. "I think *I* could manage it," she said. "Would you care to stay here for the night?" It was very nice there, and I must say I slept like a log. But do you know what happened this morning? A nurse brought my breakfast in to me. She was all grins. Do you know where I was? I had spent the night in the maternity home.'

As we were laughing the dean's door opened and the girl came out.

'Wait for me,' I said to Alcwyn. 'I'll see you later. Perhaps you can dig with me.'

I was not long with the skull-like dean but when I came out Alcwyn had disappeared.

That evening I walked about by myself in the lighted main streets of Dinas, hoping to see Alcwyn. I had never before experienced the particular longing from which I suffered, and it was hard to bear. To think of Ystrad, I found, my granny accompanying me to the bridge of Rosser's Row and my Uncle Hughie seeing me off at the halt, was a bad thing. I came back early to Boundary Villas, refused supper, said my prayers, and went to bed.

2

On Sunday morning Miss Machen, tall, stooping, the rookery of her coiffure bebowed and becombed, brought my breakfast into the front room on a tray and placed it in silence before me on the table. Her Sabbath-day dress was of some thick blackish material, very stiff, like tarpaulin or roofing felt, but wormed over inch by inch with intricate and silky black braid the thickness of tubular bootlaces. It had a high collar supported on whalebones under her figlike droppers, with narrow pleated lace showing its edge against the tortoise neck-skin. On her mannish bosom, one offering no glance-hold, featureless and inaccessible as a jail wall to the sensual eye, hung a gold-framed cameo from a golden lovers' knot, and around her wrist clinked the golden shackles of her jointed bracelets. Her bony ice-cold hands, heavily ringed, were the large and masterful graspers of a wicket-keeper, they had flat nails, and an intricate system of blue pipes tunnelling the skin of the shiny backs. The thin skin of these hands and of her face seemed to give off in that dim room a silvery, phosphorescent sheen.

Miss Machen was deaf and, apart from the awe with which her remarkable appearance inspired me, little communication was possible between us.

In the chill and gloomy front room, beneath the menace of the smoke-brown ceiling and the muddy walls, I ate my food in unhappiness and silence. Outside the sun shone and a church bell tolled near by.

I finished my meal and stared gloomily across the cauldron out of the window. In the middle of the road, right before the house, I noticed three young men drawn up. They were all hatless, two of them very tall and one short. They seemed to be engaged in discussion, but not knowing them I turned away, took out my Tennyson, and sat at the fireplace reading. In a moment or two I heard someone at the window behind me. I turned round and there with his face tight up against the glass was one of the tall young men, the bald-headed one. His nose had turned white on the pane, it looked like a fruit-stone showing pale in a glass of plum jam. His head was abruptly withdrawn when I turned, and after some discussion at the front door Miss Machen came into my room and said I was wanted outside. I went out, puzzled, and there, smiling in the front porch, his hymnbook under his arm, stood the tall baldhead.

'Good morning,' he said in Welsh. 'You are Mr Morgans, are you?'

I said my name was Morgan.

'I'm Zachy Charles,' he explained. 'My auntie told me about you. Mrs Charles. She goes to Caersalem where your uncle is precentor, in Ystrad.'

I said I knew Mrs Charles very well. Would Mr Charles come in?

'No,' he said. 'No, thank you. As a matter of fact we're going to chapel. Come here, boys,' he called. 'This is him.'

The two other young men came in

through the gate and across the area smiling and were introduced – another Charles, Zachy's cousin, called Charley *bach*, or little Charley, and Doug Edwards. The three of them, it seemed, were at the university. I shook hands with them and invited them all inside again.

'No, no,' said Zachy. 'We thought if you weren't going anywhere else you might come to chapel with us. Would you like to come?'

I said I would very much indeed. I had not promised my granny that I would go to service, she had taken so much for granted and would arrange for my letter of membership to be forwarded from Caersalem to the chapel of my choice. In a few minutes we were all walking down Boundary Villas on the way to the Welsh church in Markethall Square.

This was Zachy's third year at the university. He knew everything, and said it. He was big, blond, and talkative. His face, long and already heavily lined, had little clusters of bluish spots here and there in the skin of it, like the markings in blue cheese, and these, and his physical maturity, made me think he had once perhaps been working underground. As he talked the other two listened and laughed. Charley *bach*, small, also fair, had a scar on the bulbous end of his nose from a wound that must almost have severed it. He smiled happily at Zachy's talk, showing his teeth, large, white, and even. Doug, I gathered, was a final-year medical, a high bony man with fluffy hair and a ruddy, dug-out face with a lot of skull showing in it. All three were neatly dressed in what looked like their best suits, they had handkerchiefs at their breast pockets and well-polished boots.

'How are you getting on at Miss Machen's?' Zachy asked me. 'You've got a good place there, you know. Last term she had Decker and Pompey, that's it, and how she put up with those two I don't know.'

'She didn't, Zachy,' said Doug the medical.

'No, you're right,' Zachy agreed. 'They were not there many weeks. I wonder if Nico and Tommy are next door to you again. They're a rare pair of birds too, they are. What about Gordon, boys, shall I give him a knock?'

He left us in the middle of the road and went up to the bay window of a house, peered in as he had done to mine, and then returned.

'Not there,' he said. 'God knows where Gordon is. With the Quakers, or the Mormons, or the Mohammedans, or God knows who by this. He doesn't like Markethall any more. I remember the last time he went there, Morgans, and old

Richards the announcer asked him after chapel if he had enjoyed the service. "I didn't come here to enjoy the service," Gordon told him, "I came here to worship God.'"

'Rude devil,' said Doug.

'Miaow, miaow,' Charley *bach* began. 'Miaow, miaow,' in perfect cat-call imitation, long-drawn-out and in an agony of unsatisfied libidinousness.

We were passing a house with a lamp over the front door and a large wooden sign in the area. On both were the words 'Cats' Home.'

'Miaow, miaow,' Zachy joined in, but with inferior mimicry. Then he frowned all over his lined face. 'Not to-day, boys, it's Sunday,' he said. 'Come on, we'll be late if we don't step it out.'

All the way to chapel he talked, voluble and expansive. He had long legs, and Charley *bach* and I had to hurry to keep up with him. Several times he left us and tapped at the front-room window of some student he wished to bring to chapel, and before long our numbers had doubled. Between these visits he kept on blaming Doug, in his bantering, half-serious, loquacious way, for spoiling his conversations with Olwen last term, just as he was getting on lovely with her. He accused him of laughing if he made mistakes in English.

Doug interrupted to tell me Zachy kept a little black book in which he collected big English words, and once when Mrs Jeffreys Evans asked him how he was he said, 'Indispensable.'

Never mind that, Zachy said, he had a new overcoat with a velvet collar now, and he was going to polish up his English accent so he might stand a chance with these city girls after all. One thing he had to remember. 'That Olwen now, is not a typewriter, is she?' he said. 'She is a typ*ist*. I must remember that because it put her off me before. I am afraid though, boys, she is a respecter of persons, that Olwen. Chris Crosshands used to dig there, Morgans, a medical. Remember the night he qualified, Doug? Coming into our digs, sniffing and sneezing and his eyes running and asking Doug and me if we knew what was good for a heavy cold. I expect he'd forgotten by then. He took fifteen years to qualify. This is Markethall Square, boys,' he said with a hand-wave to the dozen of us, 'and there in the corner is the chapel.'

There were villas all around the large square and a patch of green in the middle, where, I supposed, the market hall had once stood. The chapel was a church-like building with stained-glass windows and a slated spire. We all went into the porch, combed our hair, and then up into the gallery. The inside was small, but very pretty and tasteful; everywhere, except upon the brown pews, there was paint, cream or bright green in colour. An organ decorated with gilt was playing sweetly and softly. The windows were of stained glass in lozenges of pink and pale blue. Covering the table before the pulpit was a white satin cloth with golden fringes and three bunches of golden chrysanthemums in silver vases stood upon it. The pulpit was not the sort of elevated black box which we had in Caersalem, stuck on the wall like a swallow's nest, it was really a platform or small stage with a brass rail and a velvet curtain to the front of it.

Other students were sitting in the two small galleries, one on each side of the chapel. Zachy smiled round at them all, men and women alike, and nodded warmly when he caught someone's eye.

Presently the doors beside the pulpit opened and the young minister, tall and handsome, entered the chapel and ascended the pulpit; the deacons following him, going into the big seat in front.

In a block of seats opposite us sat a dozen girls who had all come in together. I was next to Zachy. As the young women put their heads down in prayer he turned to me and nodded across at them. 'College freshers,' he whispered. 'You'll be able to persecute some of those after chapel to-night.'

The organ began the Lord's prayer and the service commenced. With our heads bowed Zachy passed each one of us a double-strength peppermint. The sweet he put in his own mouth was large and noisily unwrapped from paper and I could hear it rattling hollowly between his false teeth as he tried to chew it.

All that happened then was familiar to me, the hymns, the prayers, the sermon were similar to those I had known every Sunday since childhood in Caersalem, Ystrad. But yet here, in Markethall Square, everything seemed strange. At home, when I sat down in the gallery I saw Sunday after Sunday my uncle opposite me in his precentor's seat behind the pulpit, his skin shining, his spectacles half-way down his nose, and the bushwork of his hair rising stiffly above his brow. Mrs Nicholas the caretaker was always there, bad-tempered and red-faced, her voice in a screech when we children went with unwiped boots over the scrubbed boards of her vestry. The Barachaws, the old half-tramp, hawked and spat in every service and slept during the sermon, drop-ping his hymn-book or knocking over his walking-stick. Mr Clements the deacon, too, with his white beard, whose photo-graph, until I found it represented John

Ruskin, I thought was on our kitchen wall in Rosser's Row. Anna Ninety-houses. Doli Vaughan. Treharne Tai Mawr. Mrs Rees the Bank. All sat in Caersalem on a Sunday morning, all within the clean bare walls, all together in the building with the long plain-glass windows where nothing was decorated or ornamented, where the forms into which wood and cloth and stone had been worked were simple. Markethall, after the austere and comely bareness of Caersalem, seemed elaborate and pretty and unreal.

After the service that night all of us, Zachy, Charley *bach*, Doug, and the other students, were invited by Mr Morris the young minister into a vestry behind the chapel for coffee. This room was large and well lighted, pleasant to be in, the high-pitched roof vaulted over at intervals with arches of grained timber.

We found there many men and middle-aged women, evidently members of the chapel, as well as younger people and a good number of the students we had seen in the service. All were standing about in groups or sitting on back-to-back forms, talking with animation and drinking the coffee which was being brought around on trays by the young women of the chapel. Zachy Charles seemed to be known to everybody and he introduced me as his friend Mr Morgans, of Ystrad, a new student at the university.

The only thing I disliked about Zachy then was that he called me Morgans.

I noticed that several of the ladies he spoke to he addressed as 'Captain,' as 'Mrs Captain Davies' or 'Mrs Captain Jeffreys Evans.' This puzzled me. I had never heard anything like this in Ystrad, where our distinctive appellations were homelier, but when I whispered to him about it he rolled his eyes and answered: 'Sea captains. Their husbands are sea captains. Plenty of money.'

He pointed out with proprietary satisfaction some of the more important members of the chapel: a barrister, the wife of a surgeon, the son and daughter of a high-ranking civil servant, a newspaper editor. If I had not remembered what he himself had said about Olwen, that she was a regarder of persons, I would have thought that he too suffered from this same weakness, because when he stood up to speak to these people he did so with an amusing mixture of satisfaction, deference, and beaming self-importance. He became pink, his excitement made his bald head steam. 'Did you know Lord Lisvane was a member here?' he asked me between two coffees. 'A deacon. We call him "Yr Arglwydd." He used to teach us in Sunday-school.'

'He wasn't a lord then,' said Doug, a very

dry and factual sort of man.

Zachy looked hurt. 'I took his niece out once,' he said.

'Once,' said Doug.

'Tell Morgans about it,' said Charley *bach*, pulling his wounded nose. 'Up the Crossett.'

Zachy grinned, good-humoured again.

'She was some niece of his from up London way, stopping with her uncle for a bit. Linda she was, wasn't she, Charley? One Sunday night in here after chapel I asked her if I could show her round a bit and she said yes.'

'Zachy's not a bad-looking chap,' said Doug, winking at me.

'Well, I got on all right with her; she couldn't speak much Welsh so I was cracking my jaw a bit, to show her I could talk English tidy, and I remembered to walk on the outside, and to say, "Pardon," when I – you know. I wasn't half refined, I'll tell you...'

At the end of the vestry was a trestle table to which the coffee-cups were being returned and behind which four or five women worked at refilling them. While Zachy was speaking I had begun to watch with fascination the movements of one of these women, the youngest of them, so that I did not attend to what he had to say. She wore a dark dress with a white lace collar and cuffs. Her face was pale and oval, tapering rather to the chin, with markedly high cheek-bones and rather narrow and sloping eyes. Her straight black hair, parted down the middle, was worn in a fringe across her brow and cut in a bob which made a sort of soft frame for her face. She seemed lightly made, but yet was not small. What fascinated me was the air of silence, the solemnity almost, in which all her actions seemed to be enveloped. She poured out coffee from the large silver coffee-pot with seriousness, an impenetrable absorption; the laughter and the talk of the room and the movements about her to and fro, all seemed to be existing in a world of which she was unaware. Sometimes it became necessary for her to make contact with a person from beyond, from the busy and animated room; she passed out a coffee-cup as it were, smiling slightly, and then returned to her remote and unassailable quietness.

When Zachy had finished his story I nodded towards the trestle table and said to him: 'Who's the girl behind the table?'

He glanced over his shoulder. When he faced me again he was grinning, but he seemed uneasy and embarrassed. He took a gulp of coffee and looked at Doug in a meaningful way. Charley *bach* also looked at Doug, his white teeth in a grin, but yet rather sheepish. Doug himself had a smug smile on his bony face, which he seemed to be trying to suppress. He winked at me.

'Doug's,' said Zachy.

'Sorry,' I said. I felt bewildered and dis-appointed but I said nothing.

Presently I saw the dark girl go into a sort of kitchen behind the vestry in which the coffee was prepared. She reappeared in a few moments wearing her hat and coat and drawing on her gloves. With her was another much older woman, stooping, and with an undershot jaw, very smartly dressed, her mother I thought. The two of them came down the vestry and stopped for a moment when they reached our group.

'Hallo, Mr Charles,' the older woman said, smiling. 'How are you, Mr Edwards?' She nodded round with an inclusive smile to the rest of us. 'Back to work again, are you, all of you?'

Zachy rose to his feet, pink with pleasure to the top of his bald head.

'How are you, Mrs Pugh Pritchard?' he said. 'It's a great pleasure to see you again. And Miss Pugh Pritchard also.'

The girl standing behind her mother smiled but said nothing. She did not appear to realize that Zachy had addressed a remark to her.

'When are you coming to visit us?' asked her mother. 'You must try and come some time this term again. Will you? Are there any new students? They must come too. Shall we arrange it next Sunday? Don't forget. And good night. Good night all.'

They left us. Zachy had only time to whisper 'She's a sister-in-law of the lord,' when the young minister came up to invite us to his house for supper. He was a very handsome man, black-haired and blue-eyed, in the formal clothes he wore he looked like a distinguished actor or politician or lawyer. Zachy accepted his invitation at once and took it upon himself to assure him that Charley *bach* and I would be delighted to come too. Doug declined, and I saw the smile that passed between him and Zachy. In a few minutes we were in a large car belonging to one of the deacons, heading for the minister's home.

3

Walking down Boundary Villas the next day, Monday, I met Alcwyn. He had found digs, it appeared, in the next street. Almost the first thing he asked me was if I would go with him to the Calliper Club.

'What's the Calliper Club?' I asked.

'It's the engineers' club. It used to be serious, for debating and that, but now it's only ragging. Will you come?'

'I'm not an engineer.'

'Neither am I. Anyone can join who's sponsored and is willing to be initiated. Tonight's open for freshers.'

'How do you get initiated?'

'You have to dip your finger in a cup of methylated spirits, set it on fire and light your pipe with it, or your cigarette.'

He grinned widely at my dubious expression. 'There's no danger,' he said. 'All you've got to remember is to keep your hand vertical. If you let it hang down the flames will run up your arm and set your sleeve on fire. Coming?'

'I don't mind coming to see what it's like but I don't suppose I'll join. I don't like clubs much.'

'It's great. All the lads belong to it. Fantaz Jenkins, and Chewzy, and Legger Jones. And Nico who digs with me. He's the Sergeant. They have a hell of a time.'

'What do they do?'

'They sing and have speeches. And Legger acts the goat. It's absolutely great, they say. Men only.'

It was getting dusk when we climbed, rather late, into the shabby, whitewashed upstairs room of the Prince Llewellyn. As we opened the door the prominent features to me in the teeming, dim, and as yet unlighted place were the unrestrained babble of voices and the gloomy pall of tobacco-

156

smoke hanging under the low ceiling.

There was a noisy welcome for us. Someone suddenly howled at the top of his voice, 'Lights, Fantaz,' which produced universal uproar, deafening shouts, hoots, stampings, catcalls, whistlings with the fingers, and thunderous bangings on the tables of pint pots, until five or six electric lights of feeble power were switched on by Fantaz Jenkins, the appropriate officer, shedding dim cones of yellow illumination upon the pipe smoke and the anarchy beneath.

The clubmen sat at two long tables which ran parallel the length of the room and drank, jabbered, or played shove-ha'penny. A circle of them, sitting beneath one of the electric globes, projected meteors of copious spittle up at it and as we watched them we saw a passer-by deliver into their competition a bull's-eye from what appeared his practised ordnance. He was a tallish thickset man in heavy boots, old-fashioned clothes, and steel glasses, and his black hair was cropped down on to his skull.

'That's Nico Mathias,' said Alcwyn. 'He's in our digs.'

'Is that him?' I said. 'I walked home from college with him yesterday.'

At right angles to the two long tables was a low dais on which stood a black upright piano and a third, smaller, table. Around

157

this, under the illumination of a single globe, sat the six smoking officers of the club, of whom Nico Mathias was one. He had taken his place amidst cheering and table-bumping alongside Stonker Watkins, the presiding Lucifer, a conky bespectacled giant with a crimson nose, a healthy covering of tufted ragwork on his cuboid head, and a grin displaying large white teeth like bath-room tiles that shot their illumination through smoke and electricity.

'Whoooo-z the man with the big bent nose?' Stonker bellowed in a maroon-like howl as Nico was taking his seat, and together the chant of the Callipers sounded in thunderous response, 'Hoo-ha-hoo-ha-ha,' followed again by cheers and table-bangings re-echoing from the low ceiling and the barrack-bare walls.

The Lucifer clouted the dancing table half a dozen times with the official gavel, and heaving up his titanic form and donning his glossy topper, whose crown almost brushed the low ceiling, asked if anyone had seen Chrissy.

'In the words of Holy Writ,' he said, 'where is the scratchetairy? He's holding the proceedings up. Has anyone seen him?'

Some shouted one thing in reply and some another, some claiming Chrissy was in jail, some that he was dead, some holding he had gone north to play for Wigan. 'Never 'mind Chrissy,' Jocker called out, 'let's have Legger Jones.'

'Legger,' the Callipers shouted. 'Let's have Legger Jones. Legger. Legger.'

So Legger Jones, with presidential anvilling, was invited on to the platform to open his mouth and let it say what it liked.

Legger, a lank, rake-like individual, disguised in the sporting habiliments of the landed classes, had been sitting opposite Alcwyn and me in bow-tie, canary cardigan, and leather-buttoned green tweeds with his cap in his pocket. I had noticed with interest and had appreciated his ability to turn his eyelids inside out. His yellow hair, stiff and brushed back, glistened with oil like glassy-haired barley. He was long, blond, and loose, going on elaborate flap-tongued brogues and with a lolloping stride up to the rostrum. He bowed at the applause under the gob-cat-kinned globe and then, altering his voice, the angle of his body, the pitch of his head, he began his irreverent and fantastic mimicry. The menacing jab with a hag-like finger, the silent and suspended opening of the mouth, the abrupt flexing of the arches of his brows were enough to bring forth roars of applause and set the Callipers rolling in their seats, clawing each other chest and back with laughter.

He did first Professor Ailradd, whose sole method of historical instruction, I had found out already, was to read aloud in a hesitant and nasal falsetto from the works of Mr Prévité-Orton, an historian whose paragraphs Legger had by heart.

He did Dr Di Enaid who, dealing with Switzerland, was said to display a map of Norway on the blackboard, or considering New Zealand, hung up Mongolia, and then in growing perplexity and incoherence pawed the surrounding wall.

Professor Blwng, Legger's next character, was accomplished in a sketch of brevity and economy but also of great polish and effect. Legger shambled into the open from behind the piano with the fumbling inelegance and hesitancy of this uncouth pedagogue entering a lecture-room, took off his cloth cap and tucked it under his belt, muttering: 'Now to begin this morning, now to begin this morning—' interrupting himself to deliver a hearty belch which was echoed by the listening Callipers in a thunderous replication of dissolving ventosities.

As Professor Anfoesgar he waved an official form, bearing down upon some hypothetical student and, indicating by broadcast nods and gesticulations that he was supposed to be conducting his interview in some public place, perhaps a college corridor, boomed out questions to be asked only with the greatest reserve and delicacy. Legger stood before the piano in the well-known Anfoesgar stoop, his spine curved like a dog on his back legs eating out of a bucket, and trumpeted the professional indiscretions, as 'Now tell me, in strictest confidence, of course, now tell me, how many times has your father been in prison, for me to put it down here on this form.'

But Legger's Mr Penmoel was, for Alcwyn and me, the most rewarding presentation. Mr Penmoel, mincing, cultured, bald, and curly-sided, read aloud in class with one eye closed through a circular magnifying-glass part of a Middle English text, and presently, as his mellifluous recital proceeded, manifested symptoms of acute embarrassment, coughing slightly, stammering, scratching with the reading-glass the back of his neck, performing a sort of childish micturition dance, running his finger round the inside of his collar. Because with these posturings the learned philologist heralded the approach of a line of bawdry. Legger, standing there under the anointing light, was by some strange gift of hallucination even able to suggest the pudent port-wine blush that suffused his entire head and neck as the blunt Saxonisms were finally uttered and the steam of embarrassment which arose off the erudite cranium as off a cooking-pot.

During the resounding applause Stonker could be heard rebuking Billy Handel, next to him, for precipitating an attack of boilermaker's ear. Glancing over his spectacles, he rose and again elevated for silence towards the sooty ceiling his blacksmithlike arms.

'Spotty,' he said, 'come on. Get the cob-webs out of the brass. Come on, lad, give us a tune.'

Spotty took his French horn on to the platform and after a few preliminary roulades began, accompanied on the piano by the talon-handed Jocker Dawkins, a tremolo rendering of 'Take a pair of sparkling eyes.' The man beside me, who had all the evening given me his nape, went prowling on low bug-legs up to the platform, while Spotty played and lay down on the floor gripping him by the ankle. Spotty himself, long and angular, his drab countenance in full bud, began well, but broke down upon an exalted note and began to cry with his arm across his face. Everybody cheered encouragingly and he was led sobbing back to the table, leaving the ankle-gripper prone and asleep on the floor.

Murtagh then, summoning all Callipers to their knees, asked with uprolled orbs and blasphemous unction the divine judgment upon the head and all members of Professor Caled, a doer of ample evil, false as a bag of deceitful weights, amongst whose trans-gressions were fornication, debauchery, and failing fifty per cent of his year in subsidiary physics. Nico preached with torrid eloquence his horse-Welsh sermon on the text, *'Tenor solo i Silas, A'r hen Baul yn chwyrnu bas.'* Again Billy Handel, brandishing his churchwarden, conducted the assembly in *Sospan Fach.* So great was the animation and ebullience of his conducting that at the crash of plagal cadence he brought down the clay baton on the cranium of Jyder Davies who, with zealous conscientiousness, was contributing to the bass part right beneath him, shattering bowl and stem-piece into fragments. There arose a vociferous demand, accompanied by foot-stamping and rhythmic iron rain of pint-pot banging, that the Sergeant should now do his trick, but Nico evaded the summons with profanity and grinning reluctance. Placing his pectinated fingers across the swell of his belly he complained of a touch of Felinfoel goitre. But a swarming on-slaught billowed up and overwhelmed him from the lower tables; he was pounced upon despite dodgings and circumventions, tackled low, and dragged clumsy and cursing, but helpless with slobbering laughter, to the front of the platform below which the ankle-gripper still lay sleeping. There, by a superiority of rebellious numbers, he was being forced into immobility when the Lucifer shouted hoarsely: 'Here goes, gold watch or cork leg,' and attempted a rescue. Seeing a fellow officer assaulted and engulfed Stonker stood majestic upon a chair, spitting on his hands, intending to launch himself upon the seething scrimmage beneath him. But under his mass the frail chair, at the moment of his take-off, collapsed and pitched him under the table.

'And to think,' I heard him growl as he crawled out groping up glasses and topper, 'and to think that when I was born you could put me in a quart jug with the lid on.'

Nico's tie and collar, as he lay impotent with pinioned arms and sat-on legs, were forcibly removed and the front of his shirt opened, revealing his dark hermaphrodite dugs covered with a curling shrubbery of hairs. Gwyndaf, after ruffling up the shaggy undergrowth, set fire to it with a match. There was an evanescent flare and crackle as the little conflagration blazed up. Then Chrissy, the secretary, passing at that moment from the beer-lift with a syphon in his hand, said *'J'écrase l'infame'* and squirted a generous dash of soda-water into the burning tangle.

The Callipers were in a frenzy of hysteria and excitement. Chewzy, his appearance more negroid than ever, sprang to the platform and asked who would do what he would do. Several at once swore they would have a dack at it. He took out a needle and thread from behind the lapel of his coat and

164

showed it glittering under the electric globe.

'Look,' he shouted, 'the big act,' and plunged the needle directly into the centre of his left cheek.

There was a gasp and a tingle of revulsion, and for the first time that evening complete silence. Chewzy opened his mouth and revealed the needle protruding between his teeth. He rapidly placed his fingers into his mouth, pulled the needle and cotton through and then pushed the point of the needle back into his other cheek from the inside of his mouth.

At this point the platform sleeping pedipalp roused and seeing Chewzy above him in the act of pulling needle and cotton out of his dusky face, dropped down his head and spewed copiously on to the floor.

Everyone shouted and clapped, the plaudits were accompanied by whistlings, anguished grimaces, and writhings and some vocal criticism as, 'Where there's no sense there's no feeling.' Half a dozen Callipers hurried up to Chewzy to fulfil their promise but the landlord hammered on the door and shouted: 'Time, gentlemen, please.' To valedictory bangings and counter-cries – not initiated by the Lucifer, a dumb titan now whose aphonia condemned him to silent mallet-brandishing – of 'Whooooz the man with the big bent nose' and 'Weeee're the boys what make no noise,' the meeting broke up.

Alcwyn and I went home together. I was bewildered by what I had seen and heard.

'Wasn't it great?' Alcwyn said. 'Are you going to put up?'

I didn't answer. I was puzzled. I couldn't bring myself to say no. I thought about it until I got into bed. Then I said: 'Good-bye, Callipers.' It was interesting and amusing, wonderful as a painter's spectacle, but I knew I would never want to go there again and I was glad of it.

4

I was with Alcwyn regularly at college. Since our lodgings were so close together and our time-tables for certain subjects coincided, we often called for each other.

One day in the common room about a fortnight later I saw him, as usual with a group around him listening to him and laughing. He was now, he shouted across to me, an initiated member of the Calliper Club. Grinning, he lifted up his right arm in its sling.

I arranged to go round to his digs that night at about eight o'clock.

There were hundreds, perhaps thousands, of houses in our suburb of this seaport which appeared to be exact replicas of those in Boundary Villas and Alcwyn had digs in a terrace of them running off at right angles to it. He had two other men with him, Nico Mathias, the engineer, Sergeant of the Callipers, and Pompey Cosgrove, a medical.

I was shown in by the small daughter of the house. I found Alcwyn alone standing on the table in the middle of the room reading. The gaslight was on but the place was in semi-darkness. He had his book in his unslung hand and was holding it close up against the light. When he saw me he grinned, came down, and offered me a chair by the fire.

The room's furniture, its wall-paper, its rugs, its oilcloth, were similar to mine in Boundary Villas. Much less austere with regard to colour originally, flamboyant indeed, but, as far as I could judge in the poor light, far shabbier, untidier, more neglected. The whole place was in disorder, as though it had been stirred up with a stick. When I stepped inside everything trembled violently, every footstep I took on those jelly-like floorboards was accompanied by tinkling and rattling all around the walls from crockery inside the dresser and the cupboards, from the gas-brackets and the window-frames.

'Yes,' said Alcwyn, seeing the surprise on my face, 'one day it'll go right through and we'll all end up in the coal-hole.'

'What's the matter with your light? It isn't very good, is it?'

'There's something wrong with the gas mantle and our landlady won't have it seen to, damn her. She says we broke it and we'll have to buy another one.'

'How do you do your work?'

'We've got to do what I was doing just now. Stand on the table. In turns. The three of us. You needn't laugh. Smoke?'

'No thanks. I haven't started officially yet.'

'Haven't started? Haven't you smoked at all?'

'Yes. But I gave up when I got into the grammar-school.'

Using only one hand, Alcwyn put a long white holder in his mouth, got out his Turkish cigarettes and stuck one in it. He held his box of matches between his knees to get a light. More than once during these manoeuvres I offered to help him but he would not allow me, he kept on laughing, enjoying the novelty, and talking all the time out of one side of his mouth.

'Our landlady would love you,' he said. 'She hates smoking. She believes the roots of the tobacco plant are suckled in hell.'

I knelt on a chair and looked at the photograph of a Rugby team hanging on the wall near the chair-back. When Alcwyn was smoking he said: 'Do you play games?'

I shook my head. 'Not much,' I said. 'I like

swimming. And I'd like to be good at tennis too.'

He hollowed his cheeks and pulled in. 'I hear a hell of a lot of sport talked here. Fifty per cent of the conversation. The other fifty's about women. That's Nico, and that's Pompey' – indicating them in the photograph with the mouthpiece of his holder. 'They're both in the first fifteen. Nico's a bit fly-blown, isn't he? Or's it the light?'

Pompey the medical was handsome and dark, his expression stupid and brutal. He wore sideburns, and his black shining hair, brushed back off his forehead, was arranged in symmetrical waves upon his scalp.

Nico was thick and strong with a short neck and stumpy hair. His nose appeared to be broken. I said: 'We saw him at the Callipers, of course.'

'Yes, that's him.'

'And I've seen him in college. Are they all right?' Then I felt myself blushing.

'They're all right,' he said. 'Not many ideas. Everything done by the book of arithmetic. Both of them. Working, playing, whoring. Did I tell you? They're as lecherous as sparrows. We can't stay here in this lousy light. It gives me the screamers. Let's go down to the Queen's.'

We left the house, went down the hill running past the park, and eventually entered the main street of Dinas. Alcwyn

169

talked. He saw a lot. He criticized. In a combative, amusing way he denounced streets, buildings, squares, memorials. I rather took architecture for granted, but he observed it. He made fun of churches and municipal buildings and the series of ornate fountains in High Street, each with a lady atop fifty gazers could not abash, he said, 'though all she wears is some reeds round her waist in a sort of a sash.' What puzzled me about him was that the things he disliked, or said he disliked, seemed to occupy him far more than those he admired. He approved of very little but he made me laugh and wonder at him, at the buffoonery in him and what seemed to me the great cleverness.

Presently we came to a wide building with glass swing doors, a café, across the upper storeys of which sloped the enormous word 'Queen's,' made out in crimson electric bulbs. We went in while a commissionaire in brown and gilt held the door for us, and passed along a carpeted corridor until we reached the café. The air there was warm, it was scented and stale, it reminded me of breathing with a hot hat over my face. The room was large and rather full, the people sat at scarlet-topped tables, circular or rectangular. All round the red walls were mirrors and gilded panels alternately, giving the room space and brilliance. In a red

170

sector-shaped recess a band of strings and saxophones was playing a slow and cloying dance tune.

We got a table to ourselves and Alcwyn ordered Russian tea for both of us. Someone had skilfully and laboriously insinuated a religious tract between the glass top of the table and the wickerwork beneath it. Reading it through the glass Alcwyn said he thought there was a lot of nonsense talked about the Bible. Especially as literature. Didn't I agree? For obscurity and manifold ineptitude the Old Testament had Shakespeare and even Browning well beaten. That phrase – obscurity and manifold ineptitude – he had read somewhere and was going to use in an English essay any day now. And then think of the appalling ruffians the Hebrews had for heroes. And the prophets and the patriarchs, always whoring and bargaining with God, and eating dung and living in adultery. He thought them most objectionable. Didn't I agree with him?

I said I thought the New Testament was surely the important part of the Bible.

'Oh yes,' he said. 'It is. Jesus is admirable. But some of his followers – most disheartening. I always think Luke ought to have called his book "The Acts of the Impossibles."'

A student Alcwyn introduced as Nugent

came up. He had a fine grey suit on and he wore cuff-links, a signet ring, a pearl tie-pin, and a buttonhole rose. He was chinless and gushing and, because of his whining talk about dancing, he seemed to me a fool. I was dry in my remarks, impatient at having to endure him. When he had gone Alcwyn said: 'Look here, Trystan, I don't think you've thought out how you're going to behave in this university.'

He was grinning, but I felt hurt.

'What do you mean?' I said. 'Thought out? Must I think out how I'm going to behave? Surely I shall behave as I've always behaved.'

'How can you? This is not Ystrad. In this place there are all sorts of people. I've been here some time now, and I know how I am going to survive.'

'Well?'

'Have you read *Le Rouge et le Noir?*'

'No. Nor heard of it. What is it?'

'In that novel the hero, Julien, is repre-sented as a man of great cleverness, but in his theological seminary he becomes most unpopular because he hasn't the cleverness to conceal it.'

I understood only vaguely what Alcwyn was talking about. What had his words to do with me? He seemed to have been con-fronted with some problem and to have arrived at some decision. I was uncertain what his problem was. My own problems exercised me greatly, the question of my painting and my obligations to others, but how I should behave at the university I had never considered. It was hard to understand what made the problems of other people seem real to them. Alcwyn continued talking in the same strain, urging me, as far as I could understand him, to decide on the sort of personality I was going to present to the people around me. He seemed infinitely more grown up than I now, although when he had spoken to me outside the dean's room I had thought him boyish and irresponsible. I found it hard to accept the existence within one person of so much silliness, cleverness, and maturity.

The heat and brightness of the café were pleasant, and the drowsy-sounding band. After listening to Alcwyn for three glasses of tea and two Turkish cigarettes, I said I felt like going back to digs. Outside the café it was chilly, but we hurried and warmed ourselves.

'Come back to my place for a bit,' he said. 'We'll have crab for supper. You can meet Nico and Pompey.'

When we arrived we found the two under the dim gaslight eating their supper. Pompey was easily recognizable from his photograph, although he now looked younger and much more amiable. He had a little head with a big handsome face on the front of it.

'Let me introduce you, Trystan,' Alcwyn said, waving his slung arm. 'That, with his knife in the preserve – my preserve – is Pompey Cosgrove, captain of the college fifteen, etc. This is Trystan Morgan, Pompey.'

Pompey got up, nodded, shook hands, and smiled, pleasantly but said nothing. Nico introduced, did the same, his countenance wooden, quite unlike the person I had seen helpless on the floor of the Prince Llewellyn with his chest-hairs on fire. He was wearing his little steel glasses.

'We've met before,' I said.

Nico stared at me like a puzzled bull.

'I bumped into you coming out of college. A week ago. We came back to digs together.'

He nodded, but I could see he did not remember.

In figure Nico was tallish, long-armed and bladdery, his thick neck shortened by the structures of fat or muscle padding his lumpy shoulders. His appearance was conspicuously non-urban; he was wearing a thick jacket which seemed to be made of heavy fawn felt, or perhaps plain carpet, cut long, and with the deep vent and large patch-pockets of a farmer's town-coat. Round the neck of his cream flannel shirt he wore a long scaly tie of lizard-skin which he had found, he told me later, abandoned in the college showers. He had no braces and his black whipcord trousers – a certain clownish and endearing veracity in him confided of these also, when we got to know each other, that they had, like his father's, calico linings to 'below the knees' – his trousers were supported round his spongy hemispherical belly by an inch-wide travelling strap, and dropped their excess of length like accordion bellows over his heavy, black marching boots. These boots, sturdy, leather-laced, and rock-like as to toe-caps, presented, because of the multiple laminations of the sole, a built-up and compensated appearance; seen separately each might be mistaken for the surgical boot of a man shorter in one leg than the other.

'Sit here,' Alcwyn said to me. 'Cut yourself your own bread and butter. Everyone does here. Nico and Pompey will require speed; me, geometrical accuracy. Nico cuts wedges; Pompey digs the guts out of a loaf; me, I am an expert. Look. The loaf's horizontal as a bowling-green.'

Pompey looked at me, his film-star face bulging with food. 'I suppose he's told you already what a marvel he is, has he?'

'He noticed it, Pompey,' said Alcwyn. 'He noticed it, lad.'

Pompey made an obscene reply.

It was a good meal, although Alcwyn's crab turned out to be only cold American cheese plastered with pepper, salt, and vinegar. Pompey had been to Paris during the summer vacation and had returned with unbounded regard for what he called 'the French dames.' He described his experiences with great fullness, relish, and vividness. One morning, after a hell of a night, he found himself in his hotel bedroom wearing a white sailor's hat and a large paper bow. Dead broke and with a black eye. God knows what had happened. He remembered meeting two women, he and his brother, and taking them...

Alcwyn grinned. 'Did you go to the Louvre, Pompey?' he said.

'What the hell,' said Pompey, startled.

'The Louvre,' Alcwyn said again.

Pompey thought he had. He remembered a painting of a naked girl with a jug on her shoulder. Life size. And the *Folies Bergère*, he had been there too.

Alcwyn kept on asking him questions. I realized he was doing so merely to induce Pompey to show his stamina and carnality and his simple pride in them, and I felt ashamed. In spite of his boasting I liked Pompey very much. Taking a toothpick out of his waistcoat pocket he said to me: 'Do you play games, Trystan?'

I gave him the same sort of answer as I had given Alcwyn. 'At school we played soccer,' I said.

176

'Yes, soccer's a good game,' he agreed. 'But do you play Rugby?'

No, I didn't. 'Come on, Trystan,' Alcwyn interrupted. 'I'll see you as far as the corner.' Outside he said: 'Pompey must like you. I've never heard him refer to soccer before otherwise than as a bloody ladies' game.'

We went down the street in the direction of Boundary Villas.

'Why's Nico so silent?' I asked. 'He hardly said a word.'

'He's often like that. A complete *persona muta*. Not always! God, no! Remember him at the Callipers? Sometimes he gets going. This morning he called me a shocking foul-mouthed bastard of Effingham.'

'Where did that quotation come from, Alcwyn? You know, the one about the fountains in High Street?'

'"Up at the Villa" I believe. Browning, anyway. Do you know Browning?'

'Only the ordinary things. The only English poet I know really well is Tennyson.'

'Mm, Tennyson, as one says nowadays. And I think rightly, lad. There's some incongruity in a nineteenth century Englishman writing as he so often does. I remember the experience of my sister with regard to him. She wrote to me in her first year at the university saying it was all very well for Tennyson to chant about his Lily

Maids and Mother Idas, but she could see his dirty old pipe on the page before her the whole time. Being a woman, any disparity between the art and the man is intolerable. Incongruity, disparity, and intolerable are all words I mean to use very soon. So long, Trystan. See you to-morrow.' He was gone. I could hear him running back along the pavement in the darkness.

I went on to my digs in dejection. I felt deeply hurt to hear Alcwyn, from whom I had expected sympathy and understanding, speaking so coolly and even disparagingly of poetry which had given me such profound pleasure. Alcwyn, I supposed, did not suspect the disappointment his derisory or patronizing attitude sometimes caused me. Of course, when he made fun of what I did not cherish he sounded amusing. I knew I should resist these attacks upon things I loved deeply, and which I knew I loved deeply, and not so readily accept the standards of another person. Alcwyn seemed to me clever, but I was sure I ought not to defer to his judgments where my own deeper feelings were concerned. That Alcwyn disapproved of the poetry of Tennyson should signify nothing for me because the love I had for this poetry signified so much.

When I had begun to reject Alcwyn's pronouncements I felt happier.

5

As that term went by I wondered more and more what the purpose of the university was. As far as I could judge, the institution was concerned merely with imparting information, which indeed it did unremittingly, if also unimaginatively. Much of that information seemed to me of questionable value. Was it the most relevant to the understanding of any particular subject, I wondered? I wished to know the factors which would explain why things were so, or why events had happened in that precise way, but seldom was the illuminating word spoken, the suggestion thrown out upon which one could ponder, the idea expounded which disturbed one with its many implications. This was true even of the lectures on the history of art which I thought to me could never have been rendered dull; but all I took from them was the memory of acute boredom and of the smell of disinfectant. Two convictions forced themselves upon me. The first was that many of my teachers had never themselves been deeply disturbed by the subjects they were teaching. Secondly, many of them taught the material they gave us not because it was the most relevant but merely because it happened to be what they knew them-selves. After a little I began to believe Legger Jones was right.

When I mentioned my misgivings to some of the other students in my year they seemed puzzled and even affronted. Most of them appeared to care very little what they were taught so long as they were taught enough of it to pass their examinations. Their sole concern seemed to be not with real learning, far less with criticism, think-ing, reasoning, and speculation, but with amassing enough facts to pass their final degree examinations. I met students every day who worked hard and would, I felt sure, pass everything they tried quite satis-factorily, but who yet seemed to have no profound interest in what they were studying, who were unable to discuss their subjects intelligently, had no ideas of their own about them, and no information but what had come from their lectures and their prescribed text-books; and who had, also, no intention of pursuing any of their studies beyond the degree examination if that could be avoided.

I had never wished to be any sort of scholar, and now the masses of dead in-formation I had to master made the idea of ever becoming one repugnant to me. It seemed much more important that I should continue to see the things around me clearly and accurately, to feel and understand them as objects, to be able to bring them into moving relationships with one another when I represented them in a drawing or a painting. No one in the university seemed to think this important. When I tried to explain what I meant to other students they appeared embarrassed. Alcwyn was prepared to discuss the matter with me, but his first sentence or two showed he had not the vaguest understanding of what I meant.

6

Near the end of my first year Miss Machen brought a telegram into my room. It was from my Uncle Hughie. My grandmother was ill again. Could I come home?

I shaved off the growth of 'swot fortnight' and, although it was already late afternoon, took train to Ystrad, hoping somehow to catch the two connections I should need. I had no luggage but into the pockets of my mackintosh I slipped my Welsh *Mabinogion* which I was revising when the telegram came. I felt disturbed and anxious, as I always did when she was ill or in pain, but I could not believe my granny would die. Did the telegram mean she was going to die? She was old and often ill, but there was a permanence, a quality of rock-like immutability about her for me which meant I found it almost impossible to conceive of her death. To me she had *always* been old, yet she seemed still unchanged, no older now than in my boyhood. She would not die, not yet, not until I could imagine her death and think about it without my mind becoming blank or overborne.

I failed to make my connections and arrived outside Rosser's Row early the next morning just as the day was brightening. Everything in the valley was still and silent in the risen sun, no one was about, no smoke rose from the chimneys, only the river made its washing noise going under the little bridge. As I got out of the newspaper van which had brought me up the valley I looked anxiously over at the small square windows in the backs of the Rosser's Row houses to see if the blinds were down. But the sun shone brightly across from the opposite mountain, turning the panes of the whole terrace into squares of blazing silver, and I could not see.

I crossed the bridge and went along our front pavement. Everything was still, the people had not yet risen, and in the silence my footsteps echoed loudly on the flagstones. House after house, all had their blinds down, every parlour, all the way along to my granny's house, all had the curtains pulled across the windows or the blinds lowered to the bottom.

When I knocked at our door I could hear someone stirring inside and presently my Uncle Hughie opened it. He was wearing his crossed-over muffler, his brown cardigan, and his bedroom slippers, but he had not put his glasses on and his shaggy eyebrows were over his eyes. He looked sleepy. In his hand he carried some pieces of firewood.

'Hello, Trystan *bach*,' he said.

He could tell I knew.

We went inside to the sunlit kitchen and he put the kettle on the fire, which was burning up brightly by then.

'When was it, Uncle?' I asked.

'Yesterday, Trystan *bach*,' he said.

'Before you sent the wire?'

'She was gone when I sent it.'

He got out the things for breakfast. As he padded to and fro across the kitchen putting them on the table he talked to me. He seemed much older and slower, and more bent.

'She hadn't been feeling well,' he said, 'but you know how she is, often *anhwylus* and then better again. She was complaining of pain in her leg for the last few days. It was severe the night before last and we had to have the doctor, but yesterday when she woke up it was much better. I lit the fire for her and she dressed and came down and sat in her chair there. I made her a bit of toast and she took the plate in her hands with the toast on it. I bent down by the stand there to get the teapot to pour her a cup of tea and I heard the plate and the toast sliding to the floor. I looked up to see what was the matter. She was gone.'

His eyes filled with tears. He wiped them, took his glasses from the mantelpiece, and put them on. Then he went into the pantry again.

'Are you alone here, Uncle?' I asked.

'Mrs Williams number one is looking after me, *bach*. Yes, I was sleeping here alone last night. But you'll be here with me to-night, won't you?'

After breakfast I felt drowsy and anxious for sleep, so I went upstairs and lay on the bed. But I could not sleep. And I could not cry either. The thought of my uncle alone in the house and getting old brought me nearer to tears than the unreal death of my granny. That I could still not believe in. And soon I heard the callers beginning to arrive downstairs, tradespeople, sympathizers from the chapel, neighbours, people who had known my granny when she lived in her mountain cottage, miners working at the same pit as my Uncle Hughie, they came almost without interruption throughout the day, so that we could not even eat our meals without having to get up to answer the door.

I was glad when these visitors arrived day after day, that my feelings, because of the strange unreality to me of my granny's death, were not deeply stirred. I did not wish to cry before the women who wept in the evenings in our parlour, or in the presence of the murmuring bowler-hatted colliers who, in their own hard and enormous hands, took hold of mine in sympathy.

The night before the funeral, after all the visitors were gone, my uncle and I sat beside the table in the kitchen in silence. The gaslight was shining on the brass around the fire-place, the dark red curtains covered the back window and the fire still burnt cheerfully in the green-tiled range, although it was almost midnight. My uncle began to speak about my granny in a way he had never done before. It was sad to hear him, almost unbearably sad. That night I learnt yet more about her early life, the way she had taught herself to read both English and Welsh, her endless toil during her long widowhood as lodging-house keeper, chapel cleaner, and launderer, ironing a hundred collars, when she could get such work, for a few pence only. The mark of her religion, the valley people said, was to be seen in the work of her hands.

'Did you ever look at her hands, Trystan?' he asked me. 'Poor Mam, they were pitiful, so rough and twisted up and swollen. For fifty years they were the hands of a labourer. They brought me and your father up, Trystan, they fed and clothed us and gave us shelter when there was no one to do these things for us. Did you ever look at them, *bach*?'

I nodded. I felt I could not speak.

'Every night she prayed for you,' he went on, 'every night. From my room next door to hers I could hear her on her knees beside her bed. And every night I heard your name, every night without fail she prayed for your health and preservation and success. But above all that you might not become a child of this world, a drunkard, hard-hearted, of impure life, unfaithful. That was a thing she feared more than all. Trystan *bach*, I don't think you can realize how much she thought about you and the way you live and how anxious she was night and day on your behalf.'

Where his religion was concerned my uncle was a reticent man. Although he spent much of his time in the service of the chapel he never spoke of his inner religious experience. Those who tried to discuss such things with him he daunted with a joke or the evasion of a pleasantry. I had never heard him speak before so openly about prayer, nor had he ever shown me as now his dependence upon his mother and his sense too of the impossibility of her death. I went to bed sorrowing, deeply cast down. My uncle's grief and loneliness were heavy to bear. I loved him and I wanted to be able to do or say something to comfort him. Kneeling beside my bed, with my face against the pillow to say my prayers, I felt my heart fill with despair, I was in utter despondency and bitterness of spirit, and I wept. All night I kept waking up, thinking of my granny lying dead in her coffin in the room below me, and my Uncle Hughie, old and lonely, and awake in the darkness, weeping bitterly, I knew, and finding no comfort for his loneliness and despair.

The next afternoon my granny was buried with my father and mother in the grave we still had in the graveyard of Caersalem. The day was warm and sunny. We held first a service in our green parlour, conducted by Mr Hanmer our young minister. My uncle and I were present, with Hannah Protheroe, Mrs Williams number one, Mrs Harris and Mrs Edwards from Caersalem, and my Uncle Gomer, who had come that morning from Llansant to represent my mother's family. As the minister was praying we heard the coffin being carried out through the passage on to the pavement by the Caersalem deacons and colliers from the Ystrad pit, and the bumping sound they made against the wall is something I shall never forget. My Uncle Hughie took off his glasses and wiped his eyes. When we came out to the front doorway we found a crowd of people waiting there on the pavement, most of them neighbours, and before the funeral rose a hymn was sung. As I stood in the bright sunlight on the doorstep, my Uncle Hughie beside me, I looked around at the people gathered there, the women in decent clothes and the men bareheaded, wearing their best suits, holding their bowler hats in their hands. There was a note of triumph in their singing, and the sunlight poured down heavily upon them in our little street, and my grief was less.

Because of the narrowness of the bridge leading from Rosser's Row, and the nearness of the chapel, the coffin was to be carried on a bier. On the other side of the river we saw many more people waiting to join the funeral procession, most of them colliers again wearing navy suits, bowler hats, and black ties. In front of the procession before the flower-covered coffin on its bier went Mr Hanmer and my Uncle Hughie; my Uncle Gomer and I followed it, leading the two long lines of men. No women walked with us, the women from the chapel and the neighbours were left behind at the house, or else had gone ahead into the graveyard.

At last we stood beside the open grave and Mr Hanmer read the committal service in

Welsh. Again, with the familiar living around me, and the sun and the great sunlit mountains looking on, death seemed unreal to me. And the next day, when I had returned to Dinas and taken up my studying again, I could scarcely believe that I had been home and seen the last of my grand-mother for ever.

My examinations were approaching and I had to work hard. The weather continued to be warm but I was out of doors very little and I slept badly. Sometimes I went as far as Alcwyn's, or walked around the park after supper, but my painting, I saw reluctantly, I would have to give up while I prepared for and sat the coming tests.

I dreamed a lot and always about Ystrad and the people I had known there, often people I had not thought about for years. One night, hovering among the half-formed, ephemeral shapes that pressed about me in my dream, I saw a figure clad in the silken habiliments of a mandarin; it was little Joe the jeweller, his face masked, under his bowler hat, by a semi-transparent and rotating clock-face. He greeted me in macaronic style and disappeared into the twilight with the clockwork aplomb of the habitual noctambule.

Rain in bright pieces of water began to fall among the evanescent multitudes.

The wraith-like Maria Penrheol, her neck

hung with a crop of wens like super-
numerary breasts, nodded her head at me
out of the dim air.

Suddenly I found myself closely
surrounded by black-clothed, black-visaged
figures whom I recognized; they were the
male-voice choir of our valley; with delight I
saw Dai Herbert and Dai Twmi, Dai Gog
and Dai Total, Dai Sugar and Dai
Tatermouth, Dai Ratch and Dai Buggy, Dai
Pick-and-toss and Dai Calon-cabbage, Dai
Dorothy and Dai Emma; the peculiarity
upon the last two was that, in a land of
patronymics, they received their distin-
guishing appellations from the matriarchal
rules of their respective clans. As we moved
forward in company, harmonies of inexpressible loveliness broke from their
practised throats, my heart sang in the bird-
cage of my breast as their Lydian airs and
honeyed minor hymns floated forth into the
gathering darkness.

The weeping eyes of Knitty Evans my
teacher surged up amongst them, his long
hair hanging over his ears like bedraggled
wings, the polished lard of his head receiving on its shining surface the boiling
reflections of the heavens.

The winds worked in the thunderous
clouds like a purple-pollened yeast.

Soon now, said my Uncle Hughie, we shall
all reach the river; even Benja Bowen, I

thought, whose hobgoblin figure I glimpsed threading the shadowy multitudes, his knuckles ape-like on the grass and his nostrils pouring smoke like the holes of a censer. Even Dai the Barm, the peculiarity upon whom was that his mother supplied the ingredients necessary for the domestic manufacture of small beer; even Dai Penny-a-lump, the peculiarity upon whom was that he sold household whiting in his little back-yard at the humble rate from which he derived his name; even Dai Peg and Dai Asthma, the peculiarity upon whom was that each was named after his physical affliction or infirmity.

Complete blackness fell upon us, but the voice continued with great sweetness and power the minor harmonies of threnody, dirge and lamentation. We halted and the choir sang to the accompaniment of harp-strings. Before us the voice of the unseen River was heard sweetly and solemnly susurrant in the impenetrable night. The singing stopped, the golden vibrations of the harp-strings died away. The darkness and the silence, but for the enticing whisper of the water, were complete. It was a solemn time, the hour for the crossing of the great indomitable bird of my grandmother's spirit. The valley trembled, there was a long soft roar as though a great root had broken deep in the ground and was in agony leaving the earth. I sobbed, I wept, I cried out in unremitted anguish. I trembled to the soul like the tree into which the wind thrusts its chill arm, feeling out the shiver of its living quick. Utter darkness, complete silence, annihilation.

And then before me in the night, a faint distillation of liquid starlight gathering in intensity, so that its yellow rays lit up the green and gleaming shot-silk hills down whose slopes they poured their fiery illumination. In the splendour of this drowning dayspring we saw the waters of a bountiful broad river stealing out from among the distant ranges, advancing over the plains, its crystal current as insubstantial as the shimmer of summer rising at noonday off the sunstruck crag. Upon its surface, as it flowed in a great bow, moved flocks of swans; beside its golden beaches grew fragrant groves of fruited tulip-trees, whose scent fell heavily upon the grass. Birds bright as meteors flashed from tree to tree. In a meadow grew a clotted snowfall of daisies; in another thick buttercups glowed golden like a floating scum. The distance revealed the blueness of the sea. Pearly clouds, fragile as porcelain, floated in the blue sky, where the darkened lark-stars poured out song. Birds also sang in trees loaded with a flowery disorder of golden chains. The air embraced me, the fingers of the morning wiped the tears from my face.

As I watched, I heard beside me whispered speculation and argument, muttered metaphysics and eschatology. I saw the hemicycle of my sceptical or awestruck countrymen, the Ystrad male voice, wearing white caps, white silken mufflers, and suits of snow-white paduasoy, standing in a choir-curve around me, their rugged faces bathed in the steady refulgence the heavenly valley poured out upon them. Each wore a large lemon dahlia in his sash or buttonhole.

Dai Cocoa stood with Dai Currant-cake and Dai Bara-brown three abreast, each named after the food or drink favoured by him for jack or snap-box.

Dai Cocoa, nodding towards the valley, wondered to Dai Currant-cake what my granny, Mary Lydia, would make of the Paradise or *Gwynfa Draw*.

Dai Current-cake said he judged Mary Lydia would not think much of it unless there was a strong smell of whitelime about it and a bit of a talk now and then with Ann Griffiths or Thomas Charles or John Williams of Erromanga.

And a lot of heavy washing to be slaved at, broke in Dai Bara-brown, and a prayer-meeting every Thursday evening.

Dai Cocoa then questioned Dai Bara-brown and Dai Currant-cake as to what *they*, personally, considered existence *there* would most closely resemble. Dai Bara-brown was of opinion the nearest thing would be a long strike in a nice fine summer, and everybody drawing pay and a half: to which Dai Current-cake added – and trips to the seaside every day with the charabancs playing 'Home, sweet home,' automatic, on the return journey. With these words the discourse ended and the three protagonists nodded their ready accord.

Knitty Evans at this point, wearing white suiting and tennis shoes, advanced to my Uncle Hughie and handed him a well-used *cansan* to serve as a baton. My uncle pitched the note and the demilune of harmonious Dais broke again softly, but with unequalled attack, into mournful sequences, requiems, and doxologies. There stood bow-legged Dai Ci-du, who had the peculiarity of being attended upon all occasions and upon every errand by a little black mongrel of jovial disposition; Dai Go-to-worrk, the miners' official, stood beside him, and the pecu-liarity upon him was that during the strikes, even the strikes of universal popularity, the burden of his exhortations to the mass meetings was, 'Men, go to worrk!'...

The yellow sunlight filled up the valley like a clear tea as over our bared heads went with muffled beat the great nimbused bird of my grandmother's spirit. Our singing was of farewell as the golden-glowing, the eagle-winged, the amaranthine-coronalled made for the centre of the valley, as though with the burden of the sun-glow shining upon the powerful shoulders. With the serenity of the sailing gier-eagle it beat its way into the distance and I was with it, I felt the air about me, I saw below us the paradisiacal fields and river and the tips with a new smoothness on their velvet slopes. The singing of the white-clad descanters faded. I saw the dwarfed colliery like a ship with steaming funnels anchored in the valley. As we passed the rows of houses on the hills we were welcomed, house after house greeted us with the silver flashings of their sunlit windows, they were our salvo of silent guns. Far below, the grey tips folded their bat's-wings over their faces. The bright light around evaporated and was superseded by a refulgence even more glorious. We floated in the pure air...

7

When I returned to the university after the long summer vacation Gwydion Lloyd came to stay at my digs in Boundary Villas. For some reason he did not disclose he was a fortnight or three weeks after everyone else commencing that term. But he did tell me that he had been awarded a studentship to enable him to continue his Celtic researches.

Miss Machen stood, the afternoon of our first meeting, in the exequial gloom of my parlour and introduced Gwydion and me to each other, and Dion to the rooms he was about to share with me. Dion was not then my friend, although I knew him by sight, having seen him occasionally in college and in the streets of Dinas. He had always an air of experience and aloofness and maturity. He was much my senior, and I had watched him with fascination before we met. His clothes, although usually shabby, were somehow distinguished. There seemed nobility in his isolation and silences. He moved among the cheeping, passerine, student mobs with the sweep and freedom of some great and solitary sea-bird, indifferent alike to wonder, respect, or envious detraction. The college gossips, sensing the improbability that one of such natural distinction should have been begotten like the rest of his generation in a bed with brass knobs, discovered for him a subtropical birthplace, and credited him also with an endowment of hereditary brilliance. At the same time, a cattish counter-buzz alleged against him involvement in a suicide case and the attentions of the national press.

But Dion, whether the accusations concerned virginity-taking, or a devotion to

Chinese or to archery, remained indifferent; he always walked the Dinas streets alone under his levin-lit hair, his expression high-nostrilled and hostile, and his dark overcoat hanging down to his feet.

'Mr Gwydion Lloyd, Mr Trystan Morgan,' said Miss Machen.

Before my greedy painter's eye Miss Machen was perched, alert and skilful on the hearth-rug for the introductions, she was like a large black prey-bird who had tidied up the dusky plumage of her wings and tail.

Her horse-skull face was big, pallid, and skinny, and out of the middle of it curved a high-flanked hawk-nose, edged like a knife and polished like a hand-rail.

Her dyed and padded hair, with its side-clips, wire pins, false brown bow, and elaborately crested Spanish back-comb, was arranged around her head in the shape of an outward-spreading cushion. It was a sort of massive bird's-nest of bedroom fluff, hedge-wool, and grey horse-hair, densely inter-woven, and badged with the tortoiseshell comb and the brown bow, largely con-cealing the rigid framework upon which it appeared to be constructed as upon a skele-ton of twigs.

As Dion and I listened we nodded in silent hostility to each other. Miss Machen observed this and rolled down the reptilian membranes of her lids. She hung open her hulking horse-like underlip in a grin of conciliation and her smooth skin became plastered at once with wrinkles like blown tea.

I saw Dion's green eyes flicker at this smile, for it unmasked the gold, the wet gold crowns stopping her molars, the gold packed into the hollows of her eye-teeth, the gold rings looped round her upper fangs, securing her plate.

From her elongated ears, too, flashing beneath the pad-bolstered superstructure of her hair, dangled long droppers of engraved gold, clublike or figgish in shape, suspended by short chains from the pearl-set rosettes which hid the perforations of the lobes.

And lastly, upon the bridge of a nose curved like the slab divisions of a privy, clung her gold-rimmed pince-nez with their golden spring and finger-hold. There, as she presented us to each other and spoke with the suspicious garrulity of the deaf, her eye-glasses clung to the bridge of her nose like an insect with outspread wings flattened against a wall. A long safety-chain of thin gold hung from them and was secured to her bodice by a sort of medallion.

Before closing the door behind her she turned round and for a moment beamed upon us. Then her wrinkle-netted face, looking out through the intricate reticulations of its smile, showed in front two long, broad, and forward-sprouting horse-teeth, one of pure grooved ivory and one gone an attractive slate-grey with decay.

8

Most Wednesday evenings after finishing our work Alcwyn and I went down to the Queen's Café to drink Russian tea, to meet other students, and to talk. Alcwyn had done brilliantly in his examinations at the end of our first year at the university. I, only moderately well.

Alcwyn and Pompey were still in the same lodgings, but Nico Mathias had left them and was now next door to us in Boundary Villas, in Mrs Evans's, with a student called Decker Davies. I saw them frequently on my way to and from college; I had got to know them well and had much to do with them. In fact, because of Mrs Evans's super-stitious reluctance to accommodate it, Decker's female skeleton lay outspread beneath the couch in the window-bay of our front room.

Alcwyn seemed to me the most brilliant man of our year. Although I liked him very much I could never really understand him. He seemed to have read an enormous number of books, and to be able to discuss them cleverly, but after our previous talk in the Queen's I was never sure to what extent his actions were spontaneous and to what extent calculated. Was he genuinely as absurd as he made himself out to be, or did he invent situations for himself in which he could appear ridiculous? Were all his encounters with girls as idiotic as he represented them to be? Had his affair with Teleri quite that element of lunacy he claimed for it? Had he really tried to disillusion himself by watching a girl he was supposed to be in love with playing tennis, at which she was unusually clumsy and inept?

We went inside the Queen's. There we saw the customary evening crowd of coffee drinkers – students, clerks, typists, shopgirls, school-teachers and so on. We found a small table for two and Alcwyn ordered the usual Russian tea, and began smoking his Turkish cigarettes in the white holder which made everyone look round. He wanted to read me his current essay, but I was reluctant to hear it in all that smoke, noisy music, and talking. I had written one myself on the same subject anyway, which I would never dream of asking anyone to hear. Clever as he was Alcwyn sometimes irritated me in this way, he seemed as though he felt he had to be brilliant, or odd, or amusing all the time.

'"The meaning of tragedy,"' he began, reading the title from some sheets he had taken out of his inside pocket. '"I consider it a romantic fallacy to suppose that the value of a work of art depends upon what has been consciously put into it. Its value is to be estimated only by what is to be got out of it. This point I can, perhaps, best illustrate by means of an imaginary dialogue between Shakespeare and Shaw. Let us picture the two dramatists meeting in some celestial Mermaid Tavern."'

'You can't put that in your essay,' I said.

He looked up, surprised, the turn in his eye more noticeable than usual.

'Why not?' he said.

'The Prof. will flay you. He wants to see if we've read Bradley and understood him, not if we can write imaginary conversations.'

'Don't be narrow-minded. I'm coming to Bradley anyway.'

'How?'

'Well, the two discuss drama for a bit and I show there I've read Archer and Havelock Ellis, and then Shakespeare confides in Shaw that he never thought of half the things Bradley credits him with thinking of. And how could he have possibly thought of all the things in the shelves upon shelves of volumes written about his plays from his day to ours? The whole thing is fantastic.

Don't you see? And then think of…'

His argument went on to Vanbrugh, Shelley, and other writers whose names were unfamiliar, but I was hardly listening. Our table was near the wall, not far from the corner of the room, and against the gilded panels at right angles to ours I could see in profile the head of a beautiful girl. Her face was white, with the gilt background behind it, and on her brow and bunched behind her neck were clusters of golden curls. Her red mouth glistened. She was dressed in dark blue. She had the face of someone I had seen before and that something in me knew well, some face I had always encountered in memory or in the flesh with reverence and delight. Merely to look at her, her chin slightly uptilted and her throat sweeping down into the collar of her blue coat, was a sort of rapture, an emotion hard to endure while Alcwyn opposite me read on, elaborating his theory, bringing in Sheridan and Congreve and Synge. And I did not wish to stare too long in case the girl should turn and look at me, face to face. I realized rather than saw at first that there was another person at her table, a girl wearing a dark hat with a wide drooping brim which hid her face. This girl was almost facing me, her throat bare and long silver earrings in her ears. I did not concern myself with her, but I distinctly heard her call her friend's name.

She said, 'Lisbeth,' and then drew her attention with a nod to someone sitting near us.

Lisbeth half turned towards our table, her face serious, her shining lips a little apart, her hand dropping away from her chin. I stared at her and then began to turn my head in the direction of her glance, almost unconsciously. My movement seemed to bring her face to life, she turned suddenly and looked straight at me, her glance full of interest and pleasure. I sat still. Her face was even more beautiful, seen like this, than with the gold panel against the warmth of her skin. She smiled openly and her eyes shone. Alcwyn had reached Henry Arthur Jones and St John Hankin. 'Excuse me,' I said. 'Excuse me, Alcwyn, I've just remembered something.'

I got up and hurried out of the café and along the corridor leading into the street. As the commissionaire held open the door I could hear Alcwyn calling after me. 'Trystan, Trystan,' he called, but I went on, I took no notice of him. I ran down the steps and jumped on to a passing bus, not stopping to consider what I was doing. I went upstairs and found myself the only passenger there. When the conductor came for my fare I had my head on the back of the seat in front, pillowed on my arms. He thought I was ill. 'All the way,' I said. I felt satisfied only when the bus was moving. 'Faster,

faster,' I kept on muttering. The terminus was a long way out from the centre of the city, near a lake with a road round it and needle-thin reflections of the lamps upon its surface. I walked round the lake in the darkness. When I returned to the terminus the last bus was gone, so I walked across the city back to Boundary Villas.

When I entered the house I found Miss Machen had gone to bed, but Gwydion was in our room, reading.

'Hallo,' he said, lifting up his cool white face and giving me a stare of gathering recognition.

'Hallo,' I said. 'Sorry if I kept you up.'

'You didn't,' he said. 'Been walking, have you?' He did not wish me to answer so I said nothing. Soon we were upstairs, but I could not sleep. Dion was a silent sleeper and I listened to his quiet breathing.

I saw Alcwyn in the common-room the next day. I said, 'Sorry I had to rush off last night, Alcwyn. I just remembered something.'

'That's all right,' he said. 'I often feel like suddenly remembering something myself. Finished your essay?'

9

When I had been back at Dinas a week or

two I made up my mind to do what I had considered all through the long vacation. Now that my grandmother was dead, was I still to abide by our agreement? My sense of religious vocation was more dubious than ever and my desire to paint drew strength from my disappointment with the university. Still, I had undertaken to complete my studies and I decided that my promise was even now binding upon me. But did this promise prohibit my painting altogether? Certainly my course so far had been a demanding one, leaving me very little time for drawing and none for painting, although I had used my note-book sedulously. Finally I went down into the town to join the art school run by the council for its people. Ugly as this Victorian-Gothic building was, arched and turreted like a medieval castle, I had often passed it with feelings of envy when I saw students going in and out of its doors.

As I stood in the entrance hall wondering what to do a darkish bearded young man, wearing a badly stained smock, his arms bare to the elbow, passed. He half smiled, hesitated, and then spoke as it were over his shoulder.

'Can I help you?' he said.

He had the baldest head I think I had ever seen on so young a man; it shone as though it had been soaped and the pale skin looked so taut over the bone it might have been tightened by handscrews. But the black hair grew very thickly in a narrow strip above his ears and at the back of his neck; spread out it would have been sufficient to cover the whole cranium. His face was thin and mobile, rather small, the beard a little dark goatee. I was immediately attracted towards him because of his friendliness and the interested, quizzical smile on his face. His were not eyes that left one immediately. Their glance, dark and glittering, alighted and remained and fed.

'Can I help you?' he said to me.

'I don't know, sir,' I said. 'I came along hoping to be able to join the art school.'

'You're a bit late,' he said. 'We started a fortnight ago. What were you thinking of doing?'

His black eyebrows worked; they were not curved but pointed in the middle, exactly like circumflexes.

'Painting chiefly,' I said. 'And life. Use of the model if possible.'

'Have you done much already?'

'On my own, yes, sir. Painting. Landscape.'

'You didn't mean to join as a full-time student, I take it, did you?'

'Oh no, sir. Only part time. In the evenings.'

'I see.' He pondered a bit and then grinned wickedly.

'You're not still in school, are you? We're not allowed to enrol anyone for evening classes if they are.'

'Oh no, sir,' I said, 'I'm not in school now. I've left.'

He considered a little again. 'Look here,' he said, 'have you got any specimens of your work handy?'

'I've got one or two things in my digs. Nothing much though.'

'Well, bring along here what you've got. Come to-morrow evening. Is that all right?'

I noticed his teeth when he grinned, small and pointed as though they had been filed.

'Yes, indeed. Thank you,' I said. 'But I wonder if I could bring my work down in the morning. Then I could call later and find out whether I'm to come or not.'

'All right then,' he said. 'I won't be here myself but you can leave what you've brought with the clerk in the office.'

'Thank you, sir,' I said. 'I am grateful. Good night, sir.'

He grinned and placed his hand with the fingers spread out on the middle of his bald scalp. The hand was almost black with hairs; it was like the hairy paw of an ape.

'Good night,' he said.

I went out through the glass doors greatly pleased. I felt sure I would be allowed to join now and I liked very much one of the teachers at least.

The next morning I took down a bunch of pencil drawings and three small oils done on wood of scenes in and around Ystrad. What I enjoyed doing most then were paintings in minute detail of very small areas of landscape, say a few square feet of some Ystrad tip with a patch of thin grass on it, or a small rock-pool under a film of coal-dust, or the naked roots of a tree growing out of the earth of the river bank. No sky-line often, only the shabby couch tufted at the top, then the chocolate earth with the carefully painted basketwork of roots and at the bottom a selvage of water. Perhaps in all one square yard of landscape. Still life *en plein air* almost. I found trying to paint two or three grey, half-wetted pebbles by the water, or the patterns of nailed working-boots in the mud, or even a few square inches of the sunlit shale wall of the Rosser's Row houses something that absorbed me entirely. This was the type of painting I left at the art school.

When I called in the evening I thought the young tutor seemed not less cordial certainly than on the previous night. As I entered the school he was standing talking to a young woman on the first landing of the wide staircase leading up from the reception hall, obviously teasing her. When he saw me he excused himself and hurried down the stairs smiling. 'Hallo,' he said.

I smiled back. I knew he was going to accept me.

He told me he had liked my work very much, especially the paintings. The principal had agreed to allow me to attend. Would I come into the office and sign the forms and pay my fees?

I did this. Opposite 'Occupation' I wrote 'Clerk (university),' which satisfied my conscience. I arranged to attend two nights a week and to study oil painting and figure drawing.

I started the next night.

10

Dion seemed seldom to speak to other students.

One evening, before Decker Davies and Nico Mathias next door had got to know him, I was sitting alone in our front room with a drawing-board on my knees. Suddenly I heard a thudding in the chimney recess of the wall between our front room and Nico's, this same thudding being the academic equivalent of crude Morse or penal telegraphy tapped out with tin mug or leg-chain upon fortress piping.

I bumped back, got up, and went into Nico's to see what was amiss.

All the houses in Boundary Villas were

easy of access, and to gain admittance one inserted, instead of using knob or latch-key, one's hand into the brass letter-box of the front door and pulled at the taut string or bootlace which one's fingers there encountered.

When I went into their parlour I found Nico, yellow-faced and crop-haired, sprawled low in the cretonne comfort of his divan, smoking his calabash, arguing and practising a card trick which involved projecting the whole pack with cinematographic rapidity from palm to palm.

Opposite him was a tall, lank youth with fidgety eyelids, putty-coloured hair, and a stammer. This was Decker Davies the medical. Decker lay in a basket chair the other side of the fire-place, grinning and arguing back, his vivid bag-blue irises lit up and his large front teeth, set at an angle to one another like the prow of a boat, prominent in the dark cut of his mouth. Decker possessed an unacademic superabundance of good clothes. He was wearing now professional black coat and vest and striped trousers, a white shirt and black tie, and a pair of grey spats. He was thought to be not impecunious, and had a reputation for stuttered insubordination in his passages with the taskers of the medical faculty.

Now, as he argued and faltered, he held in his hand a pair of cutter's shears, one of the tools necessary for the killing of the mouse of number eighty-eight. A heavy poker was supported diagonally across the empty grate beside him by means of a length of fine twine. This twine was slung over the extended fire-damper and secured to a brass urn-shaped moulding decorating the fender. A few cake-crumbs and a powerful lump of cheese were spread out as bait upon the hearthstone. Decker, an ever-babbling paraphrenic, according to Dion, indulgent towards every morsel of his work-shy pia mater, passed many a pleasurable evening in this way, waiting for the fireside mouse to issue from his hole so that, with hasty scissors-snick, Decker could bring down the pendant poker on its head.

Decker and Nico, a stammering medical debating with an r-dragging engineer, were gossiping and arguing as I entered, in their obscure, canting idiom and with slangy verve, about the evening's schedule. It was the open night again, I learnt, of the Calliper Club, and the terminal smoker; and Decker held, now then, that since Nico had with vociferous unanimity been re-appointed the society's sergeant-at-arms and chucker-out, necessity was laid upon him to attend.

Nico, continuing to shoot with gathering dexterity his cards from palm to palm, maintained that at the promptings of clock and calendar, and since beggars can't be boozers, he was eagerly straining at the leash to work; and Decker too ought to consider hitting some *materia medica* flat.

Decker, who had bumped the wall, favoured allowing a spin of the coin to make decision for them; and he was prepared, now then, although still moderately well supplied with gilt, to devote his evening to the extension of medical knowledge should his shilling stand on its edge.

Nico said that, damall, the profession and theory of engineering came before pot and can and Calliper Clubs.

Decker said that Nico was a, what-you-call, a beaver for work, as hard to stop as weeping, what-you-call, eczema, but if *I* hadn't planned to anchor anywhere, now then, would I come with him to the smoker.

'Smoker me no smokers, Decker,' I said, feeling inclined to walk abruptly back out. It was my painting lesson night. Beside I knew by now, from my own experience and from Alcwyn's reports, the continued curriculum of these gatherings, the boring and repetitive bawdiness, the sophomoric blasphemy and bombast. I made my excuses, pleading that I expected Dion's return from the library.

'Now then, now then, now then,' began Decker, using one of the rhythmic phrases whose repetition had power to give his tongue consecutive utterance. 'Now then, now then, Trystan,' he said, his long features momentarily puckered and atrabilious under the buttered hair. 'Now then, now then, now then, if you don't come you'll let me down stinking.'

I shrugged my shoulders and he began the divagating commentary and incantation which accompanied his chronic para-phrenia. 'This town, now then, is lousy,' he held, clipping the shears in despondency. 'Lousy, now then, and the gravy is fast being lifted out of it. Did you, of the afterwards, know Tiny, the barmaid of the, what-you-call, the afterwards, of the Boot and Bell? The big jet-haired jane, well-developed, with the rocking-horse bulge to her eyeballs?'

I nodded a recollection of the barm-cloth covered bosom and the coaly lustre of that imperious and predatory eye. Every student knew Tiny the Boot and Bell.

'Well, now then, have you heard she is going to get married?'

I shook my head. 'I didn't even know she was in trouble,' I said.

Decker shot his arm inside his shirt and began scratching his chest.

'Now then, of the, now then, of the, if you can't come could you throw your hooks over that Gwydion, what's his name, of the show, of the show, him by night-light the local glories?'

Here Nico broke in. What's his knobs doing in college? he wanted to know. How did I feel walking through town with him the other day when he wore his Mexican sombrero? He would have loved to have been a little fly on my collar to have heard what went on. Was this Gwydion fond of his sherbet? Could he play pontoon? Was it true he wore straps round his head and claimed his father was a cardinal? Had his name been in the block letters? A frothy welcome ought to be accorded to one so superior, one who looked like a half-frozen dromedary with gingerized hair.

'Now then, is Gwydion promised forth?' Decker asked me. 'If he can be persuaded I will provide the finances of the afterwards, of the afterwards, of the celebration.'

Nico at that confessed to feelings of responsibility towards his office of sergeant-at-arms. He rose rumpled from his chair, and laying meerschaum and card-pack aside examined with grimacing distaste his twenty-one-year-old puffcheeks and charcoal chin in the overmantel mirror. He damned shaving, he couldn't go anywhere without a scrape; he had cleaned up that morning for a niner, he complained, and look at his puss now. He was like a nettle.

Decker told him, now then, not to be narky since it was either shaving or bearing children. But he agreed some academic

214

welcome should be provided for Gwydion. Did Nico remember the first-night bed and the wrecked room they fixed for Elfet, the firebricks and the biscuit tins and the ale bottles and the bedroom ware with the rambler roses? And they'd soon have Gwydion horizontal. Did Nico remember bringing Gwyndaf home and putting Dilly's garters on the bed-knobs? Nico did. Nico wanted to do all he could to welcome Gwydion. Perhaps this Gwydion was lonely, would appreciate a debauch and being shown the rounds. Wouldn't I change my mind...?

I shook my head. I knew Nico was not to be dissuaded from some sort of japing welcome. He had always enjoyed the preparation of skeletoned beds and health-salted or carbide-sprinkled chamber-pots. And one night at Mrs Wilmot's he terrified a cocky freshman to the verge of incoherence and hysteria. He awakened this boy in the blackness of the small hours holding a phosphorescent carving-knife to his throat. The boy let out a husky scream and fled along the pitch-black landing, where he was heavily tackled and brought down by the landlady, who mistook him for a burglar.

But I knew Dion was far from being such an innocent as this and what I had heard of Dan Harries crossed my mind. When Dan, a large and ruggy bullock off the phlegmatic

215

western grasses, first came to college he found rooms with Nico at Mr Regan's. One night bull-browed and -eyeballed Daniel was awakened by the brandishing in his bedroom of lights, by barefooted shufflings and low-muttered incantations. He sat up slowly in his bed, tousled and archaically night-shirted, and saw, his expression myxoedemic with drowsiness superimposed upon phlegm, Nico, stark naked and clutching a candle in each hand, performing at a prowling trot a sort of rhythmic devil-dance or corroboree in every corner of the dark room. Nico was salaaming, raising and lowering the brass candles before him, mumbling in a heavy bass the gibberish of some impromptu *ju-ju* psalm or jungle liturgy. Unmoved, Danny looked on and said nothing, and finally Nico was forced to stop chant and dance and explain he was observing this ritual because he was a Mohammedan and he had to celebrate his annual Ramadan in this way. Inarticulate Dan said, A Mohammedan? Oh, a Calvinistic Methodist he was himself, like, and turning over with animal composure went back to sleep at once.

I shook my head and was about to return to my rooms when I heard Dion entering next door. I brought him into number eighty-eight, hurriedly introduced him to Nico and Decker, and left them, not without feelings of jealousy, together discussing a visit to the Calliper Club.

When I returned to our rooms I went on with my painting, running a line of fractured milk along behind the auburn-haired stacks and industrial chimneys and the cropped herbage of the suburban chimney-pots which I could see below me beyond the recreation ground. But presently, with the dusk deepening over the trees and pitches of the park, and over the university city prickly with spires, it became too dim for me to continue so lighting the gas and drawing the purple curtains I took out my essay and sat down to work at it. I had shown it to Dion and we had argued about it.

'Trystan,' he said, 'you appear to me to be a very gifted painter, but an execrable theorist.'

I was attempting in it, for my own behoof, using a flowers-and-fizzpop version of Iwan Morgan Parry's style in his *Critique and Gloria,* to render inexpugnable the flimsy structure of my aesthetic against the resounding salvoes, barrages, and catamarans with which Dion had already begun to assail it. My assault was upon abstractionism, 'the *ignis fatuus* or quag-flare exhalation beckoning at Eden's gate.' I held the phrase 'abstract art,' since the adjective negated the noun, to be like 'young scholar' or 'happy genius,' in itself an absurdity. Window curtains, fire-place tiles, tablecloth borders, I wrote, glancing around at the swarthy and depressing furnishings of Miss Machen's parlour, were permissibly decorated, might with propriety receive the zigzaggery of Greek-key or Celtic interlacings, of serrated, curvilinear, or hachured embellishments. But abstraction, exalted and considered as great art, how was this possible? Could the abstractionist cry to me through his picture, his patchwork of gay rods, spanglings, and cuboid purples, 'I love, I love!'? Could he, before his *lobscows* colours and amorphous forms, arrest me with his soul's cry of horror? Could he even persuade my heart of his identity with those who feel? No, no, I wrote, abstractionists and designers omit too much, are too circumscribed with theory and arid dialectic; art's eunuchs, they are cut off, they lack sensuality, are not implicated with the flesh. They love – such love, I insist, is admirable in them, bereft of it they were hebete or dissembling daubers merely – they love paint, canvas, form, gradation, balance, juxtapositioning of colour, remaining unscratched and brassy-hearted before nature's earth and sea and glory-pouring baldachin, deaf to mankind's many voices, the despair and ravishment of the human breast. I proceeded then to attack for like emotional indifference to their subject-matter those clay-souled painters of heads as though they were apples, and the opulent, unbelieving craftsmen and mammonists of the Renaissance, cookers-up of gorgeous unfelt crucifixions, fakers of Cana marriages, *pietàs,* and nativities in which they had no belief.

Finally, by the adduction of personal history, I sought to amplify this contention that the abstract painting, the non-representational art-work, ignored too vast a territory of human experience. I had seen recently, I wrote, an oil entitled 'Beach,' a simple semi-abstraction figuring a promontory of railway-sleeper cinnamon and a swerve of grass and orange sand gripped by the cornflower hooks of a sea. Upon this sea rocked a flotilla of gigantic gulls and a few autumn-tinted fishing-boats with foxglove sails. It was delightful. It had the charm and sparkle of a piece of jewellery, but I was not enriched. I felt my own carnal perceptions to be more varied, more intense, and more numerous than those of the puritanical artist. What could he, with his exiguous forms and impressionistic coloration, tell me when I had seen beaches God-limned in summer and winter, at daybreak and at sundown?

During my schoolday visits to my aunts I

had watched Llansant beach at dawn, the
incandescent sun dipping its spelter on to
the splashed sea, and ships no bigger than
midges clinging against the scoop of
horizon radiance. I had seen Llansant from
above, a crawling sea-village, scaly and
monster-skinned, the dawn-glint of its
wetted limbs cast out among the pastoral
valleys; I had watched the conviction of the
brown-knuckled promontory, with the
wind-sipping wheat and the stooked barley
upon it also at grips like yellow wrestlers; I
had seen the abbey-surrounding grove,
muscular, hunch-shouldered, and elephantine...

For I knew, I said, the visionary and necromantic power of art. In my later schooldays
I had seen like a shock of sunlight, large,
solitary, and brilliant before the brocaded
back-cloth, the beautiful reproduction of
'The Beloved' in the art-shop of Pencwm in
our grim valley. My emotions on beholding
it for the first time I analysed to be those of
one who received great honour, is at once
humbled and vertiginously uplifted at
hearing his name call forth ten-thousand-
thundering applause. Further ... by reason
of my home's fastidious tutelage and a
natural pudency I was, although inexperienced at adolescence, not overborne by the
sexualism of prematurity; but confronted by
the glow-and-sex-drenched sweetness of

this picture my heart was fed, greatly agitated, it seemed ready to overflow with effusions of wonder, glory, adoration, gratitude. Ah, abstraction, abstraction, you are not food, satisfying aliment, you are the glittering, cold cutlery of art's banquet; how can you, abstraction, console or exalt the spirit, triumphantly express and answer our deepest longings, set a glow in the cold Shekinah of our hearts?

Ah well. I had shown it to Dion and he had denounced its style and its incondite formlessness, he accused me, with scorn and pedantry, out of mysterious canonical books and obscure volumes of artistic principle, of garden-flower romanticism, perhaps of wishing all art to tend to the condition of the homily, to the pronunciamentos of the great prophet-poets and artist-didacts of the Old Testament whose writings I so fervently admired.

I put my manuscript back into the drawer and went out to my painting class.

As I walked along I thought deeply about what I was doing and about its rightness. I pondered as I often did, about my grandmother and her prayers for me, and I always felt ashamed when I remembered this because of the shallowness and vanity of my life. Then my indifference to the things which meant so much to her saddened me.

Did I lead the kind of life which would enable me to have the sense of vocation she had so passionately desired for me? Was I not entirely worldly and carnal, my deepest emotions stirred by what I saw with my eyes and touched with my hands? Was it not a great weakness in my character that the face of a beautiful girl, of whom I knew nothing, could haunt me hour after hour ever since I had seen her? Was it not wrong to worship created things as I did? The folly and boastfulness and debauchery of Decker and Nico had little influence upon me. I enjoyed their talk and their stories but I was not at all tempted, as she had feared, to a life like theirs. My temptations were of a different nature. In their lives was no dedication. And I was beginning to believe that this was true of Gwydion also. But Gwydion's manifest unhappiness arose, I felt, from his own realization that this was so.

To the Tuesday and Thursday nights, when I attended the classes at the ugly Gothic art-school, I looked forward more eagerly than to anything that happened at the university, whether lectures, debates, concerts, or dances. After a week or two's attendance, I got into the habit of going a little early, ostensibly to help Mr Leyshon, the young tutor, with the easels and materials for our night-classes, but really to talk to him. He was invariably in his dirty smock covered with oil and paint, front and back, his sleeves pushed up showing his thin, hairy, monkey-like arms. We chatted in his untidy stock-room but we never at that time seemed to mention anything but painting. When I got to know him better I realized he could not be a great deal older than I was myself and that it was only his bald head and his black beard which made him appear so much more mature.

'Who's your favourite painter at present?' he asked me one evening.

'Rossetti,' I said. What I meant was that the reproduction of Rossetti's 'The Beloved' which I had gazed at day after day in the Pencwm art-shop had stirred, delighted, and satisfied me more than any other painting I had ever seen.

Mr Leyshon's roof-shaped eyebrows went up.

'Rossetti!' he said, incredulous.

'Yes,' I said. 'You seem surprised, sir.'

'I am a little. At your age people usually imitate in their own work what they admire. But you don't at all, do you?'

He made me feel guilty and I was conscious of showing it.

'Ought I to?'

'Not necessarily. But you admire the painter of 'Monna Vanna' and paint yourself little patches of mud with the marks of hobnailed boots on them, or a bit of Welsh pavement with the green moss between the flags.'

'I never thought of it like that, sir. I admire Rossetti because of the profound emotions he arouses in me. But I don't feel capable of causing those emotions to be aroused in others by my own work, sir. I don't think my work could ever give to others the really deep-down thrill that Rossetti gives to me.'

'What emotions do you wish your work to arouse in others?'

'I don't know. I think I would like people to feel respect, or reverence really, for the things I paint.'

'Isn't reverence a profound emotion?'

'Yes, I suppose so. But it's not the thrilling sort of emotion I mean, it hasn't the quality of ecstasy I feel in the presence of work like that of Rossetti.'

Mr Leyshon put his thin hairy paw outspread in the middle of his vast baldness and grinned at me from behind his elbow. Then he shook his head. I blushed to my hair. It was evident he thought me very queer. But he was so friendly towards me, he made fun of me in such an affectionate way that I was never resentful or really hurt by anything he said or did.

'Ah well,' he said at last, 'go on, get your easel up over there and try the still life. I think it's ready for you.'

He came over into the room, where

presently I and a dozen other part-time students would be at work. In the middle of the half-circle of easels was the still-life group, arranged on a blue plush cloth, a brass candlestick with pink candle, some apples and oranges in a bowl, a jewel box and, in the centre, dominating all, a chipped and dirty cast of an enormous foot, standing on three inches of solid plaster.

'God in heaven,' said Mr Leyshon. 'Look at that. Who the devil put that there? Take it back to the design room, will you, and get something a little less repulsive. You'll find lots of casts hanging on the wall there.'

I went out carrying the huge foot in my arms before me. It was hideous to look at and like lead to carry. There was not an affection of the foot from which it did not suffer – calluses, verrucas, foot-warts, bleedings. Someone had painted yellow corns on it and blue dirt under all the toe-nails, and an attempt had been made by means of skilful shading to suggest large and inflamed bunions at the joints. I wondered what I should select to replace it but decided to wait until I saw what the design room had to offer.

Eventually I came to the door which had the word 'Design' painted on it. I knocked as best I could. Nothing happened. I knocked again. I could hear voices inside talking loudly and in a leisurely manner and

I realized with profound misgivings that all the voices were those of girls. But there was nothing for it, now. I knocked a third time, louder, and at that someone shouted: 'Sylvia, Sylvia, there's somebody knocking at the door.' The inflexion of the voice suggested that the speaker felt surprise that anyone should knock at a door before entering.

I heard Sylvia on hard abrupt heels crossing the room, and then the door opened. Sylvia was a short, pretty bobbed-haired girl in a bright smock. She looked surprised to see me standing there. Then her glance fell to the foot held in my hands, my arms at full length, and she began to giggle.

I didn't know what on earth to do. I hadn't foreseen anything like this. What should I say? Desperately I tried to recall some of the casts I had seen about the college and I blurted out: 'Excuse me, I've come for the Tudor Rose.'

She giggled into her handkerchief and went inside the room. I heard her call out to her friend and I could tell by her voice that she couldn't stop laughing. I felt fresh flushes of colour going up my face. Why was everything I did so absurd?

'Erica,' she called out, 'there's somebody out here wants the Tudor Rose.'

There was silence after that and I could

imagine the convulsive dumb-show and the grins inside. I blushed in silence. Then Sylvia opened the door again and came from behind it, soberer now, but her seriousness, I thought, quite unstable, mere politeness. 'Will you come in, please?' she asked, her blue eyes bright with laughing.

I went inside the big bare room with my foot before me. Facing me were six pairs of bright and amused eyes set in six politely demure faces. The young women, all strangers to me, seemed alarmingly smart and pretty in their bright smocks and overalls. They sat behind the large drawing-boards of the design room and watched what I would do next. I didn't know what the devil to do. I thought of whistling but I was too frightened to start. I could feel the presence of Sylvia behind me. 'He wants the Tudor Rose, Erica,' she repeated over my shoulder.

Erica was a big, dark, handsome girl with enormous black and steady eyes. Her hair was pulled back over her head in a fashionable and assured way and there were large up-to-date rings in her ears. But worse than all was the cool expression on her face and the glitter to her dark bold eyes.

'The Tudor Rose,' she said. 'You want the Tudor Rose, do you?'

I nodded.

'What's that thing?' she asked, nodding at my foot.

'It's a foot,' I said. 'I'm supposed to change it for the Tudor Rose.'

There was a pause.

'What shall I do with it?' I said.

No one spoke. A pace to my right was a drawing-desk. I stepped up to it, put the foot on it and came back to my first position. I was glad to have got rid of the foot but I didn't know now what to do with my hands. I put them in my trousers pockets and pulled them out again. I had never felt so ridiculous in my life. Was my nose starting to run? I tried to smile but my mouth seemed to go up further one side than the other.

'The Tudor Rose,' said Erica. 'You said the Tudor Rose, did you?'

'Yes,' I answered. 'Mr Leyshon sent me for it.' This sounded idiotic, like a first-former on a message for teacher, so I added hastily, 'Or anything else.'

'Now where can that Tudor Rose be?' Erica said, glancing round the walls where several plaster casts were hanging. 'I don't see it here. Anyone seen the Tudor Rose? Margaret, have you seen it? Myfi? Gwen? Joan?'

The young women shook their heads but did not speak. Perhaps they were afraid to trust themselves.

'I'm afraid we don't know where it is,' said Erica. 'Would you like to look round the wall for it yourself? It's certain to be here somewhere.'

I glanced at the huge room. If I went round the walls searching I should have six pairs of eyes behind me, and silent jeering, and grins on pretty faces. And to reach the nearest row of casts I should have to cross five yards of open and polished floor-space where anything might happen. I felt incapable of moving in any direction now except backwards.

'No, thank you,' I said. 'No, thank you. Good evening.'

'Good evening,' said Erica, giving a sort of bow.

I got outside the door and then heard Erica calling me back. I was foolish enough to put my head inside.

'Thank you for the foot,' she said.

I hurried along the corridor. I could hear the girls laughing aloud in the room behind me. What the devil was I to tell Mr Leyshon? One thing I felt thankful for; I hadn't fallen over or dropped the foot on the floor. When I got back to the painting-room, I said: 'I thought a Tudor Rose would be just the thing for this group, sir, but I couldn't find one.'

He looked at me, cross and puzzled for a moment, and then he went out.

In a few moments he was back with the cast. There was a goatish grin on his face.

Every time I met Erica in the corridors after that, or in a classroom, she made me blush. 'Hallo, Tudor Rose,' she used to say. Sylvia would pass me without a word, giggling into her handkerchief.

After the lesson I walked about in the town for a little. I wanted very much to go into the Queen's to see if Lisbeth was there, or merely to be in surroundings where she had once been. But although I wished passionately to look at her again I was anxious also that she should not see me. Not yet. I merely wished to look at her, to be in her presence. She was one of the most beautiful girls I had ever seen, but it was not merely her beauty I found compelling. Mair-Ann was as finely featured, fair-haired, and fair-skinned, but about Lisbeth there was also a warmth, a radiance, some strange glow, and a gaiety and sweetness. I thought little of her circumstances, who she was, where she lived, whether she worked or not. I cared nothing about these things. She lived for me in an ideal world in which there was nothing commonplace or dull but where all was beauty and brilliance and freshness.

I came almost fully awake in the pitch darkness of my bedroom, bewildered, puzzling what night-noise, perhaps of bedspring or contracting timber, had disturbed my sleep.

Striking a match I fumbled out my under-the-pillow watch and discovered it was nearly two o'clock. Remembering the Calliper Club and the intention of Nico and Decker to bring Dion home drunk, I examined his bed, which stood a few feet from mine. It was undisturbed, and I was about to lie back again when I heard the roar of a starting car and the sudden vibrance of a trumpet shatter the almost interstellar silence of suburban darkness. Then a sharp categorical crack was delivered at the window as though the beak of some night-bird had given the glass a vindictive blow.

I was wide awake in an instant, quivering. I jumped out of bed and, standing with pounding heart behind the curtains, softly slid up the side-window of the bay. The night without was damp and intensely dark, and all I could see at first were a few dim stars, and beyond the obscurity of the park the diminished constellations of the mid-night city.

But with patient accommodation I began to distinguish a group of vague human figures directly below me near the area wall of the house. One of them was moving about and directly I leaned out of the window I heard a faint hail.

'Trystan,' someone in a penetrating whisper called up to me. 'Trystan, is that you? Come down and give us a hand, will you?'

Quietly I lowered the window. Then putting on my dressing-gown, and with throat-throbbing and deafening ingurgitations of spittle, I began silently to descend the pitch-black stairway. My heart thundered: I perspired coldly in an agony of dread that from some doorway in my rear a flood of light would suddenly burst forth and reveal the awful treachery of my descent, and the masculine voice of Miss Machen boom out behind me, demanding an explanation of my strange nocturnal behaviour.

'Give us a hand,' the call had said. I believed I had heard aright although the voice came up in an indistinguishable whisper. As I moved like a felon down the stairs I thought how the confederate craft of Nico and Decker, directed against Gwydion, had been triumphantly successful.

I crept into our front parlour, shut the door behind me, and groped my way with involuntarily contracting shins between the furniture and across to the side window. I hooked the chenille curtain over the back of the arm-chair. When I looked up, I suddenly found myself confronted out of the ambuscade of surrounding darkness by a pale face momentarily illuminated upward from its base by a match-flare. I was startled, for the moment I thought my senses were incompletely aroused. The match quickly went out and I stood staring into a darkness as black as an infinite forehead of coal. The tapping of finger-nails at the pane before my face recalled me and softly I unclipped the small side window and lifted the sash.

'Dion,' I whispered out into the darkness of the night air. 'Is it you? What's happened to Nico and Decker?'

Another match flared and I saw before me by its light once more Dion's cold and imperturbable countenance.

'Where are Nico and Decker?' I repeated. 'Haven't they come?'

He turned away without replying, bearing the match, and I caught a transient glimpse of two figures piled inside the low area wall before the flame went out.

'Give me your help to get them in out of the wet, will you?' he muttered softly from the darkness. 'Spotty, you discordant clown,' he said to someone outside, 'in heaven's name keep that damned doom-trumpet quiet.'

He came back silently to where I was still standing in bewilderment at the window. Although my emotions seemed at this hour comically and unnaturally profound, my processes of intellection were confused.

'We must haul these merrymakers in through the window, Trystan,' he said to me.

'Help Spotty and me, will you? Will you be so good as to receive Nico first?'

Before we shifted either of them Dion climbed long-legged into the parlour and helped me, in almost complete darkness, to wheel back the table, chairs and sofa, and remove Decker's skeleton and the sterile window-cauldron out of the way. Several times we stopped guiltily, fearing that the castor-squeakings had been heard, but Miss Machen was deaf and a dope-deep sleeper with her bedroom in some remote and bolted upper purdah, we believed, some inaccessible top-storey citadel of the house.

'Head first, Trystan,' Dion was whispering as Nico's head entered the room. 'Strong drink shall be bitter to them that drink it, Nico. Here he comes, Trystan, like unaccommodating carpentry or lousy bedding.' And I could feel under my hands in the darkness the powerful plush of Nico's head. Between us we hauled the dough-like body into the room and bundled it down under its harness on the double-headed sofa. Then we treated the longer, slimmer, and hyperpliable form of Decker in the same manner, cascading on to the bare oilcloth as we did so a pocketful of his coins, whose clatter curdled our blood up like a cheese.

When the two were reclining there – held in position by a couple of dining-chairs pushed up hard against them – Spotty began a sort of camel-climb into the room after them. 'Be careful,' said Dion, irritated by his curtain-clutching entry. 'Must you come in now?'

'You leave me alone,' Spotty replied, hugging the brass convolutions of his glittering French horn to his breast. 'I'm not touching you, I'm not. I've been helping you, I have.'

This Spotty was the student I had seen first during my visit to the Calliper Club, an unpopular man, depressed and unhappy, truculent in his drink, a hanger-on to such as Nico and Decker. His voice had a harsh braying quality as though frequent contact with his horn had imparted a brassy resonance to all his voice-producing organs. Upon his low, bony brow, upon his prognathous jaw and hollow cheeks were always plentiful showers of pimples and inflammatory boils; it was because of these – in size, shape, and radiance, resembling the knobs on a mastiff's collar – that he had his nickname. In summer and winter he was an habitual wearer of tight trousers and a shabby college blazer.

'Well, shut the window anyway,' Dion answered in extravagant dislike. 'There's enough air entering this room to turn a windmill. Do you think we ought to have a little light now, Trystan?'

I struck a match from the box in the pocket of my dressing-gown and lit with a plop one of the pair of painted glass brackets sticking out of the wall above the fire-place. I turned it low and its dim light accentuated the grim and shiny shabbiness of our room, the smoke-brown wall-paper, the once crocus-purple curtains, the mud-brown oilcloth, the black furniture painted as though with a viscid gum of coal-tar. The sole piece of colour was my oil-painting propped up upon the sideboard. I went to the window and pinned the curtains well across and looked round with apprehension as I turned back to the room. Decker lay with his professional suit fouled and in disarray, one spat missing, and his fair, plastered hair erect in spiny upheaval; and Nico wore slung from his neck the dirty, antique brass-and-leather bridle of some gigantic cart-horse complete with mon-strous brass-badged blinkers, triple bells, medallions, and lunate plaques of brass.

Spotty stood hesitant and swaying on the hearth mat fingering the keys of his brass instrument, but in a moment or two he fell back into the arm-chair and was soon fast asleep.

Dion sank down into the arm-chair beside the fire-place, with the down-directed gaslight glowing warm in his nimbated marigolden hair; he had already taken out a volume from the bookshelves in the chimney-recess alongside him and, holding it upon his darned knees, had begun with absorption and critical goat-nose-flutterings to read it in the dim light. For the moment the room's silence seemed at one with the external quietness of the early morning.

Sitting in my dressing-gown astride a dining-chair, facing the back with my arms and cheek resting on the decorative carving, I asked Dion what we should do now. Wait until Nico and Decker waken in the course of nature, sobered, he told me, not raising his eyes from his page, and we could dispatch them by way of our bay window and their front door into their own lodgings without disturbing Mrs Evans. To have rung their doorbell, he reasoned, would have brought down a sleepy and vindictive land-lady who would have mercilessly started them off, expelled and anathematized, upon their painful errancy again.

Laying aside his book and getting up – wrinkling up his nose as he did so as though he was walking into a drizzle – he kindled his clay pipe under the down-turned gaslight.

How did I feel, he wanted to know, palely reaching a hand again towards his book. Why didn't I go back to bed? He himself had a night-brain, bat's blood, a nocti-florous intelligence increasing in clarity and serenity from the moment the clock-points met at midnight. He was prepared to remain in the room himself. The dummies should be awake before long now, anyway...

He got up again, lifted Decker's skeleton from under the table, and laid it along Spotty's body, the skull on his shoulder and the arms around his neck.

'The essential Eve, the immutable quintessence of femininity,' he said. 'The trumpeter's bedfellow, the anatomy of womanhood, even the hottest doxy, the loveliest milk-washed quean or Byzantine empress, even warm-blooded Io, even bare-bubbed Egypt or that high-nostrilled Trojan enchantress were only these between the sheets, with a little impermanent and unessential girl-skin over them. Perhaps this, Spotty, is Joanna, or Bathsheba, or Nest, or Goewin, or Poppeia, or Lucrece, or some comparable bare-fleshed Venus, never so naked as now and never so undesired. Show her some amorousness, Spotty, you lout, cherish her, you tilted vomit, you horn-player. Here's a wench with no complexion and indifferent to those spoilers of your social aplomb, the white whelks and knobs that sit upon your cheek. And she is dumb too, your crippled conversation shall not trouble her either. Be amorous, you university half-wit, cuddle her, with your bubukled face and your no-bigger-than-a-pin's-head brain, few opportunities for dalliance and wantoning will come your way...'

We sat in silence after that, myself with my head on my arms, and Dion, with distended nostrils, reading his book under the dim shower of illumination which ignited his ruddy-golden hair into a clear and un-consuming glow. I began to succumb to an almost overpowering desire to sleep, and in an attempt to remain mentally active I asked Dion what had happened at the Calliper Club. He showed no readiness to explain and began discussing instead the book he was reading.

'What is the purpose of life if it is not to be an illumination of literature?' he asked me with his finger in the pages. 'I am content to endure it if my acquiescence will reveal the meaning and significance of *'Fermentent les rousseurs amères de l'amour'* and the *'Un drwg fydd ewin ar draeth'* passage. How is it possible that critics believe any connection other than this can exist between life and art? The sole function of art is to give us the thrill of non-recognition; of life the thrill of recognition. Art is the great enigma, the mysterious beat of the wings of great night-birds moving overhead through the dark-ness.'

Remembering the thesis of my essay I asked Dion if he believed the provision of the *nouveau frisson* to be the only function of art. But had not literature and painting at least other and more rewarding values? Would not a poem express for the relatively inarticulate what they had not the imagination and the verbal facility satisfyingly to express for themselves? Would not an adolescent, unbidden, commit love poems to memory? Did we not in plays and novels apprehend the thoughts of minds other than our own, the motions of alien hearts; did we not also recognize there our fellowship with the suffering, the humiliated, the browbeaten, the cheaply held; did we not rejoice with the virtuous, the innocent, and the fulfilled? Would not art be among the redeemers of the world, would it not by invective, parable, and exhortation convert the soul and regenerate society? Would it not be admirable even as a decorative patina covering the drab patches of our existence, might it not merely kindle our hearts as vivid colours and a candled tree delighted us in childhood? Were not artists thus the creators of human values, the unacknowledged legislators of the world?

'I believe,' said Dion, after a pause, 'that the footballers are stirring, but perhaps I am in error. Heaven forbid, Trystan,' he went on, his green eyes upon me and his eyebrows rising in mockery, 'that we should have been ruled by Christopher Marlowe,

Goronwy Owen, Robert Burns, Edgar Allan Poe, Paul Verlaine, Arthur Rimbaud, Oscar Wilde, or even by a well-meaning and fanatical fruit-eater like Shelley himself. I agree with you that the artist is the creator of values but only of artistic and not moral values. And for this reason the religious man, the political man, the philosophical man, is necessarily an impure appreciator of art, he seeks in the art-work confirmation of his own system of religious, political, or philosophical belief and, failing to find it, condemns what he has seen, read, or listened to. Such critics praise also what sustains them.'

'On the contrary, Dion,' I told him, 'the truly religious man will be free to enjoy a work of art in a way the faithless will not. It is the aesthete, bereft of religion, who seeks constantly in poem, play, and novel for philosophy, who yearns to find in literature some substitute for the religion he has lost; it is he, misled by a similitude, who bestows immoderate praise on the worthless describers to him of his own conflicts and frustrations. The religious man has his inviolable faith, and his concern, confronted by a work of art, is therefore with its complete meaning, with its wholeness, radiance, and harmony, with its entire significance as an object in whose loveliness all men can delight and not with its appeal only to those who accept the single elements of its religious, political, or philosophic background.'

'Now then, now then,' began Decker, stirring, his corn-flower blue eyes gazing around him out of fidgeting lids, 'now then, now then, I feel low.' He closed his eyes again in grimacing agony. 'What's the matter with Nico?' he continued, blinking, 'of the, of the, afterwards, he's like a fly-leaf. Was I in the smoker? What's Spotty doing with the bones in his lap?'

We explained, and as we were trying to dissuade him from going back to sleep Nico, disturbed by Decker's restlessness, gradually roused. He felt first in his pockets for his steel glasses, gazed round at us all through them and at his harness in silent perplexity, gulped hard like a natterjack, and hung on to his dishevelled head with both hands as though it were removable.

'How are you, Nico?' asked Dion.

'Only alive,' he moaned in a low and dispirited voice. His bravado and body-bounce were gone, and all his blatancy and swagger; he gazed round, abashed at the realization he had suffered at Dion's hands the dishonour of horizontal porterage. He muttered a few incoherent sentences. He disentangled his legs from Decker's, hung the massive bridle over the back of the sofa, and took, unsteadily and with cumbrous ineptitude, the two paces up to the mirror. There he stood clinging gorilla-like to the mantelpiece, examining his face out of beady and puckered eyes. He was as yellow as the sole of a foot and his tongue like tripe. Turning round again he pointed to Decker's trousers and asked him who had drenched them. Decker, observing the defilement for the first time, indignantly denounced the unknown puker and claimed condign indemnity and a new garment. Dion explained the guilty party was the *persona muta,* the lier with the bone whore, but counselled Decker to moderation since Spotty was already to be sued for a new taxi.

'Come on, Spotty,' Dion said, getting up and going across to shake him, 'you ossophile, rise and divest yourself.'

Spotty's nodose skin in the dim gaslight was the stale yellow of caked mustard, and the spent matchsticks he used as stiffeners for his collar protruded from their broken tapes. He opened his eyes, and seeing the skull in the dim half-light grinning upon his shoulder, and the bone arms round his neck, he let out a tinny shriek; at the same moment he jumped out of his chair and flung the skeleton rattling like a heap of rigging on to the rug.

'Who did that, who did that?' he demanded, shrieking, casting around his abusive regard. 'You leave me alone. You're not going to make a fool out of me. I want to go home, I do.'

It was the end. There was a silence, a hiatus, a three bars rest. Then Dion settled back to his book, asking Spotty for a fanfare, since Miss Machen's descent was now inevitable. We should all be weighed and found wanting in the scale-pans of her pince-nez. Had I, Trystan, the power to mitigate her wrath, could I induce in her a lenitive spirit, put my head on her shoulder and weep contrition into her salt-cellars? Spotty would be wise to disentangle himself and take himself off through the window.

'Now for a bit of cold tongue,' Nico groaned, hearing Miss Machen's foot resolute upon the stairs, and he sank back beside the harness on the sofa.

Dion held the door for her but she brushed past him without a glance into the room. She stopped with her poker in her hand and stood speechless the moment of her entry, gazing with pallid unbelief at the scene of disorder before her; a tall, skinny, and outraged figure, she surveyed the dimly lit room with an expression of incredulous astonishment and a blaze of bleak indignation upon her features. Her ears were divested of their pendulous figs and the rookery of her daytime coiffure had been dismantled and hung in a pair of grey plaits over her shoulders. She was wearing a black quilted dressing-gown with overflowing quantities of curtain lace at her throat; as she stood silent and stately before us with her poker-bearing arms in a knot we felt one by one the ice of her glance cast through her pince-nez upon us.

Her first words were horneted at Spotty sitting astride the window in the act of escaping. She ordered him, regally indicating with the sceptre-like fire-iron, back into the room, and when Dion with his habitual quasi-insolent manner offered his glib sophisms, she gave him an abrupt and sharp-beaked look and told him to keep his tongue quiet.

Spotty, vigorously threatened with poker and police intervention, climbed reluctantly and sheepishly inside.

She then invited us to explain this upheaval and the presence of these strangers in her house, revealing her oblong horse-teeth as she did so. I cast a tangential glance at Dion, who began the rigmarole of a dubious *éclaircissement* which I felt Miss Machen was not intended to hear – he was jealous of the good name of the house; Nico and Decker Miss Machen would recognize as lodgers of her niece, Mrs Evans, next door; Spotty was leaving in so odd a manner merely out of consideration of Miss Machen herself.

'How are you now, Nico?' he asked with solicitude, interrupting himself and turning

245

again towards the sofa.

'No change,' said Nico with a glower.

Before Dion could continue Miss Machen crossed over and turned up the gas, and for the moment her strongly marked face seemed featureless in the glare like the spotlight-sodden countenances of pallid notabilities. Then, out of the pink under-roofs of her brows, she rolled down her extensive lids and her teeth flashed their interior gold as her lips were lifted off them in a reticulated sneer and her attack upon us began.

She had kept students for twenty years, she knew the revolting smell of strong drink, at three in the morning her house was disturbed by the ringing of bells, by trumpet blasts, by the yells of some drunken maniac, her rooms were entered and quitted by louts she knew nothing of, and that by her windows, and these creatures had the effrontery to lie there stinking in their drink.

She was on the draw now as to eloquence, and before the indignation of her flashing face and the majesty of her prey-bird aspect we were mute and overborne. The departure of Nico, Decker, and Spotty was in silence after that scourging *tramontana*. The guilty hearts of all of us were touched, they were heavy as the largest stone in the wall. But, as Nico said, Miss Machen was a nice girl. Dion and I, that night expecting expulsion, received only an edge-nosed reprimand and heard the Sinai-fiat against repetition; and, before the end of his first year at her house, she came to regard Dion as a possessor not only of esoteric learning, but also of valuable mother-wit and week-day wisdom; she began to love the stimulating alternations of homage, familiarity, and suave condescension with which he treated her. In her relations with him she abandoned her domineering, landladyish pose; she nourished and cockered him; she sought, being without male relations, his advice upon financial matters, discussing with him in the remote citadel and zenana of her office-bedroom the pink-ribboned insurances, endowments, and investment bundles which she there, with ice-cold hands, took out of her roll-top desk. She considered her affairs prospered, and soon she began to regard Dion's presence as talismanic.

Then when Nico towards the end of the year again found himself shelterless after some further scamphood in which Decker had involved him, Dion, meeting him in Boundary Villas, undertook to speak to Miss Machen on his behalf. This he did, he honeyed her, he persuaded her to let the memory of Nico's past go up the chimney, he induced her to allow him to take up his lodgings temporarily with us, although

Decker, already well known to her, was expressly excluded from this protocol of oblivion.

So Nico came to us finally at Miss Machen's at the commencement of my third year at the university. In the beginning he was a little uncertain of Gwydion and me, he regretted the pontoon and inconsequence of Decker, and remembered with embarrassment too often the ironies following that Calliper Club smoker. He was silent, truculent, or over-boisterous. He complained of Dion's studious habits; he told me Dion was forty years old when he was born; he said you had to get the ice-breakers out before you could talk to Dion; he wished he could knock a few bricks off the top of the wall Dion had raised round him. And so on. But I could see they liked each other. And Nico, who had stayed in more lodgings than anyone else in the university, never moved from 87 Boundary Villas as long as he remained in college.

11

I thought continually about Lisbeth and from time to time I saw her again. At present I was content to look at her, to enjoy the radiance and sweetness of her presence without being seen by her. I did not wish then at all for acquaintance or any more intimate contact. Sometimes I visited the Queen's and watched her sitting there with her friends. Sometimes I stood outside, concealed in the dark doorway of the photographer's opposite, and waited for her to come down the two or three steps between the glass doors of the café and the pavement, to see the street lights falling upon her curls and the glowing perfection of her face. Sometimes after waiting until the café lights were all turned off and the commissionaire had carried out the steel telescopic gates, I did not see her at all. Whether she knew of my existence or not I was uncertain. Once when I passed close to her and her friend in the carpeted corridor of the Queen's she looked at me and smiled slightly, on her face the dubious expression of half recognition.

One day when I was walking rather dreamily along the park avenue on my return from college, I slipped off the kerbstone and jarred myself unpleasantly awake. I glanced round to see if anyone had witnessed my clumsiness, and there, not twenty yards away, I saw Lisbeth walking before me in the direction of Boundary Villas. I did not doubt for a moment it was she. At the sight of her I always experienced some violent disturbance, a sense of upheaval and delight at the same time, the stab and the balm together. I stood quite still, unable to see for the moment or to realize what was happening. Slowly at first and then rapidly the darkness cleared, and I walked on again. I could not bear to look at her, but walked with my eyes fixed on the gardens of the houses on the opposite side of the avenue. Both Lisbeth and I were on the sunny side of the street which, but for us, seemed entirely deserted. As she walked under tree after tree she became for a moment completely black and then at the next step the sun splashed its colours over her, upon the scarlet straw of her hat and the long blue dress with a scarlet girdle.

I feared very much that she would turn round. What if she does, I thought. Would she recognize me? Would she stop and wait for me? If she does I shall certainly stop myself. I will never be able to walk forward to her and speak. If she turns round I shall stand here. I've heard that if you think sufficiently hard about a person you can force them to look at you. But I was quite incapable of doing anything else.

I followed her in a sort of ecstasy of trepidation along the avenue, and saw her go off into Boundary Villas. I went in at number eighty-seven and stood watching her walk on and turn into Powell Street at the next turning.

At dinner I sat absorbed in a dream of her.

Opposite me Dion ate steadily and read some thick periodical concerned with Celtic studies. Suddenly I stopped eating. Like a flash I remembered that while walking behind Lisbeth I had passed Spotty in the avenue without even a nod or a word.

12

One night at the art school, the first Tuesday after half term, I was as usual helping Mr Leyshon to prepare the room before the arrival of the evening students. I got out of his cupboard the pile of folios belonging to our class and began to distribute them. One of them bore initials I did not remember having seen before.

'Who does this belong to?' I asked him. 'Is it one of ours?'

'New student,' he said, glancing over. 'Starting this evening. Put it there.' He indicated the desk next to mine and then went out suddenly, as he often did.

Soon the students in our class began to arrive. They were pleasant people, one or two clerks, a schoolmaster, two typists (sisters, these), a crane driver, a bus conductor, a shopkeeper. I liked them all very much and felt at home with them. None of them seemed to me greatly gifted, but they very much enjoyed painting and drawing and one or two appeared to have a good knowledge of art and were capable of discussion.

As I sat at my desk looking at them coming in for their lesson, Mr Leyshon entered the room, followed by the girl I had watched pouring out coffee in the vestry of Markethall Square during my first week at college, the one I had always thought of as Doug's girl.

This was a great surprise to me. Although I still went regularly to chapel with Zachy and my other friends I had not seen her since that Sunday night of my first term in Dinas, over a year ago now. Her absence, I had supposed, was due to the removal of her family from the city, since I had not seen her mother either; or had, perhaps, some connection with the irregularity of Doug's attendance in his final year when hospital work kept him away from chapel Sunday after Sunday; or with his quitting the university at the end of the summer term. All these possibilities I had considered earlier but I had forgotten almost entirely about her now and I had not expected to see her again. But here she was following Mr Leyshon into the room, calm and assured and remote, a little solemn almost, unmoved, dressed as on that Sunday night, with simplicity, her frock dark and severe but with a sort of grave fitness and elegance.

Her high-cheekboned face was still pale and her dark hair done in the style of fringe and bob, although the bob was longer now, down almost to her shoulders.

Mr Leyshon came over towards me, his face with its pointed eyebrows and little goatee like the mask of a satyr, and indicated to her the desk next to mine. 'Here you are, Miss Pritchard,' he said. 'Sit here. Mr Morgan will tell you anything you want to know.'

He gave me the sort of sharp-toothed leer he used when he thought he was embarrassing me and went off.

She nodded, put on her overall, and sat down. On the cover of her box I saw her name, Mabli Pugh Pritchard, scratched in the black paint. She painted in a steady, assured manner, using thick water-colours. Although she worked slowly, almost in a leisurely way, she was utterly attentive to what she was doing, her attitude concentrated rather than absorbed, and yet her indifference to all that happened around her in the classroom was complete. She hardly spoke a word to me all night, or looked at what I was painting, or seemed aware of my presence. She bent forward at her work, the long bob of her hair falling at the side of her face, half concealing it. I was able to look at her hands. They were beautiful, long and pink and rather heavy. The fingers, I noticed, seemed always half cupped, they lay alongside one another, continually touching, in them a heavy immobility.

During the interval she did not go out but sat cross-legged on her tall stool, talking in a desultory way to the chatting sisters on the other side of her. The rung of the stool on which she rested her heel was high and her skirt-covered knees protruded upwards. She sharpened a pencil, refilled her water-jar, and went over to speak to Mr Leyshon, who listened with his hand outspread on his baldness. To me she said nothing. It was obvious that for her all memory of our brief meeting had completely faded. Ought I to speak to her and remind her of it? I felt very strongly the absurdity of sitting there next to her and saying nothing. But she seemed so remote and indifferent, she gave me no encouragement at all to speak in spite of Mr Leyshon's invitation. Besides, if she was to be a student here there would be plenty of opportunity in the future. I said nothing.

At the end of the session she gathered up her things, took off her overall, and wished the two sisters good night. Then she turned casually to me. 'Good night,' she said, and left as she had come in, calm, silent, un-involved.

'Good night,' I said.

When I went out myself a little later, I could see Mr Leyshon grinning at me over his shoulder from the washbasin.

A day or two later Zachy was at our door on his way to the university. In his shabby college clothes, he seemed hardly the same person as stood, tall and well-dressed, outside Markethall Square on a Sunday morning talking in his fawning grandiloquent way, and with gestures, to the wives of the wealthier deacons.

'Hallo, Trystan,' he said. 'I didn't see you in chapel Sunday night.' In his voice was an element of reproof, and yet he seemed eager to tell me something.

'No,' I answered. 'I was rather busy. I really had to miss.'

'I see. This is what I want, boy. Would you like to come out to supper with us one night this week? Saturday, say?'

'To supper? Where? To your digs?'

'No. You remember Mrs Pugh Pritchard? You know, the sister-in-law of the lord? Well, she's been ill for a long time but she's better now. Hum. She's asked me to bring two or three students along on Saturday. Would you like to come? Charley *bach's* coming.'

'She's got a daughter, hasn't she?' I said. 'Doug's girl.'

The question came without premeditation. It was the first time I had ever asked anyone about the family and I was surprised to see that Zachy, a transparent character, looked affronted at it. An expression of impatience swept over his large lined face and he coloured. 'Doug's girl?' he said, annoyed. 'Of course she isn't. Ann Price is Doug's girl. Are you coming or not? It's a fine opportunity, boy. Big house and well-connected people.'

I agreed to go. I did not tell Zachy I was in the same painting class as Mabli although I could not explain even to myself why I was reluctant that he should know. Evidently, I reflected after he had gone, I had made some mistake with regard to her. That Sunday night Zachy and Charley *bach* had taken for granted my question had referred to some girl who perhaps always served at the coffee-table but whom I had not even noticed there. I felt pleased that this was so. I had received the impression from his conversation that Doug was a limited man, unimaginative, insensitive, concerned to the exclusion of almost all else with his conjoint diploma. There seemed in him a matter-of-factness, an earthiness, a lack of speculation, which made him to me quite unworthy of the sort of person I believed Mabli, on the evidence of her air and her appearance, to be.

On the Saturday night the three of us went out to Cwrt Nicol, the Pugh Pritchard home. It was plain that Zachy had been there often because even in the dark he knew the way unhesitatingly, and which buses to take. He was wearing his best suit, highly polished shoes, his overcoat with the velvet collar, and a wide-brimmed trilby. Tall and mature-faced, he appeared to me impressive and reassuring. He spoke English all the way, using, when he remembered, a remarkable nasal twang with a falling inflexion which he seemed to believe was the accent current among people of refinement and social superiority. 'For practice,' he told us in Welsh, winking. 'We never know who we'll meet there.'

I was not concerned with whom we would meet but more and more apprehensive of what would happen when Mabli and I stood face to face.

The family lived in a suburb of big houses, each in its own grounds. A maid answered the door and led us into the hall. We took off our coats and were shown into a large warm sitting-room, very beautifully and comfortably furnished, lit by two or three heavily shaded lamps set on low tables and in the overmantel recesses, which threw brilliant disks and distorted ellipses of illumination on the furniture and the carpets beneath them. There was no one present when we entered so the three of us stood and looked about. Heavy curtains of crimson velvet, fringed and tasselled, were drawn over the windows, and a good flame-covered fire burned in the fire-place. After the khaki bleakness of Boundary Villas everything here seemed warm and comfortable and generous, the deep plush settees and arm-chairs with their plentiful fringed cushions, the thick red carpets, the large vases filled with leaves, sprays, and flowers, the shelves of books, even the florid ceiling moulding and the unlit chandelier with its gilt chains and tassels of glass – all made me feel I had never been in a room at once so comfortable, so inviting, and so delightful to look at.

Zachy glanced expectantly at me, made a grimace of satisfaction, and rolled his eyes round from object to object, taking my glance with him, and nodded with pleasure to see I had observed, under the guidance of his eyes, the signs on every hand of comfort and affluence.

I gave him his satisfaction. 'Very nice,' I whispered.

In a moment or two Mrs Pugh Pritchard entered.

I recognized her immediately although I had forgotten all the details of her appearance except her undershot jaw. She was rather bent now and supported herself on a slim, black walking-stick with a silver handle. Her dress was entirely of black lace and a long gold chain went three or four times around her neck. Her plentiful hair was a dry and even grey, she wore gold spectacles, and her jaw protruded even more than I remembered it to have done. Her lips were almost black.

'Good evening, Mr Charles,' she said to Zachy. 'How are you? I'm so glad you've been able to come. Do sit down. Have I met your friends before?'

Zachy was a great bow-er. He bowed now but he was better at it with his broad-brim in one hand and his hymnbook in the other.

'How are you, Mrs Pugh Pritchard? Much better I can see. Mr Charles, my cousin. Mr Morgans, my friend.'

As I was still feeling in mine the chill of her beringed and bony hand, the door opened and Mabli entered, with her calm and unmoved stride. She came silently over the carpet smiling slightly at Zachy and Charley *bach*. Then she recognized me. She stopped and even in that subdued light I could see the painful blush deepening immediately in her face, and the look of bewilderment, of utter panic, with which she stared for a moment into my face.

'You know my daughter, don't you?' said Mrs Pritchard.

Zachy bowed and both he and Charley *bach* shook hands with her and I did the same. I was greatly disturbed now at what was happening, I was filled with remorse for the wild, agonized look which had appeared momentarily on that human face. Why hadn't I spared her that, why hadn't I spoken to her in the painting class and told her we had met before? Had I wanted to hurt her because she had taken so little notice of me? But that was impossible since I had not then known that I was so soon to visit her home. Why had I said nothing to Zachy about our meeting in the painting class? Why did I so often do these senseless things and get myself into such unbelievable tangles. What was my purpose in doing it? And how was I to reveal now, as reveal I must, to those about me that a night or two ago she and I had sat next to each other for two hours without my opening my mouth almost, although I knew all the time who she was. I felt so concerned with my own problem, so disturbed and ill at ease, that I said hardly anything during the conversation.

Zachy, Charley *bach,* and I sat in a row on a very comfortable settee before the fire. Mrs Pugh Pritchard was in one of the armchairs and Mabli in the other. Fortunately not much seemed to be expected of me in the way of conversation because Mrs Pugh Pritchard herself was a talker of great range and stamina, and Zachy also supported her with a ready fluency in every discussion in which she engaged him – Markethall Square, the university, famous preachers,

Lord Lisvane, and diseases of the heart. I was relieved to hear his downward dipping sentences come only very occasionally through his nose. From time to time Mrs Pugh Pritchard addressed herself to me, but it was obvious that she regarded Zachy as the representative spokesman of our group.

'Where did you say your friend came from, Mr Charles?' she asked, nodding to me.

Zachy inclined his bald head graciously as though granting me permission to speak on my own behalf.

'Ystrad,' I answered. 'A mining village in the Ystrad Valley. Near Pencwm.'

'How interesting. What are you doing at the university?'

'An arts course.'

'Very nice. And do you like being at Dinas?'

'I do, but not at the university.'

I sounded rather rude and abrupt even to myself but she only laughed and turned back to Zachy.

Mabli also said very little. As I sat so close to her, thinking about her, about her calmness and the inexplicable look of terror that for a moment had appeared in her eyes, I thought I sensed between her and her mother a certain antagonism, a concealed irritability. Although I did not speak to her, or look at her, I was acutely aware of her presence beside me, so much so that the other people around the fire and the vehement agreements of their conversation hardly existed for me. A few inches away from my elbow her hand lay on the soft arm of her chair, the long fingers curved and resting heavily one against another in the way I had noticed in the art school. I was able to watch it without turning my head and I remained unceasingly aware of it, of its softness and colour and the perfection of its shape. She was at ease again now and when she made a remark she seemed calm and rather detached as she had been on the two previous occasions when I had seen her.

Supper was brought in on a trolley by the maid who had opened the door to us. With it came a smartly dressed young man of about thirty speaking English with a public school accent and Welsh too, calling his mother 'Memah,' saying 'den' for 'dan,' and in words like 'tadau' bringing the accent on to the last syllable. Zachy talking to him was almost incomprehensible, and I was cheered.

When I got home that night I told Dion all about it, blushing. He stared at me, while I spoke, in his cool, hostile way. When I had finished he dropped his head and gazed at his broken shoes.

'You're an idiot,' he said. 'Come on, let's go to bed.'

13

I began my third year at the university with Gwydion and Nico as my co-lodgers. Waiting around the supper table on our first night together Gwydion read his *Othello* and Nico his *Dinas Star* aloud to me.

What always struck me most about Nico was not now so much his quaintly rustic clothing, or his gorilla-like figure, or the luxuriant pilosity of his yellow flesh. It was his inability to pronounce the eighteenth letter of the alphabet. Instead of placing the tip of his tongue behind his upper incisors and vibrating it rapidly in this position, he dragged the sound; he seemed to produce it in the region of his epiglottis; he made of *ground* and *green* each almost a disyllable. Some time later Dion said to him: 'You, Nico Mathias, you inarticulate Dyfedite, you utterer of kitchen English, you speaker of a sub-dialect of the Welsh language, by what deformity or cryptic reversion perhaps do you produce that perfect gallic *ar, l'r grasseyé*, that inachievable *r de Paris?*'

Nico was often teased and interrogated by us because his luxuriant Esauism was a feature not only of the visible skin of hands and head but of the entire surface of his flesh. When Dion was confronted, day after day at Miss Machen's with the big rounded head, massive and hairy, and the deep primrose-yellow skin – 'Your mother, Nico Mathias,' he would say, 'she suffered severely from heartburn and the water-brash when she was carrying you, did she?'

Nico's thick black hair, which he kept cropped so short that it looked like the nap on hatter's plush, came down low on his brow with a rounded point in front like the toe of a flat-iron. Each fibrous eyebrow, very firm, dense, and black, and shooting out long curling pea-tendrils, ran up continuously in a sort of dotted line from the vertex of each brow and disappeared into the low nap of the hair. The shape of his beard, although he was clean-shaven, showed clearly; it gave the shiny greyish lustre of kitchen blacklead to the flanks of his fleshy cheeks and his double chin. His nose had a wide, lateral bend in it and was hairy; and his puffed cheekbones were hairy, a fringe of dark outward-curving hairs grew in orderly profusion upon them.

As Nico, wearing with discomfort his minute spectacles, was reading the paper aloud I heard his nose emit with each gathered breath a high-pitched, involuntary whistling note. 'Nuptials at Dinas: Richards-Symons,' he read. 'The wedding was celebrated at St Paul's Church (*peep*) on Tuesday last, of Mr Thomas Richards,

Butcher, High St, Dinas' *(peep)* – (here he stopped to nibble with his incisors part of the tongue-garnered scourings of his meal. Then he continued) – 'and Miss Teresa Symons, both of Dinas. The ceremony was conducted by the Rev. J. Prifcopyn Price ("Prif-copyn"). The bride was attired *(peep)* in a navy blue *ensemble* with shoulder-spray of crimson carnations *(peep)* and accessories to match. The best man was *(peep)* –'

Nico stopped, puzzled and annoyed, trying to locate the origin of this metallic locomotive-like whistle, piping shrilly while he read, but ceasing when he held his breath to listen. I was afraid to explain because I knew I would laugh if I tried, but Dion, intoning *Othello* from his tilted-back chair, in indication of the source of the sound, tapped with his clay pipe the bridge of his nose.

Slowly Nico's beleaguered features began to relax and to acknowledge by a sort of scowl that he had understood the sense of the signalled intelligence. Laying down the paper and taking from his loaded side-pocket an immense handkerchief he spread it completely over his face and discharged into it the hairy gunnery of his nose. Then after gazing round at the unannihilated walls, he tested the result with copious inhalations of wind that rung an answering hum from the gas-shades and completely overwhelmed the tranquil monotone of Dion's recital. But not the smallest peep, hoot, or whistle sounded out of the distended nostrils.

'That's better,' he said with satisfaction, his yellow face wine-red as he called upon heaven to bless his animal exertions. Then, the room again in repose, he continued his reading.

'After the reception, held in the Central Chambers *(peep)* the bride and bridegroom left for the honeymoon in Yellow Wells. The bride, who holds *(peep)* a responsible position with a local firm of caterers, *(peep)* travelled in a brown two-piece with hat and shoes to match *(peep)*. The happy couple were the recipients of many tokens of esteem from their wide circle of friends *(peep)* –'

Nico stopped, cursed the septum nasi, the nares anterior and posterior, the ethmoidal passages, the mucous membrane, and the discharge of both his nasal orifices, and then lowering his paper again, he said: 'You recognize Miss Teresa Symons, don't you, Trystan? It's Tiny, the barmaid from the Boot and Bell.' Then turning to Dion, who maintained, indifferent to verbal interruptions or convulsive nose-blowings, his bass Shakespearian accompaniment, he began to recall the butcher's bride to our memory, describing her abundant shapeliness, her false-blonde hair, her doctored beauty, her brittle prancing action behind the bar counter as she bore her beer-tray before her with the blithe movements of the spring stallion.

As Dion lifted his head and, turning his indignant gaze on the sultry bladder of Nico's face, confessed to a sonorous remembrance of her, Miss Machen entered with the supper tray. On her head was the homespun hair halo thrusting out its eaves into space, and on her cold hands the many rings with the cat's-eye onyx entangled in threads of gold.

'To what shall you be likened,' Dion said, when she had closed the door behind her, 'half cart-horse and half bird? Your beak to the hook of the duke-nosed condor or the rough-legged kite, your protrusive muzzle to some bladdery horse-mouth, you seem equine, runtish, and knacker-bound. Your coiffure might offer a refuge to the migrant waterfowl–'

'You don't know when you're well off,' Nico interrupted him. 'You ought to have been with Decker and me. I could tell you about landladies.' And Nico did that night, for hours.

He had lodged in main street and three-piece suburb; in Westendia; in artisan's terrace and behind the sawn bathstone of middle-class slum. He knew among landladies the psalm-singer and the sponging drab; the reserved; the esurient and the anserine gaggler. He had experienced the coal-grudging widow and the light-fingered old maid; he could describe the serene and the malevolent, the unsuspicious, the censorious, and the tedious snob. He had boarded in the dog-hole of ex-*diva* Regan, a majestic, shawl-shouldering, platform-posturing, mail-opening dipsomaniac, who, drunk before noon on neat spirits, would with eloquence and shouted contumely refuse him his midday meal, and be carried pickaback upstairs by him in the evening to her maudlin bed. He had stayed in the unsoaped squalor of the trullish Mrs Watkins and her scandalous half-caste, whom he overheard threatening to finish him and Decker with knuckle-duster or knife-blade for non-payment of their rent; and who on their grim-visaged appearance together at the kitchen door, between lamp and bird-cage – this half-caste with disclaimers and abject denial retracted. He had stayed with Mrs Truscott, a pallid drug-addict and carpet-pawner, gown-clad and with her hair-tails down her back, wandering in doped indifference about her resounding barn-like villa, a buff cigarette in her mouth and her lids hung in unheeding fixity half-way down her eyeballs. So extensive had been this chronic and ignominious nomadism of Nico and Decker that they became forgetful and confused. One morning, knocking at the front door of a house in which they hoped to find new lodgings, they recoiled and fled upon beholding the ominous scowl of recognition on the outraged porridge-spotted face confronting them in the porchway; for they recollected in a flash then their peremptory expulsion with threat and insult over this identical threshold the previous term.

Nico talked long that night and kept us up late.

14

I saw Mabli regularly at the art school now and every night I walked with her after our lesson as far as her bus. We learned a lot concerning each other; she, about my life in Ystrad, and my reasons for pursuing an arts course when my ambition was to become a painter; I, that her late father had owned a couple of factories out in the rural west where Welsh rugs, blankets, and tweeds were made; that he was Lord Lisvane's younger brother and had stayed in Cardiganshire to work the family mill, resisting the attraction of the coal-fields; that the mills were now owned by a company of which her mother and her uncle and aunt were all directors; that she rejected the politics of her uncle and thought that Wales should become a self-governing nation.

She was absent the week following my strange visit to her home, but the Tuesday after she was at her desk, next to mine, again.

When she came into the room she seemed as calm and assured as usual; she was already wearing her bright smock, and her paints and her bag were under her arm. She said an indifferent good evening to me, laid out her things on the ledge of her desk, and then turned to speak to the typist sisters on the other side of her.

I said nothing to her after her greeting, I made no attempt to attract her attention or speak to her about my visit, I was only too glad to avoid all reference to it and I concentrated as much as I was able upon my painting. But I felt disturbed and uneasy, I was certain that more was to be said about what had happened, although I could not imagine what circumstances would bring this about.

I worked steadily but unsuccessfully and with divided attention until the interval. When the break bell sounded the sisters immediately got up and hurried chattering out of the room, inviting Mabli to go with them. She declined and laid down her brush and when no one was any longer near our desks she turned to me. I went on painting, and for a moment she sat on her high stool facing me in silence, I could feel her gaze upon me as I brought down the paint. Finally I stopped and looked at her.

'Why didn't you tell me you knew me when I joined this class?' she said at once.

I could feel myself trembling. I did not know what to reply. I had not foreseen that she would speak out directly and without introduction or occasion like this.

'I hardly knew you,' I said. 'I had only seen you once before.'

'But you knew who I was. You knew a lot of people I knew, too.'

If my hand had been steadier I would have picked up my brush and resumed my work. I felt guilty and miserable. But I could not tell her that her own coldness had helped to discourage me.

'I'm sorry,' I said. 'It was stupid. But I didn't think you wanted to speak.'

'Didn't want to speak?' she repeated. Her expression was troubled, the idea seemed painful to her, and colour began to show faintly in her pale face. For a moment, as she uttered the words, that look of panic I had seen once before came into her eyes, a wild look as of one lost and in complete despair. She turned away and picked up her brush and began to paint, her long hair falling down beside her face. To my surprise

271

I noticed that her hands, so beautiful and so assured, were trembling also. How could this be? I sat beside her not knowing what to do or say. The rest of the interval was an agony of perplexity and silence. I had never been in so puzzling a situation before, and all I could do was to sit there tortured with ignorance and indecision and allow time to end it. I could endure, but not act.

During the second period we said nothing to each other. I knew I was behaving boorishly and foolishly but, desperately as I wished to do so, I did not know how to break out of the entanglements of silence and misunderstanding in which I had enmeshed myself. The thought of Dion, and Alcwyn, crossed my mind but I was unable to conceive of either of them placed in so imprisoning an impasse. But as the evening progressed I made up my mind, come what may, snub, rebuff, coldness, that I would speak that very night and explain all I had to say. The time for the final bell approached and my heart began to beat furiously with fear and resolution.

With two minutes still to go the bell went off suddenly, startling me, and I got abruptly off my stool and stood beside Mabli. 'I'm sorry,' I said. 'I didn't speak because I wished not to intrude upon you. You seemed to want it to be like that. I didn't know I should so soon be visiting your house.' I managed to grin. 'I'm sorry,' I repeated.

Mabli looked up. She smiled. I was conscious of someone standing between us. Mr Leyshon had arrived silently and was flipping through his fingers the pages of a book which he then held out towards me. There was a grin in the middle of his beard.

'College magazine,' he said. 'Have you seen a copy? Miss Pritchard?'

Mabli stooped to get her purse out of her bag.

'Very interesting,' Mr Leyshon went on. I was sure his grin and the jeering pitch of his eyebrows meant that he was going to do or say something to embarrass me.

'Look at this, Trystan. "College Notes." Read it. Listen, Miss Pritchard. Let me read it then,' he said, as I kept my hands in my pockets.

He turned a few pages and then read out a satirical paragraph headed 'Tudor Rose.' The basis of the story in this paragraph was my misadventure with the enormous plaster foot, treated in a mock-heroic manner. In it 'Tudor' had become the name of a diffident, self-conscious student, and 'Rose' a verb. It was signed 'E. and S.'

To diminish Mr Leyshon's satisfaction I would gladly have remained unconcerned, but I could feel the colour going up my face as he read. Mabli was smiling although she could not have known the whole meaning of the paragraph.

'You'll want more than one copy of this, won't you?' he said. 'Come and get them at the office. Sorry I can't leave this.'

He went off, satisfied to see me colouring before Mabli. 'What's it all about?' she said, puzzled.

As we went out of the room together I told her what had happened. She laughed. 'You are too decent to them,' she said.

I waited for her in the entrance hall while the students streamed past me into the street. When she came she was wearing a black velvet tam with a golden tassel and a long tight coat of black cloth, high-collared, and trimmed with astrakhan. There was an elegance and an assurance about her which seemed to me absent from the women students I knew at Dinas, both of the art school and the university. She walked towards me with the weight of the fur edging swaying the hems of her coat about her with grace.

Together we went out through the glass doors and made for her bus stop under the lamps of the main street of Dinas. As we walked along side by side she laughed about the visit I had made with Zachy and Charley *bach* to her house. Her mother felt it her Christian duty to invite the Markethall Square students into her home and entertain them, but to Mabli the visits were matters of boredom. Many of the students seemed amusing without at all intending to be, bumptious, patronizing, cocksure, or busy acting a part. No one, she thought, could take them seriously. Particularly Zachy Charles. Except her mother, that is. No, Mabli hadn't told her mother she had already met me. Mrs Pugh Pritchard disliked what she could not understand. Best to say nothing. And the next time I came to the house I had best not make any reference to our art school meetings either.

I saw her on to her bus and then went and stood outside the Queen's in the hope of seeing Lisbeth.

15

On our saint's day and saturnalia, the afternoon of our patronal rag, yearly carnival and ball, a thousand excited, box-rattling students, male and female, swarmed the city streets, blazered or clad in sober academic dress, and, in tableaued procession, bedaubed, fucoed, and vividly costumed, walked, rode, or were lorry-borne, colour-fully masquerading as clowns, colliers, pirates, Scotsmen, Kanakas, Arctic ex-plorers, Dames Wales, dudes, Red Indians, whores, deep-sea divers, Celestials, gauchos.

The conspicuous bladder-bosomed horse-man wearing a sou'wester under pink ostrich plumes, a draught-board bodice and baggy harem-like bloomers of emerald net that showed his suspenders and underpants, was sergeant-at-arms and rag-marshal Nico. As he galloped his skewbald pony from end to end of the procession in a sort of reckless hypomania and corybantic frenzy, he was not easily recognizable, because his swerving nose and cheekbones were geranium, and he had corked on his face immoderate moustaches, kiss-curl side-whiskers, and a black obliterating beard.

The same evening the ball took place in the city hall of Dinas. Alcwyn, Nico, and I went, but Dion refused. 'Not for the golden wedge of Ophir,' he said.

On the way home after the rag I called in at Zachy's digs, since I had not seen him for several days. Although it was still only teatime he had begun dressing for the ball. He had hired a dinner suit with appropriate shirt, collar, and tie, but had forgotten about pumps. Did I think his new brown boots would be out of place? A dress watch was what he wanted, too, one of those slim ones he had heard of that you couldn't see in the pocket, much better than the fat railwayman's timepiece he usually carried on his thick chain. Didn't I think so? What was I going to wear? And Nico?

Alcwyn, Nico, and I were rather late going – Nico took a long time getting rid of his make-up, clowning over the business while we sat waiting for him, laughing at his lunacy. When we got to the city hall we found the large assembly-room crowded, the three great crystal chandeliers were blazing overhead and palms, shrubs, and flowers were arranged in the angles and spread out in beds and upon trellises. Everything looked gay and bright and glittering. The first person we recognized inside was Nugent the college dandy and authority on precedence, etiquette, mode of address, and the ramifications of the royal family, enjoying himself very much, he told us, although the pitying stare he passed over my blazer suggested that such garments were a shade too numerous for his un-alloyed satisfaction. He was beautifully dressed in tails. 'Damn it, Nugent,' said Alcwyn, himself wearing a smart dinner suit, 'go away, go away. You make me feel as though my clothes have come off a door-hook. Shoo!'

We wandered about in the crowd, greeting people. The hall was already full and rather warm and, although the band was silent for the moment, noisy with talk and laughter. In a palm-treed recess between two large fluted pillars we found a group we knew around Lorna singing, 'Happy birthday to you,' and Lorna in the middle, pretty and crying with joy. All the girls looked attractive, even the ones with funny legs and behinds had long dresses to cover them and the ones who wore glasses in college had left them in hall. We had a few dances with girls from our year for practice and then Alcwyn walked up to the principal's wife, a vivid little woman with no neck and a sparkling face and asked her for the next waltz. She seemed, from where we stood near the settees, to accept readily enough and moved off with him, laughing. When it was over we saw her introducing him to a tall thin girl who, somebody said, was her daughter. 'How did you get on, Alcwyn?' I asked him. 'Which of the old jokes did you serve up?' asked Nico.

'I told her,' he explained, 'I was only just learning to waltz and she said, "I thought so."'

We laughed.

'But she said she hoped I'd ask her again,' he added.

'Politeness,' said Nico.

'Jealousy,' said Alcwyn.

The evening was enjoyable, everything went with *hwyl* and pleasure although the hall, large and lofty as it was, seemed to become warmer, noisier, and more crowded hour by hour. We found a good number of people we knew about in the crowd, Legger

Jones, Murtagh, Billy Handel, Chewzy Hughes, Wally Oriel, and there were in addition large numbers of strangers, townspeople, perhaps, and friends of our professors and lecturers. Spotty and Gordon Anthony we discovered marooned in a corner. Like many of us neither of them could dance much but Gordon agreed after a time to be taken round by some of the women from his year. He was unteachable. Spotty stood in the background, silent and morose.

As I watched Gordon's clumsy progress amongst the dancers I became suddenly aware to my surprise and confusion of Lisbeth standing quite near, beside one of the enormous fancy pillars placed at intervals around the hall. Her face was alive, radiant, she was talking with uninhibited animation, her ringed hands moving before her, laughing at the same time. The sight of her thus almost at my side, so beautiful, so animated, sent a momentary torturing sensation through me like the deep burn of a stab. My first glimpse of her was invariably a moment of peculiar agony and joy. I turned again towards her. Although the hall was filled with women, young, beautiful many of them, she alone seemed to move and breathe at the core of an indescribable warmth and brilliancy, there was about her always a glitter, a gaiety, a unique and indefinable sweetness beyond that, it seemed to me, possessed by any other woman present. Her golden hair was parted at the side and drawn simply across her head and down upon her neck in a thick row of clustering curls. In her ears were little red flowerlike earrings, cup-shaped, like scarlet water-lilies. Her creamy dress fitted closely in the bodice but the long skirt was full and overlaid plentifully with a gauzy material which sparkled. Round her waist ran a narrow red girdle fastened with a buckle of red glass. Her shoes were of white satin, but the heels, very tall and slender, were scarlet. It was the first time I had seen her bare-headed.

As I watched her she and the dark man to whom she was speaking edged away from the pillar into the crowd and began to dance. She moved beautifully with him; he appeared to me a manifest expert, his body in its perfect jacket taut, controlled, and yet lissom, going through the complicated steps of some new dance with grace and assurance, the skill and usage of familiarity; and Lisbeth swayed and turned with him, at ease, smiling into his face, her wide skirt at each turn flaring out and falling back against her again, her red heels coming together with a little pause in the middle of the swirling movement, in perfect unison and understanding. And while she danced her expression glowed, she held back her head and laughed wet-lipped, looking into the face of her partner; her eyes shone, joy and loveliness seemed to be about her. Her dance was enchanting to watch but in a few minutes, before she had moved out of sight, the band stopped playing and, laughing and her long slender arms moving before her, she accompanied her partner back to the golden pillar from which they had started their dance.

'I say, Trystan,' said Alcwyn, 'when's supper? My stomach thinks my throat's cut.'

'Next dance is supper dance, I think,' put in Nico and was immediately confirmed.

I heard them but I felt remote and withdrawn, a little dazed. To get to the refreshment-room it would be necessary to pass within a foot or two of where Lisbeth stood and I determined to make an excuse and not to go in to supper if she did not move away. Looking in her direction again I saw clearly for the first time the face of the man she had been dancing with. He was very dark and sleek, about thirty-five, with a narrow moustache and smooth black hair brushed smartly back. He seemed distinguished, assured, and mature to me, unsmiling, very calm and handsome in his beautiful evening clothes. He was rather short, no taller than Lisbeth herself, but powerfully built, athletic, and active. Suddenly, as I was studying him, Nico

281

beside me exclaimed: 'Damn, look who's over there by the pillar,' and I saw Alcwyn's glance follow the direction of his nod. They seemed to be looking straight at Lisbeth.

'What?' asked Alcwyn. 'The one in white? Who is she? One of yours, Nico? One of the noble six hundred?'

'No fear,' he answered. 'She's not available for the use of students.'

'Not enough curves,' Alcwyn suggested. 'Who's that big-mouthed totty you were taking around when I tapped you? Where the devil is Trystan off to?'

I passed Marjorie, one of our English class, and heard her saying: 'Why haven't you asked me to dance, Alcwyn? You needn't take me in to supper unless you want. Shall we?'

I was filled with uneasiness and then panic when I heard Nico and Alcwyn beginning to discuss Lisbeth. I left the hall, hurried along the corridor that led into the street, and went out into the open air. It was quite dark, and fresh after the smoke and heat of the crowded dance, and as I came out on to the top of the steps leading down on to the pavement I could see Teddy Edwards in the little car-park below with his head under the scarlet bonnet of his car, tinkering with it. Presently he looked up, and seeing me under the lamp of the porch called out, 'Hallo, you.'

'Hallo,' I answered. 'Anything wrong?'

'Nothing much,' he said. 'Come for a ride?' He shut the bonnet, fastened it with the straps that held it down, and seated himself at the driving-wheel. 'Come on,' he urged, 'jump in. We shan't be long.'

I stepped in gladly over the minute door, about the size of a pocket-flap, and the car moved off along one of the main roads running from the centre of Dinas out into the open country. Teddy's car was famous. When he started it up in the college quadrangle he brought lecturing to a standstill. It was a sporting car, home-made, an open two-seater with headlamps like coal-scuttles and a bunch of levers on the outside. It had rude sentences and semi-nude girls in transfers upon its scarlet body-work and a naked dancer for a mascot. The wind was bracing when we got into the country and shot between the black hedges. Teddy drove furiously and my mood responded to his recklessness. As we went nosing our light before us we fetched behind a continuous loud zoom which was almost drowned under a deafening metallic clatter. I knew this direction well, it led out to the extensive fields of a Dinas seedsman, and when his wallflowers were in bloom, acres and acres of them under sunlight, I often walked out merely to smell the scent that came from them in overwhelming waves.

Teddy explained in a shout that he had come for a spin to shake down the damn bitters. He asked me how I was enjoying myself and, being a bar-boy, who was at the dance. He talked loudly perforce most of the way, taking both hands off the wheel to gesticulate in explanation. Sometimes he sang his strange songs with great feeling. I only half heard him. I was anxious particularly that he should not slacken his pace. At a village war memorial, cheesy in our headlights, we slowed down, circled the pale column, and commenced our way back. He excused his speed now by telling me at a shout the car could smell her oats. 'Take a little patience,' called a policeman as he made play with his musical horn in the traffic outside the parking-ground of the city hall. 'Where shall I take it?' he asked, and slipped in his clutch. When at length we got back to the dance hall the interval was over.

'Where the devil have you been?' Alcwyn asked me as I entered. 'I've been looking for you everywhere. I wanted to borrow money for supper. Luckily I had Marjorie. Where have you been?'

I explained, looking round for Lisbeth. I could not see her anywhere, and I thought she might not have come out of the refresh-ment-room. I stood talking to Alcwyn while my glance travelled restlessly round the crowded hall. My answers and responses, and the changes of my expression came accurately and almost automatically, although I only half heard what he was saying.

'Have you danced with the prinny's daughter?' he asked.

'No, where is she now?'

He pointed. 'The tall girl with a mop of hair. Slightly like an onion gone to seed. Very nice. Talks a lot about Girton.'

I was quite sure Lisbeth was not now in the room, but I could see the man with whom she had been speaking engaged in conversation with the principle's wife.

'Alcwyn,' I said, 'who is that talking to Mrs Prinny? Do you know? Over there, look.'

'John the Bastard, I should say,' he said. 'Although I was introduced to him as the French Consul. Or Vice-Consul. His face suggests vice. He's going to pull a stiletto out of his sleeve instead of the customary handkerchief. Wouldn't it be funny to see Mrs Prinny with a dagger sticking out of her chest like a coat hanger and saying...'

Alcwyn, greatly exhilarated, rambled until the band stopped, and a little crowd of our friends collected round us so that I could no longer see what was happening beyond them. When the music struck up again the quenching of cigarettes began and the moving off towards partners. Nico did a duty dance with a girl from his home and

Alcwyn made again for the principle's daughter. The others went one by one until in a few minutes I was left quite alone. As I looked round I saw on the nearest settee, not two yards away from me, Lisbeth sitting by herself. Although I had been searching for her I felt a little startled when I saw her sitting so close to me. I was about to move off without being seen, when she turned her head slowly in my direction and smiled bright-lipped at me, that strange radiance in her smile which I had thought so wonderful, like the warmth of an unforeseen forgiving, the first time I had seen her. I smiled back and then stared fixedly in another direction. I stood leaning against the pillar with my eyes averted for what seemed to me unending time, desiring, but fearing to look at her again. At length, when I had persuaded myself that she must have gone on to the dance floor I glanced once more in the direction of the settee. She was still sitting there but she did not see me now, because her head was bent downwards, she appeared to be doing something to her slipper. I was able to look at her steadily, but in fear, for a few seconds, at her face in the shadow and the thickness of curls filling the bend of her neck. I glanced at her heavily ringed hands and saw that the glass button had come off her slipper, and that she was trying to fasten the instep strap with a safety-pin. She looked sideways up suddenly, her eyes blue and glittering, and seeing on my face, I suppose, a look of interest and sympathy, smiled at me again. I coloured guiltily, and without knowing properly what I did, found myself walking towards her, mastered by coolness.

'My button's come off,' she said, smiling and showing up the pin. 'I wonder...' Her voice was English, hoarse and low for the moment, but in her smile once more was the warmth and glitter and animation.

'Let me,' I said, kneeling down, with her perfume about me and a strange and un-expected self-possession. I took the pin and soon managed to push it through the satin side of the red-heeled shoe. 'There,' I said, when the strap was secured. 'I think that's all right.'

'Thanks very much,' she said as I stood up. 'It's very kind of you. Isn't it funny no one ever invented a safe way of fastening shoes? Laces break and buttons come off – I think I shall have to wear elastic sides as the safest. Oh, I've promised this dance to Jimmie really, I believe. Good-bye. Thank you very much.' She smiled and laid her sparkling hand for a second on my sleeve, as she was about to pass. I looked at her. 'Then may I have the dance after this one?' I said.

'Surely, surely,' she answered. 'The one after this. I'll see you later.'

She removed her hand from my sleeve, smiled again, and hurried off.

I stood watching her. She went among the crowd of dancers and disappeared.

I did not feel like talking to anyone so I went out of the hall and waited among the smokers on the great marble stairs for the music to stop. My heart was beating painfully. When I returned to the hall I looked about in the vast crowd to see where Lisbeth was sitting so that I could go to her immediately the band recommenced for the dance she had promised me. I could not see her anywhere. I thought perhaps I had missed her in the haste of my excitement because after all, the hall was very large and very crowded, so, patiently standing on the lowest step of the band platform, I went calmly and systematically through the groups scattered about the floor and through the people spread around the sides where the chairs were arranged against the walls. Still I could not see her anywhere. Soon the band struck up again and I felt a sort of panic at having missed her. Was she somewhere in the hall looking for me, I wondered desperately, or outside in the corridor or on the stairs? I went around the edge of the dancing mass of people to the far end of the hall and then back again. I had to find her before the end of the dance. I went across and stood near the booming band once more, scrutinizing every couple that approached me; I saw Nico with a town girl painted up like a tart and Alcwyn a little later with another girl I had noticed in the principal's party, but Lisbeth was nowhere to be seen, nor, I realized, the handsome dark man with whom she had been dancing. Half-way through the dance, a valse, I went out. My disappointment was bitter, I had so much wanted to dance with Lisbeth, to know for the first time the ecstasy and comfort of her presence, alone with her in spite of the crowds around us, and she conscious of my being with her. I had longed to feel myself for a little within her warmth and glitter, to be spoken to by her, her voice mine, and her smile, for one dance all her warmth and loveliness, all the vivacity of her speech and features mine. I had trembled with the excitement and dread of it, and my heart had hammered as though with a great struggle, but now it was all over. I went out of the hall. Alongside it ran a palm-lined corridor, thickly carpeted, on the walls of which hung portraits of the mayors of Dinas. I walked down towards the cloak-room to get my hat and coat so that I could leave. In a dim alcove near the cloak-room two figures were standing. One was the short, dark Frenchman and the other was Lisbeth. The man had his back to me. As I approached along the silent corridor

Lisbeth turned slightly and looked in my direction. When she saw me a frown, a glance of annoyance appeared in her eyes rather than in any expression of her face, and she looked abruptly away.

I went by without a word. The music of the dance I should have had with her still came clearly from the hall. I got out my hat and coat and left the building.

I walked through the dark streets in misery and humiliation. At first I was incapable of thinking about what had happened, I could only endure the agony of it. And then I began to wonder if I had not made a mistake. What had Lisbeth actually promised me? Was that particular dance the one she had said I might have? Ought not I to have waited and asked her again? But then that coldness, that annoyance I had seen as I passed along the corridor, so unlike any expression I had ever imagined possible upon that lovely and untroubled face. But was this too merely imaginary, the result of my disappointment? Should I not go back and apologize, for leaving without a word of explanation?

I stopped and began slowly to retrace my steps. I had not gone far when I saw a figure I recognized at once as Nico's coming down the street towards me.

'Hallo, Trystan,' he said. 'Where you off?'

'I don't know. Back to digs, I suppose.'

'Come on,' he said. 'Let's go together.'

He took my arm.

'What's the matter, boy?' he said.

'Matter, Nico? Nothing's the matter.'

He said no more and we walked on arm in arm.

We had told Miss Machen that we would be late and she made no objection. We went quietly up to our bedroom and there we found Gwydion lying in bed smoking his pipe and reading.

'Hallo, Trystan,' he said. 'Hallo, Nico.'

'Hallo,' I answered. 'Have we kept you awake? Sorry.'

'Not at all. Nice dance?'

'Very.'

'Many there?'

'Rather. Lots.'

'Who?'

'The usual crowd. Teddy, Nugent, and so on. The Prinny's wife and daughter were there.'

'Gordon? And Spotty?'

'They came in for a short time, but they didn't stay. They can't dance.'

'I see. Gordon certainly refutes the sultanic supposition concerning honesty and dancing. Spotty passed the bar on the other side, I suppose? Was Teddy singing? Melody has certainly marked him for her own.' Dion went on in this fashion, making remarks about people I mentioned. Soon the light was out and he and Nico were fast asleep. But I remained awake tortured by the memory of what had happened, disappointed, bewildered, jealous, humiliated, knowing for the first time the bitterness of rejection.

16

The day after the dance a note from the dean of my faculty was delivered to me asking me to see him in his room without delay. I wondered very much what he wanted but could think of no reason for the summons and neither could Gwydion and Nico.

I entered his room through the door outside which I had stood with Alcwyn on my first day at college. The dean had a skull-like face, bony and hairless; he was my English professor, but I had never liked him and I sensed that he disliked me also. He was a meticulous man in speech, dress, and learning, and he always criticized my work adversely because of its romanticism, its lack of qualification and accuracy. He seemed to me cold and unemotional. I often wondered how so exact and pedantic a person had found a lifetime's satisfaction in a subject like literature.

'Sit down, Mr Morgan,' he said from

behind his desk. His voice was precise and edgy, it had the superior assurance that always made me bristle.

'Thank you, sir.'

'I have asked you to come here because I have received information about you. You may be able to assure me that the statements before me here are incorrect.'

I said nothing but I looked puzzled enough for him to notice it. He put on his glasses and looked at the paper lying on the desk.

'It seems,' he said, 'that you are pursuing a course of study at the Dinas school of art. Is that so?'

'Yes, sir,' I said. 'I do go to painting lessons there.'

He gazed at me sternly.

'Are you aware that this is forbidden?'

I didn't answer.

'You will see that you discontinue these lessons immediately. Your work in this faculty, Mr Morgan, is unsatisfactory in general, and my opinion is that these lessons may be contributing to this. Would you care to say anything?'

'No, sir.'

'Well, good morning.'

'Good morning, sir.'

I went out feeling sore, as though I had been mauled and rolled in filth. The unfairness of it, the complete injustice of his words and his verdict. Give up my painting class which I loved, where any growth and development I had experienced had taken place, not in the sterile lectures of this hair-splitting pedant. And to think of the men who wasted infinitely more time than I did, really wasted it without any official rebuke at all, drunkards, wasters, lechers, sports-mad, caring for nothing but the gratification of their obsession. Why had I to be singled out because I had committed a mere technical offence against some obscure college regulation? What about Wally Oriel who spent night after night not studying but coaching schoolboys so that he could make money for his week-ends. And in what way was my work unsatisfactory? I hadn't failed a single examination yet, and I was now in my final year. I knew I had not done brilliantly in any paper from the beginning as Alcwyn had, but it was unfair to speak as though I was merely wasting my time. It was unjust, everything he said was unjust and vindictive.

One thing puzzled me. How had the dean found out about the art school? Who could have told him? All my friends, Gwydion, Nico, Alcwyn, knew I went there twice a week but I could not believe any one of them would inform against me. My attendance was only a joke to them in fact, and I remembered Zachy looking over some drawings of the model I had spread out on the table when he came in one evening.

'Are the women naked like that?' he asked, grinning with lechery.

'Yes,' I said. 'Why?'

'How can you draw 'em? I'd be jumping right on top of them,' he said in Welsh, incorrect with excitement.

Damn the dean. Why had I ever come to this place, or entered this faculty?

That night I went to the art school, although it was not my lesson night, to collect my paintings and drawings. In the entrance hall, where I had seen him for the first time, I met Mr Leyshon who was about to go upstairs.

'Hallo,' he said. 'What's up? Not your night, is it?'

I hated telling him. I could feel myself colouring.

'I'm afraid I shan't be coming here any more,' I said.

'Not coming any more. Why?'

'Well, really I've been deceiving you. I'm a university student.'

'A university student? Well, what difference does that make?'

'I'm not supposed to come. They've found out and they've stopped me.'

'Who's *they*? Our lot here?'

'No. The university. The dean of the faculty.'

He mumbled something in his beard and

looked annoyed. 'Look here,' he said, 'can I do something? Can I write? Ask them to regard yours as a special case?'

'No, thank you. It's kind of you to think of it. Most kind. No, thanks.'

'Why not? I'm sure your case *is* exceptional.'

'No. I wouldn't ask them for any favours. I loathe them. And they'd never consent.'

The students were entering.

'Blast it,' he said. 'Come up to my room. Let's see if we can think of something.'

We went up the great staircase together and I collected my drawings and watercolours. My oils I would have to leave until some other time. I was unwilling to let Mr Leyshon petition on my behalf and in the end he agreed not to. I promised to call in to see him very soon. We shook hands. I thanked him for all he had done and left.

17

Without my painting lessons my life seemed arid, and the work I was forced to do became more and more burdensome and distasteful. I found it increasingly difficult as the year went on to remain indoors with a book before me on the table. I was rebellious and embittered when I thought of what had happened to me, at the injustice and the inhumanity of the way I had been treated. I experienced a growing certainty also that I was not going to pass in my final examinations. For my own part I cared very little about this, but I was still anxious not to deny my uncle the satisfaction of my success. It would mean a great deal to him, a fulfilment after three years of waiting. My only solace at this time was in painting, and painting was an insatiable devourer of academic time.

What added to my restlessness was that after the night of the dance I did not see Lisbeth. For several months I stood outside the Queen's, I went inside and sat with the coffee drinkers, waiting, I walked the main streets night after night but I failed to find her anywhere. Where had she gone? What had happened to her? There was no one I could ask. But I could not forget her. I was restless and despondent and often short with Nico and Gwydion. But neither of them at any time answered me back. Their forbearance was a thing that in my calmer moments I greatly marvelled at, because mockery came readily to Gwydion and jeering and eloquent derision to Nico.

A fortnight after I had been forbidden to attend the art school I had a letter from Mabli inviting me up to her house. Mr Leyshon, she said, had told her what had happened.

I was reluctant to go. I felt so dispirited and downcast that I was loath to make any such visit. I disliked her mother and her brother seemed to me a clear fool. I felt a certain amount of guilt, also, at not having myself told her in some way that I had been forbidden to attend the art school. I ought to have left a message for her with Mr Leyshon or paid a visit to the school as I had promised to do. Instead of that, although I had sat next to her for many months and had walked with her regularly to her bus after our classes, I had merely stopped attending and had not sent her a message of any kind, not of regret or greetings or explanation. So that when her letter came to Boundary Villas I felt obliged to go. She asked me to come to tea and to bring Alcwyn with me if he was recovered. I had myself introduced Alcwyn to her one night on my way with her to the bus, but I wondered how she knew about his accident. He never spoke to me about Mabli and I was very much surprised to learn she knew this about him. Once, I remembered, he had referred to her as 'the girl with the Chinese whites to her eyes,' but he had never shown me he had any interest in her.

Her house, Cwrt Nicol, or Nicol's Court, was named, Mabli told me, after the farm on which her mother was born. Standing outside the front gate was a large black car, long, low, and gleaming. The maid took Alcwyn and me through the house and out on to the large lawn at the rear. Here several people were sitting in deck-chairs, about to have tea – we were late arriving because it was a Saturday and the buses were full. It was very pleasant there, sunny, the grass clipped short and the rustic trellises around the garden a mass of pink roses. Mabli came forward. She looked tall and very pretty, her dark hair gleaming and hanging down to her shoulders and her fresh crimson dress slim and elegant upon her.

She asked Alcwyn how he was and seemed to know all about his broken ribs. Her friendliness, I thought, made him a little sheepish, although he was not the one to be overborne by a situation of such elementary difficulty for any length of time.

She took us along in front of the row of deck-chairs, presenting us in turn to the other people present – Mrs Pugh Pritchard her mother, Rosser Pugh Pritchard her brother, and a man I blushed at seeing since I hadn't been to chapel lately, the minister of Markethall Square. All these I knew. Finally we were introduced to Lord and Lady Lisvane her uncle and aunt, and to Beti Pugh Pritchard her cousin.

Alcwyn and I sat down, he stiffly because of his plaster, and everyone started to eat. Alcwyn sailed into the conversation and made the party laugh, addressing himself, it seemed to me, principally to Lord Lisvane. But there was a frankness about him, an open, eupeptic drollery, that these people, as I foresaw they would, found attractive and charming. With his white wavy hair and his ready laugh he seemed no sort of calculator; his stories almost invariably showed him in some ridiculous situation, some unfavourable light, so that none of those present suspected his cleverness, his brilliance even, in his academic work. But this brilliance also he made the occasion for tales that showed his folly and inconsequence, as when he described how he had completely forgotten to go to one French terminal examination, how he had played shove-ha'penny in his digs with Pompey all the afternoon. But I knew that he had passed very well in French all the same because he had done brilliantly in the remaining papers. This cleverness of his was something Alcwyn could bring out after he had firmly established in the mind, primarily on this occasion, of Lord Lisvane, how very human and without intellectual arrogance he was. I envied him his ability to charm people and then on top of that to make them respect him for his knowledge and ability.

As the tea-party went on I felt more and more unhappy and regretful. I failed to see what I had to do with these people, all so satisfied and assured, without doubts or struggles, all so charming, so meaningless. I had no sympathy at all with what they were saying, the whole flow of their conversation seemed empty and unimportant and pointless. Of the seven listening to Alcwyn only Lord Lisvane interested me, apart, that is, from Mabli of course. I had seen him half a dozen times in the big seat of Markethall Square, but this was the first time I had spoken to him. He was a very big man, tall and broad but loosely built and with very little flesh on him. His swarthy face was long, the face of a great clown, the skin of it very loose, giving endless mobility to his expression. A lot of this skin hung down on his throat into the gladstonian collar. A high quiff of black hair rose above his forehead shaped like half the swell a ship's bows push up in front of her and his black eyes flashed under brows as black as Nico's, as thick as my Uncle Hughie's, and with a shaggy dishevelment of their own. It was a wonderful face, expressive, volatile, responsive. A blue collier's scar was still to be seen on the bridge of the large nose and another on the prominent cheekbone, laid there when Lord Lisvane was Jim Pritchard, a miner, before he became a check-weigher, a miner's leader, a member of Parliament, a peer of the realm. Jim Pritchard the agitator! I could see him with that large loose mouth making his audience laugh or rousing them to fury.

After a while I found myself out of the general conversation and contented so, and whispering to Mabli who sat on a pouffe a little before me.

'Would you like to see the gardens?' she said. 'They've all finished tea now.'

'Yes. What about Alcwyn?'

'I mean him too. Mother, if everyone's finished I think I'll show them the gardens.'

I got up. But Alcwyn was in the middle of a story and waved us off without pausing in his talk. So Mabli and I went slowly across the lawn in the direction of the screen of roses covering the trellises.

'I wish Alcwyn had come. He's terribly amusing, isn't he?' she said.

'He's very amusing.'

'You must bring him here again.'

I said nothing. We were near the end of the lawn.

'What happened at college?' she said.

When I had explained she said: 'Mr Leyshon told me it was something like that. Why don't you fight them?'

'I don't know. I don't seem to have the will to do it. I just haven't got the energy. The whole thing is loathsome to me.'

It seemed strange to hear Mabli, so calm, so indifferent always, speaking of fighting and urging me to it.

'You liked the painting class very much though, didn't you?'

'I got more pleasure out of it, I think it contributed more to my development than anything else in this city.'

'And yet you give it up without a struggle. And you are gifted. Mr Leyshon thinks you the most promising painter in the school.'

I said nothing although I felt I ought to be pleased.

'I think so too,' she added. 'Did my coming there help you to enjoy it?'

'Of course,' I answered. 'I looked forward to our walks afterwards, too. I've learnt a lot from them. You are much more mature, much wiser, and more grown up than I am. I am glad you like my painting.'

We went through an archway of roses into the garden. It was pretty there, with green banks, a rockery, and terraces and many flowers growing in profusion, their arrangement not too rigid and formal. It was restful and the scent powerful and sweet. But all I wanted was to get away. Mabli's praise was unexpected, but it did not seem to lessen my sadness at all. As we returned to the group we saw the three men smoking, Mr Morris the minister a pipe and Lord Lisvane and Alcwyn cigars. They were all leaning forward listening to a fantastic description of Alcwyn's of the way he had been fined when the brakes of his bicycle gave way and he knocked over the policeman who was attempting to halt him at the cross-roads. The policeman had suffered shock and Alcwyn had broken two ribs. 'Decker and Nico,' he was saying, 'when I got home from hospital, Decker and Nico got me on the table in the digs and chalked broad arrows all over me.'

I remained standing, hoping that Alcwyn would get up and come away with me. I waited in an agony of suspense. Lord Lisvane questioned us about our careers, Alcwyn with interest, myself perfunctorily. Mabli's mother at last, to my intense relief, began to show signs of wishing us to go also, but the rest of the party seemed insensitive to her hints. When at last I got Alcwyn away Mabli accompanied us across the lawn to the house. She shook hands with us.

'You must come again soon,' she said.

Outside the gate I groaned. 'Oh, God,' I said.

'What the devil's the matter with you?' Alcwyn said. 'Cross and bad tempered. Why couldn't we have stayed a bit? You could see they wanted us to.'

'I'd had enough. I'm not interested in people like that. They bore me. And irritate me. Besides, I've got a lot of work to do.'

'Aw, shut up,' Alcwyn said. 'For God's sake. You say anything it pleases you to say.'

I had not the energy to reply, I was too depressed and dispirited. I said nothing. We got on to our bus in silence and Alcwyn smoked a cigarette in his white holder. We parted in Boundary Villas without having spoken further. Outside Miss Machen's Alcwyn did not stop.

'So long,' he said, passing the house.

I went in through the gate without replying.

I knew that Alcwyn would be invited again to Mabli's and that I would not be asked as one of the party. I saw him about in college and although we spoke when we met we held no conversation. In the common-room he seemed to me more vivacious and amusing than ever, endlessly joking and teasing. He had spent a week-end in London, I gathered, as the guest of Lord and Lady Lisvane, and there he had collected the autographs of many famous people – on his plaster! He stood in the common-room with his shirt up while the men crowded round and read back and front, on the grimy white casing around his body, the signatures of famous actors and members of Parliament. Alcwyn was going to auction his plaster, that's what he was going to do, auction it for the infirmary...

One day in the main street of Dinas I saw him on the other side of the street walking with Mabli.

18

And then, after three months, I saw Lisbeth again.

It was a Monday night and the summer examinations were to start, but not for me, the next morning. I was sitting with Gwydion in Miss Machen's parlour – which I had scarcely quitted during the previous fortnight – when Nico came downstairs.

He had shaved off his beard and looked clean and fresh. 'What about a night out,' he said. 'The theatre, Trystan?'

Gwydion and I glanced at each other.

'Come on,' he said. 'I'll treat you. Both.'

Only Spotty was a better poker player than Nico in the whole university.

'What's there?' Gwydion asked.

'"Two's Company,"' he answered. 'Damn funny. I saw it before in town.'

Gwydion shook his head. 'Many thanks, Nico, but not to-night,' he said.

I shaved and dressed properly and we went out. Although it was May the weather was cold.

As Nico and I walked down into town we saw children playing near the street lamps of some of the poorer districts through which we passed. On a small open space a guy had been set up and was burning brightly while a large number of little boys looked on or threw stones at it. Then, suddenly it seemed to me, as we were passing them they began chanting together, 'The Prince of Morocco, the Prince of Morocco,' while the sparks flew up, and each little figure gleamed freshly in the flickering light. It was a strangely beautiful moment, but why they should have been shouting 'The Prince of Morocco' I was unable to guess, and did not even trouble to think, being filled only with the beauty of that sight – the black, half-consumed guy, the soaring sheets of flame with upward showers of golden sparks shaken out of them, and the ruddy-edged figures, chanting loudly and in time: 'The Prince of Morocco, the Prince of Morocco.'

'Wicked little devils,' said Nico.

In the High Street we met Alcwyn and Decker. Nico did not know that there was a coolness between Alcwyn and me. 'We're going to the theatre, Decker,' he said. 'Feel like coming? Alcwyn?'

They said they would like to so they turned and walked in our direction.

We found the theatre almost full. Nico got the tickets and led us into the pit, where we sat near the front, Alcwyn, Decker, Nico, and myself, in that order. The orchestra was playing some Schubert ballet music, which a man behind kept whistling through his teeth, half a beat ahead of the orchestra, to my annoyance. But I had not to suffer long, because hardly had we settled down into comfort than the lights went out and the curtain began to rise. Just at that moment when the whole theatre was dimming I looked up and saw Lisbeth enter the lower box on the right above us, accompanied by some other person. She was in a heavily sequined frock of blue and her arms were bare. During the first act of the play, an uproarious farce, I followed the action scarcely at all, although I was not looking at the box, except for short periods of time. A strange and quiet feeling of happiness filled me, making me wish to delay all external determinations and contacts. The others, fortunately, were enjoying the play and were giving it their attention, and taking little notice of me, or of one another. Once or twice I glanced up, but I could not see Lisbeth, whom I supposed to be sitting close in on the side nearest to me and furthest from the stage, but once I caught sight of her hand resting on the red plush which padded the front of the box. When the end of the scene came I saw her leaning forward and talking to the man in evening dress who was sitting with her. He was stoutly made, a prosperous, middle-aged figure, well-dressed and well preserved, with a rosy face, and his black hair smoothly parted. Each time Lisbeth moved to speak to him her dress shot out a thousand little electric blue flashes like signals. Sometimes she looked down into the auditorium, and once it appeared to me that she was looking straight at me, but she turned her head away again, without any sign of recognition on her face.

The others were talking.

'What do you think of it, Nico?' asked Alcwyn. 'Hot, isn't it?'

'Jolly good,' he answered. 'Like it, Trystan?'

'M'm. Very funny,' I answered.

'Of the, of the, of the afterwards, the plot reminds me of that case we had in hospital yesterday,' said Decker. 'Two girls from down St Anne's.'

'Damn, yes,' said Nico. 'I never thought of that. So it does.'

'Two girls brought in yesterday,' Decker explained to us. 'Now then, sisters, one fifteen and the other seventeen, of the afterwards, both pregnant and the father their what-you-call their brother aged nineteen.'

'How horrible,' I said.

'Pretty awful,' Decker agreed. 'We've had worse though.'

'Overcrowding,' said Nico. 'Look where they live.'

'But, after all...'

'Sh!' said Alcwyn, and the curtain went up.

I was horrified at what Decker had said. Each time I thought of it I was filled with shame and revulsion at the monstrous beastliness of it. I wished Decker had not told me, because I was quite incapable of enjoying the second act of the play, thinking of it. For a time I even forgot about Lisbeth, but little by little my reflections became less painful, and I was able to say to myself: 'What's the good of worrying about it? It's nothing at all to do with me. If people are so depraved and unnatural I can't help it. It is still very shocking though.' I settled my mind with an effort on the play, which was still bright and amusing. It appeared at that point of development that the hero, a handsome young man of engaging manners, was responsible for the seduction of a pair of very attractive young women to whom he appeared to have been making love without their mutual knowledge. When the curtain fell at the end of the second act, all the evidence, except that of his own lively and ingenuous nature, favoured the suspicion that he was guilty, although we were all quite unperturbed, confident that some as yet undisclosed circumstances would finally vindicate him completely.

'Jolly good, isn't it,' said Alcwyn. 'Isn't the hero funny?'

'He's in a hell of a hole now,' said Nico. 'Look who's over there. Nugent, isn't it?'

He was sitting in the stalls a little to our right.

'Leave him there,' I said.

'You don't like him, do you?' asked Nico. 'Gwydion put you up to that, didn't he? He's not a bad feller.'

Alcwyn started looking round to see if there was anyone else in the theatre he recognized. Presently he leaned across and said: 'Nico, there's that girl who was at the dance, isn't it? In the box, look.'

Lisbeth was at that moment in full view of the four of us, her beautiful shining dress sparkling with thousands of little lights of blue. In a sort of panic, I wanted her beyond anything else to withdraw herself where she could not be seen.

'It is her, isn't it?' Alcwyn continued.

'Yes,' Nico answered. 'Who's with her to-night, Decker? She's a shocker for the men, isn't she?'

'Everyman, I will go with thee,' said Alcwyn.

'Yes,' Nico continued. 'Remember what Wally said about her?' he asked, lowering his voice. '"She's not a real pro, but she's one of the most enthusiastic amateurs in Wales." He ought to know. She's pretty though, isn't she? I wouldn't mind myself. By God, she is pretty.'

'She is,' said Alcwyn. 'What's her name?'

'Are you thinking of hanging your cap there? What's her name, Decker?'

'Now then, now then, Lisbeth Arnold,' he answered.

'Oh yes,' Nico continued. 'Dion used to call her the Fortunate Whore. They say she had a kid when she was sixteen. She won't look at you, Alcwyn lad; you wouldn't pay well enough. I think she's the prettiest tit I've ever seen. She reminds me of that barmaid down in the Welsh Harp, Decker. Doesn't she you? Only not so plump. Now shut up, everybody. We're beginning. The play's the thing. Where's that from, Trystan?'

I nodded mechanically. I was quite dazed and utterly incapable of appreciating what was going on about me. Alcwyn leaned back into his seat; and the bright stage yawned wider upon the darkness, but my mind was become too insensitive to notice except vaguely what was taking place. I experienced the peculiar sensation of having been physically crushed, except for the extremities of my body, of whose unconnected isolation I remained dimly conscious. I felt as though something had smashed into the middle of me and left me dazed and helpless. So very vivid was this impression, that I looked half-consciously down at my body. The words the little boys had chanted: 'The Prince of Morocco,' came beating upon my mind. I had no problem to solve, and I was not in any mental travail or conflict. I suffered only from a sense of not-being, of complete annihilation. I seemed to be stricken down without the energy to struggle, or to escape, or even the strength to stir my body. I went home with the others in silence, and I remained inwardly in a state of stupefaction, as though with the effects of a spell or of an enchantment, although I did habitual actions without any abatement of facility. But I did not try to work. After tea each day I made some excuse and went out by myself to wander about the streets until bedtime, not caring where I went. I wondered at times whether I was going mad. I felt as though the edges of my mind were shattered and no longer capable of cleaving into the sense of things. All this time I thought scarcely at all directly of Lisbeth, or of the conversation which had brought about the state of bewilderment in which I now lived.

Then one night, when my mind seemed again to be rousing, I knelt down and prayed passionately that what I had heard of Lisbeth might not be true. But my phrases seemed to be floating round like echoes in my empty soul and I broke into tears of anguish and despair.

During my examinations I found it difficult
to believe that what I was doing was of any
importance of even sense. I knew it was
impossible that I should pass. I left one
examination at the earliest moment permitted by the regulations. From another I
helped to carry out a woman student who
had become hysterical beside me. I did not
return to the room.

Crossing the recreation ground about
three weeks before I intended to go down, I
saw Mabli sitting on one of the seats there.
'Hallo, Mabli,' I said.

Both of us coloured.

'Hallo, Trystan,' she said.

I had no idea what to say next. I seldom
thought about her now. When I remembered her talkative and irritable mother, and
her idiotic brother and that uncle of hers,
dominant, watchful, influential, I knew
instinctively that they occupied a world
which I did not wish to inhabit. And yet I
had from the first been attracted to Mabli,
and I had got to like her increasingly during
our time together at the art school. I
wondered to see her sitting alone in the
recreation ground. She lived a long way
from here.

'I'm just going down into town,' I said.

'Are you? I intended going that way too.

Shall we go together?'

We went in silence out of the park and in the direction of the town. At last Mabli spoke.

'When are you going home, Trystan?'

'I've got three weeks again.'

'I never see you now. Not in the art school or in Markethall Square.'

'Too busy. Working. Exams.'

'You don't like coming to our house much, do you?'

I said nothing.

'Why is that? Some of the students do – Zachy, Charley, and others.'

'Oh, I don't know. I don't think your mother likes me much. I don't seem to fit in there somehow.' I thought of Alcwyn when she was naming the students, but I said nothing.

'You don't try to fit in. Your uncle works at the pit and my Uncle James worked underground for years. You ought to have plenty to say to each other.'

'But I'm bored by the sort of talk they find interesting; appointments, the best chap for that job. So-and-so a coming man – that's what the talk was the last time I was at your house. And Alcwyn, of course.'

She said nothing for a moment or two.

'Will you come to our house once before you go down?' she said. Her voice stirred me, she sounded intense, her words were sincere and urgent, not those of formal invitation. I looked at her but she kept her steady gaze directly in front of her.

'Will you?' she repeated.

'What's the good? I shall only be in this place another three weeks, and then I leave for ever. And I'm bound to say I shall have no regrets at all.'

Mabli always walked with her head high. She was a beautiful walker. Her expression was troubled.

'I'm sorry,' she said.

'Look, Mabli, I like you very much, I've enjoyed as much as anything our walks after the painting classes and I've learnt a tremendous amount from you. But I want to be an artist, a painter, and I can't see how coming to your house is going to help me. No one there, apart from you, has got the slightest interest in art. I'm like a fish on the mountain.'

'You won't come for my sake?'

'For your sake? What about Alcwyn? You see him a lot, don't you?'

We went on in silence for a little.

'I saw a good deal of him at one time. All Alcwyn wants is to use Uncle James to push him into good jobs. And trying–' She stopped.

'Trying what?' I asked.

'Nothing,' she said sharply.

'Trying what?' I repeated.

She was blushing.

'Trying to get me to sleep with him,' she said.

I could scarcely believe that I had heard correctly. God, what an Alcwyn. I was as shocked and filled with jealousy as if I had myself been in love with Mabli.

'Will you?' Mabli said again.

'When?' I asked her.

'I'll send you a card,' she said.

We parted in town. I was filled with emotions of a sharpness that puzzled and relieved me. Disturbing as these emotions were they were preferable to the daze and numbness under which I had lived for so long. For a few days, from the moment I woke up in the morning, my mind returned continually to what Mabli had told me. I was obsessed by it, it took the place of the numbness and the sense of defeat which had begun with Nico's words at the theatre. Why had Alcwyn behaved this way? Was he in love with Mabli? Could he be and still speak to her in this way? Did he want to marry her in order merely to establish a connection, a relationship, with so influential a family? Alcwyn always had the capacity for getting to know important people who might be of help to him. Or did he hope to make Mabli marry him by creating a Gretchen situation? How horrible it all seemed. I felt incapable of answering my own questions. I knew I was too ignorant and too inexperienced. Alcwyn, even when we were at our friendliest, had always been a puzzle to me and now his character had become completely incomprehensible.

I began to think with intense relief that soon I should leave Dinas for ever, my academic life would be over and I should be free. (Alcwyn I heard was returning and there was said to have been professional competition to secure him as an honours student.) I felt cheered and consoled by the thought of quitting in a week or two a place where so much that was painful had happened and where so much of my time, it seemed to me, had been wasted. I began to think with pleasure of Llansant, I thought how delightful would be a holiday there before I looked for a job, a holiday in fine weather with Gwydion and Nico perhaps, if they would come. Dreaming in this way I became calmer, I looked forward at last with excitement.

One night when the three of us were together in Miss Machen's, I said: 'Gwydion, Nico, how about spending some of your holidays in Llansant? We shall all be leaving here in a little and we might have a fortnight, say, together before we part.'

'Where is this Llansant?' asked Gwydion, although he knew.

Nico got out the atlas. 'Here it is,' he said. His own home was not many miles away.

His hirsute index traced first the curved, nine-tailed tributaried river to its mouth, and came to rest upon a little hanging uvula of land swilled in the milk-blue sea. 'It's a good place, Trystan,' he said, with Miss Machen's gaslight yellow athwart his orbicular and Buddha-like countenance. 'Tell Dion about it.'

We had finished our supper by then – an unsightly dish resembling duck's dung and warm hailstones, eaten with plentiful Welsh-cakes and spotted bread – and as I described to Gwydion the remote situation of my Uncle Gomer's sea-village and its umbrageous surroundings, Nico became involved, as was his custom, with the pappy detritus of his meal. I told Dion, with painter's enthusiasm, of the fecund hills about Llansant, the impinging roundnesses, as of a tightly laced corsage; the glowing pastures of suede-smooth emerald; the furzy wool of gold-flecked, gorse-fleeced heath-lands; and the chocolate acres under plough, formally embossed with lime in white studs arranged in rows along the tillage.

As I did this Nico's fat face assumed a long-lipped monkey-grimace, and his mouthful of tongue heaved forward again and again the whole puffy fabric of his countenance in a purge of contorted scavenging.

I told them of the Llansant square – rhombus, diamond or lozenge rather – where appear in constant succession, beside the plain villagers, the local notables and eccentrics: Charlo Pil Glas the dwarfish imbecile who blesses himself with complacent head-pattings when greeted and then spits in the roadway; the gay, glance-gathering oreads, nubile descendants of damsels once destined for the broad beds of the squirearchy; the doomed and saintly Sardis minister, coughing like a cave upon his merciful ministrations, his stoop and swarthy visage vulturine; the three young bakers in their white caps who come there cooling themselves, letting perflations of sea-breeze inflate their shirts and floury trousers; the brutish horse-breaker on his bold pony, his boozy face enflamed and ape-rump red, his bowler low on his brow like the topper of a tap-dancer.

As I spoke, Nico's tongue went rooting among his cheek-teeth, probing its way up behind the fleshy curtain of his face, shovelling the cuds out from the invisible reservoirs of his head.

I told them of the church, dedicated to the miraculous Celtic hierarch, its tower nourished with green branchings of arterial ivy, its slated graveyard full of farmers and fishermen and their buried spouses, and the putative descendants of the local princelings. I told them of the Ship Aground, the inn in Water Street with its mounting-block and tethering rings, and its external plumbing clawing the cream gable like a gigantic reptile. I told them of the broad, estuarine waters that there debouch into the bay, and the pour into them of the clear little brook, paved with green velvet; I told them of the noon coast with a sun in the air and a sun in the sea; of the glider gull and the dandled buoy; and the glittering sea-liquor lustrous against the animal muzzles of the hills; and I told them of the rounded moon seen there too, her valleys carved out of cold silvers, and the night sea with its wedge of burnish glassy beneath her disk.

The place was well, despite my dithyrambic description it found favour in Gwydion's sight as holiday abode for vacation, retreat, or *villeggiatura;* it was desirable and he would accompany us.

Nico's features, as he nodded his pleasure, screwed themselves up into a convulsive rictus that closed one beady eye and exposed the large holes in his decaying grinders.

Of my relatives, my three aunts and my Uncle Gomer, I said nothing then; to them I referred with a frequency that must have given rise to boredom although Gwydion and Nico seldom showed what they felt.

And so it was arranged as we sat crowded round our atlas in the grim mohair of our city parlour.

The Village

1

I look out of the Môr Awelon bedroom window down into the square of Llansant.

Gwydion, Nico, and I have been here nearly a fortnight. Every day we talk and eat immoderately, fly our kite, stroll down to the sands, bathe, and on our return to this house recommence the cycle of our talking and eating. The weather has been fine, almost always like to-day, very sunny and I have been able to do a good thickness of drawings. I look forward to this evening when the annual procession of the mock-sheriff will take place and more work will result.

I came to Llansant as I never remember to have done before, hurt and still at times even despairing. I began to see clearly as time went by the folly, the betrayal even, of such an attachment as mine to Lisbeth, an English whore – the senselessness and the barrenness of it, the pain and unhappiness it was bound to cause; but the cutting of myself free from my idealization of her was agonizing, it was like the hacking off of a hand become incapable of a voluntary release. But this I was doing despite the protracted agony so necessary and drastic a determination had caused me. In Ystrad, separated from Dion and Nico, living with Uncle Hughie, now sick and ageing, I was tortured with loneliness and disillusion and despair. The thought of our meeting at Llansant had lost its brief attraction. When I received the news from the university that I had failed in both my final subjects the disappointment I felt was slight. I was almost satisfied that my intuition of the professional vindictiveness was confirmed.

I had no fear of breaking the news to my Uncle Hughie and I did so immediately.

'Never you mind, Trystan *bach*,' he said. 'Don't you worry about it.' And then, after a pause: 'Couldn't you do the work, *bach?*'

'It wasn't so much that I *couldn't*, Uncle, as that I wasn't *interested* in doing it.'

'I see. Only one thing you've always been interested in, isn't it?'

I said nothing.

'It's a pity your granny made you go to that university, I always felt. But she was very determined. She couldn't have done all she did otherwise. But you mustn't worry.'

I wondered whether he really thought what my grandmother had decided was wrong or whether he was trying to reassure me.

'What will you do now?' he went on.

'I don't know, Uncle. Get a job teaching

somewhere, I suppose. I don't mind what so long as I can paint.'

'That's right,' he said. 'You will be able to be a painter now as you've always wanted to. But whatever happens you mustn't worry. Everything will turn out all right.'

I had begun the conversation speaking English but after a few words he had interrupted me with the old teasing smile on his face. 'Stop your nonsense now,' he said, 'and talk properly.' He meant that I should speak Welsh to him.

The idea that I could now become a painter was a lifting of my gloom. I had fulfilled, I thought, my promise to my grandmother. During my three promised years I had become increasingly indifferent to the sort of vocation she desired for me. The deep sense of dedication I had once seen in Caersalem was to me always a dispeller of self-delusion. I had felt myself progressively less concerned with a calling, with formal religion, with politics, and increasingly concerned with painting. And so I began to look forward once again with some eagerness to my visit to Llansant, a place where I had always found that drawing and painting came naturally to me. I have found it so again, and my friends and my uncle and aunts have been healing presences. My academic life has ended in complete failure; I have no job or prospects of a job; my unthinking, barren, passionate love of Lisbeth is over, and my three years' friendship with Alcwyn similarly. But after my first few days in Llansant the old hope and happiness and vitality, which I had expected never to experience again, began to return in the endless sunlight; and the natural loveliness and the people of this countryside brought delight if not oblivion. By the end of the first week I was painting again.

And now, as I look out, the morning kindles, becomes crystalline above, and in the deserted square below me is rhapsodic and cobwebby. Above my high head the birds pass and repass, whistling their kitchen hosannas as they seek food, hailing the day. The luxuriant graveyard wall, like a garden set up on its end in the sun, receives twittering the small grain-bearing birds into its tufted foliage. A pausing swallow holds in her little feet the glitter of a wire and, with hairy song-bag pulsing under his splayed beak, a baby starling babbles from the lace-like roof-crest opposite. Silvery cloud-fronds and fine-day featherings are spread around the blue; and there, in the high hollow, the milky herring-gull is garrisoned, observing in silence the flashing circulations of his airy ziggurat. Into the road of the square a flock of creamy, vee-winged pigeons gently descends on crimson feet, radiant enough to alight in benison upon a dozen messianic heads.

It is our Llansant fair-day, but early, the window-blinds are still down, the black heavily-beaded house-doors opposite still bolted, like rows of life-size portraits tarred all over, frames and all. With my head out of the pointed window I hear the dissonant scraping of a heavy bucket on cobblestones, and the pigeons billow up as my Uncle Gomer appears in the sunshine at the front of the house, the halting obliquity of his bearing exaggerated by the weight of his one-handled burden. An eggy-beaked blackbird flees, scalded and screaming, below me as he approaches, but the fountainous pigeon flock recognizes him and subsides.

I wait to hear his latest story. Yesterday the body of a young man drowned up at Tremyrddin was said to have been seen in the river above Llansant, so he has a new tale to tell. Gwydion meanwhile stirs in the wool behind me and his bed creaks with its contents; while Nico, awakened, clowns, and lances his inappropriate canticle into the morning. Ancestry has endowed him with the thorax and vocal organs of the *basso profundo*, but he can counterfeit the exalted registers of the castrati and man-sopranos. He now does so and his hymn, to the tune of 'Les commandements de Dieu,' is, 'The day Thou gavest, Lord, is ended.'

My Uncle Gomer, hearing Nico's falsetto, looks up, sees my head projecting under the boarding-house blue of the eaves and greets me with a good morning which I return. Even now, bearing boiled chicken-meal, the grey rings cling thick about his elegant skull with the perfection of ornate masquerade hair. His long and princely face, although unshaved, although rugged and elaborately wrinkled with a mobile webwork of grooves, fine lines, and creases, is handsome-boned, is fleshed with arched nostrils, and thick brows delicately canted outward. During momentary respite his features are benign, contemplative, and hierophantic, but always in his brown eyes he has the sparkle of a star.

'They have given up trying to find the body this morning,' he announces, slightly increasing his habitual obliquity and grounding his bucket. I raise my eyebrows, and Nico, hearing the interrogatory inflexion of my grunt, breaks off his hymns and listens.

As we wait, my uncle sinks with almost sacerdotal reverence his searching thumb and forefinger under the pocket flaps of his pendulous waistcoat, and reflectively brings out a jetty pipe, the stem bound up with narrow bandaging. This, as he speaks, he unhurriedly examines, cleans, using picked-up box-twig, fills with provident frugality from a cloth bag of cut plug, and finally, almost at the moment of departure, sets lit in his head. He wears large, dusty working-clogs, a buttonless waistcoat gleaming glassily under a lacquer of grease, and navy trousers piped with railway red, the knees bulging forward in advance of him, so that his legs appear chronically in a state of partial genuflexion. His black flannel apron has been tucked up around his waist out of respect for the properties of the square. He has no jacket or neckwear, and his grey flannel shirtsleeves are rolled up to his elbows.

Pipe-filling, he begins to remember, and as I follow the intricacies of his sprawling narrative I watch his tireless mimicry, and his uplifted features flashed over with endearing expressiveness and lambencies of stupor, drollery, anguish, delight, and apprehension. 'I have been up there in the river,' he says, 'where the poor fellow's body was seen, me and Pit Saer and the son of old Doctor Phillips, Johnny his name was, the beautiful southpaw, savaged to death at last in the champion's loose-box by the biscuit-coloured hunter' – he observes a momentary silence and rocks his face at the dismal reminiscence – 'shooting cobs we were under the red bank of Cwrt Newydd, where that French foreigner was living, sinning with the one-eyed blackess. Pit was a good swimmer then, when he had his two arms, and he had swum the river at slack water before now, nearly a mile across, with the water-bailiff and Nat the Glandwr bobby in their punt after him' – the troubled brow unpuckers and a look of drollery contracts into riant fascicles the grooves of his cheeks and his glittering eyes. 'Pit was a great one, a big, black-headed, heavy man then with bandy trousers and a plate of a backside. Pit could feel it in his bones every time a salmon swam out of the sea into the little green-bottomed brook up there, and he would leave whatever coffin he was making to land it, trampling through the village on the outsides of his feet like a prowling bear, his shirt-sleeves rolled up, the shavings all over him, and his thick, black hair like a shawl round his head.' My uncle swings a few paces up the square and returns crouching and rolling clumsily on bow-flexed legs in a stagy imitation of Pit's predatory shamble, his arms apeish, his tread ursine, his expression piratic. 'And Johnny, the doctor's son, he was clever too, and often you could see him from the Vicar's Point' – he shades his eyes, stretches his finger, and peers with absorption at the horizon of the graveyard wall – 'before the army put him in charge of the whores of Malta, sailing the old half-deck *Cymro* with his father and the twin brothers right out to the corn-boat wreck on the sand-bar, and swimming five or six miles back to the village, the three of them, with the spring tides powerful under them.' My uncle's failing breast stroke and gaspings represent the wearied co-ordination of the fatigued swimmers. 'They could swim like fishes in the village then, and the regattas were going full swing.'

Here he stops; carefully, on the toe of his clog, he knocks the coke out of his fractured pipe and, his expression suddenly withdrawn and contemplative, turns abstractedly to follow the movements of his dog Pero, sprinkling the gate-butts, and sniffing the matutinal scents of the fresh and unexplored square.

When I mutter a question about Pwlldu my uncle's waistcoat vee-piece rotates, the majestic curled head tilts up again and, milling the plug between unsundered palms, he continues his recital – 'Up in Pwlldu we had the guns in the boat, me and Pit and Johnny, the son of the doctor, it was before Pit lost his arm, because he couldn't shoot any more after they took it off for him.' He chops at his left humerus and makes loud, labial squirtings to represent the sounds of the amputation. 'He lost it another day, poor fellow, when three of us were out after sea-duck in Pit's punt, round the nose of the headland, me and Pit and Wally Wildvine' – for him the name is lilting trochaic-iambic – 'who thought of nothing but a lot of shooting and swilling beer, and persecuting the young farm-wenches for miles around. He was a proper fool, but his mother (the travelling cook she was, and as good a woman as ever stepped on Christian ground), she thought he was the pop-alley, and she nearly broke her heart when he cut his throat in prison.' My uncle's pipe-mouth travels with rapid rotation the anterior circumference of his neck. 'But there you are, even the mother crow thinks her chicks are white'– Then, having for a moment reflected, he turns suddenly to a burlesque of rapid action, and picks up with vigour an imaginary double-barrel – 'Willie snatched up a gun off the thwarts when he saw the duck coming over' – he gazes upward at the gull-hung blue and swings his finger before the echelons of the advancing migrants – 'dropped it on the boat-bottom in his excitement and fired off both barrels into poor Pit, hanging a mackerel line over the stern locker. When we examined him, his rug-head sopping with sweat and his teeth milling froth, we found his arm hanging off in the sleeve of his ganzy.' My uncle's right hand clutched into his left axilla, he dangles his relaxed limb helplessly beside him and large clots of blood blob on to the roadway.

'It is a perilous thing,' he says, 'to have a fool and a gun in the same boat.'

Again he stops and plugs in his tobacco, while Pero corners an outraged tortoise-shell, who at every bark, lunge, or pawpass squibs at him rage and defiance, and sends her hairy back up like a bag-handle.

'What happened at Pwlldu?' I ask again.

He puts his unlit pipe between his teeth and with his amputated arm picks up a gull's flight-feather from the road. 'We were up there one summer under Gwrt Newydd, by the first elbow of the river' – he holds before him horizontally, and with both hands, the brown-barred wing-feather, and rocks it gently in imitation of the motion of the anchored boat – 'and Pit wanted to have a swim. The tide had turned half an hour, and the current was rushing fast out of the river back into the sea, but Pit wouldn't listen, his head was the biggest in the village, but there was nothing much in it, poor dab, except a lot about polecats, and rabbit-snares, and salmon-gaffs, and paternosters.' Here, having stuck his feather Indian-like into his back curls, he brings out a shabby match, strikes it on the iron under-rim of his clog, and, with its invisible flame, sets fire to the plug. Then in demonstration of Pit's exiguity of intellectual powers and slowness of part he describes, laughing, the gifted poacher's attempts to master printed

English, and quotes sentences which in his Welshness he had once rendered comically italianate by a stubborn pronunciation of all mute vowels: 'Pit wouldn't listen when we told him the tide had turned, but before he had swum twenty strokes he began to swirl away in the water like a dog with the itch rolling over on his back; he was screaming for help, throwing up his arms, trying to get his feet on the bottom. We could see he had the cramp on him, so Johnny and I got up anchor and the boat spun round and round in the tide after him' – here the feather is twisted with violent eccentricity from hand to hand in imitation of the swirling craft – 'and Johnny began to peel off his clothes–'

A shout of astonishment and boisterous displeasure issues from a female throat situated in the porch-way of the house, and a loud but undistinguishable stream of angry vocables follows it into the square. My uncle drops his feather in alarm, stuffs his pipe unstashed into his waistcoat pocket, and with limping gait promptly departs, bearing in shamefaced silence his hen's-mash bucket in the direction of the rear parts of the graveyard.

2

When Gwydion, Nico, and I have finished

our breakfast we sit around the table talking.

'I admire Iwan Morgan Parry more than most,' says Gwydion, handsome and luxurious in his new clothes, 'because he has the enterprise to begin not a period, or a paragraph, or a chapter, or even a volume, but the proem of his entire trilogy with the word "But."'

'*Nage, nage,*' Nico answers back, taking his stumpy finger out of the ear of his teacup, and turning his music-stool from the circular table to spit into the grate. (Nico is a prodigal scatterer of his sputa, and his phlegm is received now into a solid iron cuspidor with bolts, formerly, its enamelled lettering testifies, among the saloon-deck furnishings of the S.S. *Ticonderoga*.) '*Nage, nage,*' he repeats, 'nothing enterprising in that, Dion *bach*, if the second word is "for."'

The dense air of my Uncle Gomer's purple breakfast room glows about us with heavy, subaqueous gloom, we and the gleaming furniture are steeped in grey light and thick tobacco smoke. The fancy leather window-curtains, still stamped in faint gilt with the zodiacal signs of the pythoness who once owned them, are drawn against the morning's brilliancy because Gwydion has been composing before breakfast; but a beam of sun, like a foot-thick slice of talc, stretches in glass-like rigidity between the window and the shabby plum-puce of the opposite wall.

Into the confined and purple cube of the room, whose inward-bulging walls seem buckled beneath the stress of elephantine leanings, are packed the limbo-furnishings of cottage, schoolroom, tavern, church, and bankrupt country mansion. An arm-chair commode, relacquered crocus yellow, glistens on one side of the fire-place; and on the other stands an American rocker, pied, and heavily antimacassared. Our meals (served on dishes bearing the coats of arms of liquidated hydros and transport companies) we eat from a mahogany loo table inlaid with brass, and spread with a green cloth of billiard baize. A bedroom washstand has become our sideboard. We recline in a chapel pew painted a forget-me-not blue. We draw our music from a pipe-and-pedal schoolroom harmonium with adjustable stool. Time is ticked out from the mantelpiece by the ornate ormolu with no hands, and the clock repaired with the oblong picture-frame. A pair of black-leaded busts of the same unrecognizable genius stands noseless on the harmonium, both, Gwydion pretends to believe, representing the poet Sir William Davenant, the knightly Shakespearian by-blow. Above the empty fire-place hangs a large overmantel, the mirror extensively mottled with lichens of rust. The glass door of the corner-cupboard is kept permanently open to accommodate the end of the curtain pole, a massive tree-trunk of polished mahogany running the whole length of one wall.

As I sit, perforce bolt upright, among the antimacassars of the rocker, I watch Gwydion, cream-fleshed and green-eyed, reclining in the blue pew with his crane-fly legs extended on the breakfast table. His abundant brickish hair, caught in the ingot-glow of the sunbeam, burns like the un-quenched bush or the rays of the fiery corposant; his narrow eyebrows are pointed upwards in mockery and the slits of his goat-nose dilate in rhythmic accompani-ment to his gentle respirations. He has the brilliant scarlet lips and the precious-stone green eyes of the hot-haired, high cheek-boned, and marble skinned. He wears now the clothes he has bought to come to Llansant for his holiday, a beautiful shirt of intense emerald poplin, and a greenish belted tweed jacket, which Nico calls the filing-cabinet, very fashionable, and decorated on the breasts with rows of up-right knifepleats. *Pen punt.* His grey flannel trousers, an ancient and impressive garment now extensively, elaborately, and colourfully maculate, are darned on both knees with large gratings of grey wool; and on his sockless feet he wears, the uppers cracked, the soles holed and almost heel-less, a pair of brown brogues, laced with yellow bias binding, from which a plentiful stuffing of dirty newspaper extrudes. He still has a mustard-coloured scarf wrapped round his right leg because he has been composing.

'I'll stick a fork in your eye, Nico,' Gwydion replies, splaying his nostrils. 'Iwan Morgan Parry's second word is "antidis-establishmentarianism."'

Fearing their wearisome term-old wrangle will recommence I desperately propose that we take a blow on the Llansant beach, but my suggestion is not complied with.

The difference between Gwydion and Nico arose originally from my foolish elaboration once in Miss Machen's parlour, of the theory that the standing-on-end of my hair at the Othellan words 'ill-starred wench' was due to the violently explosive nature of its compounded elements, that is to say, to the ambuscading oxymoron of 'starred' and 'wench.' 'Wench, Dion,' I argued earnestly, 'is a disreputable, loose-living word, blowzy and uncorseted, one that lost its innocency before it put its hair up, not long perhaps after it shed its milk teeth. Don't you agree, Dion? And Shakespeare uses this gross, earthy, deflowered substantive of one whom, with all the resources of his transcendental genius, he has striven to portray for us a lovely and patient creature, the apotheosis of womanly sweetness and virtue. That undoubtedly is the aesthetic blow to the ribs as it were, but the real uppercut is brought about by its imaginative nexus with "ill-starred." Listen, Dion, until I've finished. Because "star" belongs to a more exalted order of images, it has uplift, refinement, and nobility in its associations. We say, do we not, "on an astral plane" and, "Hitch your wagon to a star," which reveal its ambience of purity, altruism, and idealistic aspiration and endeavour. And the Moor himself says:

It is the cause, it is the cause, my soul;
Let me not name it to you, you chaste stars!

Chaste stars, you see, Dion. Yet Shakespeare lumps – no, compounds with unerring craft and subtlety – these two words, the ditch-drab "wench" and its antipole, the etherealized "starred," and produces in us a violent aesthetic explosion. And look, my hair is erect.'

Gwydion, smoking his clay pipe with the tin lid, had gazed down hard at me while I spoke with an expression that, on features less habitually arrogant and unabashed, would have meant contemptuous encouragement and compassion. But his green eyes gleamed in triumph as I finished, and his nostrils fluttered with the malign glee of the pedant about to demolish a thesis exiguously based upon imperfect scholarship and scatter-brained theorizing. 'Prospero,' he said with satisfaction, 'as example, calls Miranda a *wench* in a matter-of-fact and unambiguous manner. The word had not the dubious associations you attribute to it. Othello meant "girl" merely.'

At this point Nico, ignorant, apart from the Bible, of all literature in hard covers; imagining, according to Dion, *Daniel Deronda* to be a novel about Treorchy; but gifted with courage, loyalty, and mother wit; Nico had entered the argument as my champion, and soon engaged Gwydion in a discussion of the nature of poetry. Gwydion began his wearied apologia by reciting with consummate skill from a fifteenth-century *cywydd*, written in praise of the golden hair of a Welsh aristocrat. When Nico, who held doggedly to a conviction of the reciprocal flux and intercommunication between life and literature – when Nico asked the significance of the quotation, Gwydion replied that only his stupidity prevented him from recognizing it as a controvertion of his idiotic theories, an *exposé* of their complete hollowness and falsity. Life, Dion maintained, was a protracted humiliation and indignity for mankind, it was ridiculous always, and ugly, brutal, and corrupt in addition; our bodies and our desires were shameful, and poverty, loneliness, disease, torture, starvation, and death were the lot of the swarming generations. But literature is concerned with language, images, and words; it is shapely, formal; the little supreme literature extant, the three or four hundred lines of verse in any language which are real poetry, are perfection; they are immaculate and immortal. The verse that Trystan admires, he told Nico in my presence, is metrical prose fouled at its origin with life, belief, and dogma, and is rhymed rubbish.

Nico asked him if he had heard of an English poet called Shakespeare.

'An absurd American theorist,' Gwydion went on, 'said in a sober and lucid hour that only a short poem is possible. A long poem is in reality many short ones joined with metrical prose explaining the progression between them. The poetry exists in isolated words, groups of words, individual images, in groups of lines at the very most. The *cywyddwyr* are undoubtedly the wisest of poets, caring nothing for poems, and concentrating all their skill upon the perfection of the line or the couplet. Shakespeare, on the other hand, was a great and stupid poet who performed the stupendous literary feat of writing perhaps three hundred lines of pure poetry.'

'You ought to edit an anthology of poetry,

Gwydion,' Nico had jeered, 'a slim pamphlet, entitled "The Complete Effective Works of the English Poets." Or the Welsh poets, that would be even slimmer.'

'Yes, Gwydion,' I said, 'a unique production. On page three a couplet representing the entire poetic riches of those twenty-five thousand lines of doggerel we call the *Canterbury Tales;* and page five, halfway through, a solitary gem-like word plucked from the bleak and howling arctic of Milton's *Paradise Lost.*'

'It's always illuminating,' Gwydion had answered, 'to observe the point at which a pleasantry, a witticism, or a jest is introduced into an argument. You and Nico think, in your circumspect and academic fashion, only of the corpus of poems produced by the acknowledged writers – Shakespeare, Dafydd ap Gwilym, Whitman, Hugo. But one of the finest distichs I ever read I saw scratched on the slate slab of a slum privy. But I don't read poetry now, I only write it.'

Thereafter, Gwydion withdrew into his misty Snowdonia fastnesses of erudition, ambiguity, denial, evasion, and perversity, emerging from time to time to deliver biliary and vindictive attacks upon Nico whenever a question involving letters arose amongst us.

I pull back the leather curtains, the

mahogany rings rattling loudly on their caber-like pole, and let in the unbearable light of the morning. Beyond the bluebottle-haunted aspidistra; beyond the blue-painted woodwork; beyond the ecclesiastical panes of the breakfast-room window into whose bottom half is fitted a large oblong of framed gauze with the inverted words *Saloon Bar* still faintly discernible upon it; in the brilliant sunny corner of the square I see the maestro-gestured figure of my uncle Gomer again, eloquent before the Llansant barber who listens to him with intensity, white-aproned at his cabin door.

The bucket, now empty, stands beside him. As I watch, he gives over conducting, creeps off with a sort of skater's crouch, and returning suddenly takes hold of his own neck with both hands, and in attempted self-strangulation shakes his head to and fro with such violence that his curls are momentarily agitated. What new illustration of the work of the *cythraul canu* culminates thus? His tale of the garrotted musician is new, it is one we have not yet heard or seen enacted. As I watch he languishes against the barber's still regaining his breath, and the varnished soffit above my head cracks as Nico and Barty thunder up the stairs to our bedroom.

3

Llansant fills with people. I stand at the midmost point of the square in the warm of the morning, in the downpour of perfume and bird-song, waiting for Nico and Gwydion. I feel the sunlight's ecstatic handling of my hair, my flesh absorbs the bean-flower fragrance and the breeze, my heart hands the showery fountain of its benedictions upon the square like the multitudinous lit dew. This is not for me, I know it, the moment of the pigeoned head, or epiphany, or pentecostal fire, but the salute only of elate and harmonious flesh. Upon whom does the infidel or unregenerate heart, beholding such created loveliness, the cosmic splendour and the comicality, bestow the oblations and sweet odours of its gratitude and praise?

The surrounding architecture of Llansant I know well. The shops I have painted more than once, and the church. The four sides of the square form an elongated diamond of shops and dwellings about me, and the ivy-veined church tower looks down in benediction, its cockplumes golden, and a white flagstick stuck like a hatpin into its battlements.

Forming one boundary of the square and terminated by the barber's cabin – blessings upon that scented cane-haired perspirer – a row of small shops stands, awinged and barrel-windowed, below the level of the roadway, where the country people buy such food, garments, medicines, and farming gear as they have need of.

And now, hobbling among the crowd, his hairy face stretched upon his neck as though he were struggling to keep his head above water, comes the miniature figure of bearded Charlo Pil Glas, the dotty hermit, wearing his boyschool skullcap, two frockcoats, and dun corduroys with the fork between the knees, all filthied and in irremediable disrepair. The brace of poached rabbits hanging from his left hand, because of the disproportionate shortness of his legs, bump their snouts at every step upon the roadway.

Charlo raises his thumbstick in salutation to the tall wife of Wernddu, who bears in black her handsome man-mould down counter to him with the majestic carriage of importuned seignieur or church-prince, her head high in the military helmet of her hat, her black leather boots flashing cold fires as they bear her past the minute and deferent ragamuffin. Her sombre puff-sleeved gown-coat is fastened with a large safety-pin about her *enceinte* waist, for she is about to bring forth her ninth or tenth upon this dangerous ball. May her family flourish, may her substance increase, may the crops and fatlings of the freehold Wernddu farmlands abound and multiply.

And here comes Dafis, the *dyn hysbys* through the throng, the local wiseman, augur, and apothecary, a tall bending man in mossy bowler and green tweeds, his sharp nose furnished with side-barbs and with no meat upon the bones under the slime-green of his unshed lizard-skin. On his lean face are horny scales and flat warts, large thick lenses cover his goggling eyes, and the mouth through which, after payment, are muttered remedies, enchantments, and prognostications, is firmly shut, the lower lip fitting over the upper like a codpiece. Dafis *bach*, will you shake that glittering dewdrop off your nose and write out your knowledge of visceral toads, snowbroths, and incantations; prophesy, Dafis, in the sun, you slim wizard, you skinny warlock and medicine-man, tell us if the world will have a happy ending.

I glance from him to the young swallow on his wire and my heart burns with love for him; and for the swaying lilac tree casting its elastic shadow lacily upon the snowy wall; and for the gull riding rigid above the bumpy breeze, his wings tilting and settling like the uneasy tipping of a scalebeam. But how can I express my joy and healing without the power of flight; without the grace of a Beacon buzzard or a limber wave of dancing Severn; without the decks of a dithyrambic shooting star? Without soaring, without plunging and capering, how can I show my exaltation at the inexpressible loveliness pouring upon my soothed heart? How can I proclaim the healing glory, not only of the woman or the sailing gull, but the comparable marvel of the skip in a child's walk, and my uncle's sunlit fence patched with blue wood, and Llaethdy's dusty racehorse, the rawboned straw-wigged monster towing at an arrogant trot a tiny white milk-cart across the square? The Eternal made them all, and the little girl with the bright-handled skipping-rope, and the imbecile manikin signalling now like a tick-tack man, and Anna Wernddu counter-marching with military dignity, and the golden, green-frocked girl with the long legs, the slim bosom, and the large eyes. Let me bless, let me laugh, and let me never despise.

Adjoining the shops and built at a wide angle to them upon a narrow cobbled pave-ment I see a neat, low row of white-washed cottages. Their small windows are of green bull's-eye glass. Their framed and varnished front doors are now held open for the day by a brass greyhound, or a polished brandy-keg, or a heavy black-leaded beach-pebble, or a large pink sea-conch bristling like a porcupine. The sea is glimpsed beyond them in the glassy blue of its morning glitter.

Outside the last house, upon eighteen inches of upturned log-end, sits the captain in arthritic immobility, wearing an old blue suit of nautical cut upon his adipose and dumpy figure, and a rude hat shaped like a tweed cowbell upon the unconsuming conflagration of his face and bloated neck. Smoke oozes upwards from his pipe as though it were a chimney leading off the stokings from his immobile and combustible visage. He sits motionless in the sun as I watch, his inflamed hands swollen upon the crook of his malacca, his tweed hat and boozy head rigid upon his chalky neckbones. But his watchful eyes glitter, they jerk with lecherous electric clicks from woman to woman, and jets of hurtling spittle gush out intermittently upon the cobblestones, warm from the smouldering bonfire of his face. My blessings are upon you, too, you stumpy ruffian, may your chalks crack and your joints be flushed with their due dosage of lubrication, may you yet tumble and, rejuvenated, perform handstands through the village with the contortions of the boneless figurant.

Three doors away the twin rotundities of Twmi Prudence House's polished rear bulge into the sun like a pair of headlights from the doorway. We learn from the local skald and druid, my Uncle Gomer, that, stealing from his bride's embraces in the dawn light following the celebration of his nuptials with red-haired Elin Tanlan, Twmi had held up the pegtop trousers flung the previous evening over the bed-end; and then addressing his partner had said: 'Now, we might as well settle who is going to wear these from the start.' Elin's reply was to seize the water-jug and hurl it with great violence at her one-night spouse, accompanying her action with horrid fangy grimaces and a flood of abusive eloquence. Fortunately, the animal vehemence of her temper unsteadied her aim and the missile failed to reach its mark; but a sharp fragment of glass, rebounding off the bedroom wall, took a large chip out of Twmi's ear. Recognizing from that moment the superior dialectic skill of his mate he abandoned all intention of establishing over her the supremacy due in nature to his sex. The duplicated hemispheres of his shiny bum gleam now out of the doorway, as he kneels near the threshold washing the passage. *Ichabod, Ichabod,* should I say? – or *Beati pacifici* perhaps.

The square, not one of whose angles is approximately rectiline, is bounded on the third side by a row of larger, brightly painted dwellings. They are dissimilar in size, shape, and decoration, some are set a little out of alignment and have flower-gardens before them; some have porches and bright shutters; some roses and flowering creepers; some are tall with underground kitchens and dormer windows; all are brightly colour-washed and decorated with window-boxes or hanging flower baskets. Cambrian Cottage, Min Iwerydd, Swn y Don, San Remo, Philadelphia, Tegfan Villa, Denbigh House. My Uncle Gomer's Môr Awelon is tinted eggshell blue and the seven front windows, delicately pointed, appear to be lights looted from some moribund religious meeting-house. The little creosoted fence around the flowerbeds before the house is patched with two strips of timber on which the brush has been cleaned that painted bright blue the forget-me-not chapel pew in our breakfast-room. Now, as I watch the house, I see Nico at the upstairs window haying about, gesturing indecently to attract my attention, his fat face distorted with lycanthropic grimaces like a creature behind madhouse bars.

On the fourth side stands the leafy churchyard wall against which a dozen or more wood-framed booths with striped canvas awnings of red and green, or black and amber, are being erected and prepared for the afternoon fair. Their proprietors are cockney cheapjacks and confidence men; Hebrew dutch-auctioneers of shoes, remnants, and finery; Welsh dairymen and hawkers of woollens; and Negro quacks and mountebanks. They are piling up their stalls with goods now, emptying their fibre cases, leather trunks, and large wicker hampers. The ground is thickly littered with packing straws. On the sea-road leading out of the square stands the shooting range, the coconut-shy, and the hoop-la stall where a gipsyish man is arranging the cruets, garish vases, rag-dolls, inkstands, alarm clocks, and sugar tongs upon their little wooden pedestals.

Small assemblies of village children watch with absorption the unpacking, the brief burnishing and the displaying, and groups of young and red-faced farmers, grinning in the hot discomfort of unaccustomed hard collars, tight leggings, and hot broadcloth, stand slashing their legs with cut switches, and listening to the patter of the stall-holders, above all the corn-curing Negro. I would be happy listening to him and watching the hoop-la gipsy; and remembering the Wernddu Boadicea's processional behaviour among the crowds; and the camel-like, dung-dropping racehorse with the corrugated ribs; but I see Gwydion and Nico approaching from my uncle's house.

I move towards them. Gwydion will have no patience to wait at the fair. Gwydion in such matters is a hard, inhuman, and insouciant man. He strides now through the people in green coat and shirt and dirty trousers, with haughtiness and lofty looks, bearing his six-foot newspaper kite on his shoulder. Why, why, has Gwydion's heart its constant watchers unsleeping upon the walls? His wounds, bitterer than mine, will surely not ache in this mild psychic weather of my presence and Nico's. Why does he not let himself be healed? Wales he loves, but he has brought his anguish even here. Forget, Gwydion, for this morning the offensive generations, gravebound and swarming into oblivion; forget your sadness and disenchantment, the frustrations and futility of your existence; forget the earth become for you excrementitious and the befouled waters a cloaca; and forget the universal nockandro, the strange existence in the universe of the lower bowel; forget for a little the grave, the insatiable eater of loveliness and philosophy; forget the cosmic indifference; forget, do not believe, treading this teeming raft of a square, your *hiraeth* for the uterine oblivion, the oblivion of innocency and the oblivion of death.

I move forward towards the stalls and wait for them, and listen to the Negro delivering his patter in guttural Welsh. His Nubian face is already a painted picture. The fatty saliencies of it are pallid, his rolling eyeballs bulging and yellow as saffron and his scarlet sweater tight over the enormous yielding ball of his belly.

And to you, Nicco, walking reluctantly backwards in Gwydion's wake – seen thus from the rear, thickset and bulgy, you have the neckless appearance of a clothed snowman, of one who has pulled his skin on over some bedding – in the flower of your days, reverence the promptings of your spectral being; to you, conning the sexy equipoise of the stout Jewess's scarlet sash retreating into the crowds – blessings upon her, upon those sturdy legs that might have borne some brown-nosed Rebecca and her bundles in comfort out of Egypt's bondage – to you, I say, remember your house, and your blood, and your inheritance, and the persecutions and martyrdoms of your puritan ancestry; remember, and do not be content to remain only their sensual and decadent epigone; and remember the crag from which you are hewn; remember you belong to mankind; remember the words of Iwan Morgan Parry – 'You, golden stars and glittering systems, you, bright moon, your silver earths not enriched by grave, or burial, or honoured bones, you, as our sad planet passes amongst you, draw aside from your orbits and with muffled music or silence salute her journey across your universe, for her soil is the burial ground of our virtuous, of our mighty, and of our beloved.'

Gwydion comes down rapidly over the scattered straws on the long loose legs of the larger arachnida, his nostrils stink-distended, his coppergold hair glowing, his green eyes narrowed in the sun upon me in a thought-divining and hypnotic glitter. Because of what I have been thinking I expect to be addressed in mockery as some heroic pulpiteer or horseback Bibleman, Hywel Harris or Christmas Evans or Williams o'r Wern, but he passes me without stopping. 'How are you now, Mr Rubinstein?' is all he says.

4

'Apprehended beauty,' yells Gwydion, fleeing with the kite-string in hand, 'is what gives the artist soul its demiurgic power.'

I lie on my back in an embrasure of the gorse-bushes, rolling and kicking my feet into the air, the loud laughter of my teeth, my lungs, my belly, and my tingling skin uncontrollable and paroxysmal at the absurdity of Gwydion's behaviour.

'He is due to acquire a great reputation,' I think, but do not bawl after him, 'for the profundity and insight of his philosophic criticism.'

I believe what I wish ironically to bellow may be done. He has unusual facility in producing such phrases. He can so formulate commonplace ideas and often meaningless generalizations that they appear at first hearing to be of startling originality and infinite suggestiveness. 'The concern of major poetry,' he says, with lid-lowering, 'is exclusively with lust and religion.' Or, 'We find in modern literature, as its outstanding and characteristic feature, the apotheosis of the amateur harlot.'

The wind sweeps up the grassy slope, fresh and scented from its contact with the hidden sea, burning in Dion's blazing hair like flat flames as he plunges among the buttercups. According to Nico, the run, the undignified scuffle rather, of those concerned with culture and learning, seems stylized and conventional as the soft black hat, the baggy black umbrella, the black-rimmed spectacles, and the black brief-case, which have become the regalia of their sodality; their trot is commonly sybaritic, maladroit, and disharmonious. Running, their black-clad flesh expresses only supreme desolation of spirit.

But Gwydion's athletic haring does not deserve, now or ever, the jeers or condemnations of Nico. Now, the kite-string in his hand, he runs with the untrammelled grace of the young unicorn, the speed of the galloping dromedary is in his savage limbs. He legs it down the steep slope with fugitive

357

tie and hair blazing, his stride eating the distance, kicking the clumpy burdens of his shoes well up in the wake of him. Fifty feet behind, the paper tail garlanded like an Hawaiian welcome about his shoulders, Nico advances into the teeth of the wind, bearing above his head, in the manner of Moses displaying the stony decalogue, the tall newspaper kite which he will project upwards into the powerful air currents when Dion reaches the bottom of the slope. Nico, once the university hooker, pounds laboriously forward with steam-roller ruthlessness and muffled detonations; he advances irresistibly through the scattering flowers as though embellished with an emblematical brass horse on his breast and 'Invicta' in brass on his brow. But the heavy progression of this ponderous Rugby-raiding gait is deceptive. He is maintaining, despite the bulk and peculiar *dyn sgwar* structure of his person, the hot pace set up by the flying Gwydion. And when Gwydion, now almost at the bottom of the field, yells their pre-arranged signal, Nico heaves the long-tailed kite up into the air. Instantly it shoots at an angle into the breeze, pauses a moment above the jigging tail, trembles like a phthisic hand, darts upwards again upon another tack, and then, fluttering in a long, helpless parabola, turns gradually upside-down, and returns crashing to the field.

I fall back laughing, while Nico accuses and denounces Gwydion with heat and profanity over the intervening acreage; but finally each resumes his position and a second attempt begins. This time the long paper tail, at the moment the kite becomes airborne, entwines itself in graceful wreaths and coronals about Nico's head and shoulders, and he, running momentarily blinded and bewildered in this cocoon of head-wrappings, flounders among the molehills and crashes to the grass. At once the kite mounts and leaps away as though joyously, derisively, and with full wings, but being tailless it wags its head, abruptly turns turtle, and plunges at a high velocity to earth.

Nico sits in anger among the buttercups, unspooling the tangled tail from his brow, while Gwydion mounts the acclivity with menace in his stride, rolling the kite-string around his slim wooden baton. When Nico has completely disentangled himself he gets to his feet and runs, a revengeful and intolerant expression on his face, in my direction, pelting me with whatever comes into his hand off the surface of the field.

'Look Nico,' I shout at him, holding my ground and pointing with urgency to the heavens. 'The lark, the lark, the loveloopy lark.'

He stops dead and gazes with bewilderment upwards and I escape into the shelter of the gorse bushes.

'Your granny,' he shouts after me, 'didn't beat you enough.'

The wind curving tightly over the hill with the pressure of a powerful spring, sweeps up the scents of the hillside. The morning sky is silken, glass, and cornflower blue. I move around the slope alone, seeking a new sketching point where I can sit until our midday meal.

5

My Uncle Gomer has a steel foot.

After our ravenous eating we sit engaged in desultory and undirected argument around the loo table, the dinner dishes before us uniform only in their complete emptiness. Gwydion smokes his pipe with the little lid, and Nico is engaged in the gleaning of fish-meat lodged among his molars and in their steady manducation.

The leather curtains are drawn back off the church-like window and the bar-parlour gauze has been removed to the fire-grate, so that we can the more easily see the visitors and the crowds of country people assembling in the square for the fair-day afternoon. In the pauses of our conversation we hear bursts of sale-cries and the shouted banter of cheap-jacks and stallholders.

My uncle, cleaned, shaved, and dressed for his holiday, leans in the doorway leading from our room to the kitchen passage, having entered with his lacquered tray to remove our dinner dishes. He wears a neat, black Norfolk jacket with all the pleats and trimmings stitched down. Round his neck is a small black bow tie and a down-turned, professional collar with long points, the rubber breast attached. A white linen apron, starched out and voluminous, and tied around his body at the level of his arm-pits, reaches down to his knees. His clean and wrinkled features, caught by the strong sunlight cast back from table-top and purple walls, have a leathery prelatic grandeur, the battered theatrical nobility of his whole curl-clustered head is both comic and endearing.

Before my uncle's entry Gwydion and I had listened to the bloated lips of Nico uttering immoderate praise of women.

His back to the window and his tongue raising in his fat cheeks from time to time a low-domed protuberance like an ankleguard, Nico occupied the yellow commode, which burned in the sunlight under him, according to Gwydion, with the glow of Elen Luyddog's throne in the Dream of Macsen Wledig.

I sat in the blue pew listening, and watching my semitocymric features assume, in the rusty proliferations of the mirror opposite, the black blotches of bubukles and eruptive scabs.

Gwydion, a demi-dandy, a handsome, goat-nosed, semi-smiler, sat tilted backwards in the American rocker opposite me, he was completing, as a counterblast to Nico, the whimwham and fantasticality of a disquisition designed to prove that knowledge of physiology and coprophagous literature could act as an antidote to Nico's concupiscence. He forced Nico, with cold abuse, to face the window, and as the farm-women and the visitors passed to and fro he pointed – reminding him that all grievous discrepants were withdrawn into hospitals and asylums – he pointed to their blemishes, infirmities, and repellent habits; to the spitting in the road of one; to the outward leaning calves of another; to the pustulous skin of a third.

'Observe,' he said, 'here she comes, her sow-jowled face dipped in the flour-bag, Mari Bobgwraig, with inflamed veins branching over her, edentate, gummy in grinning, and with big nose-pores. Here she comes bald, or horse-haired, or whiskered like a grey monkey. Here she comes greasy, or cadaverous, or yellow as hogskin, or covered with hairy swellings. This is the dream and vision of fair women, here they come limping, or squinting, or with malformed noses leaky. Here they come disfigured with pigmented moles, portwine stains, and the brand of the vascular naevus. Here they come bow-legged, or hump-backed, or flat-footed, or expecting; here they come flea-marked or knock-kneed or wrynecked or goitrous. Here they come stinking or nose-picking, belching or cursing, sniffing or scratching; here they come sluttish, their tongues in their nostrils and tied up ugly. And where are those, where are they, comely as Iwan's Ceridwen, the golden and hyacinthine-haired, walking in sunshine over Cefn yr Eira or making her way towards the foam-flowered sea between the dark corn and the sacred laurels? As the church father says, all these have defilement in their ears, defilement in their noses, defilement in their finger-nails, more defilement in their toe-nails, defilement in their entrails, and defilement in every pore and cavity of their skins. What do you know about women, Nico, you bile-blooded Dyfedite, what do you know, you bull-bellied Buddha, you bulging Ainu-pelted man-boy?'

Nico grinned and held he wouldn't mind, all the same, being turned loose among that lot now, or better still with a few pints and a couple of coddled eggs inside him. 'Look at those two, Dion,' he countered, indicating a pair of plump sluts destined for premature obesity, who stood pink and in inviting prominence below the house. 'Do you call those two dolls tufted meat held up on bones?'

He hailed my uncle, who at that moment had entered the confined bathing-machine of our apartment, and beckoned him towards the window where he now stood. 'Look, Uncle Gomer,' he says (Nico has adopted without all warrant of consanguinity this mode of speech in addressing my uncle), 'tell us, who are those two janes down there. Look, those two near the black man.'

My uncle limps across from the doorway and stands at the window stroking his chin, his face assuming an expression of increasing gravity, but his eyes flashing the sparkles of shaken dew. 'What a crowd,' he said. 'Look, you could walk on their heads already. Which two are you talking about, *machgen i?* Those? They are up to no good, I can tell you that. You can see the one next here now, can't you?' Nico, with the promptitude of libidinousness, readily distinguishes the nearer of the two. 'Well,' says my Uncle Gomer, 'she is a stranger – but I don't know who the other one is.'

My Uncle Gomer is a bachelor, living in the village under the strict surveillance of my three aunts his unmarried sisters. Nico now invites his opinion on the subject of women, and at the invitation I see with dismay a clowning glitter break into his brown eye and a grin distort his unstable expression of abbatical benignity. Down in the bay the sun is drenching the sea and the white-backed Atlantic is pushing blue and shelfy up the beach. That is where I wish to be. But I know my uncle's reply will entail a prolix and pantomimic recounting of his youthful visits to Trephylip; the story of the knocking off of Gittins's bowler; and the story of the falling ham. Possibly a sense of artistic fitness will demand a recital of the reasons for his celibacy and the story of the steel foot. I begin to hope my Auntie Cutty will rattle the door-latch or my despotic Auntie Rosa bump out a peremptory summons on the bulging wall.

But at Nico's invitation he, after a hasty glance into the passage, softly closes the door behind him. His oval tray he places on the music stool. Advancing at a heavy limp towards us he loads the tray with dishes. Then, placing his hand under his apron into the pockets of his Norfolk jacket, he draws out his bandaged brier (already tobaccoed) and, stooping, kindles it at Gwydion's pipe, inverted and with the lid open for the purpose. He returns to the pipe-organ, slides one of the noseless busts along the lid so that he can get his elbow on it, and begins the elaborate rigmarole of pauses, pipe-smoking, semaphoric eloquence, and unfaltering buoyancy which constitute the aberrant cycles of his narratives.

He couldn't say much about the ladies himself – here a cloud of pipe-smoke, which appears to issue in symbolic obfuscation from all the vents and orifices of his head, completely screens his expression from us for the moment – but when he and Pit were learning their trade (a smith he was himself, of course, before he had his attacks, and Pit was a carpenter), they were very fond of courting a bit of warm earth about the country after work. Pit indeed was like a ferret after the farm girls, but when he was only a beginner he was rough with them and the young creatures were not liking him then. They were telling about Pit that when he was taking out his first young woman he was so dull with her he said: 'I don't know much about courting, Mali Pantglas, but let us start by seeing which of us can give the other one the hardest clout.'

My uncle then, after this introduction, proceeds with the story of Tomos Gittins, the Englishman who was like the Llansant sheep-dogs, he could understand Welsh but he couldn't speak it. When he came to this Gittins on the sugar sacks having his tooth extracted by Pit and Charley I glanced across at Nico and Gwydion. Both of them were staring in fascination at his representation, even Dion sat in sober acceptance before the swollen veins, the copious salivation, the powerful convulsions contorting my uncle's limbs as he sat on the organ stool. At length, hearing a step in the passage, my uncle rises, and concealing his pipe under his apron, adds an oval plate decorated with hawsers and life-belts to his tray. But the danger passes and after a few powerful inhalations he sits again and proceeds – this time with an account of Gittins's nervousness on the roads after dark. Then remote on the music-stool a few moments, he again wraps himself in pipe smoke and imperscrutable silence. Upon Gwydion's face the habitual expression of scepticism and superiority, expunged by the power of my uncle's miming, begins to re-impose itself. He imagines, I well know it, that my crafty relative is now attempting, in counterfeited serenity, to recall the point at which the incident of the knocking off of Gittins's bowler on the lonely road departed from the mainstream of his narrative. But the extensive plexus of my uncle's reminiscences is, to himself, so familiar that he is able to pick out and follow without difficulty any desired thread in the complicated webwork; he sees the whole entangled mass of characters and incidents with the clarity of a coloured diagram magnified, powerfully illumined, and projected piecemeal upon the snowy disk of his imagination. Quietly he proceeds to the incident of the ham that nearly brained him falling from a hook in Gittins's kitchen one night when he had gone there to court one of the farm girls. At last he comes to his final strophe.

'Now I was telling you that Pit and I were trying to be friendly with these new maids that old Gittins had taken on. We were not caring a bone button that the old man was thinking so low of us. Pit was wearing his father's overcoat and his box-hat that night, I remember, for to show the girls how smart he was. Well, first of all we went into the cart-shed, groping about to see if there was a ladder we could use if we wanted it. We threw a few handfuls of gravel off the path up at the window where we thought the girls were sleeping, but nothing came of it. "I hope," Pit was telling, as we crossed the lawn to the other side, "that the girls are not washing their feet to-night and throwing the soapy water out of the window over my old man's hat and coat just as we are climbing up the ladder." We threw some gravel at the other window and just as we were doing it we heard the first window opening and old Gittins shouting out: "Who is there, prowling about? Clear off, there is nobody here wanting to see you to-night." "There is nobody here wanting to see *you*, I am sure neither," Pit was shouting back at him, and at that Gittins began to curse like a tom-cat, warning us he had a couple of shots in his gun and he was willing to fire if we didn't go away. And what do you think happened then? The window of the girls' room opened and indeed a bucketful of water shot out of it and just missed us. Well, Pit wasn't liking to be made small of, he was very old-fashioned like that, and he said to me: "This old joker Gittins will have to eat what he shouted to us just now, Gomer. I am not going home until I have given him something to go on with. We will be quiet for a bit until they are all gone to sleep again." "What about the girls, Pit?" I was asking, not liking to think that things were in the mud for us. "I wouldn't have that sort now," he was telling, "and we ought to have known what Gittins's girls would be like, because where the horse rolls he is leaving some of his hairs." Well, in a short time we were creeping round to the front door and tying the big knob in the middle of it sound with halter ropes to the monkey-tree they had growing in the centre of the lawn. Then we went round to the back and tilted the water-butt, a big one they had in those days, so that it was leaning against the back-kitchen door. We waited a bit again, having a smoke in the cart-shed, and then we went up to the front and started hammering on

369

the panels, making a big riot. Of course they came hurrying down inside the house, wondering what the pandemonium was outside, but they couldn't open the front door because we had tied it so sound to the tree. They went through to the back in a hurry and when they opened the back door the butt full of water fell into the kitchen and ran all over the house. Those girls and old Gittins were up for hours before they had clent it all out, they were sweeping the water away with cane brushes and drying the mats and carpets...'

The catastrophe is over. The long, hyper-sensitive, wall-piercing antenna which burgeoned from my uncle's sensorium as he spoke vibrates now with violence at its termination; it trembles in the gusty atmosphere surrounding my Auntie Rosa's person, as she supervises with impatience the washing up of the dinner dishes in the kitchen. And my Auntie Cutty, whose eye, glittering behind its pebble, I had earlier noticed at a hip-high hole in the plank door, at the same moment opens it, and thrusting in the glowing illumination of her lit nose, whispers: 'Come on, Gomer boy, come on, Tilda is waiting for the dishes.'

Hastily concealing his pipe and filling the tray with the remaining crockery, he winks cheerfully at us all and creaks out to the kitchen on his steel foot.

6

We sit on the rocks of the Llansant beach.

Under deep azure and the metallic symbols of hung sun and moon, the bay receives endlessly into its lap the tumbled load of the sea. A few transparent clouds steam insubstantial over our heads, its base red rock in the afternoon sun.

Holiday-makers lie scattered in groups upon the sands and rock-ledges, brilliant in flowery beach-gear; or, splashing in gay costumes and water-wear, gather and scatter spangles of the glittering sea. The sombre families of a few hill-farmers sit crowded quietly together in the discomfort of their Sunday black, or with timidity paddle in the spring-tide rock pools.

I commend to the attention of Nico, sun-bathing beside me, the vividness of the scene, the rock-moithering waves, the steaming clouds, the fawn arc of beach, and without an upward glance he agrees it would be a moving sight to witness over the top of a pint of beer, with a woman behind him and his head blowsing on the softest part of created nature. 'Come on, Dion,' he goes on, lifting his sebum-sodden face off his pillowing arms, 'let's go in now.'

But Gwydion shakes his head. He sits

outstretched on the red rock ledge behind us with his back resting against the cliff, enfolded in a faded green bathing-wrap, beneath which, bandaged round his right leg, I glimpse the Dionian equivalent of best wig or rotten apples, the puttyings of his yellow writing-scarf. He is composing a sea-poem, and artificially to create the dimness indispensable to the collaboration of his muse, he wears a pair of owlish, green sun spectacles, complicated with suède side-pieces, ventilation holes and adjustable anti-dazzle eye-awnings or hooded shades. But he seems oblivious of the scene before him; the punctual gush and vomit of the waves, the ectoplasmic clouds, the gaudy beach, he derides. The surrounding quantities of un-clothed human flesh affront him. He refuses to enter the water until he has found a suitable trochaic epithet to describe some lurid and phantasmagoric beaches existing in his own inhuman imagination.

'Go on, Trystan,' Nico says to me, his eyes puckered against the sun. 'You know about poetry, you tell him what he wants.'

With tusky grimace I propose the Shakespearian *yellow*. Nico, thinking the suggestion has liquidated the problem, sits up, spits, prepares to move off, and declares he will risk swimming with his teeth in. Gwydion coughs slightly and stares in silence down at my wide grin with the mingled expression of

372

hauteur, patience, and cold compassion which at first in Miss Machen's flew a flush up my face, but which now I take pleasure in provoking. I know what goes on in his mind. 'In a poetic *dyfaliad* of Dafydd Nanmor or Dafydd ap Gwilym,' he said to me once in Boundary Villas, 'the comparisons considered suitable for the yellow hair of a girl are bush-broom, gold burdens, heaven's lightning, golden latticing, and so on and so on. But, you know, the indubitable verity is that the yellowest yellow in this universe is dog's urine on sunlit snow.' Again, during a similar discussion, he said: 'The whole nodus of the poetic problem lies in the use of words like "cream cheese" and "anthropomorphicism" in an elegy on the death of a beautiful young woman.'

Replacing his glasses he drops his head and scratches in a word.

Leaving Môr Awelon after our midday meal we made our way across the sunny square with our trunks, wraps, and bathing towels over our shoulders.

Nico, as we walked, looked about him unsuccessfully for the two young women whom he had watched from Môr Awelon. How different, I thought, was his appearance now, in his ostentatious clothing, his blue-and-white canvas shoes, his well-pressed flannel trousers, and his fine-wool navy sweater with the oval neck, from the homespun days of our first encounters.

We left the crowded village square and crossed the grove that lay between us and the sea. The beechwood floor was soft with moss and ground-ivy; and harebells and enchanter's nightshade swarmed under the boughs. The massive trees stood radiant in the sunlight, immobile upon their powerful thigh-muscles, their gigantic gull-grey trunks delicately dappled with the airy shadows of their own leaves; and the sun poured out mottles and lustre upon the vast wrinkled iron of their skin.

The choral harmonies smouldered, pulsed, and swarmed from a clearing in these beeches. In an open circle a group of people, perhaps seventy or eighty, sat spread out on the wooden rivers of beech-roots pouring into the ground. Having finished their open-air meal they sat around dying fires, singing their chapel hymns under the trees with the sun and the beech-bough shadows upon them. Many of the singers were blue-marked colliers, pale and bone-faced, wearing cloth caps; many were their wives in day-trip finery; many their children. One was a husband with a grey-plaid shawl wrapped around him, rocking himself to and fro, nursing the baby Welsh fashion as he sang; one was a beautiful dark girl wearing a white linen suit, level-browed, red-lipped, her fluffy hair glowing in a transverse sunbeam; one was a majestic cripple who leaned against a tree conducting with grace and urbanity the familiar cadences, supporting himself with his thigh-stump thrust through the fork of his crutches.

As we stood aside and listened, Nico, Gwydion, and I, the superb imagery of that hymn hovered in the flamy voices and poured upon us with an equal glitter as of Palestinian sunshine. To hear those sweet harmonies and the words of the saintly lyricist was for me, born in the valleys, to be overwhelmed. Hearing miners, workers in the Pencoedcae, perhaps, or the Three Coals Seam, or the Big Vein, or the Rhas Las Nine Foot, or the Meadow, or the Gellideg, hearing miners singing with concerted passion the exultant poetry of their faith, I dared not speak.

Iwan Morgan Parry, describing, in essay and palinode, his visit after many years of apostasy and exile to the remote highland Sunday-school of his youth, says that with the voices of the chapel elders, and of the children, falling in prayer around his bowed head, he felt his parched and disenchanted heart, 'brushed by the dawn's winged harbingers, and the sweet dew begin to fall.' Myself, I also. My every hail and acknowledgement to compassion, to humility, to the contrite spirit, to earth's visual radiance and to her spiritual loveliness, every salute to the multitudinous loyalties and heroisms of this world, every gratitude for tenderness, every prayer, worship, adoration, is expressed for me in the mysterious grandeur and sanctity of this singing, this eloquent, unconquerable *sursum corda* beneath the beech-flecks and the shadow-fragments of this sunlit wood. At the culmination, the unutterable fulfilment, I walk out of ecstasy filling my sea-ear with the sensual loveliness of breakers sounding upon the shore.

'They are drunker on the heady liquor of singing,' says Gwydion, catching me up on the beach path, 'than ever were their ancestors on battle at debatable pass, or on hanaps of mead and victorious metheglins.'

I protest against drunker, in spite of historic sanction I protest. The expression is unsuitable. We are a deeply religious and musical nation.

'Consider it, Trystan,' says Gwydion. 'I will not embarrass you by asking you to subjoin the names of our universal composers. The proportion of melodious larynxes amongst us is high, yes, we sing readily at *cymanfaoedd canu*, at *eisteddfodau*, under the boughs of exile, at dissenting chapel services, and, you tell me, at the doors of bereaved households and calamitous pitheads following flood, explosion, and communal disaster. Such a gift is common amongst primitive and unsophisticated peoples. It is not art or religion; its effect is anodynic; where conditions are worst, in the brutal and squalid industrialism of your valleys, the singing is the sweetest. You think I am guilty of detraction.'

'There are two things, Dion,' I say. 'Not only do we sing, we sing the words of Ann Griffiths, of Morgan Rhys, of Thomas Williams Bethesda'r Fro, we sing "Pwy welaf o Edom yn dod," we sing "Dwy aden colomen pe cawn" and "Fe welir Seion fel y wawr," not religiose Madelons, Sospan Fachs, and Tipperarys, but the sublime poetry of the sacred lyrics. And Dion, how are you competent to judge, you, a tall, fair-skinned Welshman who does not believe in God.'

'I do believe in God, Trystan,' says Gwydion, 'but I don't know which side He's on. The Welsh, don't you agree, singers at funerals and international football matches, are a heathenish nation of rhapsodes and fantasts bemused with Calvinism, often the drunkest men in Europe still on poetry, or patriotism, or dusty learning, or *soif du martyre* or a sense of ancient justice. Are they vocal in the further west, Nico?'

Nico had been one of a crowd hymn-singing after dark on the promenade of a popular holiday resort he told us. Councillor Rees, an annual visitor, his full face bricked up red between his panama and his three-inch collar, rises in the midst to appeal for the lifeboat. To show off he speaks in English. It was heartening now, for to see so much people coming together for to sing the songs of Seion. Rising he was, like, on behalf of the lifeboat, at the request of his friend Mr Lewis here, which he was very glad to see present this year again. Now the history of the lifeboat was entering on a new area. Perhaps some of those present had heard the phrase: 'The sea was running *mountains* high. The sea was running *mountains* high–'

'And Dion,' I say, interrupting Nico's story, *'paid a bod mor ddi-enaid.* What do you mean? I claim that seldom are the trinary experience of music, poetry, and religious fervency felt by so large a number in concert as in the singing by our countrymen of their hymns, and seldom do these three meet at so exalted a level. At the very lowest, our countrymen who know their hymn-books are cultured in a way that the foreigner who knows his is not. When I was a child, the Ystrad miners...'

I go on to describe the virtues of the dwellers in our valley and the coal-field in general with much warmth, their high culture, their erudition and intelligence, their generosity and humour, their solidarity and neighbourliness. Nico, awaiting a chance to repay me for my impatient interruption of his narrative, questions me closely, in the counterfeited accents of the valleys, concerning the cutting of headings by workers hampered with back-wings, and the hanging-place of halo or sacred tettix at the daily stripping for the coal-face.

Gwydion is pleased at this. 'Trystan's Wales, Nico,' he says, 'is a very intellectual country you must remember. The people of Gilead he claims read the *Iliad*, and of Maesycwmmer – *The Summa*.' In Gwydion there is this childish love of words, rhymes, jingles, nonsensical verses, the *migli-di magli-di's*, the *titrwm-tatrwm's*, the hey-nonny-nonny's and hi-dee-do's of language. Hearing children in the street chanting 'Om-pom-pah-ne-oh' or reciting 'Inky, blinky, boo-lah-bah' or 'Each, peach, pear, plum' he would light his pipe or make some other excuse to stop and listen. He seemed sometimes as though mankind's ancient and universal faculty of speech were to him a new and enchanting discovery. He was a dictionary reader, a neologist, an inventor of nicknames, a collector of the technical tricks of the *cywddwyr*. Any such oddity as an adjective embedded in the middle of a noun delighted him. He wrote poems by dropping water from a pipette on to words in his

379

thesaurus, and by picking, as though from a bran-tub, phrases which he had cut out of a newspaper. Reading that a well-known essayist, being short of an exercise book, had written an article in the margins of an octavo classic, he tried the experiment of copying one of his poems into the inter-linear spaces of a handbook on navigation, and then typing out the resultant, parataxis as a completed work.

Now, having started this nonsensical game, he proceeds with it regardless of veracity or probability. 'In his Rhiwbina,' he says, 'the people read Heine, and in his Gwent perhaps Sion Cent. In Trystan's Llyn, they all read Robert Green, and in Trystan's Caerphilly, John Lyly. In his Llandebia they read the *Fantasia,* and in his Penderyn, *Llyfr y Tri Aderyn.* In his Llan-drindod...'

I make for the beach by means of a bypath, weary for the moment of his lunacy and waywardness. Why must he always be a detractor? Why does he not give himself unreservedly to his love of Wales? Why is he not made whole by her? As I go I think with resentment of the shallowness of his words, remembering the voices of Ystrad men who waited outside our door wearing black for my grandmother's funeral, singing the simple Welsh hymn as she was brought slowly out of the house on to the pavement of Rosser's Row. Remembering the *cymanfaoedd* in Caersalem. Remembering the bare hot building, the floor-space of our chapel packed, the massed wooden gallery of singers divided into four voices above the head of the young conductor, all moving together to the organ's thunder in harmonies of hymn or oratorio, with the heavier resonance of bass and tenor – the image arises again – like some angelic gull-flock sweeping in mastery over the sea towards the sunlit beaches, and its undulating swarm of adroit and responsive breakers curling beneath it. Remembering a different scene, the clear airs and sweet descants of the pavilion concert, the massed, mixed choir of black-and-white clad singers spread out at the building's end in a fan-shaped keyboard, the hatted audience-heads a vast oblong of coloured pebbles, the fluid pistoning of the orchestra strings, the dark-clad conductor moving with the action of a flashing star; and then the rolling harmonies of this fan-shaped choir and its sea-song, its storm-song, its tide of trees. Remembering the constricted throat, the tingling flesh, the mingled awe and tenderness and exaltation at the singing of my countrymen. Of this, of choiring warm and intimate as the blood, Gwydion knows nothing. By the time he and Nico arrive on the beach I am stripped and sun-soothed, laid out among the naked heliolators of the bay.

7

And soon beside me, Nico, intoed, shut-eyed, the heavy plush cannon-ball of his head pillowed upon his arms and his yellow-as-hensfoot face deflected towards me, lies burning his back on the rock, clad only in the luxuriant black scrub and bushery of his natural fell and his magenta bathing drawers. In spite of his youth, the nostril presented to me is densely packed with a dark hairy plug; and yesterday, when he went for a neck-shave, I saw the anaemic wet-handed barber, with a skilful twist of the clippers, cut the tufted hairs bushing like corn-shocks out of the barn-holes of his ears. This right ear itself now, miniature, intricate, and countersunk, fits snugly into the base of the depression in the fat on the side of his head, and scarcely rises above the yellow levels of the surrounding adiposity; it is a winsome peach, a show-gem in plush, an unborn child crouching *in utero*.

While he suns himself and Gwydion composes I remember on the rock my last visit to Mabli, the day before I finally left Dinas. How strange she was. I had thought of her as cold and aloof and indifferent but I had discovered increasingly that my judgment of her over many months had been quite insensitive and shallow. When we had walked together from the art school we had usually spoken about our painting, sometimes about the university, sometimes about her relatives or my own. She taught me much, I learned something of the world in which her people moved, the managing, influential wire-pulling class into which they had entered. But I had been too often so deeply concerned with my own affairs that I had not, until the very end, paid real and sympathetic attention and respect to Mabli's life, to think of her as a human being also with problems of her own, with aspirations, capable of suffering and disappointment as I was myself. I had considered her too long as rather apart, secure, beyond conflict, assured, serene. But in our last talk at Cwrt Nicol I realized with shame my own selfishness and the extent of my arrogant absorption with my own feelings.

Mabli's mother had gone to rest for the afternoon, so we sat on the lawn together. I had not thought very much about our meeting after our talk in the recreation ground, I had been too concerned with what she had told me about Alcwyn. I hoped now that she would not refer to it. That was one of the faults in my relation with her, a desire to avoid what concerned me deeply. Mabli had on a flame-coloured frock. With her high cheek-bones, her sloping eyes, and her pale pointed face she had always seemed to me a girl of very remarkable and attractive appearance, but not until this afternoon had I seen in her the seriousness of her character, the extent to which she felt implicated and involved with what happened in our country. How had I ever been so obtuse and imperceptive as to be taken in by her mask of indifference? Why had I not realized the meaning of that glance of panic I had seen more than once in her eyes? Why had I not recognized her loneliness, her frustrated desire to serve?

'I suffer,' she told me, 'from being the different one of the family.'

'How do you mean, different, Mabli?'

'I don't seem to care about what the rest of our family think important.'

'What do they think important?'

'Well, you've seen them, you ought to know. Mother thinks Markethall Square very important, and her cloth factories, and being a bit better off than most other people. She just wants me to enjoy myself, bless her, to be as she is, only starting from a much earlier age. She's never wanted me to do anything that she wouldn't care about doing herself. And really I seldom seem eager to do what she does. I'm not at all like her really.'

I had sensed from the beginning this antagonism between Mabli and her mother, and I felt pleased to hear my intuition confirmed. 'What about your uncle and aunt?' I asked.

'I'm afraid auntie's very much like mother. She enjoys above everything being in the swim and knowing important people, and hearing of decisions and so on before they become news for everybody. And I can't talk much to uncle now because as you know I don't believe in his party any more.'

'I didn't know you were so very deeply interested in politics.'

'I dare say real politicians would call my politics mere sentiment, emotional, impractical, impracticable. Uncle does. But all new parties seem like that to older people.'

'What party are you talking about? The Party, of course?'

'Yes. You've heard me speak of it before, haven't you?'

'Yes. More than once. But–'

'But what?'

'Oh, I don't know. I can't really imagine you mixed up in politics. There are several members at the university now. But they all seem a bit queer somehow.'

'Have you spoken to any of them?'

'Oh yes, often. But they don't seem to me to make sense. They mistake the enemy. Our enemy, so we thought in the valleys, was capitalism, not England. So it seems to me still. Am I the damp cloth that goes safely near the fire?'

'I'm afraid I'm that a little myself. I want Wales to rule herself but I haven't actually joined the Party yet. I don't think I've got the courage.'

'Does it require courage?'

'For me, yes. Mother and uncle and aunt would be against it, very much so. And Rosser, my brother, of course. He's a Tory.'

I was puzzled. Had my life at the university been too self-regarding, too restricted in interest? Were there important things happening around me now of which my absorption in my own affairs had kept me unheeding and ignorant? I had never taken seriously the men who wanted to make us a self-governing nation and continually said so. Even Gwydion, whose courage, independence, and integrity everyone acknowledged, seemed to me a little unbalanced on this subject. But I thought after my talk with Mabli more and more about Gwydion and his concern for the learning of our country. Gwydion, in spite of his criticism, was, above all, Welsh, I began to realize. He was deeply conscious of it. The only thing he appeared to believe in apart from poetry was the importance and the richness of his Celtic heritage. All that he lacked was will. Why had I not realized this before? Nico was as Welsh as Gwydion so far as language and background were concerned, but Nico was not concerned with his Welshness, that was the weakness of his character it seemed to me now. Compared with Gwydion he seemed rootless, although he was the one who had spent all his life in Wales. Mabli's conversation disturbed and enlightened me. I thought a good deal of her loneliness and isolation, her unalterable desire to do something which would be of service to others and in which she herself could believe and find herself fulfilled. Her painting, I felt, would never satisfy her as it would satisfy me. I reproached myself bitterly for the trivial level at which I had so often kept the conversations between us, avoiding reference to the matters which concerned me deeply and forcing this restriction upon Mabli also. It was cheap and superficial. Why had I not sensed that the withdrawn expression, the lowering of the eyelids were often in reality a rebuke, the sign of impatience and distaste at the triviality of my conversation? How many times, I wondered with shame, had she hoped that I would not accompany her after the art school classes? This thought was painful and humiliating for me now, but how humiliating for her to be treated so often only to the lightest gossip and the exchange of the most trivial generalities. I had been stupid, greatly deceived by a calm demeanour and good taste and a gift for water-colour.

In my first letter to her I must tell her so, I must explain everything from the moment of our first meeting in Markethall Square. We had agreed that afternoon to write. I had already received from her one letter which informed me she had at last come to a decision and that she had determined to brave the displeasure of her mother and her family.

8

The three of us, Gwydion, Nico, and I, the waves and the breeze behind us, approach the beach swimming. Our view is that of returning migrants, we glimpse ahead of us over the water an awry picture of the bay and the hills behind it where the ruined abbey stands grey in its diminishing grove.

Ahead of me, on my left, Nico with crude strokes batters the ocean back. His body, large, likely, and buoyant, seems yet vulnerable and maladroit in the water, losing contact with the ground his limbs lack their athletic skill and potency. Is it in obedience to some mysterious philosophy of natation that his action is thus laboured, that he rolls alongside me with a gulphing motion and heavy, wallowing stroke? I pass under him and catch a ventral glimpse of his frog-like action in the green water, I see his red trunks and his limbs gleam palely and without grace above me. When I come up beyond him he desires webs between his toes and fingers, he importunes of providence a mouth-like aperture for unhampered breathing at the back of his neck; eyelids of transparent horn, he breathlessly holds, were a boon to the vision of the surf-cleaving swimmer.

Gwydion rides the waves before me like the flexuous sea-serpent, grim-visaged and flame aureoled.

Now, with Nico and Gwydion drawing away, I lie outspread in the glitter, I float in the fragmentary wedge of sun sparkling upon the bay. Above my head a cloud of teased-out silk floats lightly through the afternoon, an airy tuft blown off some gigantic snow-white blossom. The sea heaves, a wave swells up beneath me like the bringing-up hard of an enormous muscle, and I am rolled upon the curve.

I drop my feet and run out of the foam-patterns shedding flakes of light. I run across the swarming beach, past the magnificent Juno in the scarlet bathing costume; past the wistful boy brooding upon the rock; past the beautiful girl all bones and eyeballs, and her golden hair among the loveliest things ever caught in a net – I bless her now and I bless her when she shall be old and with bald sons – past Nico with his red shorts pulled high over the swell of his belly; past the two little bearded men in black with a Bible between them murmuring in the warm sun to each other.

Behind me the light of the torn sun glitters like lace on the water. I turn from the beach and lie once more outstretched upon the rock. I close my eyes and as a dog barks and the children call and the sea rushes I experience in the sun's warmth a flow of happiness and praise and healing, my spirit rises up and is magnified, she breaks bounds, she gives me the power of a hundred fighters, she...

'*Myn brain i*,' says Nico, climbing up alongside me, 'I could eat a suffering cart-horse between two mattresses.'

9

Boom-boom-boom-boom, down in the square goes Harry Nantfach's drum.

Above the crockery-crowded chest of drawers of Môr Awelon's upstairs sitting-room, occupying about one square yard of wall space, hangs a photographic enlargement. A rectangle of rude carpentry surrounds it in the shape of a frame – to my boyhood vision the heavy timbers seemed

390

stout lengths of door-post sawn down and handed over for decoration in bad light to the clumsier practitioners of the rural crafts – and the shadowy face appearing in it is morose and saturnine. Gloomy, wool-like hair, obliterating brows and side-whiskers, and a heavy moustache grow over the blurred features like a sombre moss. The whole aspect of the picture is dark and forbidding, the man lowers malevolently into the room backed by the spectral waistcoat buttons of the expunged camera-confronters of the group who formerly surrounded him. It was not until I was a grammar-school boy that I learnt who this repellent wearer of coal-house cobwebs was.

Môr Awelon is now the property of my mother's brother and sisters, that is to say, it belongs to my Uncle Gomer, my Auntie Rosa, my Auntie Tilda, and my Auntie Cutty. It is a commonplace of those given to aphorism that many shall eat the bread when the sower is in his grave; and in the possession by my relatives of this roomy and peculiar dwelling the adage is triumphantly exemplified. I had imagined, in the in-curiosity and innocent acceptance of childhood, that my three aunts were ladies in the maiden state, and by the discovery that my Auntie Rosa had, during my infancy, married, and was now a widow, I felt greatly shaken and unnerved. It was an idle question concerning the large picture resting upon the back of the chest of drawers which brought about this discovery. The subject of it turned out to be the deceased husband of my Auntie Rosa.

Perpetually hairy, dismal, and indistinct as he now seemed, this unknown Uncle Eben Evans was in life uxorious and possessive, the inheritor of fertile Allt y Celyn, a good hundred and fifty acres of freehold farmland and, according to the peasant standards of his neighbours, rich. But soon after this marriage to my aunt he fell into the common decline and died, bequeathing to her those compact, fruitful, and unburdened slopes which she, with hired help, maintained in profitable cultivation until her paralysis forced her to abandon them. My Uncle Gomer, soon afterwards, became increasingly aware of the shortness of his breath, of arm-pains and pectoral spasms, and decided the hour had come for him to fix his last horse-shoe and forge his final gate-hinge. Peak-widowed Môr Awelon, with the large field and garden to its rear, was bought out of the proceeds of Allt y Celyn, and the brother and three sisters maintained themselves in fair comfort there by the sale of eggs, goats' milk, rabbits, and vegetables, and by catering for holidaymakers who loved their village. Now they regarded themselves as having retired, and accommodated importunate friends and relations only out of a good-natured dislike of a refusal or from an active desire to please.

Under the dark gaze of our lichen-laden relative, with the sun pouring in through the pointed windows, and shouts and drum-beats from the crowded square beneath us ascending, we eat off an incomplete and roseate tea-service the tea to which my Auntie Rosa has invited Gwydion, Nico, and me. This large upstairs sitting-room – 'You would not paper it now,' my Auntie Tilda tells us, 'in under twelve pieces' – was once used as the general dining-room of the boarding establishment. It is long, with two church-lights looking out over the square at one end and a sort of glass conservatory or solarium at the other. The table at which we sit is set *across* the room and stands near the front windows. My Auntie Rosa, the pouring hostess, a-glitter at the head of the table, presides with composure; she confronts the timbers and unmitigable scowl of her late partner from her wheeled chair with the griffin-faced equanimity of assuetude.

Uncle Gomer, half-way up the room, stands smoking, grinning, and jawing with his back to the sitting-room door. He is to occupy the chair directly beneath his disapproving brother-in-law. He is involved now in a recital of the peculiarities of the Nantfach family.

The rotund Nico and my silent Auntie Tilda are seated side by side with their backs to the windows while Gwydion and I, opposite them, complete the circle, blinking into the reflected glare of a dazzling sill full of sunlight received full in our faces.

But where is my Auntie Cutty, that wild and homely maenad for whom a place has been prepared between Gwydion and me; where is the big-boned latch-rattler, the tall and gawky peeper through hip-high door-holes; where is she, elusive, flighty, and incalculable; where is Nico's Gliding Gwladys; where are now that incandescent nose-point, that hen-like profile, that chin on her neck-front no bigger than a bunion or a palm-corn; where is the bunned and brass-combed glarer through powerful glasses, the warmer of her stays in the kitchen oven, the waterer of the garden beds with skim-milk, the washer of her drab hair in crimson curtain dye? Where is the narrow creeper-out from under sofas, the wild flouncer through doorways like a demented hen; where is the meeter of Nico upon the stairs who greets him with: 'Everything in the garden's fine'? Where is she who employs her red fingers in the computation of her meagre accounts; who, finding difficult the mastery of cutlery, bolts down her dinner with a spoon? Where is she who yesterday in the garden disputed out steak with the pilfering cat, wiped the meat on her apron, and slapped it back in the frying-pan? We all know that most of her time is spent in the basement where, dressed in a schoolboy's navy blue jersey, a hearth-cloth skirt, and a bibbed apron, she observes through thick glasses from the barred windows on ground level all callers approaching the front porch. My Auntie Rosa turns in her invalid chair to my Uncle Gomer, and interrupting him, asks where Cutty could be now.

My uncle is observing strictly at this moment the rule that tobacco-smoking is prohibited in my Auntie Rosa's best parlour.

And yet he smokes.

Wearing his velvet cap and pink rose, his well-pressed trousers straight-legged, his Norfolk jacket heavily dandruffed and no longer protected by the outsize apron, his position and attitude are equivocal. His pipe is invisible, no cloud-wreath or smoke-plume drifts from his mouth or nostrils into the sunlit air.

And yet he smokes.

The sitting-room door, against the varnished jamb of which he stands, is slightly ajar; and with his right hand he holds his pipe out through the aperture behind him so that by standards of strict accuracy it may be said to occupy space, not in the sitting-room itself, but upon the stair-landing outside. Before answering my aunt he turns his back upon us and inserts his face into the nine-inch gap to the rear of him, and we see by the bellows-like fluctuations of his cheeks that he is sucking out a final lungful of tobacco smoke, before joining us at the table. This same smoke, after a short interval of internal circulation, we observe him to pump forth again into the passage beyond the door. Then he faces once more into the room, his brows arched up to the edge of his smoking cap, and his eyes glittering in a well-lined grin.

'Cutty,' he says, 'is gone up to bed with a pile of *Schoolgirls' Journals* and a bag of plums.'

Then pocketing his broken pipe he sits down facing Auntie Rosa, presenting his shapely nape to the scowl of his benefactor.

This upstairs sitting-room reminds Gwydion, he whispered to me one evening, of the lounge of some homely provincial *maison tolerée,* frequented by a middle-aged clientèle high in local regard. There is about it an air of domestic comfort, of shabby and dated grandeur, of oppressive respectability. Every room in Môr Awelon, because of my Uncle Gomer's incurable jackdawism, is excessively crowded. But nowhere does the redundancy appear more striking than in this parlour. The rather narrow room seems to be completely encircled with massive easy chairs, divans, couches, daybeds, and settees, bulging with comfort-promising upholstery. Underfoot we have deep red carpets, rugs, and the fleece as of some hyperborean ram. The walls, flattened by the superimposition of a deal boarding, are covered with a dainty paper of black and rose-pink bands. But large areas of it are hidden by the photographic junk of our family picture gallery.

Edacity and opsomania are not among the infirmities of my uncle's character, he approaches his food in a spirit of indifference. After importuning, with reverentially bowed curls from which the velvet cap has been removed, the presence at our table of Heaven's King, he sits and talks, with his restless eyes glittering as they pass from person to person. Subdued merriment I notice seems gently to convulse him and send its fleeting tokens across his unstable features. Absorbed in the shy silence which precedes the eating of a meal in unaccustomed presences, the rest of us only half attend to him, but when he catches my eye during the passing along of food, he winks. From his position at the door he had been relating to us, with one handed gestures, an anecdote concerning Harry Nantfach, the lame baker-boy, now the drum beater in the square below.

This Harry was a cloddish lad with highly

curved legs. His understanding was dwarfish. Once being asked in a meeting of the
Sardis young people to speak on *Charity,* he
had arisen with the confident alacrity of the
bird-brained and had disposed of the
intricate Pauline concept with these words:
'Charity – charity is a good man.' He had
then sat down. But, doubtless as the result of
a clerical error – 'And,' said my uncle, 'I
happen to know from the schoolin that he
was spelling egg with one g' – Harry had
passed his entrance examination to the
Tremyrddin grammar-school some years
before. My uncle, meeting his mother at the
time, had spoken to her about her boy's
success. Perhaps now he would begin
algebra, and even start taking physics. 'I
don't know whether he will be taking physics
or not,' Harry's mother answered him, 'but I
will be giving him syrup of figs every Friday
night just the same as I am doing now.'

I see in my Auntie Rosa's tigress eye stern
rebuke, flashings of minatory fire, and fran-
tically signalled reminders, warnings,
threats, and injunctions. My uncle, commencing a further illustration of Harry's
stupidity, observes the signs himself and
becomes silent and a little vexed and downcast. He is handed on a rosy plate his jelly
and blancmange, which he falls to eating
with sober inattention.

Glancing periodically at him to ensure his

continued silence, my Auntie Rosa subjects us to the interrogations traditional amongst hostesses.

She has long had the information, but nevertheless asks Nico with polite and long-lashed condescension if he is to be a school-teacher. He is not, he is an engineer soon to be employed by a firm engaged in the production of superior machinery belting. Gwydion? 'Not yet,' he answers, not without observable grimness settling at the corners of his mouth.

My Auntie Rosa, black in her regalia of susurrant satin, smiles. A preternatural light beams out through her dusky eyes during the meal, she uses the illumination of her glance like a baton to exhort, enliven, or subdue. With her heraldic head and hooded eye she is the hospitable and masterful hostess, she sits enthroned at the table-head in her cripple's chair with the autocratic benignity of some dark and flickering infanta, her black curtain-ring curls laid out like a dusky chain bound across her brow, her brazen face fleshless and glazed, but bloated as though with soft fawn water-pouches, under the black-beaming head-lights of her eyes. Her funeral satin, which has to run to pleats, knots, bows, tassels, and general ribbonism, winces at every move; and at every wince her adornment shoots forth sparkles from lobe, throat, breast, wrist, and finger. Her watchful spirit becomes tranquil as the meal progresses, as the talk remains polite and well distributed, and as my Uncle Gomer does not saucer his tea or upset the dishes with his posturings.

She begins talking about the Anthonys of Pentywyn. Did I know Densil was going to be a doctor?

'A doctor, Auntie?' I said, surprised. 'He's left it a bit late, hasn't he?'

'I don't know about that, but a doctor he's going to be. He's at some special school now, studying. Entering college after this holiday, they say.'

'Why has he done that? I thought he liked farming.'

'It's Mair-Ann, must be,' she said. 'You know about her, of course.'

I felt my colour going up. 'I know she's left Llansant,' I said. 'For London, wasn't it?'

'She's engaged, boy.'

'Oh yes. To whom? Stevie Ty Croes I expect, is it?'

'Oh no. Not Mair-Ann. She's marrying somebody with a title they say. A sir. His people live up there in Cardiganshire. Landowners. They met in London.'

'What was she doing in London?'

'She went to learn how to be a secretary and then she had a job.'

'She doesn't come to see you now, I suppose?'

'Oh no, not now. I've seen her passing, though. On horseback. With this fellow – that's who they said it was. I must say, she is much better looking as a woman than he is as a man. Round-shoulders, thin legs, and a little bowler hat on him. Shouldn't wonder if he didn't drink a lot by the colour of him. Whisky at that.'

She turned to the rest of the table and with pride in her voice added: 'The Anthonys are friends of Trystan's. He and Mair-Ann used to be very friendly.'

I felt as though all the blood in my body had suddenly found its way into my face. It was ridiculous. Opposite me Nico was grinning, his look of mock surprise sending his eyebrows up. Gwydion glanced at me and saw my embarrassment.

'This name Anthony seems to be common in these parts, Mrs Evans,' he said to my Auntie Rosa.

'It is,' she said. 'There are many of them about.'

'I wonder how it happens. An English name obviously, but right out here, eighty miles from the Severn. One of the group of saints' names, perhaps, like Lawrence, and Dunstan, and Eustace. We had one at college. Do you remember, Nico?'

'Yes,' said Nico. 'Gordon.'

'He was a very religious man and he wanted home rule for Wales.'

'I have heard about those,' said my Uncle Gomer, after a glance at his sister. 'They held a meeting in the square here a couple of months ago. Youngsters. Very good they were too. I would vote for them.'

'Would you indeed?' said Gwydion. 'If I had any faith in political action I would do so myself.'

As they discussed the matter I thought of the letter I had received from Mabli at the week-end. She felt, she said, she could not continue to lead her life as she had been doing. Her mind was now made up. She had decided to brave the displeasure of her mother and the rest of her family and do what she could for the freedom of Wales. She felt she must do this, cost what it may to herself and to others. And involved with this political question was the question of religion. Markethall Square she found less and less satisfying, she told me. She had read the Iwan Morgan Parry I had recommended to her and the logic of it seemed inescapable. Wales free and Catholic. Wales part again of the great European tradition. Wales fulfilling her own destiny and not trailed along behind pagan, or at best Protestant, England. Couldn't I think of serving Wales, of giving my life to my country? She had felt restless and dissatisfied and unfulfilled until she had made her decision. She had not yet told her mother and that was not going to be easy, since she was violently prejudiced, emotional, and also suffering from a dangerous disease. The rest of the family she cared less about.

Her letter had surprised me. So deeply had the image of Mabli as a conventional, unimplicated, and acquiescent girl impressed itself upon me, of an artistic personality fond of beautiful clothes, careful of her appearance, concerned with the taste and fitness of everything at her home at Cwrt Nicol, so accustomed had I been to this conception of her that it was only with an effort that I had recognized the conflict, the warm feelings which her coldness and reserve and the indifference of her manner concealed. I found it hard to realize that in her heart was that passionate hunger to do what was right, that scornful dissatisfaction with a docile adherence to the ways of her family. What would happen to her? I thought constantly about her. She made me uneasy and apprehensive and yet grateful that she felt impelled to so courageous and to me so arid and fruitless a course.

And as the talk of the tea table went on around me I wondered at myself. Why was it that I, coming from the desperate and squalid industrialism of Ystrad, had remained apart from those in college who, without themselves having lived there, saw clearly the iniquities of that industrialism and desired passionately to end them? Why had I not matured more rapidly? Compared with many of my contemporaries I seemed unawakened, not much older, except as a painter, than when I first left Ystrad. I was happy really only when I had a paint brush in my hand and a canvas before me. Or when I was receiving uninterruptedly what I could use from the shoals of impressions flooding towards me. I seemed to have been living in a world in which seeing was all, while around me in college and in the world outside went on this passionate life to which I was largely insensitive. Men, and women too, wanting social justice, others desiring that one's dedication should be to religion, others caring only that their country, small and unimportant as it might seem to the world, should be its own mistress. Was I so very self-centred, so blind, so callous even? Why did I not feel more deeply about these things? I took them for granted – religion, socialism, freedom for Wales, they all seemed so obviously desirable that I could not feel they demanded more of me than agreement. Then why was it that people wished me to devote myself to the causes in which they believed? Why were there so many voices? My grandmother had called and now Mabli was demanding a different dedication. And when a person had such an enthusiasm he viewed the whole of existence, I observed, in terms of it, everything he saw, read, thought, either confirmed and so elated him or else was antagonistic and abhorrent. The book by Iwan Morgan Parry I had lent Mabli was one that I had admired for the brilliance of its prose, for the loveliness of his descriptions, painter-like and accurate, of various parts of Wales, and these were the things I wished her to share with me. It is true that one of the essays in it concerned his conversion to Roman Catholicism, but that I had hardly noticed. Mabli and I had not been reading the same book.

Everybody round the table seemed to be talking at once, all had views on the state of our country, its language, its history, its future. All except Auntie Tilda, that is. She had said little throughout the meal, not by reason of embarrassment, or, certainly, of any shortage of conversational powers, but because her powerful jaws had been engaged wholeheartedly, and with sober pleasure, in the radical function of chewing. She is the labourer of Môr Awelon, both skilled and heavy, she at all times slogs like a cart-horse, or talks like the voluble river, or snores like leviathan, or devours food like a ravenous tiger, or laughs till she cries and wipes away the tears with the back of her hand. The hurricane currents of her being seem always to thunderbolt along a single path, great convulsions of volcanic energy sweep indivisibly and resistlessly out of her, overwhelming her tasks and occupations. She is the clamorous bucket-banger who with the din of her daily white-liming awakens at dawn all sleepers to the rear of Môr Awelon. She is the frantic boot-repairer whose handiwork we, with admiration, examine in the garden shed where she sits cobbling boots like fury and drinking tea strong enough to sit on. She, wearing Gomer's trousers, is the noisy worker on Môr Awelon's roof. She is the vigorous, dis-patchful, and ruthless washer-up, at a stoop she shoots dishes across the kitchen bench with the recklessness of a knockabout comedian; in the line of crockery-breaking, Gwydion says, she is surely unsurpassed among the drabs, helps, kitchen-maids, day-girls, cinder-wenches, landladies, and housekeepers of the Isle of the Mighty. She is also Miss Thomas Top-notes, a strong tower and kingpin of Sardis's congrega-tional singing. The volume of her penetrat-ing soprano often caused strangers to the chapel to peer round full-eyed at her in wonderment and apprehension – more than once, in boyhood, I went scarlet to the curls standing beside her, fearing these back-ward-glancing visitors should believe *me* to be the source of that powerful and unabating volume of hymnody.

My Auntie Tilda's hands now, as she sits at

the table steadily consuming all eatables within range, are brick-red and polished, her back is humped, her big-jointed arms apish as though unnaturally extended through continual lifting and carrying. Her thick bobbed hair, radiating from the crown of her head, has the rigidity of spoke-wire and the texture of thatching-straw; it is dyed at the extremities a greenish sulphur, with streaks of mustard and carrot interspersed, while the crown itself has reassumed with growth its natural shade of iron grey in the shape of a tonsure. Her rugged face, like my Uncle Gomer's, is long, bony, and mobile, but the eyes and the healthy flesh of it are unvisited by those angel-lambencies of nobility and reflection familiar upon his. Her brow is low under the forward-brushed hair, her mouth is wide, her large nose broad in the hump, and cleft at the tip. In contrast to the heathenish finery of her sister Rosa she wears a knitted jacket of grey wool over a sombre cotton dress patterned with the dark tartan of the hunting Grahams. Round her neck is a white collar whose daintiness is in sharp contrast to the homely irregularity of the features above it. She sits now large and in monolithic silence, steadily devouring her food; she is like a coastline, the rugged edge of a continent, her rocky arms are curved upon the table edge like the engulfing promontories of

Lleyn and Pembrokeshire, and the tide of nourishment piled up against her retreats like the sea sliding out of Cardigan Bay.

Watching her with affection and tenderness, I think of Iwan Morgan Parry saying that nothing is more mysterious than a man walking down a road or an open door with a woman standing in it. As for the fact of six people seated in sunlight around a table while a drum beats below them, it is to me, at this moment, so staggering a marvel that the wonder and mystery of it fill my eyes and almost prevent my eating…

Boom-boom-boom-boom.

The tempo of Harry's drumbeat increases and a series of cheers rises from the square below.

10

The fair-day has been fine and successful. When we had wheeled my Auntie Rosa to the window so that she could see the procession we went down into the front garden.

The diamond square is filled with people, but down the centre three or four constables, imported for the occasion from neighbouring villages, keep clear a passage along which shall pass the shrieval *gambos*. Spectators are to be observed at the upstairs windows, some of which have been bodily removed. A row of provoking farm boys, their corduroys astride the coping, sit barracking and chucking berries along the top of the churchyard wall.

Harry Nantfach the drumbeating dunce, dressed in scarlet and black like a flannelette guardsman, stands above the crowd, banging hard. He has heard the procession has now left the election hall at the other end of the village, and this information it is that has produced a variation in the volume and tempo of his drum-taps.

Short-statured and rhesus-bearded above the crush in his schoolboy's skull-cap, Charlo Pil Glas supports himself with his thumbstick, unsteadily, upon the window-sill of Prudence House. Twmi, the twin hemispheres of whose hinder end we this morning had observed slowly advancing in servitude along the passage, now, having evaded a moment the vigilance of Elin Tanlan, stands almost beneath our garden, revealing across the top of his complete baldness a single dark stripe of glacé hair like an inverted chinstrap. The Sardis minister has been caught in the crowd and stands helpless beside the red-necked horse-trainer. A farmer's wife, proclaiming, Gwydion thinks, her lack of faith in aneroids, wears a long spray of bladder-wrack wound round and round her hat.

In every garden on both sides of us,

among the fuchsias of Cambrian Cottage and the red roses of Philadelphia, stand groups of smiling people looking down into the square. The flocks of white pigeons wheel in the high sunlight which now no longer penetrates into the square, although it still varnishes the weathercock crowing into the south.

'Here's a click is here,' says my Uncle Gomer, sucking his pipe and at ease in the evening. 'They are sure to be standing on one another's feet. We are in the committee boat for the show just by here. You wait, it will be hooray in the village now in a few minutes when they bring Sam or Daffy up on the *gambo,* because both of them have got plenty of language. Well *tawn i marw,* there's old Edwards the Bryn, I have never seen him in a straw-benjy before. There's a wag now that old fellow is. I remember him telling me once...'

As my uncle is speaking a tweedy man under a plaited boater in the crowd below us turns back in our direction revealing a fat, round farmer-face plastered with freckles. Seeing us in the garden he waves a red hand, enlarged as though with dropsy, and shouts at my uncle.

'What's Gomer's speed to-day?' he calls, his eyes bunged up into the fat of his slit grin like new buttonholes. 'Any ducks' eggs to be had there this week?'

'Not to-day, Mr Edwards *bach*, indeed,' says my Uncle Gomer. 'I am very sorry too.'

Mr Edwards turns away. 'You wouldn't,' he shouts. 'You want to put some powder behind them ducks, Gomer.'

My uncle laughs, salutes him with his pipe, and goes on. 'Old Edwards was a farmer up there in the Bryn before he retired, and there's a card he was too. They are telling that once, to get the boys to walk from the village up to the Bryn to help him with his haymaking, he came down to the church here on the quiet one night and wired the old cockerel up there fast facing the south-east; he fastened him sound so that he was showing fine weather for nearly a fortnight, and the boys were looking at the weathercock in the morning and thinking it was worth while to walk up to the Bryn to do a bit of haymaking. I remember once he brought down the two-year-old to be shod with me in the smithy there. Well, when we were talking, he asked me if I would like a bit of pork, some spare rib now, and I thanked him very much, because another man's food will always be tastier than your own. He told me he would send it down, but two, three days went by and I didn't hear a word from him, and Tilda was getting her mouth in shape every day to taste a bit of that meat. I wasn't in the way to go up to the Bryn myself, but at last I saw one of the

Nantfach boys passing the smithy. I called him and told him to ask Mr Edwards about the spare rib. Well, he called on the way back, and what do you think he said? He said: "Mr Edwards told me to tell you the pig got better." He is a big wag about in these parts *reit i wala,* and he has won his parish as a wag, I can tell you.'

So my uncle proceeds. But it is for him really the season of receptivity rather than of creativeness, of making wood rather than of the plenitude of crop and harvest. He peers, nods his head, points with his pipe, and eases himself creaking on the path from foot to foot.

'Look at that black man,' he goes on, 'in the red jersey standing on the box in front of the stalls. What has he got in the middle of his forehead? A sixpenny bit? How is he keeping that there I wonder? Isn't that Anna Wernddu he has got on the box with him? Sure to be, I know her by that volunteer's helmet she is always wearing. Well, fair play, now, indeed, that was a good thing for him to do now, wasn't it, to get her up there like that and him a cheap-jack too. She has got her ninth or tenth, I think it is, on the way now. You are right, it is time for them to put the hood on the chimney up there in Wernddu with all those mouths to feed. She is a fine woman though, although I am always thinking she is a bit too tall. I will tell you now, to be honest, our Mamo and Dado were wanting me once to take an interest in her, when she was living with her mother up there on the Tyle. A lovely house they had too, with a little bootshop in the parlour, and everything was ready just for somebody to hang his cap on the nail. No, nothing came of it. I liked the cage but I didn't like the canary. It was just then my heart went bad too, and old Doctor Phillips, God bless him indeed, ordered me because of it to marry a small woman. Good old doctor, he was like a saint, and I will never forget the way he was with poor Mamo and Dado at the end. Ay, ay, you are quite right, that's the captain with his cane by the window over there, smoking the same as usual. Indeed there's a colour his face is, it is like the rind of a black ham now, isn't it? Yes, yes, it was in the captain's *Alice* I hurt my foot the first time. How are you meaning? I fell over when she was tacking out by the buoy in the regatta. And *tawn i byth*, when I looked down on the deck the toe of my boot wasn't in the front, it was right behind my heel facing backwards. What do you think I did? I took a holt on my boot and twisted it back where it ought to be. But I must have done some harm to it because it went from bad to worse after that until I had the operation. No, no, you are mixing them up, although fair play there is a likeness there too, but that is Pritchard the lawyer. They are saying about him that he would take the pennies off a dead man's eyes; but there is one thing, he upset Evans Ty Canol, and that is a bit of a job I can tell you. Evans met him on the road one day on his pony, and as he was passing Evans said to him: "Good morning, Mr Pritchard. Yes, it is a nice day right enough. Do you think we are going to have any rain later on?" Old Pritchard reined in the pony, looked up at the sky, and said: "No, I don't think it will rain to-day, Mr Evans"; and the next day Evans had a bill wanting payment for legal advice. Look at Charlo shouting over there, he is like somebody let loose. Those cheap-jacks have been doing well to-day, did you see one of them with a big wad of pound notes fastened in his lapel with one of those steel paper-clips? There, I knew he would do it before long, he was hitting right into the head of the drum instead of giving a glancing blow...'

But my uncle's words are drowned. Harry Nantfach's drum, a large edge-tear now in its skin, will in any event be no longer necessary, because 'Life on the ocean wave' and the cheers of the crowd announce the vanguard of the sheriff's procession. A crocodile of awkward schoolboys in red fezes, red flannelette jackets, corduroy trousers, and heavy boots trample heavily into the open space prepared by the imported constables. Each boy plays upon kazoo, rattle, cardboard trumpet, comb-and-paper, or at most a melodeon. But their restricted music is drowned beneath the brazen harmonies of the village band following in a beribboned *gambo*. The green-clad bandsmen, inflated and crimson-faced, sit facing inwards in the salmon-pink wagon and blast the *fortissimo* trumpet of the successful candidate. Behind them comes a second *gambo* pulled by a brass-harnessed and beribboned shire, grey and gigantic, his flashing headpiece shaped like the end of a row of houses. He it is who draws into the applause the sheriff's triumphal cart. Around this cart, upon whose huge wheels, the mud and dung washed off, puttee-like wrappings of red, white, and blue bunting have been wound, march the sheriff's bodyguard, a dozen young farmers armed with hayfield pitchforks, their steel points topped with flagon corks.

Wearing a grey, rose-garlanded topper, with two shaggy hearth-rugs upon him front and back, and a thick chain of clustered mussel-shells depending from his neck, the mock-sheriff sits jocosely in his elevated arm-chair, smilingly acknowledging the shouts, jeers, and applause of the crowded square. Around him in the cart stand a ring of his supporters, grinning under mangy silk

415

hats and with creased and moth-eaten morning coats donned over breeches and market-day tweeds.

The sheriff elect for the year is Sam Pantbach, Sam Sebon, Soapy Sam, an odd-job man from a lonely cluster of houses up on the hills. He is, according to my Uncle Gomer, not quite solid; once when he went to dig a cesspool for Cwrt Newydd he dug it so deep he couldn't climb out of it. 'If *he* is sound in the head,' says my uncle, 'the way they are treating thousands is a big mistake.'

He had persuaded the crowd who, in the election hall, had listened to his case, to support his candidature by making fantastic promises concerning the benefits which would follow his election to the exalted office of mock-sheriff of Llansant. He had, he claimed, arranged for a supply of gigantic umbrellas which farmers could borrow from him free of charge when the rain threatened their standing crops. He advocated, at a nominal cost to all farmers, an increased supply in the land of barbed wire and English orphans. He was already negotiating with an engineering firm for the laying on of pipes to all farms in Llansant along which could flow free and unlimited quantities of mild and bitter. He wished experiments to be performed upon local pigs with a view to inducing the species to produce their lard already packed inside bladders, and stamped with the name of their native village. He outlined a scheme by which the mussel-beds out in the Llansant estuary were to become migratory, and were to arrive each teatime almost upon the doorsteps of the villagers. He wanted flatter hill-slopes, hotter summers, multi-annual crops.

Sam Pantbach is an undersized man – my Uncle Gomer says he is a good bit taller sitting down than he is standing up – with the large grey topper low on his forehead, resting upon his cup-handle ears. But his face is not altogether without nobility. He has a large, hooked, statesmanlike nose and a clear blue eye. But his dribble betrays him.

Behind his official *gambo* comes a miscellaneous crowd in fancy-dress costumes led by an Ancient Briton clad only in a coating of gravy-browning and a hearthrug, and a grey-haired woman holding her skirts up to her knees and displaying ankle-length drawers of black sateen decorated with small silk flags of all the nations. These competitors, thirty or forty in all, laughing and gesticulating excitedly to their friends in the crowd, are followed by the people who have attended the election in the village hall.

The two *gambos* and their ribbony and phlegmatic shires come to rest in the centre of the square, and schoolchildren, pitchfork guards, and fancy-dress artists rapidly encircle them. The green band sit wiping their heads and shaking plentiful spittle out of their instruments while the mock-sheriff, shouted up to speak after the applause, repeats with the eager grin and the uninhibited eloquence of the dotty his fantastic election promises to the laughing crowds below him. One of his supporters reads a bunch of quaintly worded telegrams, greeted with laugher and wild cheers by the audience, from the heads of all the civilized states of the world, expressing their gratification at the election of Sam Pantbach as sheriff of Llansant, and their confidence that his universally acknowledged ability, now available in the high conclaves of nations, would effect a speedy termination for all time of the troubles which, since the beginning, have afflicted humankind.

Leaving my uncle, who fulfils reluctantly his promise to return upstairs at the disbanding of the procession, Nico, Gwydion, and I quit the garden of Môr Awelon and descend into the crowded square.

Daffy, the candidate whom Sam had defeated, tall, narrow, with the down-hung face of an indiarubber Hapsburg, dressed in a black frock-coat and a top-hat much too small for him, begins to express his execration of Sam Pantbach and his disappointment at his rejection at the hands of his fellow parishioners. He is well drunk and, standing on a readily provided box with his back to the stalls, he soon has a large and encouraging audience of farmers for his grievances. He denounces with savage grimaces of his half-daft and saturnine countenance the corruption and ineptitude of Sam Pantbach; he agitates his long, black arms like the branches of a stormy tree; dancing frenziedly upon his box, he weeps and howls in paroxysm of disappointment and frustration while the crowd, with cheers and laughter, urge him on to further excesses of malice and scurrility. Raucous Charlo Pil Glas, mischievously incited by some of the farm youths in the audience, begins to interject a quavering succession of jibes and irrelevant lewdnesses, which seem to drive the candidate into a condition of almost wordless fury. As we leave the square for the headland abbey, a ring is being cleared and within it orator and heckler face each other bare-fisted, their knees bent, and their slightly flexed arms held out before them. Both are fully clothed, the candidate in his undertaker's uniform, Charlo in skull-cap, two tail-coats, and bandy corduroys. But Charlo is not a willing combatant; several times he abruptly abandons his bellicose posture and hurries in dismay and querulous supplication out of the ring towards his backers, protesting in his high raucous voice against the injustice of matching one of his inches against a long-armed and incensed six-footer like the candidate. He has at last, when he had been refused the use of this thumbstick, to be forcibly held in the ring by his supporters and at the moment of our departure we see that with fright and beer he is visibly wetting his trousers.

Gwydion and I look for Nico and see him, abdominous, his burnt face yellow as footskin, in japing conversation with the calf-eyed young women we had watched beside the black man at dinner-time. This is one of the nights upon which the ritual of his Bible-reading will not be observed. He would return to Môr Awelon late, after locking-up time, and Gwydion and I would have to carve out some excuse to satisfy my Auntie Rosa at supper; inform her that he is already in bed, having retired early with an indisposition. When we should hear the rattle of his gravel against our bedroom window we would steal along the landing and haul him indoors – he softly humming 'Another day begun' to the tune of 'St Michael' – from his position on the roof of the lean-to garden shed. But, avoiding the strictures of my Auntie Rosa, he would not escape in the morning my Auntie Tilda's aloetic purge, or my Uncle Gomer's twinkling assurances that costiveness increases our spiritual distresses.

'He pretends,' said Gwydion, 'to the characteristics of the male bonellia. He is perpetually in rut. He would carnal with a statua. How eagerly he would endorse the statements of the eminent Welsh comic, if we could persuade him to read them, concerning chastity, the inappropriateness of springtime nuns, that nunnism is inferior to boscage. There is also, of course, a good deal of flannel about him. Much of his bravado, I feel sure, is a mere racing of his engine.'

We leave the crowded square discussing the young women of Nico; the blonde daughter of the tomato-canner; Dilly Saunderson with the red garters; a young woman from the chorus of *Mother Goose* lodging with him in Mrs Regan's for the duration of the pantomime; Mike's girl; Miss Cartwright, a high-nosed shop assistant; Phoebe, the barmaid, with a thick plait on her hair like plaited bread; a rush-like woman student with an expression of oriental inscrutability who worked on the same bench in the physics laboratory. We laugh beneath the sun-patterns and the delicately prancing leaves of the grove, we come to the ivy-mantled tower on the headland, watching the remoter beaks of Wales laid brooding upon the waters.

11

Silence and peace and glittering full tide. From the crumbling brink of our tower the sea far below is a lit hearthstone and the snouted promontories nuzzle in a remote half-ring upon its edges. The embers of the sinking sun are brittle and uneasy upon the water. Out of a distant headland the hot eye of a cottage pane burns back at the sun. The sunlight lies brown over the hills with the lustre of some fiery gossamer. A white, eating horse, minute in a field far below us, walks over his own table. The only sound to reach our ivied tower is the bee-humming of the waterfalls tumbling in the hills.

'You have not seen the Yangtse,' Gwydion says to me. 'The beggary of India and Persia; you have never known Mexico or Sumatra or Japan; you have never seen the ghettos, say, or District Six. You have not experienced the cheap life of the East. You have not encountered the squalor and the disease. You do not know the stink and the misery and the world's indifference. In Shanghai, the maggot-dripping stump of a dying mendicant's forearm was thrust at me beseeching alms. In Persia I passed through the stench of the lazar-hovels where the eyes of swarming pox-blinded beggars were encrusted with flies. In the Ganges I saw the unheeded corpses swirling in hundreds down the flood. In the streets of Mexico City I saw every night the children asleep in the gutters. And year after year your God permits it, Trystan. No, no, do not attempt to maintain that God does not sanction the devilry and the suffering, but only endures them. Your God is also the creator of man's brutish nature. Your fidelity arises from the supposition that the norm of existence on this planet is the life of this small enclave of your birth and upbringing; where for a brief moment some equity is regarded; where protest is possible; where conscience is permitted some tenderness. But this is in reality a minute clearing of relative justice and order into which the jungle might at any moment return. That is what life for the denizens of this cosmic perineum in reality is.'

The ruined abbey tower is half concealed among the headland trees, its coping crumbling, and thick cables of ivy snaking million-footed into the tufts of foliage clustering upon its rough walls. It was hidden thus by its founders from the arrogant longships sweeping south, and the predatory eyes peering under the brims of the winged hats. But our bell-tower, added later, triumphantly tops the hill-crest and gives us an unimpeded view out over the ocean.

Within an hour the glowing sun, hung now like a golden plummet, will sound the sea. Gwydion experiences the malaise of evening, and time, and impending departure. In my moods of petulance and judgment at his scepticism, I convict him in my heart of *hubris,* of atheism, of self-adoration. But Gwydion is not simple, there are layers and layers of him, he sees himself also as one of the humanity whom he despises. Gwydion's will is torpid with self-loathing. Gwydion believes, deeply he believes, in God, in his brutish and incalculable God, the daft, gifted, and vindictive begetter of this hideous universe. Upon our leafy paths up to our ruin he spoke, as he seldom did, of his boyhood and youth, glancing with a kind of hauteur down at me along his nose. Gwydion's nose was stiff and straight, very firm and elegant, it always looked to me a very fine nose for breathing through.

After the death of his grandparents he joined his father, whose life was spent in the service of an engineering company with contracts overseas. Gwydion's father, although most of his life an exile, was at all times a great lover of our land and its learning. At the university, Gwydion told me, grinning, his father's uncomprehending Saxon contemporaries nicknamed him the *Welsh stallion,* because, even in his student days, his constantly expressed determination was to 'serve Wales.' In Italy, in Egypt, in the Argentine, father and son conversed always in the soft Carmarthenshire dialect of their native tongue. While they lived in the Street of the Hare in Hankow, so Gwydion told me, a play concerning Iolo Goch and Owain Glyn Dwr was composed by them in Welsh. In Guadalajara a Mexican printer brought out for them two bilingual volumes of prose – both full of misprints – one a Welsh-Spanish edition of the *Bardd Cwsg,* and the other Quevedo's original with a translation done directly into Welsh without the intervention of L'Estrange. During a period of bridge-building in Hyderabad the two projected and commenced, with the help of a learned Welsh missionary, a translation into Urdu of the *Pedeir Keinc y Mabinogi.* But here, for Gwydion's father, engineering and philomathy had a termination, for he was drowned crossing the incalculable waters of the Godavari and Gwydion returned to Wales.

In our arguments Gwydion is always victorious and unconvincing. Although I know him now to be in error I have not learnt how to answer him. I do not on the instant insist upon faith's hegemonic role in the establishment of the clearing he spoke of, and the necessity of her continuance if

425

the boundaries are to be preserved. As we sit on the broken parapet high above the trees, gazing out at the lighted sea, Gwydion attacks me with a mixture of teasing and cold violence on a variety of fronts, maintaining I have the typical insensitivity of the pious painter; that nothing exists for me but *le monde extérieur* and a God-given paint-box; that I am concerned only with sensuous appearances; that I am ableptic to all that seethes beyond or beneath the restricted field of my organic vision; that my compounded stupidity and intellectual shonyism enable me to go over all philosophic difficulties as upon balloon tyres.

'You, Trystan, believe,' he says, 'that you have the Almighty living in your waistcoat pocket. You are not yet awake, although, I must say, I never saw eyes wider open. Part of your credo, I have observed it, asserts that the Eternal has afflicted one of His creatures with wry neck, another with squinting, another with gammy legs, all for your especial solace and diversion, and the enrichment of your artistic life. You, the type of the dense, eupeptic, snow-broth-blooded painter, believe life to be one long tail-wag. Why are painters never philosophers? Why has no painter ever turned against his art as writers have against writing? *Sancta simplicitas.* I give up.'

I have no gift of eristic eloquence and resource, no conception of what I ought to say, how to prove I reject the beliefs Gwydion imputes to me. Instead I recall merely to myself the faith and judgment of my grandmother; the poverty and the communal disasters I experienced in childhood; the squalor it was possible for me to witness in the city slum through which I passed on my way from Miss Machen's to the university. And the dedication of my paintings in my heart is always to the prisoner with whom I am captured, to the exile with whom I am banished, to the fugitive with whom I flee; to the women who have sacrificed their lives for others; to the incurable, to cripples, to dwarfs and monsters, and to their parents; to the parents of imbeciles; to the lonely; to the unfulfilled, to suicides, to the repressed, to the unregarded, to the cheaply held. But how shall I say this to such a man as Gwydion?

Instead I tell him I know that the howlers, the God-arraigners, the despairing weepers into their beer build no hospitals and set no captives free. Gwydion himself, Gwydion, the didymist who sees loveliness nowhere, no truth, little goodness, his pleasure reduced to the enjoyment of graffiti and a few dozen lines of verse, Gwydion, and not I, experiences the despair of aestheticism.

But I wish, when I speak to him, that I were able to apprehend reality in a manner more readily expressible in words. I do not know, when Gwydion questions me, what shall have happened to my mind when that sun, now setting fire to the sea below us, shall appear among the opening clouds only as a 'shabby ruin.' My mind feels her affinities with the imponderables of the universe; my body, compounded of milk, birds, seeds, flesh, belongs to the earth, to the sea, to the air, and will in time fume back whence it came. And my mind cannot be a nugatory buzzing inside my skull, my thinking merely the hiss as of some effervescing chemical plunged into a beaker and soon silenced. She too must have her homing flight, her circling, and her nest.

Gwydion, when I try to say this, when I speak to him further of God, of freedom and immortality, claims I mistake powerful emotion for thought. 'What is repugnant,' he says, 'is often true. Mankind has the faculty of putting a frill of philosophic glamour around the uglier facts of existence. You and all acceptors of appearances are so deceived... This evening we are confronted with the spectacle of nature copying Richard Wilson.'

I do not reply and we both look out. The full sea holds the image of the nearing sun. The hills around us rust in the sand-red light, and the woods glow green like gardens of subaqueous coral. The heavens' hollow, apart from a few strings of incandescent cloud, is ungulled and blue and immaculate. The sun gently buffets the water. Here, on our lonely grey wall, the fragile breeze passes the cheek like velvet, it sets a brilliant water-glitter in the tower ivy-tod.

Gwydion takes his tin-lidded clay pipe out of the filing-pleats of his jacket, fills it with fine-fingered hands, and begins smoking. His smooth, white face in the sunset has a delicate blush upon it, and his faintly stirred hair has turned the hot colour of rusty tins. Staring at the sun he lowers his lid, he halves, quarters, and obliterates his green eye. 'Your excellent uncle, Trystan,' he says, 'if his thumbs were secured behind him, would be inarticulate.'

12

I gaze out of our bedroom window, waiting for Nico. The square below is unlit and deserted; after the fair-day, peace and darkness lie over the village. Behind me Gwydion reads beautifully his Goronwy Owen by candlelight. 'Cywydd y Farn Fawr,' the Great Judgment. He can make even his own lines sound like poetry.

Nico's bed is the middle one. When we

tease him and prevent him from sleeping he makes a whip out of a walking-stick and his braces and slashes us into silence right and left.

It would be easy to sleep but one of us must remain awake until Nico returns. Through the darkness I hear the delicate noises of the night, a distant sheep bleating and an owl floating out a soft hoot from the hill behind the house. Gwydion mumbles. Orion marches out of the sea with military glitter. Into the heart-shaped bullring of the square below they drift, here all must reveal the patterns of their lives, reverse and obverse, all recite their *vidimus;* millions mass in the galleries like a fair-day crowd, all who have ever dwelt in the great tabernacle of breathing, occupied a moment the all-embracing trysting-tent of the universe.

An orchestra, composed of drums, harps, and a harmonium, sweetly plays in the square below and a white-clad collier-choir, occupying a wide sector of the encompassing galleries, hums delicately the sacred harmonies of *Calon Lan, Cwm Rhondda,* and *Crugybar.* About the floor of the arena move angel-forms, they fly bearing dossiers and shed their perfume over desks and tables of the court. Soon every seat in the sky-reaching galleries is filled. The minute faces reach back bank upon bank into outer space, an assembly not to be told or numbered for multitude. And round the edge of surrounding eternity stands the ring of golden trees.

Now, at a silver call, all is stunned, the whole universe rushes into silence. Both in the arena and in the infinite galleries all is mute and motionless. A powerful angel-smell drenches the court, like an incense. A honey-haired kherub arises and the voice of this roll-caller rings through the cosmos and the replies float down from the galleries – Ellis Bellis Brown – Here; Roderick Broderick Bowen – Here; Evan Bevan Bowen – Here; Ithel Bithell Bowen – Here; Eynon Beynon Bowen – Here; Lloyd Bloyd Bowen – Here; Owen Bowen Bowen – Here; Harry Barry Bowen – Here...

Under the awnings below me are hidden the righteous who shall sit in judgment upon the earth and I recognize the gnarled hands laid in the glaring light upon the table.

The stately cream-clad recorder comes to Gwydion Lewis Lloyd, Gwydion Lewis Lloyd.

Presently Gwydion is seen slowly drifting down in diminishing circles into the middle of the court from the upper darkness, reclining on the back of an immense paper kite. His eyes are protected by dark glasses, and he has the yellow kite-tail entangled about his left leg. He wears a gown and sombrero and carries a large sack of green baize upon his back. Touching down in the centre of the court he bows in all directions with hauteur and supercilious mien; doffing his hat, he then takes his stand in the blue pew. From beneath his gown he unrolls a large painting of the head of a beautiful woman. To the cheek of the lovely face is held a magnifying glass which reveals the skin beneath to be not smooth and pink but yellowish, roughly pitted, and corrugated into an ugly *crêpe*. Under the picture, which Gwydion hangs over the front of the dock, are printed the words, 'The skin, an organ of excretion.'

Then with nonchalance he up-ends his green sack, and thousands of books, folios, quartos, incunabula, thunder out on to the floor-boards of the dock. These he begins arranging like a bricklayer in a wall around him, calling out the title of each volume before he sets the book in its place – *Early Vaticination in Wales; Antiquae Linguae Britannicae Rudimenta; Math vab Mathonwy; Zeitschrift für Celtische Philologie; Vagantenlieder; Canu Rhydd Cynnar; Les Mabinogion; The Myfyrian Archaiology; Cerdd Dafod; Braslun o Hanes Llenyddiaeth Gymraeg hyd 1535; Cywyddau Dafydd ap Gwilym a'i Gyfoeswyr; Pedeir Keinc y Mabinogi; Cyfranc Lludd a Llefelys; Recherches*

432

sur la poésie de Dafydd ap Gwilym; Thesaurus Palaeohibernicus; Essai d'un Catalogue de la Littérature Celtique; Canu Llywarch Hen; Tudur Aled; Études Celtique... By this time the Callipers in the galleries are chanting in derisive unison, *A handbook of British Dragons, Karl Kratchen ar Aryaniaeth Dafydd ap Gwilym, Recherches sur la poésie lyrique du Bardd Cocos.*

From under the green-and-white-striped awning a blast blows and the wall of books flies out over the heads of the millions like chaff into outer space. Gwydion shrugs his shoulders, looks round the court with his nose in the wind, and awaits his examination.

Voice: Your name is Gwydion Lewis Lloyd?

Gwydion bows.

Voice: You have studied at the university?

Gwydion bows.

Voice: What did you study?

Gwydion: I studied an assumption.

Voice: What was that assumption?

Gwydion: That connection exists between learning and culture, knowledge and wisdom, virtue and art.

Voice: You have read the poetry of four or five nations and with much studying you have studied it?

Gwydion bows.

Voice: You believe poetry to be a method

of apprehending or embodying ultimate Truth?

Gwydion: The poetry I admire is concerned with lies and glory.

Voice: You have considered the love of man and woman?

Gwydion: Pish on it, I say, passion. *Cynghanedd draws.*

Billy Handel *(shouting from the gallery)*: What's that *cynghanedd* you're always talking about, Dion?

Gwydion *(turning to gallery)*: Cynghanedd, my friend, *cynghanedd* is an attitude of mind.

Voice: You have no desire to marry?

Gwydion: I shall marry a woman competent to write my literary history.

Voice: You come of a race given to triple wisdom and triadic utterance. What three things in the sublunar world have you greatly loved?

Gwydion: You have set the figure too high. Upon earth it comes harder to bless than to blast.

Voice: What three things have you hated?

Gwydion: Most art, mankind, and living.

Voice: This mankind which you hate. Tell us what sets you against it.

Gwydion: Its unspeakable lousiness.

Voice: How can you substantiate this?

Gwydion *(sighing)*: Directly the human organism imagines itself alone and unobserved it begins to hawk and spit, to pick at itself, and to scratch its furry parts.

Voice: This concept of man is a profound conviction?

Gwydion: My profoundest conviction is that mankind is a bad lot.

Voice: Yet, since you are one of that race, to which class, if you had your choice, would you belong?

Gwydion: To the lucky draft.

Voice: You have no sense of consecration or dedication?

Gwydion: I have the ambition to write the history of the Cambrian Railway between 1880 and 1900.

Voice: Have you anything you could say as enlightenment, purgation, or defence?

Gwydion *(shrugging his shoulders):* I have not practised augury and witchcraft. I have not frequented priests, mediums, and wizards. I subject my prose to purple-purging, and am guilty only of intentional catachresis. In one sea-poem I wrote 'night's blunt knees' and 'the dark osmundas of defeat'.

Stonker *(crying from the gallery):* How can you have a blunt night, Dion?

Gwydion: You can have a sharp morning, can't you? I didn't mention a blunt night.

Voice: Proceed.

Gwydion: Neither in writing nor in conversation have I ever referred to the joke about the cuckoo, the College by the Sea, *yr*

Hen Iaith, the Premier County, taters, the name Dai, the Act of Union, the nationality of Monmouthshire, Gelert, leek or daffodil, Dewi Sant, Welsh drama, Cardis, North v. South, Coalopolis, the first Prince of Wales, Fluellen, Snowdonia…

The roll-call recommences. Gwydion is no longer seen. When the stately voice arrives at Thomas Hugh Morgan there is no reply and silence falls in the hall. One with wings swans to the portals of the court and floats out his call. 'Thomas Hugh Morgan, Thomas Hugh Morgan, Thomas Hugh Morgan,' goes bell-sweet and trumpet-clear to the echoing periphery of space. There is no reply, and in the silence my Uncle Gomer, who sits at the harmonium, arises and, putting down his pipe, addresses the court.

'Now being that my relation Thomas Hugh Morgan is not present here yet,' he says, his face as full of cracks as the canvas of an old master, 'perhaps it would be in order for me now to tell you something that came to my mind a few minutes ago.'

For a moment he pauses and stares down at Pero, who lies in a state of winking dormancy like half a dog on the ground before him; he looks as though the under half of his body, including his legs and his bottom jaw, have been at one slice removed, so profoundly has he sunk himself into the floor beneath him. After a moment's affectionate contemplation my uncle proceeds.

'It is the little harmonium here that is calling what I am going to tell you to mind and it is about Williams, Sardis, our old minister down there in Llansant. And I hope I might say he will win the peace of God, because I have heard our Mamo and Dado saying a hundred times before they closed their eyes that he was like salt and sunshine in our village for forty years. Well now, they were talking in those days about having a little organ in Sardis, in the chapel, for to help with the singing, but some of the old saints living in the district in those days were against it, God bless them, because they were thinking an instrument like that would be worldly and wicked. But at last Williams persuaded them all and indeed they got the organ to please him. Well the very next mart day who should Williams meet in town but Parry *bach* Noddfa, a sour, shrivelled little preacher he was, from the back of the country, always very full of his coat and with a tongue sharp enough to break a bone. "Well, Williams," he was saying, "I hear you have got an organ in Sardis now." "That is right," says Williams, smiling and thinking no harm. "Well," said Parry *bach*, "all you want now is the monkey." "All *you* want," said Williams back to him, "is the organ."'

With drumming of working boots my Uncle Hughie clatters at these words on to the floor of the arena, wearing his working clothes and carrying his tin box and jack. Out of the dim and awful interior of the awninged bench he is summoned forward and the voice of my granny rebukes him with love and tenderness.

Granny: Thomas Hugh, Thomas Hugh, you are late again as usual. Why have you kept the court waiting?

Uncle Hughie (*on his face are the furry arrowheads. Tilting his head, upon which mounts the grey fortification of his hair, he sings*)*:* Ba se lah! Ba se lah! Ba se lah! (Loud laughter breaks out throughout the galleries of the whole universe.)

Granny (*sternly*)*:* What are you joking about, Thomas Hugh? What do you mean by that old 'Ba se lah!'?

Uncle Hughie: Mam, you know Caersalem mixed choir, don't you? Well, Harris the grocer is one of our first tenors, isn't he, and in the first tenor part they have to sing 'Ba se lah,' three or four times in one of the eisteddfod test pieces. But Harris, *druan,* is very weak on his 'Ba se lah,' very weak indeed, and so on the way home from work now jest I stepped inside the shop and asked him to sing 'Ba se lah' a few times for me for practice, we had a little singing school down there in the Crown Stores, him on one side of the counter and me on the other.

Granny: *Ach y fi,* you ought to be ashamed of yourself. Fancy asking the little man to sing like that in front of all his customers and you in your working clothes. Go and sit down up there in the middle next to Anna Protheroe until your turn comes for you to be called. And mind you don't tease her now. No nonsense.

My Uncle Hughie moves off and finds a place beside Anna Ninety-houses in the front of the chapel gallery. As he sits Anna rises from her seat in her straw hat and puff-sleeved overcoat and shouts big-toothed across the court in the direction of the judges under the awninged pulpit.

Anna: Mary Lydia, how are you feeling? There's a nuisance, isn't it? I meant to go up to Pencwm to see about the houses and this have come along. I didn't know to-day was going to be Judgment Day, did you?

Granny: Every day is Judgment Day, Anna *fach.*

Recording Kherub: Hugh Pugh Price – Present; Hywel Powell Pryce – Present; Harry Parry Pryce – Present; Henry Penry Pryce – Present; Humphrey Pumphrey Pryce – Present; Richard Pritchard Pryce – Present; Anthony Pantony Pryce – Present; Hopkin Popkin Pryce – Present; Rhydderch

Prydderch Pryce – Present; Rotheroe Protheroe Pryce – Present; Rosser Prosser Pryce – Present; Roger Proger Pryce – Present; Rhys Preece Pryce – Present...

One tears round the floor of the court like a high-powered lunatic. As he passes the section of the gallery given over to the Callipers there is cheering and thunderous rattle-ratcheting. Stonker Watkins, the Lucifer and fugleman, rises, but the puce-winged marshals quell the demonstration.

Nico takes his stand in the dock looking like Dyfed's Buddha, dressed in shorts and a red-and-black-barred rugger jersey. Swotting now for his examinations he shaves only on Tuesdays and Saturdays. As we watch him stand behind the brass rail we see his huge body blaze with energy, his eyes flash, his yellow skin sprouts as though his vitality pushes out in shoals his luxuriant quantities of hair. As he is being questioned he shaves his lumpy face with a blow-lamp.

The voice speaks to him out of the awninged dais.

Voice: You are John Nicholas Mathias, an engineer?
Nico nods.
Voice: You are the son of Nicholas Mathias, the schoolmaster of Llanddafydd?
Nico nods.

Voice: The grandson of John Mathias, farmer of the same parish, the great-grandson of Nicholas Mathias, farm labourer, the great-great-grandson of Nicholas Mathias, farm labourer, all of the same parish?

Nico shrugs his shoulders and is bewildered.

Voice: You are the friend of Decker Davies, Stonker Watkins, Billy Handel, Murtagh?

Nico: Yes, and Gwydion Lloyd, Trystan Morgan, Trevor Rees, and Joe Humphreys, they are my friends too.

Voice: You are a boarder of Miss Machen in Boundary Villas?

Nico: I was, and Stonker says you can tell all the other lodgings me and Decker have been in by the scratches round the keyholes.

Voice: You answer from the point. Why were you the friend of Decker Davies?

Nico: He made me laugh and taught me pontoon.

As he speaks a tall, lank figure in a wraprascal, sou'wester, and one spat sways across the court, scratching himself and muttering as though suffering from sailor's delirium. On his breast is a large enamel bone, the first metatarsus, the badge of the medical school. Decker passes.

Voice: Would you regard this Davies as a good doctor?

Nico: I wouldn't let him cut my toenails.

The sound of cosmic tittering tapers off into the distance. Loud thunder rolls. A cold shudder passes through the Judgment, and the teeming galleries fall into awed silence. The tension is like an ache and my heart pounds with the strength of three. Nico begins to sob, upon his face a look of unremitted anguish. My bowels yearn towards him. The verdict is to be delivered. I hear my granny speak out of the judgment seat and in a flood of tears I try to intercede.

Granny: He shall be judged and his expiation promulgated. He is condemned for his indulgence, his forgetfulness, and his neglect. Where is his reverence, his devotion to a cause? Are five generations of sacrifice to be rewarded only with horse-loving and complacency and indifference? You lover of women, beer, and easy religion, you shall know the history of your race. You shall learn concerning your ancestors, the *taeogion* of the princely *cywyddau;* you shall read how you were borne off to Ulster in the slave-ships, crowded among the yellow hunting-dogs; you shall learn of the centuries of your labouring, a traverser of farmlands, despoiled and plundered, the victim of the merciless princes and of their conquerors alike, your barley-crops burnt,

442

your few sheep driven off the war-annihilated territory. You were robbed on the toll-roads, fastened in stocks, evicted for exercising a legal right, imprisoned, deported, punished for speaking the language of your fathers. You were ridden down by your own countryman, the squire, who could not speak his native tongue, umbraged at your undoffed cap. You are the third generation of your race to read books. You are the second to live without the fear of poverty and old age. You are the first to choose the work you wish to do. In the carouse, in the debauch, in the love-grip, in the sweat of lechery, you shall remember. Not for you the loss of paradisial meadows, not for you the sulphur and eonial fire. You shall learn and remember...

The laniferous harpist and the harmonium break into music and the awed silence of the galleries is broken. Nico leaves the box slowly and with chastened tread. The white-clad colliers croon a soothing lullaby.

A foot falls. On a breeze that lifts my hair Nico's morning hymn softly ascends. The sea mutters on the Llansant beach. 'Are you sleeping, Trystan?' asks Gwydion. In the square below me Nico motions me round to the back of Môr Awelon.

GLOSSARY OF WELSH WORDS

Cwm, valley

Cymal, joint (in finger, etc.)

Barachaws – *Bara a chaws,* bread and cheese

Bach (a diminutive), little, or dear

Ardderchocaf Ach Anac, most excellent family of Anak (*see* Numbers xiii)

Bechgyn Beilchion Bendigeidfran, proud sons of Bendigeidfran (*see* Mabinogion, second branch)

Cewri Cedyrn Cymru, the strong giants of Wales

Yn enw'r Tan, In the name of the Fire

A'r Mwg, And of the Smoke

A'r Yspryd Drwg, And of the Evil Spirit

Tawn i marw, 'If I were to die'

Tad, father

Fach, fem. form of *bach* (q.v.)

Cwbs, slang Welsh for colliers' train

Y Foelas, Wernddu, names of farms

Gambo, farm wagon, hay wain

Arfaeth fawr, a theological term, lit. 'the great design'

Cymanfa ganu, hymn-singing festival

Cwtsh y geifr, lit. the little pen for the goats: the name given to remote or unused seats in a chapel, always upstairs and normally occupied by very infrequent attenders

Cariad, term of endearment, 'dear,' 'darling'

Tenor solo i Silas, A'r hen Baul yn chwyrnu bas, 'A tenor solo for Silas, and old Paul growling out the bass' (*see* Acts xvi)

Anhwylus, unwell, not 'up to the mark'

Cansan, teacher's cane

Lobscows = olla podrida

'Un drwg fydd ewyn ar draeth,' 'Evil is the foam on the beach.' A line from ap Gwilym

Tadau, fathers

Hwyl, (here) 'with a swing'

Nage, no

Pen punt, lit. 'pound head,' i.e. his head is in the pound class, but the rest of him is rather ragtag-and-bobtail

Cywydd, a Welsh metre – seven-syllabled lines, accented rhyming with unaccented, etc.

Cywyddwyr, writers of the *cywydd* metre

Cythraul canu, the devil of the singing, i.e. the bad feeling that singing causes, through jealousy, etc.

Dyn hysbys, village 'wise man' or quack

Hiraeth, longing, nostalgia, home-sickness

Dyn sgwar, lit. square man, i.e. a square-figured man

Machgen i, my boy

Dyfaliad, term in Welsh prosody: a heaping up of imagery

445

Cymanfaoedd canu, plur. of *cymanfa ganu*
(q.v.)

Eisteddfodau, plu. of *eisteddfod,* competitive
festival of poetry, singing, drama, etc.

Paid a bod mor, ddi-enaid, lit. 'don't be so
soul-less,' i.e. so stupid, or obtuse, or insensitive

Llyfr y Tri Aderyn, 'Book of the Three
Birds.' Welsh prose classic

Myn brain i, very mild oath

Reit i wala, right enough, sure enough

Tawn i byth, lit. 'if I were never'

Cynghanedd, term in Welsh prosody

Yr Hen Iaith, lit. The Old Language, i.e.
Welsh

Druan, poor one, or poor chap

Ach y fi, expression of disgust, like 'Ugh!'
in English

Taeogion, serfs

The publishers hope that this book has given you enjoyable reading. Large Print Books are especially designed to be as easy to see and hold as possible. If you wish a complete list of our books please ask at your local library or write directly to:

Magna Large Print Books
Magna House, Long Preston,
Skipton, North Yorkshire.
BD23 4ND

This Large Print Book for the partially sighted, who cannot read normal print, is published under the auspices of

THE ULVERSCROFT FOUNDATION

THE ULVERSCROFT FOUNDATION

... we hope that you have enjoyed this Large Print Book. Please think for a moment about those people who have worse eyesight problems than you ... and are unable to even read or enjoy Large Print, without great difficulty.

You can help them by sending a donation, large or small to:

**The Ulverscroft Foundation,
1, The Green, Bradgate Road,
Anstey, Leicestershire, LE7 7FU,
England.**
or request a copy of our brochure for more details.

The Foundation will use all your help to assist those people who are handicapped by various sight problems and need special attention.

Thank you very much for your help.